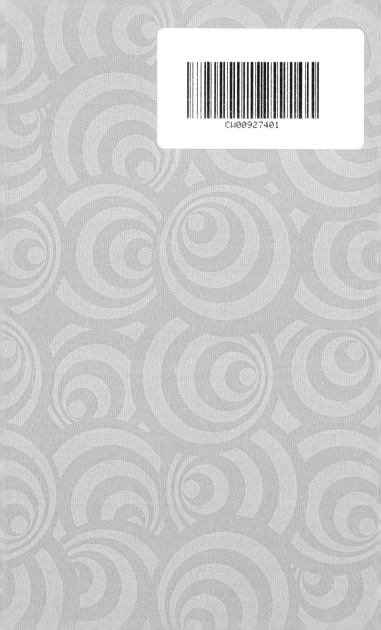

STORIES OF
PEOPLE & CIVILIZATION

CELTIC

ANCIENT ORIGINS

FLAME TREE PUBLISHING
6 Melbray Mews, Fulham,
London SW6 3NS, United Kingdom
www.flametreepublishing.com

First published and copyright © 2024
Flame Tree Publishing Ltd

24 26 28 27 25
1 3 5 7 9 10 8 6 4 2

ISBN: 978-1-80417-619-1

Cover and pattern art was created by Flame Tree Studio, with elements courtesy of
Shutterstock.com/svekloid/Tanvir Ahmed Siddique. Additional interior decoration courtesy
of Shutterstock.com/Pavel Miller.

Judith John (lists of Ancient Kings & Leaders) is a writer and editor specializing in
literature and history. A former secondary school English Language and Literature teacher,
she has subsequently worked as an editor on major educational projects, including *English
A: Literature* for the Pearson International Baccalaureate series. Judith's major research
interests include Romantic and Gothic literature, and Renaissance drama.

A copy of the CIP data for this book is available
from the British Library.

Designed and created in the UK | Printed and bound in China

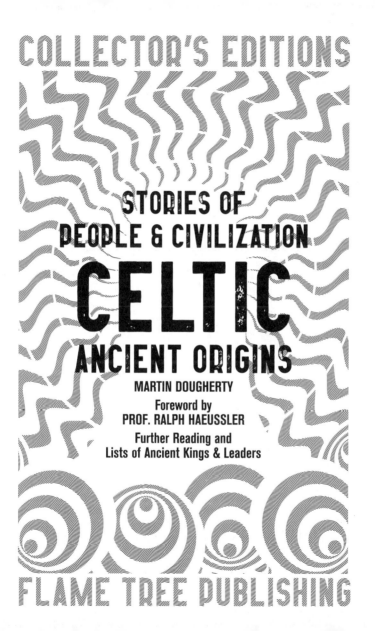

COLLECTOR'S EDITIONS

STORIES OF
PEOPLE & CIVILIZATION

CELTIC

ANCIENT ORIGINS

MARTIN DOUGHERTY

Foreword by
PROF. RALPH HAEUSSLER

Further Reading and
Lists of Ancient Kings & Leaders

FLAME TREE PUBLISHING

CONTENTS

CONTENTS

STORIES OF
PEOPLE & CIVILIZATION
CELTIC
ANCIENT ORIGINS

SERIES FOREWORD

Stretching back to the oral traditions of thousands of years ago, tales of heroes and disaster, creation and conquest have been told by many different civilizations, in ways unique to their landscape and language. Their impact sits deep within our own culture even though the detail in the stories themselves are a loose mix of historical record, the latest archaeological evidence, transformed narrative and the unwitting distortions of generations of storytellers.

Today the language of mythology lives around us: our mood is jovial, our countenance is saturnine, we are narcissistic and our modern life is hermetically sealed from others. The nuances of the ancient world form part of our daily routines and help us navigate the information overload of our interconnected lives.

The nature of a myth is that its stories are already known by most of those who hear or read them. Every era brings a new emphasiz, but the fundamentals remain the same: a desire to understand and describe the events and relationships of the world. Many of the great stories are archetypes that help us find our own place, equipping us with tools for self-understanding, both individually and as part of a broader culture.

For Western societies it is Greek mythology that speaks to us most clearly. It greatly influenced the mythological heritage of the ancient Roman civilization and is the lens through which we still see the Celts, the Norse and many of the other great peoples and religions. The Greeks themselves inherited much from their neighbours, the Egyptians, an older culture that became weary with the mantle of civilization.

Of course, what we perceive now as mythology had its own origins in perceptions of the divine and the rituals of the sacred. The earliest civilizations, in the crucible of the Middle East, in the Sumer of the third millennium BCE, are the source to which many of the mythical archetypes can be traced. Over five thousand years ago, as humankind collected together in cities for the first time, developed writing and industrial scale agriculture, started to irrigate the rivers and attempted to control rather than be at the mercy of its environment, humanity began to write down its tentative explanations of natural events, of floods and plagues, of disease.

Early stories tell of gods or god-like animals who are crafty and use their wits to survive, and it is not unreasonable to suggest that these were the first rulers of the gathering peoples of the earth, later elevated to god-like status with the distance of time. Such tales became more political as cities vied with each other for supremacy, creating new gods, new hierarchies for their pantheons. The older gods took on primordial roles and became the preserve of creation and destruction, leaving the new gods to deal with more current, everyday affairs. Empires rose and fell, with Babylon assuming the mantle from Sumeria in the 1800s BCE, in turn to be swept away by the Assyrians of the 1200s BCE; then the Assyrians and the Egyptians were subjugated by the Greeks, the Greeks by the Romans and so on, leading to the spread and assimilation of common themes, ideas and stories throughout the world.

The survival of history is dependent on the telling of good tales, but each one must have the 'feeling' of truth, otherwise it will be ignored. Around the firesides, or embedded in a book or a computer, the myths and legends of the past are still the living materials of retold myth, not restricted to an exploration of historical origins. Now we have devices and global communications that give us unparalleled access to a diversity of traditions. We can find out about Indigenous American, Indian, Chinese and tribal African mythology in a way that was denied to our ancestors, we can find connections, plot the archaeology, religion and the mythologies of the world to build a comprehensive image of the human experience that is both humbling and fascinating.

The books in this series introduce the many cultures of ancient humankind to the modern reader. From the earliest migrations across the globe to settlements along rivers, from the landscapes of mountains to the vast Steppes, from woodlands to deserts, humanity has adapted to its environments, nurturing languages and observations and expressing itself through records, mythmaking stories and living traditions. There is still so much to explore, but this is a great place to start.

Jake Jackson
General Editor

FOREWORD

The 'Celts' are a fascinating people! A people that once shaped much of Europe. We find 'Celts' from the Mediterranean Sea to the North Sea, between the Atlantic and the Black Sea. Still today, we refer to many towns by their ancient Celtic place name, including large cities, like Milan, Lyon and Paris. And how many hundreds of Celtic words do we still use in English, French, Italian and German today?

But the 'Celts' are also the most misunderstood people. There are so many negative accounts of their behaviour which were largely created by the ancient Greeks – from drinking undiluted wine and cutting off the heads of their enemies to the 'Wicker Man'. And it was the Greeks who coined the term '*Keltoi*' ('Celts') for these 'barbarians'. The Romans, who called them '*Galli*' ('Gauls'), reiterated these barbarian stereotypes to legitimize their brutal subjugation of Celtic populations across Europe.

But who are these mysterious Celts? What do we really know? What defines them? Can we create a pan-European history of the Celts? First of all, they did not call themselves 'Celts' but used a multitude of ethnic names. We are dealing with hundreds of peoples, many of which can surely be classified as states. What unites them is above all the Celtic language. But this does not mean that they could understand each other, just like in the surviving Celtic languages nowadays when a Welsh speaker cannot understand an Irish speaker and vice versa. The earliest evidence for Celtic comes from inscriptions around Como and Lugano from around 600 BCE, at a time when all our evidence for Latin in rather spurious.

We also see early urban centres, like Castelletto Ticino or the Heuneburg, which show how complex and advanced Celtic cultures were, even in the early Iron Age. Craftsmanship, metal working and mining – like the famous salt mines in Hallstatt – demonstrate the level of expertise and sophistication of these Celtic-speaking populations at a time when Rome was still a small town on the Tiber. Archaeological research of the past thirty years has provided so much new evidence to challenge the old Celtic stereotypes. And while we see many unifying factors, there is also an enormous amount of regional diversity, for example, how various Celtic peoples were living or which gods they worshipped.

It is therefore important to provide a new, comprehensive picture to rethink our understandings of these mysterious 'Celts'. And with most Celtic languages being extinct today, we ought to promote and cherish the last surviving Celtic languages in Wales and Britanny, Ireland and Scotland, to preserve our living Celtic heritage for future generations.

Prof. Ralph Haeussler

STORIES OF
PEOPLE & CIVILIZATION
CELTIC
ANCIENT ORIGINS

INTRODUCTION
& FURTHER READING

INTRODUCTION TO
CELTIC ANCIENT ORIGINS

The Celtic people of Europe are familiar to most modern readers, yet at the same time mysterious. Celtic music and art goes in and out of fashion, and Celtic mythology informs much of our entertainment. Viewers may not realize a monster in a TV show is inspired by a Celtic legend, but the influence is certainly present. The average person has heard of Druids and leprechauns but probably knows little about them beyond a general impression that has been distorted by time and the agendas of other cultures.

That general image of a Celt is of some kind of barbarian, with red hair and swirly tattoos, living in a hillfort and perhaps battling Romans; while Celtic societies had Druids and bards but no written language, worshipped strange gods and organized themselves into tribes. This impression has truths within it, but the reality of the Celtic people is bigger and more complex than most people would imagine. They belong to the distant past, but their actions helped shape the modern world.

DESCRIPTIONS BY OUTSIDERS

Much of what we know about the Celts comes from accounts written by outsiders. The statement that they had no written language is partially correct; they had none of their own. However, in many regions a Celt who wanted to record something or send a message would write in Greek, which was widely understood throughout the ancient world. They did not leave much in the way of a written record, but this was not due to ignorance or stupidity; it was simply not their way. Important information was stored in the minds of bards who recited it at need. Like the Norse peoples of Scandanavia, the ancient Celts believed important information was better stored in living memory than written words.

The writings of outsiders are by definition unreliable. The perceptions of, say, a Roman historian would be filtered through their own preconceptions and prejudices. A people who lived in huts with no underfloor heating were naturally considered to be backward and brutish, and Roman observers simply could not comprehend some aspects of Celtic culture.

Most notable among these was the willingness of the Celts to be ruled by women. Roman society was extremely sexist, to the point where the Roman historian Tacitus (56–c. 120 CE) describes a people ruled by women as having sunk below even a decent level of slavery. He is willing to repeat what he heard about lands of dog-headed men without comment, but finds gender equality too much to accept.

CONTEMPORARY HISTORIANS

Some contemporary historians were in the habit of translating what they heard or observed into familiar terms.

Tribes are noted as worshipping Roman gods when they almost certainly did not. A vaguely similar deity might be described as being Mars or Mercury, for ever muddying the waters and passing up the chance to create an accurate record of Celtic religion.

There is also deliberate bias on the part of many writers. Julius Caesar's (c. 100–44 BCE) *Gallic Wars* is an important source on the Celtic people the Romans called Gauls (because they had settled in mainland Europe in an area the Romans called Gaul), but it was written by someone who made war upon them for his own gain. Caesar could hardly be expected to be truthful about the matter; not when he had deliberately provoked the Helvetii tribe into war so he could profit from crushing them. His subsequent campaigns might have been brilliant, but they were largely unnecessary, and his writings about them are more self-glorification than dispassionate history.

BIASED HISTORY

Much of what we 'know' about the Celtic peoples is filtered through such bias. Accounts of the Druids as bloodthirsty savages who practised human sacrifice may have been simply made up to justify breaking the power of the Celtic tribes in Britain. Records of expeditions into the far north are couched in fearful terms, as if the land and the sea conspired against intruding Romans and an ambush lay behind every tree. The Celtic people certainly earned a reputation, and when the victors wrote the history books they were cast in the role of antagonists at best – and often as outright villains.

ARCHAEOLOGICAL HELP

Archaeology can tell us only so much. We have recovered fragments of brightly patterned clothing and beautifully made jewellery. We have opened burial sites and examined the grave goods. We know the shape of structures and what they were made from. What archaeology cannot tell us is what the builders talked about as they worked; what they feared and what they aspired to. This can only be inferred, and a modern archaeologist can still be misdirected by unconscious bias.

TWO THOUSAND YEARS AND A WHOLE CONTINENT

Who Were the Celts?

Attempting to answer the question 'who were the Celts?' provides an immediate problem. Celtic cultures have been identified from Eastern Europe to the Iberian Peninsula, and also in the British Isles. A population eventually settled in what is today Turkey. These groups were subject to widely differing influences as a result of climate and interactions with other peoples. The influences changed over time; the Celtic people dwelling just north of Greece in 1500 BCE lived in a different world to the Britons who faced Saxon invaders in 500 CE.

Generalizations are necessary to an understanding of any topic, but as more of the 'big picture' emerges details are lost and exceptions to the generalization emerge in ever greater numbers. Eventually, the big picture becomes so vague and the exceptions so many that the whole thing becomes meaningless. It is therefore necessary to focus on regions, and to do so within a restricted time frame. This is entirely acceptable since there was never an overarching 'Celtic Nation' nor a single culture. The Celtic peoples had much in common with one another, but they were never monolithic.

Social Constructs

A typical member of one of the Celtic cultures would identify first with immediate family and then with a clan, which would include close and distant relatives as well as those who had married into the clan or joined by choice. Above the level of the clan was the tribe, which might be thought of as a loose proto-state whose member clans had something in common. This might be a blood relationship but could just as easily be economic ties or acceptance of a common leader. A mixture of these factors was probably at play in most tribes.

Some of the groupings listed as tribes might actually be tribal confederations, which sometimes came to be known by the tribal name of their leaders. These confederations would gain and lose members over time, but they were the most powerful social institutions in the Celtic world. A dispute with a member clan or tribe might or might not escalate, but if it did the confederation could bring to bear an impressive military force.

Celtic Characteristics

The people we today identify as Celts have certain characteristics which point to their 'Celticness'. However, there were groups living alongside definite-Celts who did not share all of these characteristics. Some of these can be considered Celts-by-association, while some groups which are genetically identical to the Celtic people are sufficiently different in cultural terms that they must be placed in the category of not-Celts.

Physically, Celts are generally identified as being of large stature with fair skin and light-coloured hair. The general stereotype is of various shades of red, but blonde and light brown are also common. Blue, grey and green eyes are also considered 'Celtic' traits. Culturally, organization into clans and tribes and a preference for brightly coloured clothing suggest Celticness. Styles of art and metalwork also can suggest that a group is 'Celtish' in nature. However, these are indicators only. It is difficult to put even a general date on when a Proto-Celtic society became 'real Celts' and when a group ceased to be Celtic in nature. This is inevitable over such a wide area and extended time period. It should be possible to identify Celtic groups by their language, but even this would be subject to drift over time and outside influences from other peoples.

CELTIC GROUPS AND ERAS

Hallstatt-Era Celts

The earliest known Celtic, or Proto-Celtic, people are identified by the name of an Austrian town, Hallstatt, where evidence of their culture was first unearthed. The Hallstatt-Era Celts were a mature Bronze Age culture who interacted with the Greeks to their south. Indeed, it was the collapse of the Greek civilizations around 1200 BCE that forced a move from bronze to iron, as the Hallstatt Celts obtained tin from Greek groups.

It was from the Greeks that the Celts got their name. The Greeks called them *Keltoi*, which means 'barbarian'. However, the connotations of this were linguistic rather than cultural. Foreigners who could not speak Greek were said to make 'bar bar bar' sounds. The term barbarian now has connotations of squalor, stupidity and a tendency to set fire to other people's villages, but originally it meant little more than 'people who do not know how to speak our language'.

La Tène-Era Celts

By 450 BCE, the Hallstatt culture had been supplanted in the same area by what is now known as the La Tène culture. This name, too, derives from an archaeological site where significant evidence of this culture was first unearthed. La Tène-era Celts were skilled in iron working and interacted – sometimes rather vigorously – with the emerging city-states in Italia. (*Note*: Throughout this book, current names are used for modern countries such as Austria and Italy, whereas archaic references are used for more general regions of the ancient world. Thus 'Iberia' refers to Spain, Portugal and the associated islands, 'Gaul' refers to modern France, Belgium, Switzerland and parts of northern Italy and the surrounding region, and 'Italia' refers to the Italian peninsula and its immediate surroundings.) When these coalesced into the Roman Republic, the 'Gauls', as the Romans called them, were sometimes allies, sometimes trading partners and sometimes enemies of the new state.

In the third century BCE, La Tène-era Celts began migrating south-eastwards into the Danube Valley. This was some of the best land in Europe, and from it Celtic groups pushed onwards towards Greece. A diplomatic mission to Macedonia resulted in the wise decision not to challenge the empire of Alexander the Great, but after his death Celtic warriors overran much of Greece and the surrounding areas. This period of warfare came to an end with a series of Celtic defeats. Some of the survivors settled in Thrace and others went to Asia Minor as mercenaries. There, they settled in a region that became known as Galatia – a 'land of the Gauls' in what is now Turkey.

Celtiberians

Large numbers of Celts dwelled in what is now France, and more made their homes in the Iberian Peninsula (today's Spain and Portugal). These are generally known as Celtiberians, since they had a different culture to the people of France and Eastern Europe. The Celtiberians were a mix of Celtic and Iberian people, often dwelling in close proximity or even intermixed. Determining who was and who was not a Celt in this region is practically impossible, and it is likely to have been irrelevant to the people of the time in any case. Relations and conflicts due to previous interactions were more important than who belonged to a notional cultural group.

The Celtiberians began to come under Roman control from around 200 BCE, though they were difficult subjects prone to rebel on the slightest pretext. The iconic Gladius Hispaniensis, the short sword of the Roman soldier, was adopted after the Romans encountered it in Celtic hands. Wars with the Celtic peoples forced a reform of the Roman army into the form widely recognized today. By 72 BCE, the Celtiberians had been vanquished and were gradually Romanized.

The Gauls

Much the same happened to the Gauls of what is now France and Switzerland, though they were victims of internal Roman politics. Having bankrupted himself buying popularity and power, Gaius

Julius Caesar engineered a war with the Helvetii tribe, which escalated into a general conquest of the Gauls. This brought about changes on both sides; Caesar's actions precipitated a civil war which led to the establishment of the Roman Empire, and the Gauls were, to some degree at least, Romanized.

The Celtic peoples of the British Isles were aware of the expansion of the Roman Empire through trade with their Continental counterparts. At first the threat seemed far off; minor Roman expeditions were easily dealt with. Eventually, however, Roman might was turned against the divided tribes of Britain. Some found it more beneficial to side with Rome against their fellow Britons, especially when generous 'donations' to the tribe were made. Mainland Britain was gradually Romanized, but what are now Ireland, Wales and Scotland resisted.

The Caledones

The Caledones, as the Celtic people of what is now Scotland were called by the Romans, were repeatedly defeated but refused to remain so. Again and again they rebelled, causing one Roman historian to despair that they would never be conquered so long as there were two of them left to stand together. Tacitus records a great Roman victory in 83 or 84 CE at a place called Mons Graupius. Long thought to be in Perthshire or nearby, a location further north is now considered more likely. The extent of the Roman victory is debatable, and the Caledones were not brought under Roman control.

It was this inability to vanquish the Celts of Scotland that led to the establishment of the first border fortifications in the Roman Empire. These lay along Gask Ridge in Perthshire, which lies more or less on the border between Lowland and Highland Scotland.

The chain of fortifications at Gask Ridge was constructed around 70–80 CE, suggesting a time of great conflict. Hadrian's Wall, constructed much further south, was begun in 122 CE, and other permanent fortifications followed. The construction of these border defences is considered by some to be the beginning of the Roman decline. If so, Celtic resistance in southern Scotland was a major factor in the history of the Empire, and therefore in the history of all Europe.

The Franks

The declining Roman Empire was unable to deal with mass migrations across Europe caused by the arrival of the Huns from the east. Some regions within the Empire had by this time developed a new identity. One such was the former Gaulish holdings in modern-day France. Now identified as Franks, these people were ostensibly part of the Roman Empire – but when Rome sent to them for help against the Huns it was a request to allies, not a command to subjects.

A Romano-Frankish army defeated the Huns at the Catalaunian Fields in 451 CE. The Huns retreated eastwards, many eventually settling in the Danube Valley. These events were not only the death knell for the Roman Empire; the Hunnish invasion sparked a period of migration and conflict known as the *Volkswanderung*, with whole peoples displaced. By the time it was over, the cultural map of Europe had been completely redrawn. Germanic and Slavic people were now dwelling in what had been Celtic areas, with an inevitable mixing of genes and cultures. The Celtic peoples of mainland Europe did not cease to exist, but they were largely absorbed into the new societies that gradually emerged.

The Gaels

The Celts of Ireland remained free of Roman influences and had a history very much their own, interacting with the British and European mainlands from time to time. This branch of the Celtic family tree is often referred to as the Gaels, or Gaelic people. The Gaels established a kingdom in western Scotland and north-eastern Ireland known as Dál Riata, which eventually became part of the Kingdom of Alba. By this time, the Celtic identity was merging with other cultures to create new societies which may have had Celtic influences but were not truly Celtic.

The coming of Christianity to the Gaelic lands created a unique blend of a very formal 'Roman' Church with Celtic traditions. For many years the Celtic Church vied for supremacy in the British Isles, gaining popularity among Britons as well as in Scotland and Ireland. However, in 644 CE King Oswiu of Northumbria decided that his kingdom would follow Roman traditions rather than those of the Celtic Church. The Celtic Church declined thereafter.

Romano-Britons

After the Roman departure, the Celtic people of mainland Britain did not revert to their traditional ways. They had become 'Romano-Britons', with many influences from the Empire, though they did retain a Celtic flavour. These post-Roman kingdoms were gradually eclipsed by Germanic peoples from the Continent. Exactly what happened is open to debate. Some sources cite waves of invaders, others imply incursion by smaller numbers. What is clear is that the Anglo-Saxon 'invaders' gradually took possession of eastern Britain, and there was conflict.

The Britons were gradually pushed west, into Devon, Cornwall and Wales, while Anglo-Saxon kingdoms replaced the

Romano-British ones. These in turn came under threat from the Norse kingdoms in what are now Denmark, Sweden and Norway. While Norsemen and Anglo-Saxons fought for possession of Britain, its former rulers were sidelined and never regained their importance.

Mainland Britain changed hands again in 1066, with the invasion of the Normans under William the Conqueror. After gaining control of what is now England, the Normans attempted to conquer Wales. This met with fierce resistance and a number of rebellions; a pattern that continued after the Norman dynasty ended a century later.

LITERATURE

A significant body of literature exists concerning the Celtic people in the post-Roman world, but it is important to note *who* created these records. Literacy was largely the preserve of the clergy, and the Church can hardly be considered unbiased. Even if they wanted to create a true and accurate account of a culture or set of events, churchmen had to conform to the overall agenda of presenting their faith in the best possible light, which inevitably meant that non-Christians would be portrayed as uncivilized, stupid or just plain bad.

The Creation of Arthur

One of the main sources concerning the Saxon incursions into Britain was written by Gildas, a notable clergyman who died around 570 CE. His *De Excidio et Conquestu Britanniae* (*The Overthrow and Conquest of Britain*) blames the Saxon invasion on a lack of piety and good sense among the political and religious leaders of the Britons. The later *Historia Brittonum*, possibly written by Nennius around 800 CE, also covers these events and presents a figure who may be the first reference to the mythical King Arthur. A war chief rather than a king, Arthur despatches a huge and oddly precise number of Saxon warriors. His feats are credited to divine inscriptions on his weapons and fighting on the side of right more than personal prowess.

Arthur appears again in the *Historia Regum Britanniae* (*History of the Kings of Britain*), written by Geoffrey of Monmouth (d. 1155 CE) sometime around 1136 CE. This work purports to be an accurate history but weaves a tale starting with the siege of Troy and the wanderings of Aeneas as told by the Roman poet Virgil in his *Aeneid* (*c.* 29–19 BCE). Aeneas's descendant Brutus then founds the city of Troyes and discovers Britain.

A series of kings follow, some of whom may have been based on figures from actual history, until Geoffrey of Monmouth reaches more recent times. Later inclusions in the *Historia Regum Britanniae* are based on remembered tales and Roman records and are somewhat more accurate. However, the work does include prophesies by the wizard Merlin and other supernatural elements.

The Matter of Britain

The tale of Arthur and those associated with him is the focus of a body of literature known as the Matter of Britain. Early writings are in the action-movie genre, with grisly descriptions of lances bursting through armour and the man beneath, and in many cases are only peripheral to the tale of Arthur and his knights.

Le Morte D'Arthur

The definitive version of the tale is generally considered to be *Le Morte D'Arthur*, written by Sir Thomas Malory (d. *c.* 1471) around 1470. It is heavily influenced by the society and technology of the day, representing the Knights of the Round Table in a manner recognizable as being of the time of writing. The original mention of Arthur was as a war chief among the Britons, equipped perhaps with chain mail armour. Malory's knights belong to an era of courtly etiquette and articulated plate armour.

There are innumerable anachronisms in the tale. Arthur and his followers are depicted fighting Saxons – and also conquering the Roman Empire, discovering Iceland and regaining the crown of Norway for one of Arthur's friends! The tone also changes, especially during the quest to find the Holy Grail. By this point, Arthur has morphed from a vigorous war chief to a passive and rather ineffectual figure whose knights are the focus. Gone, or at least massively downplayed, is the graphic violence of earlier tales. The knights do win battles, but these are mostly over and done in a few lines and followed by several pages devoted to the heroes receiving a good telling-off from a hermit for their lack of piety.

The evolution of the tale of Arthur provides an insight into the distortions inflicted on the history of the Celtic people in Britain. Arthur's change from a barbarian warrior to a cultured, plate-armoured knight reflects the way society came to perceive what a great leader should be. Or perhaps it represents the agenda of churchmen who preferred that victory be divinely conferred rather than won by rough force of arms.

The Mabinogion

King Arthur and those associated with him appear in the *Mabinogion*, a collection of Welsh folktales published in 1840. The stories are much older, first appearing in written form in the fourteenth century in the *Red Book of Hergest*, but derived from oral traditions dating back at least several more centuries. Some of the tales of the *Mabinogion* use the reign of King Arthur as a backdrop. However, it is entirely possible the original version of these stories was set at another court; that of a Welsh or Irish king perhaps, or one of the Celtic tribal leaders. Other tales concern Welsh mythology and are filled with magical creatures, enchanters and strange happenings.

The Celts Through a Distorted Lens

The Celts did not leave us a neatly written history of their people, but they did pass down tales that reflect some aspects of their lifestyle and worldview. It may be that we know too little about them, and that much of what we think we know is incorrect. We must view their world through the distorted lens of outsiders trying to document what they saw, perhaps without understanding it. Even the name we call them – Celts, from the Greek *Keltoi* – was given by others and probably not used by the Celtic people themselves.

The popular image of brightly dressed, red-haired barbarians is only a small part of the picture. We must infer and deduce the rest as well as we are able. We do know one fact for certain – the Celts were indeed barbarians. After all, that is the meaning of the name the Greeks gave them. As we learn more about their society and achievements, however, we may come to realize that 'barbarian' does not mean what we think it does.

FURTHER READING

Alcock, L., *Kings and Warriors, Craftsmen and Priests in Northern Britain AD 550–850* (Society of Antiquaries of Scotland, 2003)

Aldhouse Green, Miranda, *An Archaeology of Images: Iconology and Cosmology in Iron Age and Roman Europe* (London and New York: Routledge, 2004)

Armit, Ian, *Celtic Scotland* (London: B.T. Batsford, 1997)

Bradley, Richard, *The Prehistory of Britain and Ireland* (Cambridge: Cambridge University Press, 2007)

Caesar, Caius Julius, *Caesar: The Gallic War (Loeb Classical Library)* (Cambridge, MA: Harvard University Press, 1917)

Caesar, Julius, *The Conquest of Gaul*, translated by S.A Handford, revised by Jane P. Gardner (London: Penguin Classics, 1983)

Chrétien de Troyes, *Arthurian Romances*, translated and with an introduction by William W. Kibler (London: Penguin Books, 1991)

Chadwick, Nora K., *The Celts* (Harmondsworth: Penguin Books, 1970)

Collis, John, *The Celts: Origins, Myths & Inventions* (Gloucestershire: Tempus, Stroud, 2003)

Cunliffe, Barry, *The Ancient Celts* (Oxford: Oxford University Press, 1997)

Cunliffe, Barry, *Iron Age Britain* (London: B.T. Batsford, 2004)

Ellis, Peter Berresford, *Celtic Myths and Legends* (Philadelphia: Running Press, 2002)

Fraser, J., *Caledonia to Pictland: Scotland to AD 795* (Edinburgh: Edinburgh University Press, 2009)

Geoffrey of Monmouth, *The History of the Kings of Britain* (Penguin Classics, 1973)

Harding, D.W., *The Archaeology of Celtic Art* (London and New York: Routledge, 2007)

Haywood, John, *Atlas of the Celtic World* (London: Thames & Hudson Ltd., 2001)

Jackson, Kenneth Hurlstone, *A Celtic Miscellany* (London: Penguin Classics, 1971)

James, Simon, *The Atlantic Celts: Ancient People or Modern Invention?* (Madison: University of Wisconsin Press, 1999)

McNeill, John T., *The Celtic Churches: A History A.D. 200 to 1200* (Chicago: University of Chicago Press, 1974)

MacBain, Alexander, *Celtic Mythology and Religion* (Folcroft, Pa.: Folcroft Library Editions, 1976. Reprint of 1917 edition, published by E. Mackay, Stirling, Scotland)

Müller, Felix, *Art of the Celts 700 BC–AD 700*, with contributions by Sabine Bolliger Schreyer (Antwerp: Mercatorfonds, 2009)

Roberts, Alice, *The Celts: Search for a Civilization* (London: Heron Books, 2016)

The Mabinogion (Oxford World Classics, 2008)

Williams, Rowan and Gwyneth Lewis, *The Book of Taliesin* (London: Penguin Classics, 2020)

Whittock, Martyn, *A Brief Guide to Celtic Myths and Legends* (London: Constable & Robinson, 2013)

Martin J. Dougherty (author) is a widely published author specializing in history and mythology. His works include histories of the Celts and the Norse people as well as books on the mythology of several major cultures. Martin is the current President of the British Federation for Historical Swordplay, and teaches regularly at historical fencing events.

Prof. Ralph Haeussler (foreword) is an archaeologist, ancient historian, author and research fellow at Winchester University. Having completed his PhD at University College London in 1997, he taught at the universities of Oxford, Osnabrück and Lampeter. He is a specialist in ancient and Celtic religions, cultural interactions and 'globalization'.

THE WORLD OF THE CELTS

Various conflicting theories exist about the origins of humanity. It is widely held that the earliest humans evolved in Africa and spread out across the globe to occupy whatever land was available. By around 200,000 years ago these people were anatomically modern but lacked some behaviours associated with modern humans. Were it not for the Ice Age we might have remained on the cusp of behavioural modernity for ever. The great advances that occurred 40,000 years or so ago were, in all likelihood, a survival mechanism during the harshest conditions experienced by our species.

THE LAST GLACIAL PERIOD

The Last Glacial Period, also known as the Last Ice Age or just the Ice Age, was one of many such events in the long history of planet Earth. It is considered to have begun 110,000–120,000 years ago, but events on such an extended time scale cannot be precisely dated. The ice advanced at different times and rates in different areas, and retreated at varying times too. What is popularly called the 'Ice Age' is actually a glacial period within a much longer Ice Age which has been estimated to have started

2.5 million years or even longer ago. Our current era may be an interglacial period, with the ice set to return in the relatively near future.

There are many questions still to be answered about the Last Glacial Period. However, what is known for certain is that the ice coverage reached its greatest extent – the Last Glacial Maximum – between 19,000 and 29,000 years ago. Large areas became uninhabitable for humans. The British Isles and Scandinavia were covered in ice, but at the same time reduced sea levels created new lands for habitation.

EMERGENCE OF MODERN HUMAN BEHAVIOURS

At some point during this harsh period, modern human behaviours emerged: abstract thought, art and music among them. It is probable that this great advance in intellect was spurred by survival needs, but it has much greater implications. The development of abstract thought and the language required to convey it meant that early humans could ask questions and answer them, and could wonder, 'What if …?' in a manner that seems to be unique.

The ability to communicate saved time and averted danger. Young members of the group could be instructed rather than having to go through the potentially fatal process of making their own mistakes. Perhaps with the assistance of cave paintings, a hunt could be rehearsed ahead of time and hazards reduced by warnings. The most important tool a primitive society had was information – where and when the best hunting conditions would arise, when to forage and when to set up fish traps. Efficient transmission of information facilitated not just survival but progress.

Likewise, abstract thought meant that humans could conceive ideas rather than responding to events they had witnessed. The higher animals might make the connection between heavy rain and a rising river, but humans could extrapolate from available data: Heavy rain is common at this time of year, swelling the rivers; as the waters fall again there will be fish trapped in the drying pools, unable to reach the river and escape, which makes for more food. Perhaps more importantly, they could tell one another it was going to happen.

Abstract thought also facilitated the development of tools and other technology. Many animals can use tools, but typically this is improvisation with whatever is around them. Making a tool to make a better tool is a great leap forward, and pondering how to fashion a tool to solve a predicted problem or to improve efficiency is one of the most important strides forward made by early humans.

Archaeological evidence indicates the development of new weapons, tools and techniques during the Last Glacial Period. By the time the ice sheets began to retreat, humans were equipped with the same cognitive abilities as we have today. They had only primitive technologies to work with, but they could solve problems by improving and developing them. At a time when every project began with searching for a suitable rock to chip away at, progress was slow. Nevertheless, these Stone-Age humans were able to expand into the new lands that opened up as the ice retreated.

IMPACT OF CLIMATE CHANGE

The ice retreated rapidly, at least in geological terms, from the Last Glacial Maximum. The warming trend was reversed in events known as the Elder and Younger Dryas, the cause of which is not fully understood. It is widely believed that a period of rapid global warming took place beginning around 14,700 years ago, melting the ice sheets and creating vast freshwater lakes held in place by ice dams. The melting of these dams released vast quantities of cold fresh water which altered the characteristics of the seawater it encountered, causing a climate fluctuation.

A very rapid cooling event took place, perhaps over as little as a century, resulting in a return to ice age conditions for the next 1,300 years until warming resumed. The Younger Dryas is considered to have ended some 11,700 years ago, ushering in the Holocene Epoch. This is characterized by conditions suitable for humanity to flourish and create complex societies. Everything our species has achieved beyond survival took place over a mere 12,000 years or so, and recognizably Celtic societies existed for at least 2,000 of those years.

The melting of the ice sheets released large amounts of water which raised sea levels quickly. Land bridges disappeared and people were forced to relocate ahead of the waters. Every cultural group on Earth has tales of a great flood, which might be folk memories of this era. However, it is notable that most humans live near bodies of water and that flooding – albeit on a less epic scale – is inevitable at some point. It is possible that the worldwide memory of a tremendous flood is not due to the same event but instead something that was going to happen to everyone sooner or later.

REPOPULATION OF NORTHERN EUROPE

Doggerland

As **the ice sheets retreated**, new lands opened up. At first these were barren, but as plant life spread into them animals followed, creating a new environment where humans could flourish. Land bridges existed at the time which are now deeply flooded, and some of these were sufficiently large to be considered entire regions in their own right. Doggerland, now submerged beneath the North Sea, connected what are now the British Isles to the mainland. There was also a land bridge between Ireland and the British mainland.

Doggerland was a low-lying, swampy region which no doubt had good opportunities for hunting and foraging. Steadily rising sea levels would cut off parts here and there, creating islands separated by narrow stretches of shallow water. This would not initially force much of the population to relocate, though some would drift away over time. Doggerland stretched from what is now Denmark and the Baltic Sea to points south-west of modern Ireland and north-east of modern Scotland.

By around 8,500 years ago, Doggerland was becoming inundated. Its people were semi-nomadic, moving between hunting, fishing and foraging grounds as the seasons changed. Widening swamps and waterways would impede their movements to the point that a larger proportion began to search for higher ground. It was well for them they did, since Doggerland was inundated and submerged by a tsunami occurring somewhere between 8,400 and 7,800 years ago. This was likely the result of an underwater landslide off the coast of what is now Norway.

Some geologists contest this theory, but what is certain is that Doggerland no longer exists. Anyone trapped there when the inundation occurred was doomed. Artifacts of their lives are routinely drawn up by fishing vessels, notably on the modern Dogger Bank.

Land Bridges and Shallow Waters

This event ended overland access to the British Isles. The land bridge between mainland Britain and Ireland was apparently submerged around 12,000 years ago, by which time animals had crossed into Ireland from the Continent to take advantage of the new plant life flourishing there. Humans are thought to have arrived in Ireland around 9,000 years ago.

Many other land bridges existed, along with areas where what are now islands were inland hills. Shallow waters could be crossed in simple boats. This gave the people of the emerging post-Ice Age world many routes into Europe. It is likely that some arrived by way of what are now the Greek islands and some crossed into Spain from northern Africa. Large-scale migrations westward from Asia took place as fertile new lands became available.

Population Migration

This was not a deliberate movement of population but the natural result of climate change. People followed their food sources, gradually moving north as the animals they hunted did. Where there was abundant food, groups would make their homes. Communities of this time were semi-nomadic, returning to the same areas year after year as seasonal resources became available. Archaeological sites such as Star Carr in North Yorkshire have yielded a wealth of information about the people of the era. They had an advanced Stone-Age culture, making barbed points for projectiles used in hunting and working wood to create weatherproof shelters.

Around 9,000 years ago, agriculture began to replace hunting and foraging as the primary support for communities. There is evidence of a westward migration into Europe, perhaps early farmers seeking new lands to cultivate. They settled where the land was suitable, displacing or absorbing semi-nomadic groups who had previously used the area. By 5,000 years ago the process was more or less complete; settled agricultural communities were the norm.

Semi-nomadic groups did still exist, and there was small-scale movement over a large area. Decorative items and well-made tools were traded over great distances, more likely by being passed from one community to the next than in long-distance trade caravans. As settled communities developed, distinct populations became associated with their home areas. These groups influenced and learned from one another but where terrain created natural boundaries those within them developed their own culture, language and way of life.

PROTO-INDO-EUROPEANS

Most of the languages of Europe can be traced back to what is now referred to as Proto-Indo-European, spoken by people who probably originated on the Pontic-Caspian Steppe. This region stretches from what is now western Kazakhstan to modern Bulgaria. There is some debate about the timing and location, but it appears that the Proto-Indo-European people migrated from their homeland into Europe, Asia and India.

The Proto-Indo-Europeans brought with them their language and their stories, and also their religious beliefs. This may account for the similarities between the deities associated with very different areas. As the Proto-Indo-Europeans spread out and settled, they interacted with the populations already present. Local cultures and distinct languages began to emerge.

It is likely that divergence from the Proto-Indo-European language began around 2500 BCE, though as always there would be regional variations. One of the daughter tongues was Proto-Celtic, from which all the Celtic languages are descended. Other groups evolved their own languages which further diverged into local variations. There is some speculation about when Proto-Celtic morphed into the various Celtic languages such as Breton, Old Welsh and the Gaelic tongues. This was a gradual process which took place at different rates in different locations. It seems likely that in 1500 BCE most if not all of the Celtic people could understand one another to some degree.

CELTIC LANDS AND LANGUAGES

The Continental Celts

The Celtic people of mainland Europe are collectively known as Continental Celts. The original population probably dwelled in the Upper Danube region, gradually spreading downriver and into neighbouring areas. The ancient Greeks called them *Keltoi*, whilst the people of Italia preferred the term 'Gauls'. The

Danube Basin was among the most fertile land in Europe, capable of supporting a large population even with very basic farming methods.

At this time the heavy valley soil was difficult to plough with the tools available, forcing farmers to work the lighter and thinner soil of the hillsides. The valleys provided grazing for animals and the waters were a means of transportation. Forestation was much more prevalent than today, and much thicker. The woods were a dangerous place where a traveller might get lost or fall foul of wild animals. Movement overland was thus something of a problem, creating a pattern of habitation dictated very much by proximity to watercourses.

The Celts did spread out, however, through the great forests of northern Europe and into northern Italia as well as along the Danube and its tributaries. They reached modern France and Belgium, which, broadly speaking, had similar conditions to the original homeland. Some Celts settled in Iberia and others pushed eastwards, and some crossed to the British Isles.

The land bridges were long submerged, but crossings of the narrow seas between the mainland and the British Isles were entirely possible in the watercraft of the time. There are accounts of transits between Iberia and Ireland, but these are unlikely to have been direct. Hugging the coast as far as possible and making the shortest crossing was the only safe option in a small boat.

The Insular Celts

The Celtic people of the British Isles and Brittany are referred to as the Insular Celts. The Insular/Continental divide is important to the study of Celtic languages. Those of the Continent are all

47

extinct but the Insular languages are still spoken. All of the Celtic languages can be traced back to Proto-Celtic and thence to the Proto-Indo-European language, but there is doubt as to whether there was ever a universal Celtic language as such.

Development of Celtic Language

The oldest known Celtic language is widely thought to be Lepontic, though scholars are divided as to whether it was a distinct language or a derivative of Gaulish. Lepontic inscriptions have been found in the areas where it was spoken, northern Italia and Switzerland. There is a case to be made for Lepontic being the universal language of the Celts for a time, but divergence is a natural result of the distance between groups and the influence of the peoples they interacted with.

There is much debate about when any given tongue came into existence or diverged from the wider Celtic language family, and indeed there are two differing theories about how the linguistic situation came to be. The Continental/Insular theory holds that Continental and Insular languages became separate first, with differences between members of each group occurring later. The P/Q theory states that the first divergence was the replacement of initial Q sounds by P in some Celtic languages, with further linguistic drift occurring afterwards.

Celtiberian appears to have diverged very early from Proto-Celtic. Like other Continental Celtic languages it is extinct, with few written records to work from. Gaulish was vastly more widespread, being spoken in some form across most of Celtic Europe. The languages of the Insular Celts have survived into modern times. They can be grouped into the Goidelic (Q-Celtic) and Brythonic (P-Celtic) families.

The Brythonic languages were primarily spoken in Wales and Cornwall, with speakers also in Brittany after significant numbers resettled there. In the more northerly parts of Britain, notably Scotland and Ireland, the Goidelic or Q-Celtic family emerged. It includes Irish and Scottish Gaelic as well as the Manx language. Manx became extinct as a native language in the 1970s but has since been revived. Although the dominant language of these regions is English, significant numbers of native speakers exist and information is often presented in both English and its Celtic counterpart.

The extinction of the Continental languages places the focus on the Goidelic/Brythonic groups. These are associated with the Insular Celts but may have been more widespread or at least influential upon the Continental languages. Given that there was contact between northern Europe and southern Britain, a degree of language commonality and influence is likely. More importantly for posterity, history, legend and culture from the Continent would be transmitted to Britain and perhaps preserved there.

Romanization

The Roman conquest had powerful implications for all of the Celtic world, but Britain was not so heavily Romanized as the European mainland. Indeed, some parts of the British Isles successfully resisted the Roman invasion and some, like Ireland and northern Scotland, were never threatened. Roman imperialism extinguished the unique 'Celticness' of its subject peoples in Gaul and Iberia, though such interactions are always a two-way street. The Celtic people of the Continent were absorbed into the Empire but at the same time the Empire was influenced by their culture.

TECHNOLOGY

From Stone to Bronze Tools

By the time Proto-Celts emerged as an identifiable group, bronze-working was the standard for tools and weapons throughout Europe. The transition from stone to bronze was not instantaneous, nor did it happen at the same time everywhere. Stone tools were laborious to make but could be highly effective. Likewise, bone was an effective material which was widely available. Bone needles allowed hides to be sewn together to create better garments, while horn and antlers made handles for tools.

Stone tools were effective for hunting, shaping wood and carrying out the other subsistence tasks facing a human of the Neolithic (Late Stone Age) period. Copper was the first metal to be used, but it was of limited use. Copper can be found in its native state, requiring no processing other than extraction from the surrounding rocks. These can be bashed away with other rocks, and the resulting copper worked by hammering – again, rocks will suffice for this task – into whatever shape is needed.

Copper could be made into basic dishes and would take a sharper edge than most stone, but it would not hold it for long. A flint axe head might be useful for years, but copper needed reshaping on a constant basis. Copper simply could not replace stone in all the areas of its usefulness. However, copper dishes and cooking vessels were effective as were sharp tools for intricate tasks.

The discovery that heating metal made it easier to work was followed by one of the most important innovations in human history: adding a little tin, and sometimes other materials, to copper made bronze. Bronze could be worked at relatively low temperatures compared to iron, placing it within the technological capabilities of the Proto-Celts. Bronze is relatively heavy, but it is durable and will hold a sharp edge. It could be hammered or cast into almost anything the Celtic people needed and enabled huge advances in other areas of technological development.

Metalworking

The implementation of large-scale metalworking required specialized facilities and experts to use them. Experienced metalsmiths taught apprentices, who also performed much of the mundane work required for the forge. Apprentices would hone their skills on simple tasks, freeing the master smith to undertake fine work. One of the jobs given to apprentices was riving: drawing metal through a series of increasingly small holes to create wire. The time of an expert was wasted on such tasks, but they were certainly necessary.

A forge would thus have a stock of mundane items made ahead of time against predicted need. Nails, needles, tools and cooking vessels would always be in demand, as would repairs to worn items. The ability to work metal finely allowed decorative items to be produced. Gold, silver and bronze were used to create jewellery and other status symbols. This is one of the indicators that the Celtic people were anything but the savages implied by the modern perception of 'barbarian'. Anyone might need a cloak pin or brooch, but to make these items beautiful took extra work. This means that society was capable of meeting its basic needs sufficiently well that disposable income or its equivalent was available.

Metalworking also directly contributed to economic output. Better tools such as metal-bladed ploughs increased the amount of work someone could do, which increased personal wealth as well as the number of experts a group could support. These might include smiths or potters, producing necessary goods but also items that would generate wealth through trade. Metal coins also facilitated transactions both internally and in trade with other groups.

Pottery

Metalworking was not the only important technology, of course. Pottery is a great enabler, allowing convenient storage of food and small items as well as cooking some dishes. Certain methods of food preservation, such as pickling, require suitable vessels which can be made by a potter. The Hallstatt-era Celts were using a slow wheel which allowed basic vessels to be manufactured, and when faster wheels were introduced from other cultures it became possible to do finer work.

Celtic pottery was usually decorated in dark colours with simple designs, though highly decorative pieces were made for the upper echelons of society. Animals, or fantastic distortions of animals, were popular. There was considerable cross-pollination of ideas from beyond the Celtic world, with items produced by other cultures traded and perhaps copied for those who found them pleasing. Celtic pottery thus varied in design and character according to local preferences and the influence of other societies.

Weaving and Woodworking

Weaving was another important technology. Basic looms were in use in the fifth century BCE, producing textiles more quicky than was previously possible. These became more advanced and complex over time. Woven garments were often decorated in bright patterns which were available to ordinary people. Cloth fragments found in Hallstatt-era mines indicate that bright patterns of red and yellow were worn for routine work. This is another indicator of a stable and affluent society: even those working in occupations that would be very hard on their clothing could afford to dress well.

Some of the tools available to the ancient Celts were little different from those of today, other than their power source. Lathes for wood turning were powered by pedal action, pushing a springy stick which would rebound. A cord around a spindle delivered this power to a wheel, enabling a woodworker to quickly turn whatever was required. Metal tools could produce a finish as fine as anything possible with a powered lathe.

The Iron Age

These technologies were available to the Bronze Age Celts and continued to develop as the Iron Age dawned. The move from bronze to iron was made out of necessity and did not immediately result in better tools or weapons. Bronze-working was a mature technology requiring relatively modest facilities whereas iron was harder to work. Early iron items were no better than bronze, and even though ironworking was possible it was largely used for novelty and decorative items whose value was in the difficulty of manufacture rather than utility.

The collapse of Greek civilization around 1200 BCE was the main catalyst for the move to iron as the primary metal. Copper ore was available in the Hallstatt region but tin, necessary to turn it into bronze, was imported from Greek sources. The collapse meant that bronze-working became difficult and prompted the move to iron. By the time tin was once again reliably available, iron was the norm and the enhanced facilities needed to produce it were in place. There was simply no need to go back other than for decorative items.

Water Transportation

Water transportation was available to the Celts, becoming more sophisticated as time went on. The simplest boats were logboats, or dugout canoes, made by hollowing out a tree trunk. The earliest example found thus far dates from around 7000 BCE. Such vessels were suitable only for navigating rivers and small bodies of water. Similarly the coracle, a round or oval dish-shaped boat made by stretching hides over a wooden frame and sealing with tar, was useful for fishing on calm waters but could not be used to travel any great distance.

More seaworthy vessels eventually emerged, constructed from planking over a wooden frame. Among them was the currach, which survives to this day. These boats were small and open, suited to operating on rivers and in coastal waters. They were capable of crossing narrow seas with some risk and carrying a little cargo, making it possible to maintain contact between the British mainland and Ireland and the Continent. There is evidence for the existence of seagoing boats by around 1500 BCE.

Early Celtic boats were not well suited to warfare or raiding. By the time of the Roman invasion of Britain, ship design had reached the point where open galleys could be made large enough to carry a complement of fighting men or to land a force on an enemy shore. These ships were primarily powered by oars, with a square sail for use when conditions were right. Their range was short and seaworthiness rather poor. Coupled with the lack of a reliable system of navigation in open waters, Roman-type galleys were restricted to following the coast or making short dashes across narrow seas.

These vessels could be copied by the Celts who encountered them or modified to suit local needs and resources. By 700 CE, the people of Scandinavia had developed boats that could directly cross the North Sea, ultimately leading to the discovery of Iceland, Greenland and the North American continent. These vessels, too, became available to the Celtic peoples who encountered them.

Crossing the Ocean

Despite the wild claims that surface from time to time, it is certain that the Celts did not cross the Atlantic to the New World, and never encountered the people who dwelled there. By the end of the 'Celtic Age', the technology necessary for a risky crossing by way of Iceland and Greenland did exist but there was simply no need to make the attempt. The Continental Celts had faded into the emerging cultures of the time while the Insular Celts were more concerned with repelling Germanic and then Scandinavian invaders.

There are accounts, however, of religious figures crossing between Ireland and Scotland in traditional Celtic boats during the period 400–800 BCE, and of a community of Irish monks already present when the Norsemen arrived in Iceland. The monks left soon afterwards, possibly to return to Ireland or to move to the Hebrides. Their voyages to and from Iceland represent the likely pinnacle of Celtic seamanship.

MODE OF DRESS

Celtic clothing varied over time and by location. The popular image is of a cloak, and trousers or breeches of brightly patterned material, worn without a shirt. This may well have been the case at times, but Celtic clothing also included tunics or shirts and skirt-like garments, which are sometimes referred to as kilts, although they were different to the modern kilt.

Greek influences are obvious in some areas, with women wearing a loose-fitting dress or shawl in the style of a peplos. This may or may not have been worn over a tunic. The 'bog dress' was also common. This garment gets its name from the fact it was ubiquitous and would be worn for everything from social occasions to cutting peat in the nearby bog.

Personal Grooming

Wool and sheepskin were widely used, along with leather for shoes and some garments. It is clear the Celts were concerned with their appearance; preserved bodies are rare but many of those found show signs of good grooming. Trimmed nails and tidy hair are common, and there is even evidence for a form of hair gel made from pine resin. Brooches were highly decorative and worn with torcs and arm rings of precious metal. Shoe decorations of gold have also been discovered on the body of a chief.

Clothing and Social Rank

While possession of personal jewellery is associated with wealth and status, there seems to be no correlation between brightly patterned clothing and social rank. Some Roman and Greek writers commented on how all Celts delighted in their showy clothes, though others painted a different picture. According to these accounts, the Celtic people of Britain never wore clothes other than a belt to hang equipment and weapons from. Given the climate of Britain, this does seem somewhat unlikely.

DIET

The Celtic people farmed and kept livestock, hunted and foraged. Their exact diet would have varied between locations, but modern analysis suggests that most people had a similar diet within an area. There does not seem to be a correlation between social status – as indicated by grave goods – and any particular set of eating habits.

Cereal Crops

Cereal crops were the basis of the Celtic diet. Barley and wheat were cultivated along with millet, oats and rye, although which of these a given community had available depended upon its location. Soil was prepared for planting with a plough or ard. An ard, or scratch-plough, scrapes a furrow in soil but does not turn it over in the manner of a plough. The early ploughs used by Hallstatt-era Celts were not well suited to heavy soil, and ploughing was always a heavy job. Indeed, in some Celtic societies it was held that no promise made while drunk was binding, except an agreement to help plough a field.

Vegetables

Vegetables such as peas, beans and turnips were grown and livestock were kept. There is some evidence that chickens may have been available, though the majority of bird meat appears to have been hunted in the wild along with boar, deer and small game. Analysis of Celtic remains along with associated refuse suggests that other meats were eaten at least occasionally, including dog. Where shellfish could be gathered, or fishing was possible, the diet would include these items.

Livestock

Domesticated cattle were useful for farm work and milk, which required breeding the farm's cows. It is unlikely every stead would have a bull; the owners of a suitable animal would make it available in return for goods or services. Particularly fine bulls would have a special status, which has found its way into Celtic folklore. The tragic tale of 'The Cattle Raid of Cooley' begins with a dispute between the king and queen of Connaught over who is the richest, with possession of a magical bull being a major part of that wealth. An attempt to balance the scales by stealing another magical bull has disastrous consequences for all concerned – including the bulls.

Sheep and goats would also be kept. Like the cattle of the time, these were the ancestors of modern breeds. One of the breeds that has survived into modern times, albeit in a limited location, is the Soay sheep. These are notoriously difficult to herd, and, if their ancestors were the same, Celtic herdsmen would have had a difficult job.

Wild boar were hunted, and were sufficiently dangerous that they became warrior emblems. Domesticated pigs were also kept, though there is some debate about pig-keeping practices. These animals were valuable and could not be wasted, so roasting whole animals was unlikely other than at large gatherings and special occasions hosted by the tribe's leaders.

Meals and Feasts

More commonly, meat would be preserved – often by salting – when an animal was slaughtered, and used a little at a time. The most likely form of day-to-day meal would be a stew of vegetables and a little meat, cooked in a large pot with additional items added when necessary. This would make it possible to obtain food value from almost anything and to make unpleasant-tasting items at least somewhat palatable. Bread could be used in the manner of a plate and eaten along with the stew. Cereals were also used to make porridge and fermented into beer.

Roman accounts speak of grand Celtic feasts and, oddly, seem critical of the amount of food consumed at them. Roman observers would likely have overlooked or never seen the mundane daily life of Celtic people and would naturally be treated to a feast when they visited tribal leaders. In addition to the diplomatic importance of laying on a feast, hospitality was an important part of the Celtic world. Failing to feed a guest was failing to honour them, and was just as major a gaffe for a farmer as for a king.

CELTIC SOCIETY

Celtic society is usually described as consisting of families, clans and tribes, though different terms would have been used depending on locality. In simple terms, extended families formed the basis of the social order. These were grouped into clans, which in turn formed part of a tribe. Tribal confederations also existed in some areas. These had some similarities to kingdoms and similar social institutions but differed considerably from the modern concept of a nation. Modern nations are geographical constructs as much as social ones, and whereas a tribe might claim an area as its territory, membership of the tribe was more a matter of kinship than locality.

Political Divisions

In ancient Ireland the tuath was the main political division, and can be considered equivalent to a tribe. Every person who owned land or property was entitled to join an existing tuath or try to create a new one. Once formed, a tuath would elect its leaders who conducted its affairs until replaced. Those who were dissatisfied with the situation could leave and join another tuath or push for a change in leadership.

A similar situation existed across most of the Celtic world. Membership of a tribe was by mutual choice, at least in theory. Families or whole clans might change their allegiance, but becoming outsiders might pose problems in difficult times. Tribal membership was therefore often a matter of birth. Any child born to a woman of the tribe was considered legitimate and eligible to be part of the tribe no matter who the father was. Adults might marry into a member clan of the tribe or be adopted by association.

The tribe existed as a people bound by ties of kinship and duty towards one another. It interacted with other tribes and other cultures as a political body in its own right. There was no 'Celtic Nation', but a sense of who was 'like us' and who was 'not like us' could be a factor in relations. To some extent, this stemmed from language and expected behaviours; other Celts could be relied on – mostly – to obey social conventions and behave as expected, whereas outsiders might not feel bound by the requirements of honourable conduct.

Social Status

Most of what we know about Celtic society comes from the observations of outsiders, typically by Roman historians and early Christian scholars relatively late in the Celtic era. There are few records of how the Hallstatt and even the La Tène-era Celts organized themselves. However, the basic social strata seem to have remained intact and it is reasonable to infer a similar system was in place in earlier years. As with most other cultures of the era, leadership was based on the ability to protect the tribe and to defeat others or, less charitably, the ability to back up demands for greater status with sufficient force. Authority could also be derived from religious importance or economic factors, but in the sometimes-violent world of the Celts it was those skilled in war who rose to the top of the social heap.

Hereditary ownership of land and goods granted status among the elite, along with kinship to those holding the highest positions. Below the leaders lay a professional class including religious figures, warriors and highly skilled individuals. The majority of the population were ordinary farmers and workers, with slaves in varying numbers below them. Social mobility was entirely possible for most people; a farmer might join the warrior class after distinguishing himself in battle, and disgrace was always a possibility for the higher members of society. Even slaves might be freed to become tribe members, and their children would be adopted by the tribe. There was no concept of slave status by way of ethnicity or race; slaves were usually taken in war and would typically come from nearby communities.

Leadership

Overall, Celtic leadership appears to have been mostly patriarchal, at least in terms of who is recorded as leading any given action. Female leaders certainly did exist and there appears not to have been much opposition to this from within the Celtic world. Outsiders, notably the Romans, were confused and troubled by the concept of female leaders, but it would appear the Celts were happy to follow whoever led them well. Although wealth and birth were factors in attaining high status, keeping it required remaining worthy of those following. A weak or incompetent leader was a threat to the whole tribe and risked being sidelined or worse.

There are hints that a female-dominated 'shadow government' may have existed within Celtic tribes. Warriors and warrior-leaders might posture and get into petty fights with other clans and tribes, but once a situation began threatening the stability or wellbeing of a tribe the women became involved and things got very serious. It has been said that exchanging blows or spear thrusts with a Celt is part of life, but when his wife becomes involved you need to carefully examine the reasons for the conflict and what the outcome is worth to you.

This does create an image of Celtic men showboating and women reining them in, or, if necessary, escalating a situation according to the counsel of cooler heads, which may be an artifact of the observers' preconceptions about gender roles. The reality was probably much more complex. It may be more accurate to say that individual egos were exercised in minor conflicts and disputes, but in matters that concerned the tribe as a whole it was necessary to listen to everyone, or at least consider the implications for the entire tribe. Those who failed to do so would lose the confidence of the population.

LAW AND CUSTOM

There are no records of the majority of ancient Celtic law, but some assumptions can be made. Their society was stable and prosperous, so there must have been some means of regulating behaviour. Some actions, such as theft and murder, threaten the stability of a society and thus are always opposed by whatever passes for a body of law in that time and place. However, the laws of the ancient Celts might better be considered as customs and traditions to be respected rather than carefully worded statements which can be loopholed and twisted by a clever legal mind.

Enforcement and Punishment

Enforcement of the law therefore depended on the wise governance of leaders. The letter of the law was not important; what mattered was perception of the incident by those who imposed penalties and how the matter would be seen by the tribe as a whole. Someone who carried out a forbidden act might plead a case for necessity and receive lenient treatment on the decision of the tribal leaders, which created an opportunity for corruption. However, Celtic leaders answered to their followers and those who displayed excessive favouritism might lose their position.

Ancient Irish and Welsh law is generally similar, largely based on the payment of compensation to the victim or their family. Some aggravating factors increased the level of fine to be paid while certain actions – poisoning for example – were punishable by death. This was rare, however. The payment of blood-money was considered preferable wherever possible. If it had not been paid, the kin of the victim were entitled to launch a legitimate blood feud and take the law into their own hands.

Where someone was injured by the actions of another the level of compensation was determined by a physician's examination and report on the effects of the wound. This was made after nine days, to give time for the situation to become apparent. If long-term or permanent medical assistance was required, this was factored into the punishment, as was the social status of the injured person.

Custom as Law

Some customs were as binding as laws. The duty of fealty to a military leader and mutual assistance to fellow warriors underpinned Celtic warfare. Hospitality was also particularly important. A stranger or new arrival could expect to be fed and given a place to sleep, and if there was nothing to spare then the host might go hungry in order to uphold the laws of hospitality. Hospitality was about more than food, however. A guest was under the protection of the host and was expected to refrain from harmful conduct. Betrayals of hospitality or the use of a pretence of hospitality to stage a murder are recorded as the worst of deeds in Celtic legend.

It was the custom for leaders to reward their followers generously, particularly successful warriors. This might take the form of gifts of livestock, jewellery or weapons, but the feast was also an important part of the social contract. Leaders were obliged to hold feasts to honour individuals or the tribe as a whole. The most prominent tribe members, or those being currently honoured, sat closest to the host and had the finest food and drink. The greatest warrior was entitled to the best cut of meat, from the thigh, though another could challenge for it if they dared.

The feast was important to maintaining the social order. The host demonstrated they were fit to rule by displaying their wealth and generosity. The positioning of guests in their proper place helped remind everyone of their role in the tribe but also created a desire for advancement which translated to greater efforts in that role. Recognition at a feast might not be a tangible thing like a gift of jewellery or weapons, but it served to remind tribe members that their efforts had been noticed. It seems the ancient Celts understood just how demotivating it is to work hard without recognition, and were keen to avoid insulting their tribe members in this manner.

Feasts were also useful in external politics. In addition to showing off the wealth (and therefore by inference military strength) of the tribe they were an opportunity to have the bards tell tales of the great deeds done recently and in the past. A good feast was a form of propaganda or a PR exercise as well as an opportunity to have a good time.

MARRIAGE AND FAMILY

Most of what is known about Celtic marriage practices and sexual preferences comes from traditions that survived from later Celtic cultures, notably in the British Isles, and from the writings of outsiders. Some of these accounts contradict one another, but the overall impression is that the Celts were open and permissive in their relations but at the same time tried to protect any children that resulted from a marriage or liaison. A child born to any woman of the tribe was considered legitimate; there was no distinction between those born to a married couple and those who were not. Nor was monogamy necessary in a marriage, though couples might well decide so by mutual agreement.

Handfasting

Modern interest in what might generally be termed 'paganism' has sparked a revival in concepts believed to have been Celtic in origin. These have in some cases been misunderstood, misrepresented or mangled beyond recognition by those with an agenda. However, there is evidence for at least some of the presumed practices of the ancient Celts. One such is handfasting, where a prospective couple declare their intention to marry in a public ceremony. Today's mainstream equivalent is the presentation of an engagement ring, which until recently was normally a private matter for most couples. There seems to be a current trend towards public displays, often using social media, and it is possible to find parallels to the ancient handfasting.

The handfasting was of importance to the clan and tribe as it clearly established the relationship and intent to marry. The couple pledged themselves to one another with their hands bound together and thereafter lived together in what can be described as a trial marriage. At the end of a year, the couple could formalize their marriage with a wedding ceremony or go their separate ways without stigma. An honest but failed attempt to make a marriage work was far better than an unhappy relationship carried on out of duty.

Opinions among historians are divided about handfasting. The idea that it was the beginning of a trial marriage has been challenged, usually with the assertion it was actually a wedding ceremony. The truth may never be known and may in fact vary from place to place and time to time. Trial marriages may not have been observed in some areas, and the binding of hands is a part of wedding ceremonies in many cultures – some of which could not possibly have been influenced by Celtic traditions.

Wedding Ceremonies

A variety of practices and ceremonies have been invented throughout history to mark the occasion of a wedding and to create a sense of legitimacy, but in some Celtic societies all that was necessary was for both participants to make a public declaration of their marriage. This was no small matter; a declaration of marriage was legally binding and made solemnly before the community.

The wedding ceremony – which might be no more than a public declaration – and the celebrations that surrounded it were and remain different events. Today, there are extensive laws about what exactly constitutes a legal marriage and what is an associated tradition or currently fashionable practice. In Celtic times, it came down to the marriage being recognized by the couple and their community.

One custom associated with marriage was called jumping the broom, which literally involved the newly married couple passing over a broom laid on the ground. There are varying opinions about what the broom represented, and whether it originally was a broom as such or a bundle of certain twigs that were often used in brooms. There are connotations of crossing a threshold involved, and in some cultures jumping backwards across a broom could signify the end of a marriage. The idea of jumping a broom as a marriage ceremony exists in other cultures as well, notably in parts of West Africa.

Enslaved people, who were not permitted by their owners to marry, may have used the practice in secret to perform their own ceremony and signify their commitment. There is certainly no link between these cultures, suggesting a universal concept – two people who pledge themselves to one another in a manner accepted by their community are married in a way that no pieces of paper or formal laws can supplant.

Most and Least Desirable Unions

There were traditions, at least in the later Insular Celtic societies, about which marriages were most and least suitable. The term 'marriage' in this case may refer to a situation in which children might result, rather than a committed long-term relationship. The most desirable marriages were between people of equal wealth. If one partner were wealthier, it was considered desirable that it be the husband, but a stable and solid marriage between a richer woman and a poorer man was still a 'good' marriage. Other situations were considered less desirable, in some cases because they might create children but be incapable of properly providing for them. Some marriages were disapproved of because they were likely to cause trouble for others.

Least desirable was a union between two people who were mentally ill or prone to irresponsible acts. This would pose a risk to children and require others to intervene in the inevitable drama. 'Marriage' resulting from a rape was scarcely less undesirable. It is notable that the penalty for rape was usually a requirement to support the victim rather than punishment for the crime, although failure to meet these obligations might result in severe punishments including execution or castration. A rape and subsequent support might create a marriage-like situation, but it would be anything but a happy one and therefore undesirable.

A 'soldier's wedding', or a one-off liaison, was considered undesirable – again, because it might result in children of the tribe being without adequate support. A marriage or marriage-like situation could result from a decision to cohabit without being declared as such. This was considered better than most other informal marriage-like situations but created uncertainties.

A marriage could also begin with a voluntary elopement against the wishes of the families involved, or an abduction. The former might cause trouble that could affect others although it was voluntary, while an abduction was likely to result in violence or even long-term feuding. An abduction was not an auspicious beginning to married life, but would still be recognized as a marriage for legal purposes. This might be important if the couple decided – unsurprisingly perhaps – to separate.

Separation and Divorce

A marriage was considered an agreement between two parties, and one that could be ended like any other. Anyone had the right to declare before the tribe they were no longer married. While a marriage was usually a matter for mutual consent, the freedom to leave was personal. In the event of a no-fault divorce, property was divided up according to who had brought what into the marriage at the start, with anything gained since then to be apportioned as fairly as possible. A couple could admit their attempt at marriage had come to an end and move on with their lives.

If, on the other hand, one party gave the other grounds for an aggrieved separation the situation was quite different. It was necessary to convince a suitable adjudicator that a party had been wronged, but if successful that party might leave with most or even all of the couple's estate. A man who struck his wife hard enough to leave a mark gave her grounds for an aggrieved divorce, as did a wife who betrayed her husband to his enemies. Bad breath and bad words were also reasons; satirizing one another or speaking ill of them in company were grounds for divorce as well.

Sex and Homosexuality

Sex was considered an important part of marriage. Couples might not be monogamous – indeed, it was permissible for a man to have more than one wife and his wife to have more than one husband. Property ownership might have been a little tricky to keep track of between multiple partners, but the situation was otherwise entirely acceptable. However, a man was expected to be able to satisfy his wife's desires. If he routinely became too drunk or was too obese, or otherwise incapable of performing, his wife could leave him with grounds for an aggrieved divorce.

Celtic society was not greatly concerned about same-sex relationships. There are references to groups of 'special friends' among Celtic people of the same sex, and relationships that may or may not have been sexual. This was seen as entirely normal behaviour, and could be beneficial in strengthening the bond between warriors. One example from Irish mythology is the bond between the hero Cú Chulainn and his foster brother Ferdiad Mac Damann. Even when forced to battle one another they dressed each other's wounds and slept under the same blanket. It is possible to interpret such references in different ways, but overall the Celts seem to have had no hang-ups about same-sex relationships.

However, a man who entirely neglected his wife in favour of other men gave her grounds for divorce. Liaisons with other men were acceptable, but there was still a duty to perform within the marriage. It is often stated that homosexuality was grounds for divorce, but it might better be said that neglecting the wife was the actual reason, no matter who the husband was with. A woman who discovered her husband with someone else was deemed not to be committing a crime if she attacked either or both of them, providing she did so within three days. The marriage might or might not continue afterwards, perhaps on redefined terms. Betrayal of an agreement to be monogamous was likely to be seen as grounds for an aggrieved divorce.

CELTIC SETTLEMENTS

The majority of settlements were on lower ground than the hillforts. This is due to the practicalities of daily life. Extreme measures may seem worthwhile in times of war but livestock must still be grazed, fields tended and firewood gathered. How the ancients Celts built their settlements varied over time and according to the local resources, but all were driven by the same basic requirements.

Village Makeup

In many areas the settlement pattern was of villages and small farmsteads, which would naturally evolve into a pattern based around the provision of necessary crafts. Most people were farmers or herders, working or grazing their animals on the land surrounding their stead. As far as possible, the inhabitants of a stead would do everything they could for themselves. Elementary repairs to tools and structures were carried out when they were needed, with a view to everything lasting as long as possible.

New tools or major repairs would require the attention of a smith, who would be a highly respected and important member of the community. Smithing required specialized facilities and years of training, so the smith and other skilled people would trade their work for the produce of the farms. A village smith had to be versatile but would focus on mundane items for the most part. The best smiths could earn their place at a major settlement.

This required an organized society. Without social order and the prevention of widespread thievery no higher functions were possible and everyone would have to operate at the subsistence level. The smiths of the Celts were able to make extremely complex jewellery and there were those rich enough to afford it. Such endeavours require stability and strongly suggest that for the most part Celtic society was stable and peaceful.

Dwelling Construction and Layout

In many areas, the dwellings of these villages and farmsteads were constructed on a wooden frame to create the characteristic 'round house', with minimal internal partitioning. Walls were typically of wattle and daub – interlaced sticks filled and coated with mud – while roofs were thatched. Modern reconstructions indicate that these dwellings were surprisingly weatherproof, to the point where in some cases openings had to be made in the walls to provide ventilation for a fire.

A dwelling would have areas for storage and sleeping, and a fire pit which provided heating and some light. Animal hides and meat were hung to tan and cure using the smoke from the fire, while the floor was covered with animal skins or straw. Primitive by modern standards, the round house provided a secure, dry and warm living space for an extended family. Most work was done outside, using natural light, with the family retreating to their home at sunset.

Variations on the round house theme existed in many areas. Stone walls were used instead of wattle and daub, and in some areas the round house was replaced by a more conventional rectangular structure. This is characteristic of Celtiberian dwellings. A variation on the round house theme was the crannog, essentially a round house built on piles driven into a lake bed. A narrow bridge from the land provided the only means of access, while easy access to water was useful for fishing and transportation.

In the north of what is now Scotland and the associated islands, an alternative structure known as a broch was used. These were constructed entirely from stone without any binding material, essentially a conical drystone wall. The origins of the brochs are debated, with their construction placed around 2,000 years ago, or perhaps much earlier. There is also some debate about who built them and whether they can be considered a Celtic creation.

Land Use

The dwellings of a stead or village were surrounded by land used for various purposes. The immediate vicinity of the dwellings might house and feed small domestic livestock or contain working areas, with a wider range of land for agriculture, herding and foraging. Steads and villages might or might not have some form of defences in the form of walls, a palisade or earthworks. Protecting a whole village was a huge undertaking relative to the number of workers available, so would likely be undertaken only if there was a perceived need. Fences to keep animals from wandering off were easier to create and would be in place in most settlements.

Most of Europe was heavily forested at this time, so a village would almost always be within easy reach of a wooded area. This made timber and firewood easy to obtain but also meant that many species of animals would be close to the village. This was a mixed blessing; on one hand it meant hunting for meat could be conducted relatively conveniently but at the same time there was a threat to anyone venturing into the forest. Predators might be attracted to a village, requiring they be driven off or killed.

Many of these animals were highly dangerous. Bears, wolves and wild boar posed a very real threat to a hunting party, to the point where there are still local legends about a particularly troublesome creature from the distant past. With little light and perhaps literal wolves at the door, the nighttime world of the Celts could be frightening indeed. The home offered the reassurance of good walls, companionship and a fire.

Street Layout

Many modern cities are built over the remains of thousands of years of occupation, which can sometimes be detected in the street patterns. Unless part of a settlement or city was destroyed completely, perhaps in a major fire, there would never be the opportunity to rebuild on a more rational pattern. Newer dwellings and businesses replaced older ones in a steady progression, with the occasional major alteration when an area was cleared and repurposed.

The overall effect of this was that the pattern of roads between the buildings was retained as the centuries passed. Round houses with wattle-and-daub walls might be replaced by a line of stone buildings but the urban framework remained. The car-unfriendly layouts of some modern cities may have their origins in an ancient Celt's choice of where to build his cattle shelter, or perhaps in his decision to build his house on the site of a pre-Celtic settlement.

Site Selection

The requirements for a useable settlement do not really change. Ground needs to be reasonably flat, without obstructions, and not prone to flooding. Only in relatively modern times have we taken to clearing large swathes of forest or building on land liable to be flooded without extensive defences being put in place. The ancient Celts built in logical places, and those places remain logical today. It is therefore hardly surprising that many of their ancient settlement sites are still occupied.

Traces of the Celtic people can also be found in place names. In the British Isles, a fortified place might be known as a Dun in the north and Din or Caer in Wales. Some places have retained their old names in some form, such as Cardiff (Caerdyf) in Wales and Dundee (Dun Daig) in Scotland. There are many towns in Britain with Pen in their name, or Coombe (cym). These are Celtic words for prominent geographical features – hill and valley respectively. Others are on the site of a Celtic settlement but have been given newer names, often by the Roman, Anglo-Saxon and Norse invaders. Modern Europeans may be separated from the Celts by time, but we live on the same land – and often in the exact same places.

HILLFORTS

Military, Civilian, or Both?

The strong places of the Celts were hillforts, created by strengthening the natural defences of high ground. There is, however, some debate about whether the forts were continuously inhabited or if they were military structures. Some of the forts were sizeable and contained a large number of dwellings. These may have been fortified towns, but many forts were too small to contain a significant number of people on a long-term basis. It is probable that most of the population lived on lower ground, with the fort as a refuge or seat of power.

There is evidence that many hillforts were occupied only when necessary, or that they may not have been fortifications at all. It is possible that what are assumed to be fortified hills were actually religious sites. Dwelling at the top of a hill can be inconvenient, and while inconveniencing attackers is certainly beneficial, a hillfort may not be practical for day-to-day life. Water can be difficult to obtain, livestock will need extensive areas to graze, and basic necessities must be hauled up and down a hillside daily. This is particularly true for forts built atop small, steep hills.

On the other hand, a hill is a natural defensive position and offers a vantage point to observe the surrounding lands. Projectiles launched from above have greater range than those coming from below, and the defenders are protected from incoming fire even if there are no deliberately constructed fortifications. Often there will be a limited set of practicable approaches; anyone trying to run up the steeper parts of the hill will arrive tired and off balance even if they do not slip down or fall victim to the defenders on the way up.

Defences

These practicable approaches can be improved by simple means. A boulder rolled into the right place can create a choke point on the only path up a hillside, slowing an enemy's advance and causing a force to bunch up where it will be an easy target. Defenders might even practice throwing weapons or shooting arrows at a known point in anticipation of a stalled or slowed assault at that location.

Some hillforts were nothing more than this; a naturally occurring position strengthened by well-positioned obstructions.

Some were far more elaborate. Ditches and earth ramparts go hand in hand and are relatively simple to construct so long as enough tools and labour are available. Earth dug out of a ditch can be banked up and compacted to create a rampart, with the ditch increasing the relative height of the obstacle.

Earthwork defences of this sort cannot prevent a determined enemy from getting in, but they impose delay and fatigue, acting as a force-multiplier for the defenders. Additional protection is provided by wooden stakes projecting outward or linked into a palisade. The construction of fortifications and their maintenance requires a great deal of work, and is only worth doing if there is a perceived need. This implies that conflict was common in the Celtic world, but that may not necessarily be the reason.

Impact and Access for Visitors

Members of tribes visited one another as traders or diplomats, or for festivals. Witnessing first-hand or hearing from someone who had been there that another tribe had good fortifications would impress, especially if the hearer knew just how hard these defences were to build and maintain. This might have a deterrent effect on military ambitions, but it also increased prestige in a wider sense. A tribe that could afford to sink countless hours into digging ditches and building ramparts was clearly strong, organized and affluent. This, then, was a friend worth having. A good hillfort might pay for itself in prestige and trade revenue.

There was also the consideration of day-to-day security. Thievery was not unknown, on a large or small scale, so limiting access to places and items valuable to the tribe made sense. In more modern times, city walls were often more about controlling the movements of visitors and the local populace than keeping out armies. Traders who could only access a settlement by one gate would be easy to regulate and perhaps impose a toll upon.

Hillfort Variations

Variations on the hillfort concept include 'marsh forts' which take advantage of limited possibilities for an approach due to flooding and soft ground, and more commonly cliff or promontory forts. The latter typically wall off a section of a promontory and are defended on most sides by sheer cliffs. The only practicable approach is defended by a wall built from loose stone or earthwork defences. Such fortifications are usually in places unsuited to daily life and were probably intended only for use in an emergency.

This implies the tribe would rush to the fort in times of conflict, but that may be a false impression. Rather than securing everyone behind the defences, a tribe might send only weaker people and livestock under the protection of a few warriors. This would leave the majority in place to go about their normal business or to move to intercept intruders on their land. In this case, a fort was not a passive defence but a place of security for non-combatants which freed the majority of adults to take more active measures against a threat.

Early hillforts were for the most part 'univallate', bounded by a single ditch and rampart, which might not completely surround the fort if terrain offered protection from some directions. Later forts might be 'multivallate', with two or more layers of defences. A prime example is Maiden Castle in Dorset, UK. There is evidence of some kind of enclosure, presumably defensive in nature, dating back to 3500 BCE or so, and of later habitation on the site. It eventually became a hillfort in the classic sense, though it was only one of a great many in the region.

Originally having a single rampart, Maiden Castle was developed into a sophisticated layered set of defences surrounding a large, inhabited area and encompassing a second hill. Like many such fortifications, it had defensive structures at the entrance. Burials at the site include individuals who died by violence, which has been taken as an indication that the fortifications were attacked by Roman troops during their invasion of Britain. This is debatable, however.

WARFARE

Metalworking allowed the creation of advanced weapons and the creation of a social group whose role was fighting other people – at least some of the time. Fights between bands of semi-nomadic people undoubtedly occurred, almost always over access to locations where food could be obtained. These would have the character of a hunt rather than warfare, and would be fought with the weapons of the hunt rather than specialized man-killing tools.

The Warrior Class

The rise of the warrior would not have taken place purely due to technological capability. Training for war took an individual out of another role, probably an economically productive one. Warriors, even if they were also part-time farmers, needed support from their community. They were a drain on the local economy most of the time, and therefore a need must exist for them to be worth having.

Even those of the Celts who fought for a living could not be considered professional soldiers as such; they were full-time warriors supported by a leader. They had time to train and practice as individuals and as a combat team, but did not engage in the drill required to carry out complex battlefield manoeuvres. Warriors fulfilled a social role much of the time. A group of warriors flanking a chieftain not only protected their leader but also made the point that he was important enough to need that protection. Warriors might also be used as representatives, perhaps sent to a nearby village to resolve a problem on behalf of a busy leader.

Ordinary people were too busy making a living to engage in much war training, but weapons handling was a respected skill and instruction was available from older relatives or combat veterans. This was a harsh world where violence was always a possibility. Even those who never fought other humans might have to deal with dangerous animals, while slaughtering livestock was a basic necessity.

Once well-armed and skilled individuals existed, they tended to rise up the social hierarchy to become leaders or the followers of leaders. Their capabilities allowed them to maintain their social position. They were also necessitated by politics. A growing population in fixed locations created interactions that had not occurred before. Disputes might arise over territory as before but there was also the possibility of conflict for other reasons. Failure to honour a trade deal or to punish tribe members who raided the lands of another might lead to war, as might an insult to the reputation of a tribe or its leaders.

The Style of Celtic Warfare

Celtic warfare was heroic in nature, with prominent individuals attracting a band of worthy followers and everyone else just doing their best. Leadership was by example, and tactics were for the most part simple. On the field, the usual approach was to close with the enemy and fight it out; complex manoeuvres were not possible even if orders could be conveyed in time.

This does not mean that Celtic warfare was entirely disorganized or amateurish. War bands were experienced at working together and trusted one another. On the small-unit scale these groups could be highly effective, and enough of them working together created a formidable army. Fighting Celts was not like battling a Greek phalanx of tightly ranked spearmen; it was a fluid situation with small groups exploiting whatever advantages they could find and supporting one another as they saw the need.

Celtic tactics might be straightforward in terms of battlefield manoeuvres, but they were capable of ingenuity and subtlety in large-scale warfare. Ambushes and attacks intended to provoke an enemy into pursuing into unsuitable terrain were favoured gambits. If an enemy force could be drawn into a marsh, its advantages in mobility and organization would be greatly diminished. The Celts were prideful people but not stupid. Hit-and-run raids were an accepted tactic in the face of a superior force, and there was no shame in retreating from a bad situation.

Behaviour in Battle and Its Social Ramifications

A questionable decision on the part of a leader might result in accusations of cowardice and a loss of confidence among followers, but a Celt with a reputation for prowess and boldness could defend a decision to retire more readily than one known for hesitancy or hanging back. This could lead to recklessness, accepting greater risk and the inevitability of casualties in return for maintaining a reputation. The same applied to the ordinary tribespeople who made up the bulk of any force. Enduring danger in a short battle was better than losing the respect of peers for all time, and a well-timed spear thrust might earn great rewards if noted by someone of influence.

There was a great deal of social pressure on a Celt in battle. His fellows might be just as terrified as him but if no one was willing to be the first to run they would stand – and perhaps die – together. If another was seen pushing forward quickly, there was a perceived need to do the same. The result was a tendency for a battle to quickly break down into multiple small actions. More organized opponents such as the Romans wrote with scorn about these disorganized scrambles, and this contempt still exists today among some historians.

Many modern writers take the stance that Romans had uniforms and marched in step and are therefore worthy of respect, while the Celts and other barbarians were a bunch of dumb brutes with over-inflated egos. The truth is that these were two entirely different approaches to warfare, and each worked in context. Rome was an organized state which could afford to pay professional troops and keep them under arms on a constant basis. The Celtic mode of warfare was suited to their tribal society and made economic sense for a smaller polity. When there was no fighting to be done, the majority of the tribe's spear-strength went back to economically productive activities such as farming, herding and crafting.

Fighting Naked

Some sources state that the ancient Celts fought naked, or that some of them did. One Roman writer claimed this is so they would not be slowed down by clothing that snagged on briars and the like. This idea seems questionable, since briars will snag flesh just as enthusiastically as they will cloth. Charging through the spiny undergrowth naked seems like an excellent way to put yourself out of action before reaching the enemy.

While it is possible that some Celts did fight in the nude, it is more likely that the concept arose from second-hand information. The terms 'bare-chested' or 'naked' might refer to being without armour and have become mistranslated or misunderstood. Likewise, Greek depictions of naked Gaulish warriors may have owed more to the Greek preference for nudity in statues than an attempt to accurately record the accoutrements of the subject.

Celtic Armour

Little armour was worn by the early Celts, most of it made of leather or quilted cloth. Some sources mention bronze or iron cuirasses (armour covering the chest and back) of a sort similar to those used by the Greeks and early Romans. The Celts also made use of – and may have invented – chain mail. They were capable of making wire through the riving process, which could then be formed into rings that were butted or riveted together. Chain mail is heavy and, more importantly, does not distribute its weight well, which can impede the user. Nevertheless, it provides good protection and would be sought after by those expecting to be involved in combat.

Some Celtic groups, notably in Italia, made use of helmets constructed from leather and bronze, but head protection seems to have been unpopular in other areas. A number of highly decorative helmets, including the one and only horned helmet from the era ever found, have been unearthed by archaeologists in various Celtic lands and there are written references to others. These seem to have been ceremonial rather than practical items, though some might have had a disconcerting effect upon an enemy. Among these is a design with a mechanical bird atop its crest, which flapped its wings as the wearer moved.

The Celtic Shield

Much more prevalent was the use of the shield. The Celtic shield was usually tall and broad, providing good protection from blows and projectiles at the cost of weight. The simplest designs were of wooden planks with a central boss to provide strength and position for a handgrip. Lighter versions used wood mainly as a support for layers of leather whose resilience might be greater than that of a simple wooden shield.

Use of the Spear

The primary weapon of war was the spear, with a bronze or iron head. Spears are often denigrated as weapons for the poor, but they are perhaps the most effective all-round battlefield weapon. Even high-status warriors and leaders would enter combat with a spear, switching to their swords for close-quarters combat or when their spears were expended.

Two main types of spears were used. Lighter spears, often referred to as javelins, were thrown at the enemy. Roman sources refer to Celtic warriors holding two of these spears in their lead (left) hand, at times in addition to the shield. A warrior could run forward a few paces, hurl his spear and quickly grab another one from his shield-hand to throw again, or could retreat behind his shield to re-arm or avoid counter-fire.

The heavy spear varied in length according to local preferences but was considered a potent weapon in the hands of a skilled user. The flexing of a spear shaft provided a boost to a spear that encountered resistance, enabling it to spring aside a weakly braced shield or punch through body armour and flesh. A long spear also provided advantages of reach against some enemies and allowed cavalry to be fended off or attacked if they ventured too close. The bow appears to have been used much more for hunting than warfare, though it would have been pressed into service at need. The sling was also used by some Celtic groups.

Use of the Sword

The Celts were primarily famous as swordsmen, even though the sword was a weapon for personal combat more than the battlefield. Iron weapons were used alongside bronze during the Hallstatt period and replaced them over time. Roman accounts of 'Gaulish' weapons of this era speak of poor-quality weapons that frequently bent upon delivering a blow. This may have been a result of the transition from mature bronze technology to new iron. The Hallstatt-era Celts were excellent metalworkers who developed pattern-welding techniques to create a form of steel which was both flexible and strong. Early attempts might not have been so good, however.

The Celtic sword was, for the most part, fairly short and designed for cutting strokes, as is common in battlefield weapons. There was little hand protection in the form of a crosspiece. The sword could thrust, but this would likely be reserved for a finishing stroke against a wounded or otherwise open enemy. A warrior who overextended on a thrust might find his weapon pushed aside by a shield, or an agile enemy might dodge into position for a return stroke. A sword tip lodging in the shield of an enemy might account for some of the bent blades described by Roman writers.

There was a tendency towards shorter swords which were little larger than overgrown knives in the late Hallstatt/early La Tène era, with longer weapons being prevalent in later periods. Those of the Celtiberians were short and handy at close quarters, and impressed Roman observers by being so springy that a wielder could bend his weapon over his head to touch both shoulders without damaging it. Roman respect for this weapon, the Gladius Hispaniensis (Spanish Sword) as they called it, was such that it was adopted as the primary infantry weapon of the Roman army.

The Celts had other influences upon Roman military equipment and practice. The classic Roman helmet is designed to deflect overhead blows such as those delivered by a tall man using a sword. Similarly, shoulder protection against such blows made the weapons of the Celts less effective. They may have ultimately been defeated by the Romans. but the European Celts made their mark on their enemies in terms of both doctrine and equipment intended to counter Gaulish ferocity.

Celtic Cavalry

Celts fought primarily on foot, but some Celtic groups developed a fearsome reputation as cavalry. The stirrup had not been invented at this time, so Celtic cavalry depended on their well-designed saddles and their horsemanship to remain seated. Long spears could be used to stab enemies from a distance at which they might not be able to respond. It is possible that the spear was at times couched under the arm in the manner of later, stirrup-equipped cavalry, but it could also be used to thrust to the sides, jab down from overhead or be swept as a sharp-sided club.

Javelins were also thrown from horseback. Some Celtic groups became adept at harassing enemies and even forcing them to change position, limiting their options or drawing them out to be overwhelmed. There are records of a sophisticated casualty-handling system, whereby a wounded rider could be brought out of the fight and his horse used by someone else, or an unhorsed warrior might be brought a fresh mount.

Use of Chariots in Warfare

In the British Isles, horses were used for war, but the chariot did not fall out of favour as it had elsewhere. In some Celtic societies the commander of the chariot drove it, with warriors protecting him and striking at the enemy. In other areas the commander was the primary fighter, with an expert charioteer to take him where the fighting was. Heroic stories of warriors running up the pole between their horses to strike at the enemy may or may not have been based on feats performed either in demonstrations of skill or actual combat.

Chariots could also be used as 'battle taxis' for a force of elite warriors. Thundering along the front of an enemy force with javelins hurled at intervals, they would frighten and dismay an enemy, perhaps disordering their ranks. The warriors would leap down, launching a fearsome attack, then sharply retreat to jump aboard their waiting transport. Such a way of fighting surprised the first Romans to land in Britain. Far from being an anachronism retained only for sport as they were in Europe, chariots proved surprisingly effective in skilled hands. Chariots could also be used to quickly create an improvised field fortification.

The 'scythed chariot' may or may not have been a reality. In theory, a wildly racing chariot with blades on the axles could cause carnage and disorder among close-ranked infantry. There is no clear archaeological evidence that the Britons attached huge blades to their chariots, as well as several practical reasons not to do so. Aside from the danger to friendly warriors and their own chariot-horses posed by an imprecisely driven chariot, the mass of blades on the axles might cause stability problems or even cause the wheels to come off.

However, there are accounts in traditional Celtic mythology and some Roman writings that they did indeed use chariot blades. It is possible that it was done as an experiment or an expedient, and was misunderstood to be common practice. It might also have been a wild tale told by veterans of their hair-raising adventures, or a retelling of traditional Celtic tales.

Psychological Warfare

The ancient Celts also practised psychological warfare. Tattoos or drawings on the skin, and hair spiked up with lime, gave the user an air of wild ferocity and otherness that could be unsettling. They took the heads of enemies as trophies and even used the skulls as drinking vessels, displaying them at feasts to remind everyone of their previous conquests. Some warriors are said to have carried the severed heads of enemies on their horses or hurled the head of a family member into an enemy's fort as a combination of curse, challenge and insult. This straddled the line between warfare and religion.

GODS, HEROES, BARDS & DRUIDS

CELTIC GODS

The ancient Celts left virtually no written record of their religion, though there are many carvings and other images which grant some insight. The later Insular Celtic mythologies and beliefs were recorded by literate people, but they were in many cases churchmen whose mission was to supplant the older pagan gods with their own Christian deity. Such records must therefore be approached with caution. Folktales handed down through the centuries and finally recorded by secular scholars offer further information but, as always, the passage of time has resulted in distortion.

The religious beliefs of the Continental Celts were recorded by Roman scholars, notably Julius Caesar, but again they are being seen through the lens of writers who found it convenient or expedient to equate Celtic gods to Roman ones. This may have been an effort to simplify the subject for the reader or a misunderstanding of what they saw and heard reported. Alternatively, the Romans may have been following an age-old habit of conquerors: If the subjugated people can be convinced their gods are actually the same ones as their conquerors worship, or if they can be converted to the conquerors' religion, then they will be more easily ruled.

Simple and tidy equivalents are questionable in this regard. There is a possibility of commonality, however. The Celts were an Indo-European people whose beliefs derived ultimately from the Proto-Indo-European religion. Much of Roman belief and mythology was influenced by or derived from Greek mythology, which in turn owed a great deal to the Proto-Indo-Europeans. So when a Roman writer states that the Gauls worship Mercury this is both inaccurate and over-simple – but perhaps not entirely untrue.

Celtic versus Roman Deities

In his *Gallic Wars*, Julius Caesar records what he knows – or chooses to state – about Gaulish (Celtic) religion. He identifies five primary deities, naming them as Mercury, Apollo, Mars, Jupiter and Minerva. Of these, Caesar states that Mercury is the greatest and most prominent. Mercury – or the Gaulish Mercury-equivalent – is a god of trade and travel, and of the arts. The god identified by Caesar as Mercury was known by different names, including Lugh and Llew.

It is notable that while Romans worshipped Jupiter as the king of the gods, the Gauls, according to Caesar, considered one of Jupiter's servants as their most important deity. The 'Jupiter' of the ancient Celts was Jupiter Taranis, a god of thunder and the sky. He is also referred to as Turenn. The name Mars seems to have been applied to any Celtic god with connotations of war and combat, and also sometimes healing. One example is Mars Camulos, or just Camulos, who was worshipped in Britain and Gaul.

Apollo is unusual in having the same name in both Roman and Greek religion, and is identified by Caesar as a Celtic god of healing and wisdom. The Celtic version is sometimes known as

Grannos or Grannus. Another candidate for Apollo-equivalent is Belenus, a god of fire and renewal after whom the Beltane festival is named. The Roman goddess Minerva is equated with Athena in Greek mythology and Sulis among the Celts. She is credited with overseeing law, knowledge, insight, and of being a patron of a civilized or at least organized society. As with other Celtic deities, it is entirely possible that 'Minerva' was in fact several different local goddesses associated with wise and learned leadership.

The goddess Epona was associated with horses, and apparently was worshipped on the Continent before becoming popular with non-Celtic members of the Roman hegemony. She has aspects both of fertility, as the mother of horses, and war. It is probable that Epona worship came to the British Isles in Roman times, imported by auxiliary troops rather than spreading from one Celtic community to another.

The Roman account of Celtic religion is biased at best. Some observers might have tried to comprehend and accurately relate what they observed but others, like Caesar, had their own agenda. His are works of self-aggrandizement, intended to create a legend. He is not unduly concerned about analysing the Celtic religion, he just needs to say enough to paint a picture of those he conquered which will be acceptable to his audience. If they seem like ignorant savages in desperate need of some Roman civilization, this suits his agenda better than an account of people with a rich and diverse culture.

Similar Gods, Different Names

Dozens of Celtic gods, perhaps hundreds, are now thought to have been worshipped. Some of these were local and minor, and in others there seems to be an overlap. It is not possible to say for certain whether a particular god was known by different names in different places or if they are separate but similar gods. Some appear in legends in one region which have no parallel elsewhere, but that does not rule out the idea of one god worshipped under different names and in different ways by various Celtic cultures.

One example is Coventina, a goddess associated with springs and water sources in the British Isles. As such, she would be essential to Celtic communities and was probably worshipped in some form over a wide area. Inscriptions found on the Continent may or may not refer to Coventina. Linguistic differences make it difficult to determine if two apparently similar words or names are actually related. If so, her worship may have been even more widespread and, if not, there would have been local deities associated with water sources which might be conflated with her.

The Continental Celts may not have had a sea-god, as the majority of their home regions were far inland. The Insular Celts, on the other hand, lived close to the sea and were subject both to its bounty and to Atlantic storms. The Irish Celts recognized Manannán mac Lir as the god of the sea and protector of the Blessed Isles. These were said to be located somewhere in the Atlantic Ocean and were home to ancient Greek heroes. Manannán mac Lir had much in common with the king of the Norse gods, Odin. He possessed a chariot or boat that could travel over the sea without needing to be guided and a horse that could run on water. He was also associated with warfare, gifting armour and loaning his magical sword to Lugh for his battles with the evil Formorians, a race of supernatural giants.

The Gaulish god known as Sucellus was associated with death and fertility, and is sometimes depicted in the company of a three-headed dog similar to the Kerberos of Greek mythology.

There are obvious parallels, since these depictions are associated with modern-day Hungary, whose Celtic people were heavily influenced by their Greek neighbours. The Continental Sucellus seems to be equated with the Irish Dagda, a benefactor who had a cauldron of plenty along with a harp that played itself and could change the seasons. Dagda's club could slay any man – or nine at once – and could also bring the dead back to life. He is identified by the Romans as Vulcan, the forge-god, but is much more important in Irish mythology than Vulcan was to the Romans.

Antlered Gods

Depictions exist of one or more 'antlered gods'. These are humanoid figures with horns or antlers, which may or may not be the same being in each case. Only one inscription has been found relating to a figure of this type, naming it as Cernunnos. Cernunnos is depicted on the Gundestrup Cauldron, a vessel comprised mostly of silver that was found in a peat bog in Denmark, and appears to be associated with nature and death. It is possible that Cernunnos is the same figure known as Herne the Hunter in Old English mythology. Cernunnos appears to have been a rather dark nature-god, in keeping with an era when nature could be dangerous and frightening. As a powerful pagan god he was naturally seen as an opponent of and a threat to Christianity, leading to conflation with the Antichrist.

War Gods

It is likely that the many gods identified as Mars or Mercury by the Romans were local in nature, perhaps an ancestor or protector of a single tribe. As such, they would be associated with war, trade or leadership but might not be worshipped elsewhere. Likewise, there were many local gods associated with bodies of water, regions of land or areas of interest such as healing, agriculture and trade. One possible example is Danu, known in Ireland as the mother-goddess of the Tuatha Dé Danann – the mythical tribe that drove out the Formorians and claimed Ireland as a Celtic homeland. She may also be associated with the River Danube, as a goddess of the original Celtic homeland.

Some deities are known from only a few sources or even a single one, and then at second hand. The goddess Andraste is one such. She is said to be a goddess of war and leadership worshipped among the Iceni tribe of Britain and invoked by their queen Boudicca during her revolt against Rome. Andraste is one of several deities who have become associated with chariots and may be conflated with other war goddesses.

The Morrigan

Other deities are highly complex, or accounts of them are confusing. Morrigan, or the Morrigan, is one such being from old Irish mythology. Sometimes portrayed as a deity and sometimes as a shapeshifting mortal sorceress, Morrigan appears in a number of tales. She is generally followed by misfortune and death, and sometimes takes the form of a raven. In this guise she will wait near a battle site or other location where bloody deeds are expected. Sometimes the Morrigan raven brings warnings, though whether this is an attempt to help or a way to make events more complex and violent is an open question.

Morrigan appears in a number of Irish legends, sometimes as the wife of Dagda, but is not specifically named in other mythologies. There are parallels, however, such as the sorceress Morgan le Fay from some versions of the King Arthur story. In some versions,

Morrigan is identified as a tripartite goddess comprising Badb, Macha and Nemain (or Danu), while other variants hold that she is the sister of these goddesses. The confusion is increased by a habit of referring to any woman with supernatural powers as a Morrigan; but given the enigmatic nature of this being, she probably would not be displeased.

Badb seems to particularly delight in causing warriors to panic. Appearing as a raven, crow or hag, she bears dire warnings of slaughter and terror to come, and can cause warriors to flee with her cries. Nemain has similar powers but can also drive warriors into a battle frenzy, amplifying the degree of bloodshed. Macha is another tripartite goddess in some accounts, and is often conflated with Danu. She is associated with reproduction and motherhood as well as conflict, and in concert with the other parts of the Morrigan can bring down a rain of fire upon her enemies.

Macha's legends speak of a time when she was the victim of the boasts of a man. Her husband or lover Crunniuc, a farmer, bragged that Macha could run faster than a horse. Naturally the king of Ulster wanted to see this, even though Macha was pregnant. She won the race but, in some versions, died immediately afterwards while giving birth to twins. From that time on, the men of Ulster were cursed to feel the pains of childbirth during their most desperate moments.

CELTIC RELIGIOUS PRACTICE

Celtic religious practices and festivals generally occurred at specific times of the year, based on the Celts' agrarian culture. While these festivities were meant to celebrate life, warmth and light, because they were pagan, they were distorted by later Christian writers.

Roman Interference and Co-opting

Roman writers in particular have painted a picture of the Celts as bloodthirsty barbarians who engaged in questionable or downright savage religious practices. This is a little hypocritical in an age when blood sacrifice and even human sacrifice were not uncommon, and were more about propaganda than truth. Quelling barbaric practices and imposing civilization at sword-point – and later at bayonet-point – has long been a favourite practice used by conquerors.

In recent years, there has been a revival of interest in Celtic religion and the associated festivals, and some ancient Celtic practices have survived into the modern era through a process of being co-opted by other religions. In particular, holy sites belonging to a native religion are targets for the invader or new social elite. Some, particularly in remote areas, can be destroyed, but the real victory for an invader religion is to take possession of the predecessor's holy places or redirect the population away from them.

There are several reasons for this. The most obvious is social control. Worshippers of the invader religion are subject to its influence, and locals are more likely to join the new religion if they cannot access the old one. There is also a mystic aspect: by taking control of the holy places the new religion not only supplants the old one in the hearts and minds of the people but also in the supernatural world.

Many Celtic holy places were associated with nature, notably sacred groves and bodies of water, but religion was practised wherever people lived. By building their own temples and churches nearby, perhaps even on the same site, invaders were able to channel the spiritual energies of the local population. Destroying sites such as the Druidic stronghold of Anglesey removed the alternative to worshipping in the Romans' temples as well as breaking the power of the Druids themselves.

Religious festivals could also be usefully co-opted. There is little to stop people from continuing observances of their old religion in private or in secret, but if they are in a church or other holy place being led in a different form of worship – perhaps one that retains some of the trappings of the old festival – they can be redirected to the new religion and the old ways robbed of their power. Ironically, perhaps, the reverse has also happened in modern times. The site of Stonehenge greatly predates the Celtic people and their religion but is today a centre for Celtic-revival festivals.

Celtic Festivals and the Seasons

The Celtic festivals are in general associated with times of the year that are significant to people of that technological era. The passing of winter into spring is particularly important to people depending on agriculture, and is marked by celebrations in many cultures. There are conflicting opinions about when the Celts celebrated the beginning of a new year, but significant evidence points to it being on or around the winter solstice. This falls in late December and is the shortest day of the year.

The Midwinter festival, known as Yule, represented the hope that the worst of the winter was over and warmer weather would soon return. The Yule log tradition derives from the ceremonial fires burned during the festival to drive away evil spirits and celebrate the return of light to the world. This was also a time when there would be indications about the coming year. The winter might be milder or harsher than expected, and stocks of food may have been more or less depleted.

A mild winter might allow the people to be a bit more generous in using up their preserved food, leading in turn to optimism about the coming year, whereas a particularly cold Yule meant that stocks had to last longer and livestock would suffer more. A heartfelt cerebration of warmth and light would not only raise morale but might influence the gods and nature itself to be generous.

In a time without modern calendars, solstices and equinoxes provided a useful way to measure the year and were a logical time for festivals. The midpoints between these significant days were also important. The fire festival of Imbolc was held midway between Yule and the spring equinox, at the beginning of February according to modern calendars. Like Yule, Imbolc was co-opted by the Christian Church – in this case becoming Candlemas.

Spring Equinox

The day of the spring equinox was considered the first day of spring and named Ostara. This was the beginning of the agricultural year, a time to hope and pray for healthy herds and abundant crops. Ostara was co-opted as Easter by the Christian Church. It was followed by Beltane, midway between the equinox and solstice. This was another fire festival, in which people and livestock passed between large fires in a purification ritual intended to keep bad influences from blighting the coming months.

There is evidence for fire festivals of a similar sort in other cultures at the same time of year, which is logical given that everyone experienced similar conditions wherever they lived. This was the best and most joyous time of the year, or at least the time when the average Celt was least likely to be cold and hungry. It was a propitious time for handfastings and weddings, and for other new endeavours such as building a house or trading with another tribe.

In modern times, Beltane has been revived by various groups with different interpretations of what the festival should be. Fire is a universal element, but beyond that opinions seem to differ. There are those who claim they are accurately recreating the ancient festival and those who are more concerned with the general spirit of the day. Some incorporate neopagan elements of questionable veracity and some simply do what seems natural at such a time. It is not possible to say any of them are wrong; a festival of this sort is arguably a concept that transcends any one culture and while it was observed by the ancient Celts it was not owned by them.

Autumn Equinox

The festival of Lammas marked the beginning of autumn. It is also named Lughnasa after the Irish sun god Lugh, and both celebrated the harvest and prepared the participants for the darkening days ahead. It was followed by Mabon, on the autumn equinox. The descent into winter was marked by Samhain, which fell midway between Mabon and Yule. There are those who contend that the Celtic new year began at Samhain, but Yule is a more logical candidate as a time of renewal.

Beltane and Samhain are important in some mythologies as times of great change in the supernatural world. In Irish mythology the mystic Otherworld is dominated by two groups known as the Seelie and Unseelie Courts. The Seelie Court, which ruled from Belane to Samhain, was composed of powerful but not directly inimical beings. Whilst dangerous and capable of doing harm to humans, the Seelie did not go out of their way to cause trouble.

At Samhain the Unseelie Court took control. Just as powerful and capricious as the Seelie, the Unseelie wanted to cause harm in the mortal world and would actively seek out victims. The cold, dark half of the year between Samhain and Beltane was a fearful time for mortals.

There is some evidence that the ancient Celts believed these were times when the veil between the natural and supernatural worlds grew thin and strange events occurred. If so, clustering together around a fire would have been a great comfort. The festival of Samhain was co-opted by the Christian Church as All Hallows' Eve (Halloween) on October 31 and All Hallows (or All Saints') Day on November 1. This was a time when saints would be venerated and prayers offered for those who had died but not yet entered heaven.

Some pagan practices were still followed in later Christian Halloween celebrations. In parts of Scotland and Ireland, gifts were left outside for roving otherworldly creatures in the hope of propitiating or distracting them. People would also dress up as monstrous creatures as a disguise to hide from them. As belief in the supernatural waned, these practices became more social and fun than fearful. Today, Halloween is commercialized almost beyond recognition, but its origins can still be traced back to the pagan fears of supernatural danger.

FUNERAL AND SACRIFICIAL PRACTICES

The ancient Celts engaged in various sacrificial practices, some of which have resulted in a greater modern understanding of their society than might otherwise have been possible. Items were sometimes thrown into bodies of water, presumably as offerings. Whether or not the location was sacred to a particular god is an open question, but being submerged would place the offerings beyond retrieval and therefore outside the mundane world.

In some cases, large collections of offerings have been found by archaeologists, including expensive items such as swords and jewellery. Recovered swords are in many cases bent in a manner unlikely to have occurred after the sacrifice was made, suggesting they were deliberately made unserviceable as part of the process. Other items appear to have been constructed specifically for use as sacrifices, such as shields that are richly decorated and too light to be useful in battle. These water sacrifices give an insight into many aspects of Celtic society. Swords, for example, were expensive to make and to obtain, so anyone sacrificing one must be both devout and prosperous.

Use of Fire

As in many other cultures, fire was used by the Celts in religious observances – though not always in a destructive manner. There is evidence that some sacrifices were made by placing an object, animal or – according to some legends – a person in a prepared pyre then lighting it. These might be votives, representative objects, or actual items to be given up in sacrifice. The fires would typically be large and constructed with care to ensure there were no embarrassing failures, but they would be of a conventional bonfire configuration.

The idea of the 'wicker man', a humanoid statue imprisoning humans and animals for sacrifice by burning, is not supported by much in the way of evidence. It is described by Caesar, with references by other writers, but may have been the product of misunderstanding or misrepresentation. Some kind of cage, perhaps of wicker, might have been used to contain votives and of course there is no likelihood of archaeological evidence given the nature of the festival. The practice of burning a wicker effigy has become normal in modern 'Celtic revival' type festivals, though with a noticeable lack of human sacrifices.

Fire was part of religious festivals for pragmatic reasons as well as spiritual ones. Whenever people gathered they would need to cook food, and the food they were given might become part of the observance. Light was also necessary when night fell, for practical reasons as well as the symbolism. At Beltane, for example, people and animals passed between two fires to be purified. The warmth and light of the fires would drive away evil spirits and the passage had connotations of rebirth and renewal. Torchlight processions, combined with music, helped create a truly spiritual experience.

Human Sacrifice

Outsiders have recorded that the Celts practised human sacrifice. This is true, but it was not a common practice. It seems that in times of great need a sacrifice was made, with the severity of the situation determining the level of sacrifice required. It is not clear who most of the sacrifices were, but extreme circumstances would require a leader or king as the subject. Various 'bog bodies', recovered from and preserved by swampy areas, show signs of an excessive amount of force used to kill the subject. These bodies are typically bound, mutilated and stabbed multiple times and/or subjected to blows to the head. This might be construed as torture of a particularly disliked enemy but more likely represents a ritual sacrifice to ward off a run of bad fortune. There are references to a 'threefold death' inflicted on the subject in order to fulfil spiritual requirements.

Some of the 'bog bodies' recovered by modern archaeologists may have been accidental or attempts to cover up a murder rather than ritual killings. Those who died under more normal circumstances would usually be buried or cremated. It was believed that the deceased would move on to another life, but might also try to return to this one. That was undesirable, so measures were taken to prevent it. Heavy rock slabs barred the way into tombs and limbs were often tied to prevent the corpse wandering around. In some legends, the dead return as apparently living people who may have supernatural abilities. Their presence is rarely beneficial.

In the right and proper order of things, a deceased Celt would begin a new life somewhere else. Some sources suggest this to be a magical land far away or deep underground, whilst others suggest the person would return to the same world in a distant region. It was apparently possible to take goods and perhaps even people into this next life. Grave-goods were generally suited to the station and occupation of the deceased; weapons for warriors and jewellery for rich and powerful leaders. Animals and at times other people have been found in the graves of important individuals. At times, these seem to have been servants or family members but other burials may have contained defeated enemies.

Beliefs about what happened after death changed over time. It is not clear exactly what the Hallstatt-era Celts believed, though the fact they buried grave-goods with the deceased suggests they expected some form of afterlife or reincarnation. In Irish mythology the island of Tech Duinn was considered to be a portal to the Otherworld, whereas the Welsh Annwyn (alternatively, Annwn or Annfwyn) is sometimes portrayed as a land of the dead. It seems that some Celtic groups believed that the deceased spent some time at least in a land ruled by a god of the dead, perhaps whilst awaiting reincarnation.

There is some crossover between realms of the dead and worlds of supernatural beings. According to legend, far away across the western sea lay Tír na nÓg, the land of eternal youth. This place is sometimes associated with reincarnation but does not appear to be an afterlife as such. Tír na nÓg was visited by Oisín, son of the hero Fionn mac Cumhaill. He was taken there by Niamh, daughter of the king of Tír na nÓg, and spent three years with her. Upon returning to Ireland for a visit, Oisín discovered that three hundred years had passed and he began to age rapidly. The concept of a magical land where great people can go instead of or after dying appears in other Celtic-inspired mythology. In the legend of King Arthur, the mortally wounded king is taken to the magical land of Avalon to wait for a time when he is once again needed.

HEROES AND SUPERNATURAL BEINGS

Celtic legend is replete with heroes and other beings with supernatural powers. Some of these are difficult to define, being represented as deities at times and powerful, but mostly mortal, at others. This may have more to do with modern perceptions than conflicting accounts; perhaps the nature of these beings was perfectly obvious to the average Celt hearing their tales. Alternatively, it may be that the stories varied from place to place, over time, and according to the teller.

Some of the heroes of Celtic legend have at least one divine parent, a feature common in several mythologies. Early contact with Greece may have resulted in some commonality of mythical elements, though these might go back even further to the Proto-Indo-European people. They are also frequently equipped with magical weapons and treasures. The concept of a semi-divine hero with powers above those of mortals is a powerful storytelling device, allowing a hero to perform exceptional deeds but also to encounter difficult challenges.

The most famous of these is Cú Chulainn. There are multiple versions of the story of his birth, all of which are exotic and magical, and give an insight into Celtic society of the time. Cú Chulainn's mother was Deichtine, sister to King Conchobar mac Nessa. She was the king's charioteer, and was with him when he hunted a flock of birds that had been causing trouble. Caught in a snowstorm, the party sought shelter in the home of a hospitable young man whose wife and horse were both in labour. Despite this distraction the young man looked after his guests.

In the morning, the house and the young couple had vanished, leaving behind the two colts born during the night and the newborn baby. Deichtine tried to raise the child but it died, and soon after a small creature of some kind leapt into her mouth as she was taking a drink. This was one of several occasions in Celtic mythology upon which a woman became pregnant by swallowing something.

The god Lugh appeared to Deichtine and explained that he was the young man she had met and she was pregnant with his child. Her brother found her a suitable husband but Deichtine was ashamed at carrying the child of someone other than her husband so crushed the child within her. She was then made pregnant by her new husband, and from this strange chain of events came a demi-god child who would one day be the hero Cú Chulainn.

Magical parentage is a useful device for storytellers. A typical mortal, no matter how skilled or clever, is limited by the capabilities of their flesh and blood. If they need abilities beyond the capabilities of their body, they will need to seek divine favour, magical assistance or to transcend the mortal frame. A supernatural hero has the capability to do this, though typically their story will require them to undertake dangerous journeys and make sacrifices to unlock or learn what they need.

This trope is repeated again and again through myth, legend and fiction. It is the core concept of many video games, movies and novels. Often the hero is advised by what might be termed an oracle; someone or something that provides cryptic and occasionally misleading information that eventually leads to whatever the hero is trying to achieve. They may interact with dangerous beings and often cause more problems than they solve. While not unique to Celtic mythology, the hero-saga is alive and well today, and owes much to the tales told by ancient bards.

One factor in many of these hero-sagas is the influence of magical items. These range from weapons such as swords and shields to chariots, boats and items of clothing that can protect against threats or grant special advantages. Similarly, supernatural creatures and beings provide a level of opposition suited to a hero with a magic spear. A fight between ordinary warriors could still make an exciting tale, but one in which the hero must overcome obstacles to discover the secret weakness of his enemy is likely to be much more interesting.

A common plot for hero-sagas – whether a movie, a video game or an ancient Bardic tale – revolves around a threat too fearsome for mortals to face. Even the hero must seek some advantage in order to stand any chance. Guided by what turns out to be unreliable advice, the hero undertakes journeys to find whatever allies, talents or items are needed, then returns to face the foe. Sometimes the real solution is not the thing the hero thought he needed to find. This format has been used and reused endlessly, but if the details are interesting enough the story never gets old.

As an example: Lloyd Alexander's *Chronicles of Prydain* is derived from Welsh mythology. It charts the progress through five novels of an assistant pig-keeper named Taran. Surrounded by enchanters, bards and warriors he is thrust into great events and is completely out of his depth. Taran's parentage is unknown, and he dreams of discovering he is of noble family. He never does, however, but along the way his sacrifices and courageous decisions turn him into a hero. This is a welcome change from the 'Chosen One' trope so common in fiction; Taran is 'just some guy' who rises to become someone important through his own efforts.

Some of the supernatural beings of Celtic mythology have become part of modern mythology used in games and entertainment. Among these are creatures such as the banshee and the various 'fairy folk' who interact with humans according to their nature. The nature of these creatures has been adapted to fit the lore behind the story being told, creating a distorted image in the minds of modern observers.

DRUIDS

Very little is known today about the Druids of Celtic society. They can be traced back to what is now Wales, but it is likely a similar or even identical social class of learned individuals existed in other Celtic societies. Roman writers painted a picture of savage and terrifying priests who delighted in slaughtering human sacrifices in a variety of inventive and unpleasant ways, but the reality seems to have been rather different.

Druids were the scholarly class. They fulfilled vital roles in society as lawyers, translators, physicians, spiritual advisors and at times emissaries. It is possible that some Druids specialized in one of these areas and that some had no spiritual function, though overlap seems likely. It is certain they were highly educated by the standards of the time.

Apart from a knowledge of medicine, which was vital to any functioning society, Druids also needed a working knowledge of meteorology and the seasons. They would be able to advise on whether to plant now or to wait a few days to avoid adverse weather conditions, and on similar matters regarding harvesting. This knowledge might have had a supernatural or spiritual content, but in the ancient world this was normal. Some of today's world religions include advice on what might seem like non-spiritual subjects such as courtly etiquette, warfare and how to make a home. To an ancient Celt the spiritual aspect and the mundane overlapped to a degree where they were inseparable.

Druids in legend are generally advisors or the source of magical assistance, and often have supernatural powers. Typically this is in the form of foreknowledge, though it is rarely perfect. This tradition has survived into modern fiction and legend. Today the term 'Druid' has connotations of closeness to nature and the ability to form a rather rustic form of magic, but the most famous magician in Western literature – Merlin, in the saga of King Arthur – has his origins in this Druidic tradition.

Early in the Roman occupation of the British Isles, Druidism was outlawed. It is recorded that the Druids retreated to Anglesey where they were assaulted by Roman legions in 61 CE. The Druidic tradition was all but extinguished, with surviving Druids driven into hiding and likely hunted down over the next few years. In so doing, Rome hoped to remove a potential rallying point for British resistance and to hasten the Romanization of Britain. The vilification of the Druids was largely propaganda to justify this act.

As custodians of knowledge, the Druids could remind their people of their lineage and previous triumphs. They had the ears of chieftains and kings, and were respected by the general population. In an era of superstition, the spiritual leaders of the tribes were highly influential in ways that might not seem obvious today. Frightened people were more likely to rise up if they thought they could win, and the Druids were a supernatural ace in their hand. There was also the possibility that they might curse those who did not stand with them. By eliminating this threat the Romans weakened the Celtic spirit as well as making resistance less likely.

Some aspects of the Druidic function were taken over by bards, and others by professionals in the Roman style. Medicine and the preservation of knowledge continued, but the uniqueness of the Druidic class was extinguished. A modern revival of interest relies on a mixture of conjecture and wishful thinking, and despite the claims of some individuals to know ancient Druidic secrets, modern Druidism is exactly that: a modern invention.

Modern Druidism includes concepts that were never connected with ancient Celtic Druidism. For example, large gatherings are held at Stonehenge which predates the Celtic people by many centuries. As with the festival of Beltane, modern Druidism is an interpretation of what it might have been like. Some of those involved have undertaken good work of a scholarly fashion and made reasonable conjectures about the subject. Others just enjoy dressing up and playing at being Druids. Unfortunately, there are some who insist on muddying the waters with false claims and pretences aimed at making money or gaining influence over the more easily persuaded members of the Celtic Revival community.

BARDS

In modern times the term bard might be used to describe a great poet or literary figure. William Shakespeare is widely known as 'The Bard' by those who consider him the pre-eminent British literary figure. The bards of the ancient Celtic world were more than just poets or storytellers; they were living repositories of knowledge and powerful figures in society.

As with certain other cultures, such as the Scandinavians of the same era, the Celts did not entrust their histories and other important information to a written form. Instead, it was learned and recited at need by the bards, who used rhyme and metre to ensure fidelity to details. A wrong name or word would stand out and highlight an error in poetic form and would be obvious even to those who did not know the story being told.

Training and Experience

Bards were trained and served an apprenticeship with more experienced individuals before seeking their own path. Many were retained by leaders and lords, though some bards made their living as wanderers. Anyone could expect to be fed and given a bed for the night wherever they went under the laws of hospitality, but the worry a bard might carry word of a settlement's stinginess might grant them a better welcome than other travellers.

A visiting bard would entertain the host community and bring news of events elsewhere. This might or might not be accurate; it was not uncommon for a lord to send out bards to speak of his great deeds or to ensure that a poem written by his household bard was repeated elsewhere. The line between accurate reporting and telling a good tale might be blurred at times.

The Work of a Bard

A bard might be trusted to tell the truth to the people who mattered about genealogies, precedents and important events, but the rest of the time he was a professional entertainer and storyteller. A bard would sing, recite poems and tell tales he felt were suited to the audience. In the Bardic tradition a tale was remembered in outline, with the details filled in with every retelling. As a result, there are many versions of the old Irish and Welsh myths that survived into the modern era. The same individual might have a different adventure, or the same set of circumstances might revolve around entirely different people. The bards kept the tales alive in a way that paper never could, and they ensured the stories evolved.

The story of Diarmuid and Grainne is one example. In this tale, Gráinne is unimpressed by an elderly Fionn mac Cumhaill, to whom she is betrothed. Instead she falls for one of his warriors, Diarmuid. The two run off but are caught by Fionn mac Cumhaill, who is persuaded to spare them. He cannot contain his jealousy, however, and allows Diarmuid to die of an injury instead of using his magic. The tale is retold as that of Tristan and Iseult in the Arthurian legends, though with a different piece of treachery at the end. In this version Tristan is wounded and can only be saved by Iseult. He instructs his friend to fetch her, and to come back with white sails on his ship if she is aboard. Tristan's jealous wife, also called Iseult, lies about the colour of sails, causing Tristan to give up on life and Iseult to die of a broken heart.

There are parallels in the modern world. Reboots of the same movie series or remakes of a classic video game may become tiresome eventually, but this is in the Bardic tradition. The classic science-fiction story *Battlestar Galactica*, filmed in the 1970s and rebooted in the 2000s, bears a strange resemblance to ancient tales of mariners escaping the sack of Troy to seek a new home. *Hansel and Gretel: Witch Hunters* is a ridiculously brilliant example of the Bardic art, featuring the orphaned children from the classic fairytale battling witches using a medieval gatling gun. A good bard would take the basic story and run with it, to the delight of the listeners. Lesser bards might only be able to recite the tired old version of the same tale.

The bards were not all tall tales and folk songs, however. In addition to preserving important records – which might be the resolution of disputes between tribes or kingdoms – bards were a regulatory force upon even the leaders of those kingdoms. A bard could satirize someone to punish them for poor behaviour or to force them to take actions they did not want to. This included kings and great lords as well as heroes and ordinary people.

Satirization

Satirizing was a general term for disrespect and ridicule, which might mean speaking plain words about the person in question or otherwise making them look foolish. However, a Bardic satirization was more serious. It might mean altering an existing tale to reflect badly on someone, but the most potent weapon in the bard's arsenal was a custom-created satirical poem. There were bards, according to legend, whose poems were powerful enough to curse individuals and bring misfortune upon them without the need to alter public opinion.

Satirizing a marriage partner unjustly was grounds for divorce, but bards appear to have been able to satirize anyone with impunity. Presumably there was an assumption that someone who killed a satirizing bard was demonstrating their lack of worth; certainly there were heroes and kings who did terrible deeds rather than simply spearing their satirist.

The bards could also create a poem of praise which would either counteract earlier satirization or help resolve a dispute. They might be used as a form of back-channel negotiators, allowing two powerful figures whose pride would not allow them to back down to be influenced by the words spoken by their respective bards about one another. A clever bard might carefully select the sort of tale or poem to be presented in order to modify the mood, and was assisted in this by a choice of music. In the Irish tradition, bards played the harp using the Three Noble Strains which could induce sadness, happiness or sleepiness.

The bards of the ancient Celtic people might be considered the ancient equivalent of the internet. A source of entertainment for everyone and reliable information for those who knew how to get it, they were also a means of mass communication and the ability to defame enemies or manipulate people through misinformation – or a clever choice of what information to present.

Taliesin

The most famous of all bards was Taliesin, a semi-mythical figure based on a real person who apparently was born in the latter part of the sixth century CE. A great many poetic works and other writings are attributed to this 'real' Taliesin, though it is possible his was simply a handy name to assign as the originator. His body of work is more likely to be a collection or conflation of traditional materials, with only part of it actually written by Taliesin himself.

The mythological Taliesin is a highly influential figure whose tale is told in *The Book of Taliesin*. According to legend, Taliesin was an ordinary servant who suffered an accident while handling a potion created by the witch Ceridwen. He spilled three drops on his thumb and instinctively licked them off, gaining beauty, wisdom and wit in the process. It was as well it was only three; any more would have killed him. As it was, Taliesin had to flee his angry employer. The Bardic inspiration he gained allowed him to transform himself into other objects, but still he was unable to escape. Instead, he attempted to hide by turning himself into a piece of grain.

Ceridwen ate the grain and became pregnant, eventually giving birth – or rebirth – to Taliesin. She forgave him his error and sent him to be raised by the lord of Ceredigion in what is now Wales. Taliesin grew up in Ceredigion, receiving an education and developing his poetic abilities.

His prediction that High King Maelgwn Gwynedd would die of disease proved correct and he was sought out as an advisor to the courts of the time. Among those he served was the legendary King Arthur, and Taliesin's son became a member of Arthur's court.

Merlin

The bard Taliesin is sometimes conflated with the magician Merlin in the tales of King Arthur. Both give wise advice and make predictions, though Taliesin is generally depicted as a talented man and Merlin as a supernatural force. Taliesin also appears in a number of modern stories as an advisor or legendary origin of an item or piece of cryptic information. He is also the subject of the second album by rock band Deep Purple, *The Book of Taliesin*, which was released in 1968.

Phelim Brady

Another legendary bard lived much later. This was Phelim Brady, the subject of an Irish ballad. According to the tale, Patrick Donnelly had the misfortune to be made Bishop of Dromore in 1697. This was the year of the Banishment Act, which forced hundreds of Catholic churchmen out of Ireland and sent others into hiding under threat of being charged with treason. Rather than leave Ireland, Donnelly reinvented himself as Phelim Brady, a wandering bard, and hid in plain sight. A defiant folk song about his life emerged in English in the mid-nineteenth century, but may date from much earlier. As is common in the Bardic tradition, there are multiple versions of the lyrics.

THE KELTOI &
THE ANCIENT GREEKS

Proto-Celtic people migrated into the Upper Danube region in modern Austria from around 2500 BCE and by 1500 BCE were firmly established there. They had knowledge of bronze-working, though exactly when the technology was discovered is open to some debate. Bronze-working is thought to have been practised as early as 3200 BCE around the Aegean Sea, and was widespread by 2000 BCE.

While tools made from copper were useful for some purposes, the ability to make durable items and weapons from bronze may have been the single most significant technological breakthrough in human history. Metalworking enabled a great many other technological leaps forward. Bronze-bladed ploughs revolutionized agriculture, while metal tools allowed precision work in fields as diverse as cloth-making and carpentry. Metal picks improved mining output, in turn facilitating more metalworking.

Making Bronze

In simple terms, bronze is made by mixing copper and tin, with other metals added to give the alloy desired properties. Typically, the mix is 90 per cent copper to 10 per cent other metals, which might be aluminium, nickel, tin or zinc. Molten bronze can be cast in a mould, requiring a temperature in the range of 1,000 to 1,150 degrees Celsius. Just getting to this stage required a significant amount of work.

The Celts of the Upper Danube Basin had access to copper ore, which could be pounded out of the rock with stone hammers. A Celtic copper mine followed the deposits, with galleries where the copper could be extracted linked by vertical shafts. Galleries would follow the deposits, twisting and turning as they went.

Once extracted, copper ore had to be purified by smelting. Once the majority of attached rock was bashed away, a mix of charcoal and ore was placed in a furnace, with air blown over the mix using bellows. Modern experimental archaeology has shown that it is possible to achieve suitable temperatures this way, but only at the expense of considerable effort. Smelting would be a team job, ensuring the bellows did not weaken as operators became exhausted.

The result of a first smelting process was highly impure copper. A second smelting in a crucible allowed gases to be released and impurities to rise as slag to the top of the liquid, where they could be scraped away. Hammering the cooled ore could also break out the worst of the impurities. Once ingots of reasonably pure copper were produced they could be used or traded to other communities.

A properly trained metalworker would be able to produce basic items reliably enough, but the ability of a master smith to create more durable, more effective and more beautiful work would place him far above the ordinary practitioners of his craft. Experience was the only guide, with temperature estimated by colour and the behaviour of the metal being forged.

Trade and Commerce

Equipped with bronze tools and weapons, the Proto-Celtic people of the Upper Danube were prosperous and well prepared to trade on equal terms with their neighbours. These included the people of what is now Greece and the Balkans. The Danube provided easy transportation for goods in that direction, and the ancient Celts are known to have traded along the great rivers of Europe. They traded salt in particular, but also copper, gold, textiles, hides and slaves.

The Celts of the Upper Danube were rich by anyone's standards. They imported luxury goods such as wine and olives, glass and silver, and exchanged rich gifts of crafted items with those they favoured. Some items, such as amber from the Baltic region, were used in jewellery or traded onwards. By 1500 BCE, the people of the Upper Danube were very much part of European society. As such, they were affected by events that took place far from their homelands.

THE HALLSTATT CELTS

The Celtic people of 1200–450 BCE are often referred to rather generally as the 'Hallstatt-Era' Celts, though there are subdivisions marking changes in technology and society. The period from 1200–800 can be termed the 'Bronze-Age Hallstatt' or 'Urnfield' culture, while 800–450 BCE is 'Iron-Age Hallstatt'. These and further subdivisions are useful to archaeologists and are based on finds of significant items in the same region.

At that time, there was a significant population dwelling in the Upper Danube Basin whom we now identify as early Celtic. This society seems to have been decentralized and settlements mostly quite small, but the presence of a salt mine at Hallstatt may have made it an economic centre.

The 'Hallstatt' generalization is a reference to major archaeological finds in the region of Hallstatt in what is now Austria, and not an indication that Hallstatt itself was of any particular importance to the Celtic people as a whole. The archaeological finds give an indication of what these people were like at that point in history, but of course any discovery is just a snapshot of how things were at a particular moment. The Hallstatt-era Celts lived in a time of great change and progress that would affect them, for the most part, indirectly. Perhaps the greatest influence came from the collapse of the Greek civilization to their south-east.

Interaction between the Hallstatt Celts and the people of Greece was common enough to be routine, though both cultures developed separately. The Greeks referred to their northern neighbours as Keltoi (barbarians), which, as already noted, was not indicative of savagery. However, the Celts drank their wine neat rather than watering it, which the Greeks considered to be the hallmark of civilized people. Drinking habits aside, whilst some conflict was inevitable, both cultures benefited from their relationship. In particular, the Celts imported tin from Greece, making this trade necessary for the production of bronze.

There was of course no Greek nation at this time. Greece and the surrounding lands were dominated by what is now termed the Mycenaean culture, centred on cities such as Mycenae, Athens and Thebes. This was a feudal-type society ruled by kings and with a strict social hierarchy, but relatively little is known about it for certain. What is clear is that the Mycenaeans were both warriors and traders, and a powerful force in the eastern Mediterranean. Presumably, they respected the Keltoi sufficiently that they preferred to trade than to fight.

THE BRONZE AGE COLLAPSE

Around 1200 BCE, the eastern Mediterranean suffered an upheaval that had serious effects on the Hallstatt Celts. Archaeological evidence and some ancient records point to a series of devastating attacks by sea-borne raiders. The identity of these 'sea peoples' remains unclear, and it is not certain whether they were the cause or a symptom of the wave of disaster that swept the eastern Mediterranean.

It has been suggested that the Sea Peoples originated in the lands surrounding the central or western Mediterranean and were driven east by drought, war or famine in their homelands. They may have been dispossessed people driven from their homelands by conquerors, and different groups might have had entirely different origins. It appears that they were not solely warriors but had families with them in at least some cases, in which case this was a violent migration rather than a period of raiding or conquest.

What is known from the archaeological record is that cities along the Mediterranean and Black Sea coasts were plundered and destroyed, and civilizations fell. Among them were the Hittite, Minoan and Mycenaean civilizations. Ancient Egypt was able to withstand the assault, building a navy to keep the ships of the Sea Peoples at bay. If drought or famine were involved, the ability of Egypt – and also the Assyrian civilization – to survive may also be attributed to extremely fertile lands along the great rivers that flowed through them.

Among the cities that were apparently destroyed was Troy. Long thought to be a myth, Troy has been identified with reasonable surety at a location in what is now modern Turkey. It has cast a long shadow over many other cultures, some of them very far away. Archaeology has identified a settlement on the site of Troy dating from around 3000 BCE; the very beginning of the Bronze Age.

Although the site is today inland, in its heyday Troy benefited from a coastal location on the Dardanelles, giving access to the Mediterranean and the Black Sea. It became a major trading port, with all the accompanying wealth and prestige. Despite its power, Troy was sacked around 1180 BCE and lost to history until modern times. The Greek poet Homer, writing after the end of the Greek Dark Age, wove a tale of war between the Greeks and Trojans which has remained influential to this day.

It may be that Homer was relating old folk stories dating from before the Bronze Age Collapse, and that there is some truth to the tales of the Trojan War. Either way, Troy has found its way into European legend in some peculiar places. According to Old English writers, the kings of the Britons could claim descent from Trojans who escaped the sack of their home city by way of Rome and Carthage. In all likelihood, the use of the name 'Troy' was a handy shorthand for storytellers: a mythical place of heroes a listener might be vaguely familiar with. Such references allowed the teller to get on with the tale without explaining someone's backstory in any real detail.

Whether or not the Trojan War ever happened, something smashed the civilizations of the eastern Mediterranean. The Hallstatt Celts were not, it seems, directly affected by these events but their trade with Greece was interrupted for several generations. From 1200 BCE to 800 BCE or so, Greece suffered a 'Dark Age' in which cities were abandoned and written records were lost. The most important consequence of this for the Keltoi was the interruption of trade in tin, which impacted the ability to make bronze. Since bronze was the cornerstone of Celtic technology, a replacement had to be found.

IRON

Greece was not the only possible source of tin, but the Danube and its tributaries made transportation of the heavy ingots much easier than carrying them overland from elsewhere. Bronze-working did not cease, but the difficulty of obtaining raw materials meant that some forges might stand idle. It would be possible to switch to making decorative items from gold or silver, but this did not fill the requirement for tools and weapons.

The same situation has occurred in modern times due to rising costs and material scarcity. Some goods have gone permanently out of fashion due to a temporary interruption in supply. It was not so very different in the ancient world, though the inability to replace worn-out tools might have more immediate effects than a rise in the cost of living.

Iron was an alternative to bronze but working it was much more difficult. There is evidence of some ironworking as early as 3000 BCE, but in many cases these were decorative items prized for the difficulty of making them rather than their usefulness as tools or weapons. Bronze-working was a mature technology and items made from it were durable. Perhaps more importantly, the quality of bronze implements was more reliable than early ironwork.

Bloomery Furnaces

The key to working iron was the bloomery furnace, which took the form of a chimney-like structure of stone or clay. A bloomery furnace did not produce temperatures high enough to melt the iron, instead creating small lumps of iron mixed with slag which could be hammered away. Repeating the process eventually produced iron pure enough to work with. This would in modern terms be called wrought iron. It has been estimated that as much as 20 kg of usable iron could be smelted from its ore per day using this process.

The iron produced by a bloomery furnace can vary in purity and quality, making it likely that early weapons and tools might not come out as intended. Some would bend easily, as Roman writers observed, while others were brittle. The simplest answer would be to mix iron of different purity levels by melting it, creating a homogenous material out of a variety of ingots. However, iron melts at around 1,150 Celsius, and with the technology of the day it was not possible to produce sufficiently high temperatures to melt the metal. This also made it impossible to cast iron by pouring it into a mould.

Pattern Welding

The answer, discovered by Celtic smiths, was a process known as pattern welding. By using strips of varying purity, perhaps selected by colour, it was possible to create a composite material whose overall properties were an average of those of the component parts. Soft iron was blended with harder and more brittle material, creating a better and more consistent end product.

Pattern welding required heating the metal to near-molten temperatures and repeated hammering and folding, a laborious process which did not always produce great results. However, as the Celtic smiths gained experience, they became capable of reliably producing high-quality items. By the time the Romans encountered the Celtiberians, the latter were able to produce sword blades flexible enough to be deliberately bent almost double without damage.

Quality Smithing

The twin characteristics required by an effective sword blade are sufficient hardness to retain a cutting edge combined with the flexibility to withstand impacts. A blade that is too hard may survive contact with weapons, helmets or shields for a time, especially if it is correctly aligned, but sooner or later it will crack or shatter. On the other hand, a weapon that is too soft will bend easily and not return to its proper shape.

This can be mitigated somewhat by the skill of the user. When a blow is struck, physics dictates that the same forces act on the weapon and the target. However, a correctly delivered cut with the edge well aligned, or a well-delivered thrust with the point of a weapon, concentrates force against the target in a manner which will cause the maximum damage while the opposite force is directed against the strongest axis of the weapon. A poorly made spear point or sword blade may still crumple even if a thrust is delivered directly along the weapon's main axis, and likewise a weak blade may still bend even if force is concentrated along its strongest axis, but failure is far more likely if the contact is made at a bad angle. Of course, a fight with weapons is an inherently chaotic situation in which no stroke is guaranteed to land as the wielder intends.

Higher-quality equipment offered the user multiple advantages; it held its edge longer and in the case of armour provided better protection for the same weight. However, the opposite side of the coin may have been more important; good-quality weaponry did not fail and leave the user vulnerable as frequently, increasing the survival rate of the users. By the time the Greek Dark Age was over and it was again possible to obtain sufficient tin, the Celts had fully adapted to iron and could use it to make superior equipment. Some bronze-working continued but the Iron Age had truly begun.

WEAPONRY

Swords

Although the spear was the main battlefield weapon, and with good reason, the Celts were known for their swords. These varied in design over time, and it can be difficult to define exactly what is, and what is not, a sword. It can be generally agreed that a sword is a long-bladed weapon designed for cutting, thrusting or both. The 'business end' is made from metal and there is some kind of handgrip of other materials fixed to the tang, a projection from the rear of the blade.

A degree of hair-splitting is sometimes necessary; a relatively long-bladed weapon whose handle is in parts pinned to the tang might be considered a knife rather than a sword. This became important in medieval times, when non-nobles were not allowed swords but could own long-bladed 'great knives' necessary for work. Weapons like the Germanic Grossemesser are in many ways similar to shortish swords but are knives under this legal definition.

This was not specifically an issue in Celtic times, but resulted from the stratification of society which did exist in that era. A desire to preserve and gatekeep the privileges of the upper echelons – and to restrict access to the most effective weaponry – made weapons like long-bladed swords into formal badges of office whose possession was prohibited to the lower orders. In Celtic times the main barrier was the ability to afford something that was expensive and, most of the time at least, not all that useful.

A tribesman who answered the call to war was well enough equipped with his throwing and stabbing spears, shield and perhaps a knife. Most people owned a 'working and eating' knife which could be used at need to stab someone in a close-quarters battle. Longer and heavier fighting knives did exist and were an alternative to the sword in some situations. Some of the Celtic peoples are noted as also using hand axes in combat.

Professional warriors would be expected to possess a sword, perhaps one given to them for service or inherited from a relative. The standard sword weapon of the early Iron Age was relatively short, with virtually no hand protection and a leaf-shaped blade. The ancient Greeks used a similar weapon, known as a Xiphos, as a sidearm for their Hoplite infantry.

The shape of the blade concentrated force at the 'point of percussion' near the tip while keeping weight down, and the slight curve of the blade contributed to its slicing action. Some swords had a blunt tip and were little use in a stabbing attack, but others possessed a point. Such weapons could deliver a deadly thrust with a wide wound track, while their short length made them less likely to bend. These were in no way 'fencing' weapons; they were intended to be used on the battlefield in conjunction with a shield, and at very close quarters. The design originated with bronze weapons and was replicated in iron.

Celtic Fighting Style

There are few surviving indications of how Celtic warriors fought, but it is possible to reconstruct a reasonable facsimile from Greek depictions of similar weapons and a certain amount of experimental archaeology. Some Greek warriors carried their swords on a strap under the left arm, allowing it to be quickly deployed for a downward thrusting motion. It is possible some Celts did likewise, though the Greeks favoured close-order phalanx warfare whereas the Celts operated in a more fluid and individual manner.

Surviving accounts speak of swords carried on straps or chains on the right side of the body. A right-handed warrior could not draw a long sword from this position, but the shorter weapons of this era could be carried in a greater variety of ways. It is notable that when the Roman army adopted a similar weapon after meeting the Celtiberians they also chose a right-side scabbard position.

In all likelihood, the sword was deployed only after the spear was out of use – perhaps left behind in someone's shield or body. Assuming the sword was held in the right hand, the Celtic warrior would present his weak (left) side forward covered by his shield, with the sword held back, the tip alongside the shield or resting on the top rim. The shield could be used to deflect a blow of course, but could also be pushed forward to obscure the enemy's view of the sword and allow an unexpected strike.

Other techniques for sword and shield combat include striking with the shield rim or boss, charging an opponent to stagger him or stabbing around the shield in close combat. Cutting with the sword rather than thrusting often required stepping through to present a strong-side-forward stance, increasing reach and power at the temporary expense of protection. Skilled warriors would have been adept at launching such a stroke and getting back under the cover of their shield.

Celtic swordsmanship was an influence on their enemies' choice of equipment. The Roman pilum, a throwing-spear of relatively complex design, was a potent man-killer but was also very difficult to dislodge from a shield. Even if the pilum did not disable an oncoming enemy it might deprive him of his shield or at least make it unwieldy. Roman helmets and body armour were designed to deflect overhead strokes aimed at the head and shoulders, which were often the only targets available behind their large shields.

Spears

It is likely that the Celts used specific terms for different types of spear, though these are known to us only from the writings of outsiders. The throwing spear, or javelin, is variously referred to as madaris, mataris, matara, lancia or saunian by Roman observers. Designed purely for throwing, it had a relatively small and narrow head. A heavier version, encountered in the hands of Gaulish tribes, is sometimes referred to as a gaesum. A javelin could be used as a fighting spear at need, or thrown from horseback. However, in the Hallstatt era it was primarily used to harass enemies or soften up their formations before a decisive clash.

The long spear had a greater variety of heads, and could be used for more than thrusting. Sharpened edges improved penetration and recovery and might permit a slashing stroke to inflict some injury in the event of a missed thrust. However, the main benefit of sharp edges was in penetrating flesh and any cloth or leather covering it. Dragging a spear sideways with a one-handed grip is inefficient and unlikely to achieve much more than a distracting injury. The art of the Celtic spearman was in the thrust and recovery, getting back behind the protection of his shield and continuing to pose a threat to those in front of him.

CELTIC INVASIONS OF GREECE

t is unclear why the Celts did not expand into Greece and the surrounding regions during the power vacuum caused by the Bronze-Age Collapse and the Greek Dark Age. It is likely there were some incursions, but perhaps there was little pressure for anything more. Expansion is usually driven by overpopulation and migration by external threats. Neither seems to have applied to the Hallstatt-era Celts, though the introduction of the iron plough permitted a major population growth which might have led to later expansion.

The iron plough was capable of turning over heavy soil which was more fertile than the lighter soils previously worked by the Celtic people. More food naturally leads to an increase in population, so by the time ironworking was a mature technology, there would have been pressure to move into new lands. However, by this time the Greeks were recovering from their catastrophe, and peaceful interaction was probably more profitable than violence.

As they recovered, the Greeks began exploring and colonizing the Mediterranean world. Several major modern cities started out as Greek trading colonies. One such is Marseille, known in the ancient world as Massilia. Founded around 600 BCE it became a major point of trade between the Greeks and the Gauls (Celts) of the region. Sea trade could bypass land obstacles such as the Alps, with the result that the Celts of the Upper Danube Valley could maintain contact with their cousins in Gaul more easily by way of Greece than through the European mainland.

Again, this was a time of upheaval. Expanding populations created competition for resources which could be resolved by warfare. Conflict began as raiding expeditions but gradually became a migration down the river valleys into the Balkans. Conquest was followed by settlement, giving access to the luxury goods previously imported from the Greek city-states. Newly Celtic regions could trade with the established homelands for weaponry and tools, funding further expansion with plunder and resources gained by conflict.

By around 400 BCE there were new and aggressive Celtic populations in Cisalpine Gaul, south of the mountains. Their interactions with the early Roman state are detailed in the next chapter. Conflict with the emerging power of Rome was a driving factor in sending the Celts south and west down the Danube into the Balkans. There, they encountered the powerful kingdom (and later empire) of Macedonia.

The Macedonians and the Celts

Philip II of Macedon (383–336 BCE) inherited a declining and troubled kingdom beset by internal politics as well as invasions from Greece and Illyria. Celtic incursions were also a major problem. Under a different leader Macedon would have perhaps fallen to the Celts, but Philip was a shrewd diplomat and a military innovator. He bought off some of his enemies to gain time to crush others, and by a series of campaigns placed himself at the head of a united – if not entirely unified – Macedonian/Greek kingdom. His son, Alexander III (356–323 BCE) led such campaigns of conquest that he is known to history as Alexander the Great. The Macedonian Empire did not survive his death, however.

Although there was some conflict between the Celts and Macedon, the Celtic people wisely avoided conflict with the emerging superpower. They pushed into Illyria, overlaying their culture on a broad region along the Aegean coast in what are now parts of Albania, Bosnia and Herzegovina, Croatia, Kosovo, Montenegro, North Macedonia, Serbia, Slovenia and a small slice of modern Hungary.

Celtic warriors were highly sought after as mercenaries by nearby rulers, partly for their effectiveness against the ruler's enemies and partly to reduce the chance of raids by unemployed Celts. Their performance was generally very good, earning them the respect of those they served and perhaps providing a little second-hand protection to their new homelands by way of their fearsome reputation.

Greek depictions of Celtic warriors dating from this time are influenced by Greek artistic preferences. The famous *Dying Gaul* sculpture depicts a naked warrior, collapsed from a wound to his chest, with an athletic physique and characteristically 'Gaulish' features. He wears a torc, presumably of gold, around his neck and is well-groomed with spiked-up hair and a neatly trimmed moustache. Some of these elements are probably accurate, but the idea of running into battle naked might have been more a Greek concept than Celtic.

There are records of Greek warriors entering battle wearing only their armour of helmet, breastplate and greaves. In the summer climate of Greece this might provide necessary ventilation, and it certainly demonstrated a level of confidence that might dismay an enemy. The Greek sculptors who depicted naked Celts might have been influenced by accounts of their naked battles, or may have been offering a compliment based on their own warriors' near-nudity. Alternatively, the sculptors may have depicted the dying Gaul through their own artistic style… or perhaps they were following the age-old adage that sex sells.

Be that as it may, the Celts were familiar with the situation in the Balkans and the breakup of the Macedonian Empire upon the death of Alexander the Great. This was an opportunity too good to pass up, and the Keltoi took it for all it was worth. The invasion was not the march of an army but a migration and takeover attempt. It has been estimated that as many as 85,000 Celts moved towards Macedon in 280 BCE, though this figure includes families and other non-combatants. Macedon was at this time no longer the heart of Alexander's great empire. Upon his death in 323 BCE, the Empire was divided up among his commanders, who are collectively termed Diadochi, or Successors.

The Ptolemys and the Celts

Ptolemy Soter (366–283 BCE) took Alexander's body to Egypt and proclaimed himself ruler there, becoming Ptolemy I. He was a successful ruler, adding to his territory at the expense of other Successor states, and founded the Great Library of Alexandria. His dynasty controlled Egypt until conquered by Rome in 30 BCE. Seleucus (c. 358–281 BCE), allied to Ptolemy, controlled Mesopotamia and was successful in war against Antigonus Monophthalmus (382–301 BCE) who had taken control of the Middle East and most of modern Turkey. In its heyday, his Seleucid dynasty ruled from Thrace to India but was greatly diminished by the time it was overthrown by Rome in 64 BCE.

Antigonus was for a time the most powerful of the Diadochi, and the one most able to reunify the Empire of Alexander. His death in battle at Ipsus in 301 BCE marked the end of any realistic chance of this happening and opened the way for other powers – including the Celts – to rise. Initially, Cassander (c. 355–297 BCE) was in control of Macedonia and Greece and Lysimachus (c. 360–281 BCE) held Thrace, but the death of Cassander resulted in a power vacuum which was briefly filled by Ptolemy Keraunos (d. 279 BCE).

Ptolemy Keraunos was the son of Ptolemy I of Egypt, and originally his heir apparent. Accounts vary but apparently Ptolemy Keraunos fell out of favour and was replaced as heir by his brother Philadelphus. There may or may not have been plots and intrigue at the Egyptian court, but it is known that Keraunos went to the court of Lysimachus in Thrace where he was initially welcomed. Further internal politics resulted in Keraunos fleeing to Babylon and the court of Seleucus.

Keraunos's blood ties to Thrace and Egypt gave Seleucus a pretext for invasion. In 281 BCE he invaded the territory of Lysimachus. After killing Lysimachus in battle, Seleucus crossed the Hellespont into Thrace and would certainly have conquered it – and Macedon too – if he had not been suddenly killed by Ptolemy Keraunos. According to some accounts this is how the name 'Keraunos' (thunderbolt) came about, though it may have originated with another stabbing. On that occasion the young Ptolemy was asked to execute his nephew Agatholes, son of Lysimachus.

It is likely that Keraunos's treachery was provoked by fears Seleucus would recreate the Empire of Alexander but give Keraunos little or no place in it. Afterwards, he had little difficulty in gaining the throne of Thrace, and with Macedon in political chaos it rapidly followed suit. What little resistance emerged was easily crushed, and by a combination of diplomacy and opportunism Keraunos began to establish himself in his new realm.

Bolgios and Macedon

In 280 BCE, a large force of Celtic warriors entered Macedon under the leadership of one Bolgios. Like many Celtic figures, little is known about him for sure. He may not have even existed, though someone must have led the invasion. As such he can be considered a quasi-mythical figure, perhaps created out of an amalgamation of real leaders or an idealized spirit of Celtic leadership. The name Bolgios can also be rendered Belgio or Belgius, in the context of 'Leader of the Belgae' – a Celtic people who eventually migrated into northern Europe and gave their name to Belgium.

The people of the Balkans and Greece were rightly respectful of Celtic military prowess, but Ptolemy Keraunos was from Egypt and perhaps thought the invaders were mere savages. The Dardani, who lived between Thrace and Illyria, harboured no such illusions. They offered the new king of Macedon an alliance and 20,000 warriors to fight the invaders. Keraunos refused, perhaps out of arrogance and perhaps because he hoped the Celts and the Dardani would weaken one another sufficiently to enable a campaign of conquest.

Seeing which way the wind was blowing, the Dardani then sent 10,000 warriors to join the invading Celts in return for an agreement they would not be attacked. Again Ptolemy Keraunos could not accept there was a real threat. When Bolgios sent emissaries offering peace, Keraunos's terms were the surrender of the Celts' leaders and an immediate retreat. This was not quite what Bolgios had in mind. His was just one of the large forces involved in the invasion, and even so it outnumbered the Macedonians by a considerable margin.

War Elephants

Bolgios's army grew even larger as non-Celtic tribes from Thrace and Illyria joined the march. It appears that Macedonian rule had not suited these people; none joined the Macedonian side. Still, this was a barbarous host – presumably disjointed and lacking in discipline – while the Macedonians had conquered the world with their military professionalism. If soldiers had their doubts, Ptolemy Keraunos did not. His army was composed of phalanxes of pikemen supported by lighter troops, with heavy cavalry to deliver the fatal blow to an enemy force. Alexander conquered the known world with such tactics, and Ptolemy Keraunos additionally possessed a force of war elephants that would be terrifying to anyone who had never encountered them.

The elephants, however, proved to be a liability in battle. Exactly how the Celts dealt with them is not directly recorded, but there are numerous historical records of elephants being panicked by fire and noise, and being poked with long spears. Roman records from the era also speak of another tactic: slathering a pig or wild boar with pitch and setting it alight, causing it to run amok, squealing loudly, and thereby disrupting enemy formations or frightening elephants. The first part of this statement is undoubtedly true, though burning pigs are a rather random weapon which begins its panicked rampage closer to friendly forces. Whether the Celts used this expedient, and to what end, is unknown. However, they did succeed in turning the Macedonian war elephants back on their masters.

Fighting the Phalanx

The pike-bristling phalanx should have been a very difficult target for looser-order Celtic warriors, and on paper should have been able to drive anything in front of it off the field. Provided the flanks were held by lighter troops or cavalry, the Macedonian phalangites could have every confidence of victory. However, the Celts were not foolish enough to try to tackle the phalanx head-on.

Heavily armoured phalangites knew they would be vulnerable if they broke ranks, a fact endlessly – and literally – drilled into them. The phalanx therefore had to manoeuvre as a whole. This permitted more lightly armoured warriors to harass the formation with javelins then retire out of range. This tactic was effectively used against Greek and Macedonian phalanx formations throughout the era, but unless the phalangites could be induced to break ranks it was unlikely to produce a decisive result.

Rough ground, flank attacks and the possibility of drawing out some members of the formation in pursuit offered some opportunities to nullify the advantages of close order and long spears. In this case, however, it is likely the decisive factor was the Macedonians' own elephants. Frightened and running amok they could scatter an infantry formation, allowing Celtic warriors to ply their short swords at an advantageous range.

For his part, Ptolemy Keraunos is said to have fallen from his war elephant and was captured with multiple wounds. He was beheaded and his head displayed on a spear, at which point his army disintegrated. The fall of a king or great leader was a serious blow to morale which in this case completed or perhaps even caused the Macedonian defeat. It may be that the Macedonians were still entirely capable of winning when their king fell from his panicked elephant, and that reliance on the great beasts indirectly resulted in the collapse of morale as well as directly disrupting the army's formations. Whatever the truth may be, the Celtic cavalry conducted a close pursuit, killing or capturing large numbers of Macedonian soldiers.

The Celtic host was unable to exploit this great victory, enabling Macedon to assemble a new army for further resistance under a rapid succession of leaders ending with a nobleman named Sothsenes. Bolgios's invasion of Macedon was ultimately unsuccessful but it brought about the end of Ptolemaic ambitions in the region, and the Celtic invasion of the region was by no means complete.

BRENNUS IN GREECE

The Celtic invasion of Greece was reportedly led by their king, Brennus. This name appears elsewhere in Celtic history and cannot possibly be the same individual – if indeed either really existed. Brennus, like Bolgios, may be a quasi-mythical figure based on a title rather than a personal identity. Some sources state that the central Celtic force was commanded by Brennus and Acichorius, though little is known about this individual. Joint leadership was not uncommon in Celtic times, but it is equally possible that Acichorius was the name and Brennus the title of the overall leader.

What is clear is that a large force of Keltoi entered Greece in 279 BCE and encountered only patchy resistance. The wars of Alexander and his successors had left the cities of Greece and the surrounding area weakened, and the often-vicious internal politics of the Successor states sowed the seeds of mistrust and disunity. Some local rulers submitted or paid large sums to be left alone, while other polities were overrun and plundered. Resistance in Thrace and Illyria was quickly crushed, and although the invasion of Macedon was less successful it prevented intervention from that direction.

The Invasion

Ancient sources agree that the central thrust into Greece, under the command of Brennus, consisted of some 150,000 warriors on foot and a large number of cavalry. This is placed at anything from 10,000 to 62,700 in number. One reason for this large discrepancy is the Celtic practice of supporting their mounted warriors with specialized servants. These would bring a fresh horse to rescue their master if he lost his mount or was wounded, and might join the fight in his stead if he were killed.

Brennus's army swept through Thessaly, reaching the Aegean Sea, and pushed south. Resistance finally firmed up under the leadership of Athens, which naturally felt threatened by the Celtic advance. The Greek army took up position at the pass of Thermopylae, where the Persian Empire had met defeat two centuries earlier. It is no accident that the same locations are fought over throughout history. An expedition sent out from a stable society can go almost anywhere but a migrating people or an army can only follow certain routes. The Greeks were therefore able to predict the Celtic advance and challenge it on favourable terms.

It was obvious to Brennus that his army could not break through the narrow pass without taking unacceptable losses, if at all. There were other options than a head-on attack, however, forty thousand Celtic warriors were detached from the main army, descending upon Aetolia to wreak havoc. This drew off the Aetolian contingent of the Greek army, though the raid was very costly. More than half of the detachment was killed, captured or decided to slink away with whatever loot they had garnered.

Marching to Delphi

In the meantime, the Celts were able to find a way around the strongly held pass of Thermopylae and marched on Delphi. The defence of an obstacle – typically a bridge or a mountain pass – lies at the heart of a great many heroic tales both of antiquity and modern times. In this case, however, Brennus was unwilling to play to the stereotype of brave but dumb attackers mindlessly surging in waves against the defenders. Instead, he set his sights upon the fabled treasures of Delphi and bypassed his chance to be the villain of a heroic defence.

However, Delphi was strongly held against the Celts, whose siege was hampered also by earthquakes and storms. This bought time for an army of Greeks to arrive and heavily defeat Brennus's army. It is said he was seriously wounded in the battle and committed suicide out of shame. His force was then harried out of Greece.

THE GALATIANS

Other **Celtic forces** were commanded by Cerethrius, Lutarius and Leonnorius, about whom little is known. It may be that the names reported by writers of the time were actually titles referring to the groups they led or to their reputed exploits. Alternatively they may be a best guess on the part of a scholar who had little concrete information about these violent foreigners to work from.

These groups were successful in Thrace and gradually pushed eastward to establish a homeland. There, they encountered the forces of Antigonus Gonastus (born *c.* 319 BCE), who was the grandson of Antigonus Monophthalmus. While Greece and Macedon were struggling to repel the Celtic invasion, Antigonus saw an opportunity to continue the politics of the Successor states by capturing Macedon. In 277 BCE he sailed with his army to the Hellespont and landed near the town of Lysimachia. There, his force was attacked by Celts who had settled nearby, under the command of Cerethrius.

It is likely that Cerethrius thought Antigonus had come to dislodge his people. He led his force against Antigonus's camp but found it deserted as Antigonus had moved his troops inland to a concealed position. As the Celts began destroying Antigonus's ships they were attacked in the rear and trapped against the sea. Having shattered Cerethrius's force, Antigonus was able to move on Macedon and take its throne. There was no significant opposition from the Celts, who were at that time being driven out of Greece.

The Celts failed to establish themselves in Greece, and were ultimately driven out. Most returned north and west, but some pushed further east. This included the force under Lutarius and

Leonnorius. They crossed into Anatolia in what is now Turkey and set up an enclave there. This became known as Galatia, and developed a culture of its own as a result of interactions with other local populations.

LEGACY OF THE KELTOI

The Celtic invasions took place against the backdrop of what might be called the post-Alexander era. The breakup of that great empire was not in any way caused by the Celts, but they played a part in determining the fate of the Successor states. Without Celtic pressure on Macedon and Greece there might have been a resurgence based on Macedon and Thrace, and this more unified Greece might have challenged the expansion of Rome.

The early Roman Republic fought several wars against Greek states, notably in the region of Italia known as Magna Graecia. Had its expansion been stymied there, perhaps there would have been no Roman Empire at all, or perhaps the Roman state might not have been able to defeat Carthage and take control of the Mediterranean world. Ironically, perhaps, that might in turn have prevented the conquest and Romanization of Gaul and eventually the British Isles.

Speculation is interesting, but all that can be said for certain is that the Celts were a major influence on events in Eastern Europe and the Balkans until their failed invasion of Greece, and much less so thereafter. Trade continued, and Galatian or Keltoi mercenaries were sought out for their prowess in battle, but the Celtic people of the region were diminished and gradually overtaken by history.

GAULS & THE ROMAN REPUBLIC

In the time of the Hallstatt Celts, Rome did not exist. However, its emergence as the centre of the ancient world had enormous implications for the Celtic societies it encountered. Conflict between Rome and Carthage decided the fate of the Celtiberians, and the ambitions of Julius Caesar led to the eclipse of the last of the Continental Celts.

The exact date of the founding of Rome is unclear, but legend places it at 753 BCE. This date is a best guess compiled by Roman scholars and is based on mythology as much as history. According to legend, Rome had its origins in the Trojan Wars. In 19 BCE, the Roman poet Virgil (70–19 BCE) wrote the definitive version in the epic poem the *Aeneid*, based on much older Greek accounts.

THE FOUNDING OF ROME

According to Virgil, Aeneas and his followers fled the siege of Troy to seek a new home, undertaking a perilous voyage along the Mediterranean. They paused at Carthage, where Aeneas had a tragic love affair with Queen Dido, before finally reaching a suitable site on the shores of the Italian Peninsula. In some versions of the tale, the surviving

Trojans had their wives with them, and it was the women who decided the expedition was over. They burned Aeneas's ships and forced him to settle in Italia. Other variants state that it was Aeneas who decided it was time to settle down and build a new home.

Be that as it may, the *Aeneid* states that Aeneas married the daughter of King Latinus and thereby joined the local nobility. This is mythology, which may or may not have had its origins in reality, making dates for the people and events difficult to pinpoint beyond 'sometime between 1180 BCE and 750 BCE'. According to Virgil, Aeneas's descendant Numitor ultimately lost his throne and his daughter Rhea Silvia was forced to become a Vestal Virgin (a priestess of the cult of Vesta, goddess of the hearth, who remained a virgin for thirty years) to prevent any offspring who might challenge for the throne. This was unusually lenient for the period, in which killing anyone who might someday present a challenge was commonplace.

Rhea Silvia produced twin sons despite being sequestered. She stated that the war-god Mars had raped her and that the boys were divine. They were named Romulus and Remus. The usurper Amulius, younger brother to Numitor, naturally wanted the boys out of the way but was hesitant to simply slay them in case he angered Mars. His solution was second-hand murder. The boys were to be taken and drowned in the River Tiber, distancing Amulius from the killing.

Romulus and Remus were not killed, but set adrift rather, washing up on the banks of the Tiber where they were fed by a woodpecker and a she-wolf – both creatures associated with Mars. The boys were adopted by a shepherd and his wife, and became prominent figures of the local community.

Romulus and Remus

As children of Mars, Romulus and Remus were inevitably drawn into conflict. They fought rival shepherds serving King Amulius. The dispute escalated until Amulius was slain, at which point Romulus and Remus were offered his throne. Instead, they reinstalled their grandfather Numitor and set out to found their own city. They disagreed on the site, and Remus was slain either by the gods or by Romulus himself, depending on the version of the tale.

Romulus constructed a city, which he naturally named after himself, and set about attracting new citizens. To secure the future of the community he invited the Sabines and the Latins, powerful local tribes, to a feast where he took their women captive. This event is known as the Rape of the Sabine Women, with 'rape' in its ancient context of 'carrying off'.

The Sabine women rather conveniently decided they were happy to marry their captors, sealing an alliance with the Sabines in which their leader, Titus Tatius, became co-ruler of Rome with Romulus. Perhaps unsurprisingly, Titus Tatius was assassinated a few years later, leaving Romulus sole ruler. He inherited more lands from his grandfather Numitor and added greatly to the power and prestige of Rome. He was something of a tyrant, however, and became unpopular among his people. Depending on the account, he was either assassinated by his senators or ascended to become a god.

Romulus was followed by a series of elected kings, not all of whom were successful or popular, and at some point the tale crosses the line from mythology to possible history. In 509 BCE, Lucius Tarquinius Superbus (d. 495 BCE) was overthrown by a revolution. Having had their fill of kings, the people of Rome implemented a republican system that lasted over 400 years before the actions of Julius Caesar (100 BCE–44 BCE) resulted in a conversion to an empire.

Myth and Truth

The tale begins in an era of myth, though there may be truths embedded in it. The *Aeneid* offers legitimacy to Rome as the rightful successor of Troy and the enemy of Greeks. How much of it is true will never be known. What is clear is that the site of Rome was occupied long before the traditional founding date, and that the Etruscans were the original civilization in the Italian Peninsula. They dominated an area from the Arno River in the north to the Tiber, and were probably the source of early Roman culture and learning.

Other parts of the peninsula were occupied by a variety of tribes, with a significant Greek presence in the region known as Magna Graecia, which lay along the southern and eastern coasts. Rome gradually came into conflict with these groups, incorporating defeated city-states into its Republic. There was no deliberate expansion plan; conflicts were resolved and Rome's influence grew. New members of the Republic supplied troops who in turn made new conquests.

Roman Forces

The early Roman army was quite different from its later professional form under the late Republic and the Empire. Etruscan and Greek influences are obvious, with the main striking arm being close-order infantry armed with long spears. Their sidearm was a machete-like weapon known as a *falcata*. With a bellied blade, the falcata could deliver a powerful slashing stroke. It and similar weapons were in use from Greece to Iberia.

Military service was a civic duty tied to wealth and status. The richest citizens could afford to outfit themselves with a horse and functioned as cavalry, with those who could afford a full set of armour and weapons holding the highest status among the infantry. Poorer citizens with lighter equipment filled out a force as skirmishers and flank guards. The system was cost-effective in many ways, since the state did not have to pay for a standing army, and those in the top echelons of society fought hard for victories to avoid personal shame.

On the other hand, removing the richest citizens from their businesses and political posts imposed a hidden drain on the economy, which gradually became worse as campaigns were carried out further from home. Greek-style heavy infantry was not well suited to operations in the hills of the Italian Peninsula, which eventually forced a revision of doctrine. However, it was this kind of force that first encountered the Gauls of northern Italia.

THE SENONES AND THE SIEGE OF ROME

By around 400 BCE, Celtic people had crossed the Alps and settled in northern Italia. The Romans and their allies called them *Gauls*, with similar 'barbarian' connotations to the Greek *Keltoi*. Their ways were different to those of the city-states and Italian tribes that the Romans were accustomed to, and their martial prowess was greatly underestimated by the Roman leaders.

The Senones, a powerful Celtic tribe, were reputedly led by a man named Brennus, who, like others of his name, is probably a quasi-mythical figure based on real leaders. Brennus led a conquest of the Po Valley and laid siege to the city of Clusium, which requested aid from Rome. Rome responded by sending a diplomatic party who demanded to know what right the invaders thought they had to attack the Etruscans. This was something of a hypocritical question, given the love of conquest by Rome, and the answer was what they should have expected – force of arms gave Brennus and his warriors the right to do as they pleased.

Diplomatic Debacle

What followed was a diplomatic gaffe of the worst kind. The Roman diplomatic party joined an attack on the Gauls, killing one of the Senones' leaders. To the Romans this was acceptable behaviour, but to the Gauls it was absolutely not. The incident had the desired effect in the short term; the Senones pulled back to consider their options. When their demand that the diplomats be turned over for justice – breaking a truce was no small matter – was declined, the Senones decided to march on Rome itself.

The decision to refuse Gaulish demands had much to do with Roman internal politics. The diplomats were the sons of Quintus Fabius Ambustus (dates unknown), Roman politician and commander, and while many considered the demand reasonable, Fabius Ambustus was unwilling to see his sons put to death by a bunch of savages. He brought his considerable influence to bear and, rather than being surrendered for judgment, the failed diplomats were given command of an army.

Brennus and his army marched on Rome in 390 BCE, bypassing other city-states and leaving them unmolested. As a result, the Gaulish army arrived at a point 11 miles from Rome without meeting much opposition. It was there, at the confluence of the Allia and Tiber Rivers, that the Roman army made its appearance.

Roman writers are divided on exactly how many troops Rome had mustered. The highest estimates are around 70,000, including a great many with no training and minimal equipment. More reasonable figures suggest around 15,000 to 24,000. Of these, the main force was made up of heavily armoured infantry equipped with long spears and fighting in a phalanx formation. These were supported by lighter allied troops and some cavalry. The Celtic force may have numbered anything from 10,000 to 70,000, depending on the source.

The Siege of Rome

The Senones opened the battle in a typically Celtic manner, attempting to intimidate their foes by their appearance and the noise they made. Some sources state that warriors stripped off their shirts or even all their clothes as they brandished their weapons and shouted challenges. Despite their contempt for barbarians, the Roman force must have been affected by this display. There were other morale disadvantages; in the rush to confront the invaders, the proper pre-battle divinations were not carried out.

According to Roman sources, the Senones outnumbered their foes, forcing the Romans to extend their lines in order to avoid being outflanked. The Senones' force was more uniform than that of their opponents, being comprised almost entirely of warriors equipped with spear and shield. Less heavily protected than the Roman hoplites, these men were more mobile than the heavy troops and perhaps had more fighting power than the lighter-equipped elements of the Roman force.

The first blow fell against the Roman reserves, positioned on a hill on the right of the line. This attack was intended merely to clear the flank, but it proved decisive. The reserves were inexperienced and poorly equipped, and the Roman force overall was ineptly led. As the reserve broke and was routed, the opposite wing of the Roman army also collapsed. A general charge by the Gauls routed the Romans right along their line, with some Roman writers lamenting that none of their soldiers actually died fighting. They were cut down from behind or chased into the river, where many drowned.

Dogs and Geese

It is estimated that around two-thirds of the Roman force was destroyed, and the remainder was unable to prevent the Senones from reaching Rome just days after the disaster at the Allia. Much of the city was undefended and quickly overrun, though the Capitol Hill held out. The Senones implemented a siege and attempted to infiltrate the defences. To this end they befriended and fed the dogs that the defenders intended would raise an alarm, but when the Gauls attempted a night infiltration they were thwarted by geese from the Temple of Juno.

The geese raised such a ruckus that the attack was discovered and had to be abandoned. One outcome of this incident was a festival held for many years in which dogs were ritually punished for their ancestors' betrayal, often by crucifixion. Meanwhile, geese were venerated for their role in saving the capitol.

More immediately, Brennus's army began to suffer from disease and negotiated a withdrawal in return for a huge ransom. As this was being weighed out, the Roman diplomats protested that the Celtic weights and measures were different to those used in Rome.

According to legend, Brennus promptly placed his sword on the scales and announced, 'Woe to the vanquished!', suggesting the Romans had better take the deal, however bad they considered it, because the alternative would be worse. The ransom was paid and the Senones departed.

Consequences of Celtic Victory

The disaster at the Allia was a shock to Rome, and one that had far-reaching consequences. The hoplite-style army was clearly unsuited to fighting barbarians in the hills of Italia, and was replaced with a more flexible formation made up of sub-units called maniples. Roman troops drilled in manoeuvring maniples within a larger formation, increasing tactical flexibility and mobility in the face of a fluid enemy.

The sack of Rome inspired several subject peoples to revolt, and shattered the myth of Roman invincibility. The result was a long series of campaigns to regain control of the Italian Peninsula, setting back Roman expansion by decades. The defeat at the Allia also cost the lives of a great many prominent citizens, creating turbulent internal politics and damaging the economy of the Roman Republic for many years to come.

Afterwards, the Senones returned to northern Italia where they established a homeland. Relations with the Roman Republic were not good, with the Senones assisting enemies of Rome either as mercenaries or allies on various occasions. It is possible to see the Senones as 'enemies of civilization', but the reality was that the tribes took advantage of opportunities to reduce the level of threat posed by Rome and to profit from the situation. Rome was not so much a constant enemy as a target of opportunity.

THE SAMNITE WARS

The **Roman heartland** was Latium, a region bounded in the north by Etruria and to the south-east by Campania. To the east and north-east were lands occupied by various tribes including the Samnites. Relations with these tribes varied over time. A tribal confederation might ally with Rome against a mutual enemy but later become a bitter foe. So it was with the Samnites.

The sack of Rome ushered in a period of around 40 years in which Roman forces suppressed revolts and brought former allies back to its side. By 350 BCE, Latium was more strongly held than before and the situation in Etruria was more or less what it had been before the Senone invasion. In 354 BCE, the Samnites entered into an alliance with Rome but by 343 BCE the first of a series of wars began. The Samnites were equipped and fought in a similar manner to the Celtic tribes, which enabled the Roman army to develop effective tactics against such opponents.

The Senones sought allies against Rome, and by the Third Samnite War of 298–290 BCE they stood at the head of a coalition that included the Senones as well as forces from Etruria and Umbria. The Samnites were initially successful but Roman expeditions against their homelands drew off some of their allies. The Senones remained steadfast, however, and took the right of the battle line at the decisive Battle of Sentinum in 295 BCE.

Facing the Senones, Consul Publius Decius (d. 295 BCE) commanded the left flank of the Roman army. Quintus Fabius led the right against the Samnites. Fabius was content to fight a defensive battle, hoping to let the Samnites exhaust themselves against his solid infantry. Decius preferred an aggressive strategy, and was initially successful. Roman cavalry drove off their Senone equivalents, but became over-extended and were routed by a counterattack by the Senones' chariots.

Infantry followed up the chariots, driving the Romans back in disorder. The situation was restored by Publius Decius, who is recorded as performing the Devotio, essentially making himself a warlike sacrifice to the gods. He charged the Celtic force alone, and whether his example shamed and inspired his followers or the gods did favour him, his troops rallied.

In the meantime, the tactics of the older and steadier Quintus Fabius Rullianus (d. 291 BCE) paid off. As the Samnites tired, he launched his cavalry on a flanking attack into their rear. Combined with pressure from the Roman infantry, this broke the Samnite force, enabling Fabius's force to wheel into the Senones just as the Romans at their front renewed the fight. The result was a decisive victory for Rome, and within a few years the Samnites had been subjugated.

THE GALLIC WAR

The Senones continued to be a problem for Rome. After a decade of peace, they entered into a conflict known as the Gallic War (284–283 BCE), about which few records survive. It appears that the Senones had expanded their territory and were besieging the town of Arretium (modern Arezzo in Tuscany) when a Roman army arrived to break the siege. Few details are available, but it is known that the Romans were heavily defeated and prisoners taken. Negotiators sent to secure their release were murdered by the Gauls.

The Roman response was to march on the Senones' homeland. The Senones were assisted by the Boii, another Celtic tribal group that had become concerned about Roman aggression. Even with these and Etruscan allies, the Senones were defeated at Lake Vadimon in 283 BCE. This victory for Rome was followed by the creation of a new city known as Sena, the first Roman colony in what had been the lands of the Gauls. Within two decades, Etruria was fully subjugated and the Senones were no longer a threat to Rome. However, the Boii were now enemies and Rome had other problems.

THE GAULS AND THE PUNIC WARS

The city of Carthage in what is now Tunisia is traditionally held to have been founded in 814 BCE by Phoenician traders. It rapidly grew in importance due to its strategic location, supporting shipping that moved along the North African coast and across the Mediterranean by way of Sicily. As early as 509 BCE, Rome concluded a commercial treaty with Carthage in which Rome was clearly the inferior power. A near-identical treaty in 348 BCE was similarly concerned with economic matters; Rome was not yet seen as a military rival.

Later treaties reflected changing realities in the Mediterranean world. One signed in 306 BCE was later denounced as false by Roman writers, but was followed in 279 or 278 BCE by a treaty agreeing to respective spheres of influence. Clearly by this point Rome was seen as a major power even by mighty Carthage. The treaty did not prevent conflict, however.

The First Punic War

Using a dispute between the cities of Messana and Syracuse on Sicily as a pretext, Carthage established a presence on the island and began expanding its control. Rome could not accept this situation and launched a military expedition, resulting in what became known as the First Punic War. From 264 BCE to 240 BCE, both sides fought what was essentially a maritime campaign. Rome had to develop a navy and techniques for fighting at sea but was eventually victorious. In 240 BCE, Carthage withdrew from Sicily and accepted Roman dominion there.

Rome continued to expand its territory in Italia and, beginning in 232 BCE, launched a campaign of conquest in the Po Valley. Known as Cisalpine Gaul, this region was home to Celtic tribes whose numbers were swelled by migrants moving south over the mountains. Population pressure would have brought about major conflict at some point, but the situation was pre-empted by a Roman decision to conquer the region.

The Second Punic War

In the period 224–220 BCE, Cisalpine Gaul was brought under Roman control, more or less, and expansion continued westward along the Mediterranean coastline. This ultimately led the Romans into the Iberian Peninsula where they encountered the Celtiberians. Carthage, too, had sought new territories in Iberia after being forced to withdraw from Sicily. Tensions between Rome and Carthage had not abated, and, despite a treaty signed in 226 BCE, the two were soon at war.

The flashpoint was the siege of Saguntum in 219 BCE by Carthaginian forces. Saguntum asked for Roman help and, despite it being within the Carthaginian sphere of influence as agreed upon just a few years previously, Rome responded. Diplomacy took the form of demands which were rejected, and in 218 BCE Carthage declared war. Confident in their superiority at sea and on land, the Romans began a two-pronged campaign against both the Carthaginian holdings in Iberia and their North African homeland.

There are few records of what the Gauls and the Celtiberians were doing during this period. It is virtually certain they had their own inter-tribal conflicts, and tribal societies tend to have a narrower worldview than those who wish to create trading or political empires. The conflict between Rome and Carthage was likely to have been seen as an opportunity for some mercenary work but otherwise not particularly relevant to most of the Celtic tribes – at least until it was being fought on their land.

The Gauls Support Hannibal's Invasion of Italia

Recognizing that the economic might of Rome meant it would ultimately be victorious, the Carthaginian general Hannibal Barca (247 BCE–c. 183–181 BCE) embarked upon an ambitious campaign to take the war to the Roman homeland. Unable to move an army by sea against the powerful Roman fleet, he marched overland and crossed the Alps into northern Italia. Hannibal's army famously contained war elephants, though few survived long into the campaign.

Roman commanders expected Hannibal would be delayed or even turned back by resistance from the Gaulish tribes, but he was able to secure safe passage by means of clever diplomacy. On the other hand, Roman forces marching to intercept Hannibal were hampered by Gaulish resistance. Had the Gauls not agreed to Hannibal's request he might have been unable to cross the River

Rhône before a Roman army intercepted him, in which case his brilliant campaign in Italia might never have happened at all.

Gauls also joined Hannibal's army as he marched towards Rome. By the time he reached Italia, thousands of Gaulish warriors had swelled the Carthaginian ranks. They were ferocious fighters, but prone to quit the field if the day went against them or to wander off in search of plunder. Nevertheless, they were highly effective if handled properly.

At the first major battle of the war, the Battle of the Trebbia River in December 218 BCE, Hannibal's army of about 42,000 men faced off against 30,000 Romans. At the centre of the Carthaginian force was a body of some 8,000 Gaulish warriors, with additional Gauls on the flanks and among the cavalry contingent. An unknown number of Gauls were among the Roman contingent as well. Their positions are not recorded, though it is likely the Romans used them as flank guards and relied on their own heavy infantry to break the enemy line.

Both sides had cavalry on the flanks, with the Carthaginian elephants deployed there as well. The cavalry engagement is generally thought to have been one-sided, with the Roman force driven back quickly. This freed the Carthaginian light infantry to envelop the Roman flanks, reducing the chance of the numerically superior heavy Roman infantry flanking their opponents. What remained of the Roman light infantry tried to hold the flanks but required assistance from the heavier troops, weakening the main thrust.

The issue was still in doubt, with the heavier Roman infantry pushing the lightly equipped Gauls back in the very centre and making headway against the Carthaginian heavy infantry on each side of them. At this point a force of around 2,000 Carthaginians, concealed before the battle for just such an enterprise, attacked the rear and were joined by the victorious cavalry. As the Roman flanks collapsed, their central units burst through the Gauls in front of them, driving their opponents from the field. This force, including the commander Sempronius, was able to fight its way off the field and re-cross the Trebbia to safety. Some sources state these were the only Roman survivors of the action.

It is certain that the Roman force suffered very heavy losses, as did the Gaulish contingent in the Carthaginian centre. However, the Roman defeat inspired other Gauls to take up the fight, joining Hannibal in his advance into Italia. The route he chose was a difficult one, passing through marshes near the Arno River. Although this resulted in losses due to disease, it enabled Hannibal to draw out another Roman army, this one under a new commander, Consul Gaius Flaminius (d. 217 BCE).

Hannibal Wins Again

Flaminius was newly appointed and inexperienced, and – worse, according to Roman tradition – he had been in too much of a hurry to march against Hannibal to carry out the proper ceremonies expected of him upon taking command. Hannibal, on the other hand, was to become known as the Father of Strategy. He manoeuvred his army so as to make Flaminius think he had an advantage, whereas Hannibal's position on the shore of Lake Trasimene was in fact a trap.

In heavy fog, Flamininus's force pushed through a valley towards Hannibal's waiting infantry, neglecting to scout or properly cover the flanks. As the infantry clashed, Carthaginian cavalry positioned above the valley charged into the Roman rear elements and routed them. Elements of the main Roman body fought through the Carthaginian lines but were captured soon afterwards, as was a detachment of reinforcements sent from Arminium. The remainder of the Roman force was driven into the lake and either cut down in the muddy shallows or drowned trying to cross deeper water.

Rome was all but defenceless at this point, though Hannibal cannot have been sure of that. Rather than advance on the capital of the Republic, he attempted to induce Roman allies to join him as the Gauls had done. He pushed into southern Italia, demonstrating Roman weakness in the hope that local city-states would defect. The hoped-for rebellion did not immediately transpire, however.

The Fabian Strategy

At this point neither side could afford to risk a decisive battle. Rome needed time to assemble an army capable of defeating Hannibal, who was not likely to receive additional troops unless he persuaded local forces to join him. If Hannibal's force could be tied down for long enough it would be eroded by the inevitable friction of war. Men would get sick or be lost in minor engagements, supplies would run short and equipment would wear out. If the Gauls with Hannibal's army became bored or disaffected, or lost confidence in his ability to win, they might defect or simply go home.

Rome thus embarked upon a campaign of manoeuvre and counter-manoeuvre which earned its instigator, Quintus Fabius Maximus Verrucosus (d. 203 BCE) the nickname 'Cunctator', or 'Delayer'. This 'Fabian' strategy kept Hannibal from establishing himself in Apulia or Campania, and from triggering a general revolt, and in the long run would likely have been successful in wearing down Hannibal's army. His Gaulish allies needed victories and plunder to keep them from deserting, and shortage of supplies would eventually force Hannibal to take excessive risks. However, not everyone had the patience for such a strategy. A Carthaginian army marauding about Italia made Rome look weak, and weakness might cause allies to break away.

The Battle of Cannae

In 216 BCE, Rome deviated from this Fabian strategy and sent another army against Hannibal, this one around 80,000 strong. Hannibal accepted battle at Cannae, on the banks of the River Aufidus in Apulia. He deployed his 50,000 or so troops on terrain that constrained the Romans onto a narrow frontage, with his Gaulish and Spanish infantry in the centre flanked by Carthaginian professionals. The Roman centre was an unusually deep formation of heavy infantry, with cavalry on the flanks.

As previously, Hannibal read the character of his opponents. Consul Aemilius Paullus (d. 216 BCE) was a steady and experienced commander, but his colleague Gaius Terentius Varro (dates unknown) was overconfident and keen to win glory. With their two Consular armies combined into one huge force, the Consuls commanded on alternate days. Varro decided to make the most of what he thought was an opportunity and ordered the attack Hannibal expected.

The dense Roman centre pushed back Hannibal's centre, with heavy casualties falling on the Gauls and Iberians there. As they were driven back, the Carthaginian infantry on their flanks wheeled inward against the Roman flanks. Meanwhile the Carthaginian cavalry had defeated its Roman opposite numbers and attacked the rear. The Roman force was pushed in on itself and unable to fight effectively. It is estimated that Rome suffered some 50,000 casualties at Cannae. Most of the 5,700 or so lost by Hannibal were Gauls.

The Celts Ensure a Victory

The 'double envelopment' tactic used at Cannae is widely lauded as a brilliant piece of strategy, and rightly so. However, the great victory owed much to the resilience of the Celtic fighting man. Had the centre broken, the Romans could have fought their way out of the trap and might even have won the battle. Had this happened, the story would have been quite different. As it was, the disaster at Cannae triggered a widespread revolt throughout southern Italia, though the cities of Latium remained loyal to Rome. Hannibal had hoped more Gaulish tribes might join him if he won a great victory, but this did not come to pass.

Although important cities such as Syracuse and Tarentum joined the Carthaginian cause, support from Carthage itself was not forthcoming. The difficulty in getting troops and supplies ashore in Italia against Roman maritime resistance was significant, and the Carthaginian leaders sought gains elsewhere. As a result, Hannibal's force was gradually ground down and confined to an ever-smaller area of operations.

Carthaginian defeats in Iberia and Sicily made reinforcing Hannibal even more problematic, and the entry of Macedon into the conflict made little difference in the long run. With Roman forces victorious in Iberia and threatening Carthage itself, a force was landed in Italia to attempt a junction with Hannibal. However, Roman naval power forced it to land far north of Hannibal's remaining territory, and the reinforcements were defeated in Cisalpine Gaul in 203 BCE. Hannibal was recalled from Italia to lead the defence of Carthage. This was to no avail, and after a resounding defeat at the Battle of Zama in 202 BCE Carthage submitted to Rome.

The defeat of Carthage left Rome unchallenged for control of the Iberian Peninsula and in command of the whole Mediterranean. The third and final Punic war, fought in 149–146 BCE, was little more than a formality as Rome finished off its old enemy at leisure. A series of wars against Macedon eventually brought Greece under the dominion of Rome as well, though this had little effect on the Celtic people of the region.

PACIFICATION OF CISALPINE GAUL

The Gauls living south of the Alps were a clear threat to Rome, and vice versa. Rome's territory was so large by this point that it had to deal with events from Iberia and North Africa to Macedon, and it was against this backdrop that the campaign to pacify Cisalpine Gaul was conducted. As always, the situation was complex. The Cisalpine Gauls might be a nuisance and a threat, but they were also a buffer against more distant Celtic people. In 230 BCE the Boii repelled an incursion across the Alps from other Celtic tribes, but resentment of Roman policies continued.

The Roman treaty with Carthage, signed in 226 or 225 BCE, was a result of tension with the Boii and their neighbours the Insubres. The Celts had hired mercenaries from among the tribes on the other side of the Alps and marched into Etruria. After a period of unopposed plundering, the Celts were confronted by a Roman army and retired. The pursuing Romans were roughly handled by Celtic cavalry and only saved by the timely arrival of reinforcements. This action is known as the Battle of Faesulae, though the only place of that name lies far from the battle site.

The Battle of Telamon

Unaware that an additional Roman army had arrived, the Celts accepted battle a second time near Telamon. While contesting a hill in their rear, the Celts became aware that they faced two enemy forces. The Boii and their allies stood on the defensive against the original Roman force, improvising a defensive barricade from wagons and unmanned chariots. To the rear the Insubres and a mercenary force from the Transalpine region made up of warriors from the Gaesatae tribe attempted to hold off the second Roman army.

The fight for the hill was decisive. At first it went well for the Celts, with the Roman commander killed and his head displayed on a spear. However, eventually the Celtic cavalry was driven off and the victorious Romans charged into the flank of the infantry. The Celts were tired at this point, having driven back repeated Roman assaults, and they finally collapsed under this new attack. Casualties are estimated at around 40,000 dead and 10,000 captured, from which the Boii and their allies never recovered.

Celtic Defeat

After their victory at Telamon in 225 BCE, Roman forces entered the lands of the Boii and demanded their surrender. They had no choice, but the Insubres continued to defy Rome through 224–223

BCE. In 222 BCE, after rejecting peace overtures, the Romans besieged the city of Acerrae. With no prospect of relieving the town, the Insubres, along with Gaesatae mercenaries, advanced on Clusium and placed it under siege. This drew off part of the Roman force from Acerrae.

The Celtic commander was reportedly one Verdomarus (d. 222 BCE). He challenged the Roman leader to single combat and was slain. His disheartened force was then defeated after being outflanked by the Roman cavalry. Acerrae fell soon after, but a Roman advance on the Insubres' capital at Mediolanum was pushed back. Nevertheless, the Insubres were forced to surrender. Roman settlers were given much of their land, beginning the process of Romanization.

In the short term, however, the Boii and the Insubres remained rebellious. Hannibal's invasion of Italia seemed to offer an opportunity to regain their independence but, although a great many Celts died fighting alongside Hannibal, it was not to be. While some of their brethren were with Hannibal in southern Italia, additional Celtic forces joined a Carthaginian expedition which landed in the north. Initially successful in sacking the city of Placentia, this force was confronted at Cremona by a Consular army. An attempt by the Celts to flank their enemies failed due to counter-manoeuvres, after which the Roman heavy infantry outfought and routed the Celtic force.

The last hurrah for the Cisalpine Celts was in 194 or 193 BCE, at the Battle of Mutina. Although the Gauls inflicted heavy losses on their Roman opponents, they were defeated and thereafter increasingly Romanized. Celtic forces never again challenged Rome in Italia, though they continued to be a potential threat to the frontiers.

THE CELTIBERIANS

It is likely that the Celtic people arrived in the Iberian Peninsula around 1000 BCE, and that they migrated there in significant numbers until around 600 BCE. This would place the new arrivals in the category of Late Hallstatt or pre-La Tène Celts, though it is not possible to precisely define their culture. It appears that the earliest migrations were into the south-eastern part of the peninsula, with later arrivals settling in more northerly locations.

THE IBERIANS

The Celts were by no means the first people in the Iberian Peninsula. They encountered a local population which today is normally referred to as the Iberians, although there is no record of their own name for their culture, if they had one. The term 'Iberian' was first used by Greek observers, perhaps in connection to the Ebro River.

Given that the Iberian language was not derived from Proto-Indo-European, it is likely these people arrived from North Africa rather than migrating west across Europe from the Kazakh Steppe. They may alternatively have been descended from a non-Proto-Indo-European population dwelling in central and Western Europe who moved west over the Pyrenees.

Exactly who was a Celt in Iberia, who was an Iberian, and all the shades in between is open to some discussion. Most of what is known comes from ambiguous archaeological finds and the records left by Greek and Roman writers who may not have been working from first-hand observation. Some scholars contest that the 'Iberians' as such never really existed. Perhaps a variety of entirely different cultural groups existed when the Celts arrived. Even so, the term 'Iberian' is still useful when referring to the indigenous population(s) of the Iberian Peninsula.

ARRIVAL OF THE CELTS

The arrival of the Celts was a gradual migration rather than a mass conquest. Conflict would have occurred, but there was no immediate Celtic takeover. Instead, groups settled where they could, perhaps driving off the local population or assimilating them – or being assimilated into their society. As increasing numbers of Celts arrived, they came to dominate some regions, while newer arrivals pushed on past these new homelands in search of their own places to settle.

Some regions remained more or less Iberian, notably in the south of the Iberian Peninsula. However, the Iberian culture was basically obliterated by contact with the Greeks and, later, the Carthaginians. Other areas, particularly in the north, became distinctly Celtic. Cultural intermixing was a factor everywhere, and resulted in a society that was different to that of the Gauls on the other side of the Pyrenees but still noticeably Celtic.

Between the two primary areas there was a great deal of intermixing, creating a 'Celtiberian' society in which distinctly

Celtic groups might live next to definitively Iberian settlements without any real distinction being made between them. In many cases, the mix was so complete that it was impossible to tell who was a Celt, who was an Iberian, and if it mattered at all. A local language subfamily grew up in Celtiberia, diverging from the Celtic languages spoken elsewhere in Europe.

THE CELTIBERIANS

While some of the Iberian groupings seem to have had a tendency towards urbanization, perhaps as a result of Greek influences, the Celtiberians preferred the usual system of small settlements. They built hillforts, which Roman observers referred to as *castrum*, giving us the modern term *castro* for the forts themselves and for the culture of north-western Iberia that produced a great many of them.

Most buildings within a settlement of this period were round. The earliest building method was probably wattle and daub, as elsewhere, but Celtiberian structures are often characterized by stone walls. The apparently haphazard construction of buildings was dictated by suitable ground and the need to surround each with its associated storage, animal pens and vegetable gardens.

As the population grew there was a move in some areas towards rectangular buildings and larger fortified settlements known to the Romans as *oppida*. The term is derived from the Latin for an enclosed space and can have slightly different connotations; one oppidum is not necessarily like another, especially when they are in different regions.

The move towards larger and more regularly aligned settlements suggests a growing population and a certain degree of social organization. This would have to exist in order for it to be worth Phoenician and Greek city-states setting up trading colonies along the coast. There is no evidence to support the legend that Lisbon was founded by Phoenician traders, but the economy of Iberia was sufficiently strong to make regular trade expeditions worthwhile.

Trade and Exploration

The key to this was movement of goods inland. A certain amount of money might be made at a trade port, and a small amount of local goods obtained, but without a functional trade network the volume of goods would be too small to be worthwhile. This was clearly not the case; trade ships plied the length of the Mediterranean and explorers occasionally pushed beyond.

Despite wild claims that Celtic explorers somehow reached the New World, ships of that era were largely restricted to coastal waters. A dash across the Mediterranean was possible, though risky, but setting off westwards in the hope of finding land was a death sentence. Ships did follow the coasts north and south, and there is evidence these mariners had a reasonable working knowledge of the nearby coasts of Iberia and Africa.

Explorers reached the British Isles and the Baltic, so there is a case to be made for trade along the Iberian and Western European coasts. Indeed, there is evidence of populations moving from Iberia to the British Isles. Ancient legends speak of a migration from Iberia into the British Isles, and there is genetic evidence to suggest that this happened on some scale.

THE CELTIBERIANS AND CARTHAGE

Carthage was founded as a trading colony by the ancient Phoenicians, whose own origins are open to debate. Rather than create a political empire as many of their neighbours did, the Phoenicians built a trading network based on their cities at the eastern end of the Mediterranean. Phoenician shipbuilding techniques were a factor in driving the history of the region. Their early vessels were clumsy and short-ranged, but by 1000 BCE new designs were appearing which extended both range and carrying capacity.

This opened new markets and necessitated the construction of forward bases such as Carthage. It is likely that the Phoenicians reached the Azores and navigated some way around the coasts of Europe and Africa. It is even stated that an expedition funded by Pharoah Necho II (reigned 620–595 BCE) sailed around Africa.

This would be an arduous and risky undertaking in rowed ships, but it was achievable with the technology of the day. Following a coast allowed ships to seek shelter in bad weather and obtain supplies by foraging. Navigation was a matter of keeping the land on the correct side of the vessel. While certainly impressive, the circumnavigation of Africa in no way suggests the people of the era were capable of sailing across open oceans to reach other continents. Although cited as 'proof' of the 'Celts in America' concept, Necho's escapade demonstrates only that the Phoenicians and their successors were capable of taking the coastal seamanship of their time to an extreme.

The Phoenician cities in the eastern Mediterranean survived and retained their independence by paying tribute to the currently dominant Empire. They survived the rise and fall of Assyria,

Babylon and Persia, but were diminished as the Persian Empire declined and was overrun by that of Alexander the Great. This left Carthage as an independent mercantile power in the central Mediterranean region, carrying on the Phoenician tradition of trade rather than conquest.

Carthage Rivalry with Rome

Carthage established trading colonies along the southern shores of Iberia and in the Balearic Islands, and for many years was content to make money rather than war. Rivalry with the emerging Roman Republic forced a change of policy, and after defeat in the First Punic War of 265–241 BCE Carthage embarked on a mission to obtain new territory in Iberia. The decades of wars between Carthage and Rome is important to Celtic history, as the fate of the Celtiberians was decided by these conflicts.

The ambitions of Carthage were probably a mix of wanting to protect its holdings for commercial reasons and fear of future Roman conquests. Sicily, Corsica and Sardinia had all been lost, and Rome was demanding reparations for the war. Financial setbacks had very real political consequences; Carthage depended on mercenaries for much of its military capability, and inability to pay them led to the brutal Mercenary War of 241 BCE. This in turn resulted in political upheaval and ensured powerful families such as that of Hamilcar Barca (d. 229 or 228 BCE) would continue to dominate Carthaginian policy.

It is likely the leaders of Carthage feared conquest of their home, which only military power could forestall. Curtailing Roman expansion might also give some teeth to the treaties Carthage had agreed to with its rival. The architect of this new Carthaginian Empire in Iberia was to be Hamilcar Barca, who had performed well during the First Punic War and the reassertion of Carthaginian power in North Africa that followed.

Hamilcar Barca

Hamilcar was accompanied by his son Hannibal (247–c. 181 BCE) and son-in-law Hasdrubal (d. 221 BCE). The campaign opened in 237 BCE, with a landing at Gades (modern Cadiz). From this base Hamilcar's army was able to capture coastal towns and push inland. These victories gave Carthage access to the Spanish silver it had previously traded for, which was used to raise additional forces and to grease the wheels of diplomacy.

Not all of the local population opposed Hamilcar. Several tribes rallied to his banner for their own political reasons or as mercenaries. However, despite taking control of most of southern Spain by 232 BCE the Carthaginians faced resistance. Notable among his opponents were the Lusitani, a Celtic people renowned for their rapid mobility and ferocity in battle. It was against the Lusitani that Hamilcar met his demise. Counterattacked during a river crossing the Carthaginian army was defeated and its commander drowned in the confusion.

Hamilcar was replaced by Hasdrubal, who founded a naval base he named Carthago Nova (modern Cartagena) and continued the campaign. The success of Hamilcar and Hasdrubal worried some leaders in Carthage, who were concerned the national interests were being subordinated to personal ambition. Rome was also alarmed, resulting in the 226 BCE Treaty of the Ebro.

Hannibal Takes Command

Hasdrubal was assassinated in 221 BCE, a deed attributed to an unknown Celt, and command passed to Hannibal. Hannibal was a staunch enemy of Rome, having been raised by his father to see Rome as the greatest threat to Carthage. He was not impressed by the claim that the city of Saguntum had placed itself under Roman protection. The city was, after all, within the Carthaginian sphere of influence agreed by the Treaty of the Ebro. He launched a siege of the city in 219 BCE and captured it early in 218 BCE.

Treaty or no, Rome declared war on Carthage over Saguntum, bringing about the Second Punic War of 208–201 BCE. Information from Iberia indicated Hannibal had crossed the Ebro, though at first it was assumed he intended to operate against the pro-Roman tribes in the area. Once it became apparent Hannibal intended to march all the way to Italia, a Roman army was sent to Massilia (modern Marseille) at the mouth of the River Rhône. Massilia was founded around 600 BCE as a trading colony, on land leased or bought from the local Gaulish tribes. It became an important trading port in its own right, though it did not achieve the status of an independent power as Carthage had.

Had Hannibal been forced to fight for passage and harassed as his force attempted to forage, his march would have been greatly slowed and his campaign doomed to an early failure. Even having to forage would result in delays. The decision of the Gauls to not oppose Hannibal, and indeed to let him purchase supplies from them, was therefore a quiet but potent influence on the course of the war.

The Roman response was therefore a little late. Rather than preventing a tired Carthaginian army from reaching the Rhône, Roman cavalry pushing north from Massilia won a skirmish against their opposite numbers and discovered that Hannibal was already camped on the banks of the river. Hannibal wisely chose not to wait for the Roman army to advance towards his camp. If he gave battle he might well win a victory, but it would be largely meaningless. His mission was to get his army into Italy where it could achieve strategically important results, not to fight every Roman it encountered.

Hannibal pushed on, entering the foothills of the Alps, and the Roman army did not follow. This was a pragmatic decision; the Romans were not equipped for fighting in the mountains. Besides, crossing the Alps would wear down Hannibal's army, and large Roman forces would be available to challenge what was left when it emerged. Instead, most of the Roman force was sent to Iberia. The commander who made this decision was Publius Cornelius Scipio (d. 211 BCE). He personally returned to Italy to prepare for Hannibal's arrival, sending his brother Gnaeus Cornelius Scipio Calvus (d. 211 BCE) to command the Iberian detachment.

The outcome of this decision has already been related. Hannibal entered Italy hoping to trigger a widespread revolt against Rome, and heavily defeated Publius Cornelius Scipio at the Battle of the Trebia River before embarking on his long campaign whose high point was crushing a large Roman army at Cannae.

Scipio Marches Inland

Meanwhile, Gnaeus Scipio moved his force to Iberia by sea, catching the Carthaginian forces there out of position due to a revolt by the pro-Roman Bargusi tribe. Unable to oppose the Roman landings the Carthaginian force remained inland, in the territory of friendly tribes, where it recruited Celtiberian warriors and awaited reinforcements marching from Cartagena. After capturing or taking unopposed possession of several towns, the

Roman force marched inland, picking up additional forces from friendly tribes along the way.

The Carthaginian force offered battle near Sissa, possibly because the allegiance of the local tribes was wayward. Delay might result in some drifting away or large numbers being neutralized by Roman diplomacy. This proved to be an error; the heavily outnumbered Carthaginian army was defeated in a simple set-piece battle. This gave Rome control of Iberia north of the Ebro, where the local tribes were for the most part already friendly, but that control was not uncontested.

Carthaginian forces and their Celtiberian allies raided across the Ebro, causing some pro-Roman tribes to reconsider their allegiance. Roman responses were aimed at cementing control over these tribes and harassing Carthaginian coastal holdings. Rome had gained a secure foothold in Iberia, and its naval superiority meant that a long march through potentially hostile Gaul could be avoided. Naval superiority permitted a Roman victory over a powerful Carthaginian expedition at the Battle of the Ebro in 217 BCE.

The Battle of the Ebro

The Carthaginian force was under the command of Hasdrubal Barca (245–207 BCE). This Hasdrubal was the brother of Hannibal, and should not be confused with his brother-in-law who had the same name. Hasdrubal benefited from large numbers of local allies, while the Romans under the command of Gnaeus Scipio had received no reinforcements since their arrival. A land battle was very much in the favour of Carthage, so Gnaeus Scipio decided to attack the supporting fleet. The fleet accompanied the army as it marched along the shore and beached at night under its protection.

The Roman counter came as a surprise attack launched as elements of the Carthaginian fleet were ashore foraging for supplies. Crews rushed back to their ships but the fleet was disordered at the start of the action and the situation only became worse. The Carthaginian force collapsed, with many crews beaching their ships to seek the protection of the land forces. Some of the beached ships were dragged off the shore and towed away by Roman vessels, adding to the humiliation.

The defeat of the Carthaginian fleet permitted Rome to strike wherever it pleased along the coast, forcing Hasdrubal to cancel his expedition. Allied tribes also rebelled now that Carthaginian prestige had been so badly shaken, distracting Hasdrubal from his main goal of expelling Rome from Iberia. Instead, he was forced to campaign against his former allies, fighting Celtiberians for control of the region. He was ordered to move his force to Italia to assist Hannibal but could not do so for fear of further rebellions.

Celtiberian Allegiance

The allegiance of the Celtiberians was vital to the Carthaginian war effort in Iberia, but the need to keep them on side meant that forces were not available for operations elsewhere, such as supporting Hannibal's campaign in Italia. Carthaginian reinforcements were sent to Iberia, permitting Hasdrubal to go on the offensive once again in 215 BCE. His force clashed with a Roman army at Ibera where it was resoundingly defeated.

Hasdrubal placed his allied Celtiberian infantry in the centre, flanked by his Carthaginian professionals. Although this worked exceedingly well for Hannibal at Cannae, at Ibera it was a disaster. The Celtiberians broke at the approach of the Roman heavy infantry, enabling them to punch through the centre and wheel into the Carthaginians. Most of the infantry were lost, with only the cavalry able to make an escape.

Some historians have suggested that this was the point Carthage lost the war. Reinforcements bound for Italia were once again diverted to Iberia, giving up a chance at victory due to the necessity of avoiding defeat. Rome was freed to continue its conquest of the local tribes while Carthage struggled to retain the allegiance of those it had previously won over.

The year 211 BCE was a decisive one in the Second Punic War, and thus critically important for the Celtiberians. Roman forces were by this time commanded by Publius Cornelius Scipio alongside his brother Gnaeus. They had solidified their control over Iberia north of the Ebro but were not receiving reinforcements from Rome due to the campaign of Hannibal in Italia.

Having captured Saguntum in 212 BCE, the Scipios went over to the offensive. Some sources claim they operated south of the Ebro in 215–212 BCE, others that they did not. What is known is that King Syphax of Numidia (d. 201 BCE) joined the Roman cause in 214 BCE, creating a new problem for Carthage. Syphax eventually rejoined the Carthaginian side and fought against Rome in North Africa. He was defeated and eventually captured by his rival Massinissa (c. 238–148 BCE), who had commanded Hasdrubal's cavalry in Iberia.

Celtiberian Mercenaries

The Roman contingent in Iberia was at this time facing severe shortages of funding and troops, but managed to find the money to remedy the latter problem with 20,000 Celtiberian mercenaries.

Carthaginian forces were dispersed as three armies, enabling the Roman commanders to split their own force but retain a numerical advantage.

Aware of the approach of Roman forces, Hasdrubal ordered a concentration of his Carthaginians and friendly Celtiberians near Castulo and bribed the Romans' allies into abandoning them. He then conducted a campaign of harassment using his cavalry while remaining in the safety of his fortified camp. He sent Indibilis (dates unknown), an Iberian chieftain, to flank the Roman force. Indibilis was a staunch enemy of Rome, who had become a captive after the Battle of Cissa. After being freed he led his tribe in harassing those favouring Rome.

Some ancient sources seem to suggest that the Celtiberians preferred guerrilla tactics to a stand-up battle, or even that they could not face an organized enemy head-on. This is not the case. The Celtiberians were as martial as anyone else, but they recognized that there are other ways to defeat an enemy than by charging onto his spear points. Campaigns like that of Indibilis created the impression of the wily Celtiberian ambush specialist but this was only one aspect of their mode of warfare.

The Roman force attempted to break out of its difficult position by attacking Indibilis's warriors. This brought about a night battle in which Indibilis's force suffered badly but was rescued by Numidian cavalry under Massinissa. With the Romans now pinned, the main Carthaginian force launched an assault which routed them. Publius Scipio was killed in the fighting. This action became known as the Battle of Castulo, though it is often grouped with the Battle of Ilorca, which took place a few days later, under the title Battle of the Upper Baetis.

Even before hearing about the catastrophic defeat and death of his brother, Gnaeus Scipio began to retire. He hoped to evade the Carthaginians by abandoning his camp at night, but was located and harassed to the point where the Romans took refuge on high ground near Ilorca. This was to no avail; the heavily outnumbered Romans were overrun and Gnaeus was slain.

Roman Retreat and Regroup

After the Battle of the Upper Baetis, the remnant of the Roman army retreated northwards. They were eventually reinforced by around 13,000 troops, bringing Roman strength in Iberia back up to about 20,000. Hasdrubal did not follow up his victories for reasons that remain unclear, enabling Rome to send another 10,000 men under the command of Publius Cornelius Scipio (c. 236–183 BCE) – son of the previous commander of the same name, who was destined to be known to history as Scipio Africanus.

Scipio tried to draw out elements of the Carthaginian force but was unable to create conditions for battle on his own terms. He decided to force the issue by marching on Carthago Nova in 209 BCE. An attempt to prevent Scipio from getting into position for an assault was crushed, after which the Roman force attempted to assault the city's defences. Although initial assaults were unsuccessful, a force was able to capture a gate, after which the defence collapsed.

The loss of Carthago Nova was a severe blow to Carthaginian prestige in Iberia and was also of material benefit to Rome. The city had been built as a base of operations and would now serve Roman interests – as would the supplies and funds captured within it. Scipio also freed a large number of Celtiberian hostages who had been held at Carthago Nova to ensure the loyalty of their tribes. This was yet another setback for Carthage.

After the capture of Carthago Nova, Rome no longer struggled to support its forces in Iberia. Loot from the city provided all necessary funding and the city itself was an excellent base of operations. Meanwhile, the Carthaginian armies in Iberia remained separate, giving Scipio the chance to defeat them one piece at a time. He began in early 208 BCE by marching on Hasdrubal's force, which was in winter quarters near Baecula.

Outnumbered, Hasdrubal withdrew to a position on high ground to await the attack. It appears he underestimated the strength and capabilities of the Roman force, or perhaps thought the steep sides of his position were a sufficient obstacle. The defence collapsed, forcing Hasdrubal to fight his way out past a Roman detachment positioned to prevent his escape. As usual, the heaviest casualties were among allied Celtiberian troops.

Battle at Metaurus River

Hasdrubal escaped defeat at the Baetis with a combat-capable force but chose to march towards Italia rather than contest Iberia. Along the way he recruited warriors from the Gaulish tribes, entering Italia with an army comprising mostly Gauls and Celtiberians. Hasdrubal hoped to join forces with his brother Hannibal but was confronted by a Roman force at the River Metaurus in 207 BCE.

Accounts of the battle vary, in some cases giving impossibly high casualty figures. It appears that Hasdrubal's war elephants caused dismay and disorder in the Roman centre, but his flanks could not withstand the Roman onslaught. Hasdrubal was killed during the ensuing rout, and his severed head was hurled into

Hannibal's camp in a piece of psychological warfare. Gestures of this sort are commonly associated with the Celtic people; it is not clear whether the Romans were influenced by what they had heard about the practice or if they came up with it themselves.

In 207 BCE another Carthaginian army arrived in Iberia, and as usual recruitment of Celtiberian troops began almost immediately. Although Hasdrubal's army had departed, there were still two potent Carthaginian forces in the field. Attacking either risked exposing the rear of the Roman army to the other, but doing nothing would allow them to concentrate and attack at their convenience.

Scipio solved this problem with a fast raid against one force, surprising the Carthaginians in camp and routing them. This force might coalesce and regroup at some point but it was not significant for the immediate future. Scipio hoped to smash the other during this window of opportunity, but was unable to bring the Carthaginians to battle.

Battle of Ilipa

Even more Carthaginian reinforcements arrived in 206 BCE, opening the campaign with a cavalry raid that was repulsed with heavy losses. Days later, the two armies clashed near Ilipa in what would be the decisive battle of the campaign. As was typical, both armies formed up for battle several days before the actual event, and Scipio used this time to create a deception. After letting his Carthaginian opponents see that he had, as usual, deployed his Roman legions in the centre flanked by their allies, on the day of battle Scipio reversed this formation.

He launched an immediate attack with his light troops, giving the Carthaginians no chance to realize their centre was opposed by Celtiberians and their flanks faced assault by Roman heavy infantry. After a period of skirmishing, the main Roman attack began. The centre was held back and the flanks pushed forward, with cavalry and light troops extending the line.

The elite of the Carthaginian army was pinned in place by the presumed threat of attack by heavy Roman infantry, while the real legions were driving back the recently raised and not very effective Celtiberians on the flanks. By the time Scipio committed his centre, the battle was already won. A Carthaginian withdrawal became a collapse, though heavy rainfall permitted the surviving Carthaginians to retreat to their camp.

It was the Celtiberians who decided what would happen next – by deserting in large numbers. Had they stayed to fight, the Carthaginians' fortified camp might have been defended or at least taken only at heavy cost. With too few troops to attempt such a stand, the Carthaginians attempted to withdraw under cover of darkness. This was detected and a vigorous pursuit all but destroyed the Carthaginian army. The survivors took refuge on high ground but were soon forced to surrender.

The Battle of Ilipa spelled the end of Carthaginian ambitions in Iberia. Scipio faced a rebellion by local tribes once it became clear Rome intended to control Iberia and was in fact a conqueror rather than the liberator it had portrayed itself as. Once the region was pacified, Scipio returned to Rome and began a campaign in Africa. His brilliant victory over Carthage earned him the nickname 'Africanus' and a reputation as one of the greatest military commanders of all time.

The power of Carthage was broken, though it would not be fully subjugated until the Third Punic War of 149–146 BCE. Perhaps the Celtiberians might have met a different fate if Carthage had continued to contest Iberia or if Hannibal's expedition had provoked a wider Gaulish revolt against Rome. As events transpired, Romanization was the only possible outcome once Carthage was no longer a counterbalance. It was no easy process, however.

ROMANIZATION OF IBERIA

Rome divided its territory into provinces along geographical lines, using natural borders such as mountain ranges or rivers. The province of Hispania Ulterior lay along the eastern coast; Hispania Citerior was on the southern coast. Both were easily accessible by ships plying the Mediterranean, while the rest of Iberia was not.

The Turdetani Rebellion

Although many of the tribes living in these regions had allied with Rome, living under its rule was a different matter. The Turdetani rebelled in 197 BCE – a serious matter since they were the most powerful group in the region. The Turdetani had enjoyed a cordial relationship with Phoenician traders and adopted many ideas similar to those prevalent in the Greco-Roman world. Their cities were fortified and their military powerful.

In 195 BCE, Marcus Porcius Cato (Cato the Elder, 234–149 BCE) became governor of Hispania Citerior and set about ending the rebellion. After defeating the Turdetani in battle he demanded all their cities immediately demolish their walls, making them highly vulnerable to attack if they continued to defy Rome. Most complied, and the revolt was soon under control. However, within little more than a decade Rome found itself involved in a protracted series of campaigns against the Celtiberians.

The First Celtiberian War

The first was against the Lusones, whose territory lay north-east of modern Guadalajara. This conflict became known as the First Celtiberian War, pitting the Lusones at the head of a confederation of the Arevaci, Belli, Pelondones and Titti tribes against Rome from 181–179 BCE. The Lusones besieged the town of Caravis with around 20,000 men. A Roman expedition sent to break the siege was attacked by other Celtiberians, though without success. This time Rome took a different approach to pacification after defeating the tribes, making an attempt at conciliation which was the basis of formal treaties.

Rome still faced resistance in Iberia, notably from the Lusitani. It is not clear whether these were a Celtic people, though they undoubtedly had some Celtic influences resulting from long contact. They had fought against Rome from 194 BCE and participated in the First Celtiberian War, though relations improved for a time after it ended. The Lusitani were famed for their ferocity in war and are noted as preferring the falcata as a hand weapon rather than the short swords of many Celtic peoples.

After the end of the First Celtiberian War, Roman treatment of the Lusitani and other tribes was generally fair and respectful. However, a succession of governors saw their position as a chance to enrich themselves at the expense of the local barbarians, for whom they had little or no regard. Wearying of the situation, the Lusitani became increasingly hostile and around 155–154 BCE they launched a raid into Roman territory under the command of Viriathus (c. 180–140 BCE).

The Lusitani Attack

The Lusitani were highly successful, at one point attacking Roman holdings in North Africa, but the cost was high. In 150 BCE, the Lusitani attempted to make peace with Rome. They were offered what looked like a good deal, including relocation into better land and assistance in making a home there. The Lusitani were separated into three groups, marching under Roman escort, and once out of sight of one another they were massacred.

Few of the Lusitani survived the betrayal, though Viriathus was one of them. He rose to prominence leading resistance to Rome. He almost met with disaster in 147 BCE during a raid into the lands of the Turdetani. Caught between Roman forces and the River Barbesula, Viriathus was offered generous surrender terms that might have been genuine. He was unwilling to place his people in Roman hands after their earlier treachery, however, so he resolved to fight his way out. The Lusitani cavalry made a series of demonstration attacks, distracting the Roman force until the infantry was able to break out of the trap.

Once the Lusitani army had regrouped, it retreated ahead of the more heavily burdened Roman force, drawing them up the Barbesula Valley until Viriathus found a suitable ambush point. Warriors concealed on the valley sides attacked the flanks of the Roman column while the cavalry charged down the valley. Strung out in marching order, the Roman force was overwhelmed, losing half of their 8,000 or so effectives before managing to escape.

Viriathus used this tactic repeatedly, inflicting further defeats on Roman forces in 146 BCE. Other tribes were inspired to join him or to launch their own revolts, gaining a fearsome reputation. Some Roman accounts may be exaggerated or based on hearsay, such as the tale of how a lone Celtiberian warrior became surrounded by Roman cavalry and responded with such terrifying violence that they retreated.

Viriathus Offers Terms

However, Rome had just finished off Carthage for good in the Third Punic War of 149–146 BCE, and could afford to replace the losses the Celtiberians inflicted. The balance shifted back and forth until Viriathus trapped an army commanded by Fabius Maximus Servilianus (dates unknown). Tired of the long war the Lusitani offered very generous terms, asking only that they be recognized as friends of Rome and their borders respected.

Viriathus's terms were agreed to, and a treaty ratified, but Rome was not willing to accept the humiliation inflicted upon it by the Lusitani and other Celtiberians. Conflict broke out again in 140 BCE, and Viriathus sent three of his friends to negotiate with the Romans. Rather than making a deal with Rome, they were bribed to murder Viriathus, which they did in 139 BCE.

The death of Viriathus disheartened many of the rebels and more or less ended the war. Perhaps wisely, Rome honoured the peace terms this time, and generally left the Lusitani alone for over a century. It was not until the Republic had become an empire that conquest of all of Hispania would be attempted.

The Belli

In the meantime, other tribes had mixed fortunes. Around 153 BCE the Belli began fortifying their capital, which was not permitted by Rome. An expedition was launched to force the Belli to comply with orders to desist, causing the Belli to abandon the work and instead lay an ambush in conjunction with their allies, the Arevaci. This was successful in causing serious casualties among the Roman force, though the Belli leader was killed in the fighting.

As is often the case when an overlord suffers a setback, other tribes took advantage of the situation to launch their own rebellions. The Arevaci tribe had fortified their own capital at Numantia and were able to resist attempts to quell their revolt. Numantia became a symbol of defiance and an embarrassment to a succession of Roman leaders from 153–137 BCE.

The first was in 153 BCE, when Consul Quintus Fulvius Nobilior (dates unknown) was sent to pacify the Belli. Although his force succeeded in destroying the Belli capital at Segeda, he lost about 6,000 of his 30,000 troops and was unable to prevent the Belli from joining their allies at Numantia. An attempt to besiege the city was unsuccessful, and trying to use war elephants against the defenders resulted only in the panicked beasts trampling the besiegers.

Roman consuls held office for one year, during which time they had a chance to win glory and advance their careers. This could lead to a certain recklessness and a tendency to pick fights where they were not necessary. Nobilior's consulship was a complete disaster, and his defeat at the hands of the Belli was sufficiently shocking that the date – August 23 – was thereafter considered inauspicious. After a miserable winter, Nobilior was replaced by Marcus Claudius Marcellus (d. 148 BCE), whose grandfather – of the same name – was known as the 'sword of Rome'.

The Second Celtiberian War

Marcellus, who had served as a consul twice before, appears to have believed the best interests of the Roman Republic would be served by making peace with the Celtiberians. He was able to negotiate a treaty, which the senate refused to ratify. The Celtiberians attacked Nerobriga and Marcellus retaliated with a siege of Numantia. This ended with a renewed offer of peace from the Arevaci, Belli and Titti tribes. Marcellus quickly accepted before his replacement arrived, ending what would become known as the Second Celtiberian War (154–151 BCE).

Lucius Licinius Lucullus (dates unknown) was a more typical high-ranking Roman. He wanted a war and had been sent with an army to fight it. On the flimsiest of pretexts, or sometimes none at all, he attacked nearby tribes and carried out massacres of those who surrendered. He also involved himself in the war against the Lusitani despite this being beyond his remit. Along with Sulpicius Galba (dates unknown), governor of Hispania Ulterior, Lucullus betrayed and massacred the Lusitani in 150 BCE.

Behaviour of this sort was rarely punished, due to the power and prestige of those involved. Consuls might be elected but it was not a real democratic process; candidates came from the elite and were chosen by those who had something to gain from granting them office. As a result, the Roman Republic made a rod for its own back on many occasions. Individual consuls would not have to deal with the mess they made unless they were re-elected in a later year and sent to the same war zone.

The Third Celtiberian War

Having antagonized people who were willing to make sacrifices in return for peace, Rome enjoyed only a few years of relative quiet in Iberia before the Third Celtiberian War erupted in 143 BCE. It did not go well for Rome, with a series of defeats under successive commanders. In 139 BCE, Consul Pompeius Aulus (dates unknown) was forced to bargain for his survival. His actions were not authorized by the Senate, and Rome refused to acknowledge the peace agreement. His replacement was Hostilius Mancinus (c. 179–?), who unsuccessfully besieged Numantia in 137 BCE.

Mancinus's campaign went no better than that of his predecessor and was crowned by a decision to surrender to the Celtiberians. This was apparently prompted by a rumour that additional Celtiberian warriors were approaching his force. The terms agreed to included recognition of the Arevaci as the equal of Rome, which was never going to be accepted by the Senate. Indeed, Mancinus was recalled in disgrace and replaced by the other consul for that year, Aemilius Lepidus (dates unknown).

Lepidus arrived and began pillaging the local countryside despite there being a peace agreement at least theoretically in place. Eventually the Senate decided the treaty was invalid but, in the meantime, Aemilius Lepidus managed to disgrace himself. War was obviously not desirable, even to the distant Senate, but had Lepidus furnished a victory he might have avoided censure. In the event his force ran out of food and had to retreat in disorder.

Change in Roman Consul

The Senate recalled Lepidus, too, and wrangling over who was most at fault went on for some time. Eventually Rome offered to deliver Mancinus to his enemies, who were not interested in such a gesture. Hostilities continued in a desultory manner until 134 BCE, when Scipio Aemilianus (c. 185–129 BCE) was assigned the task of pacifying Iberia.

This required a change in the law, as consuls were permitted only to serve for one year at a time though they could be elected again in the future. Scipio Aemilianus was already consul, but such was his reputation as a military leader that he was permitted to serve another year. He was familiar with conditions in Iberia, having served there as a tribune under Lucius Lucullus. He was also the grandson of Scipio Africanus and continued his family's work in the third and final Punic War.

Scipio Marches to Numantia

Scipio found the Roman forces in Iberia to be ill-disciplined and demoralized, and incapable of taking on the fearsome Celtiberians in their current condition. Turning them back into a useful fighting force required getting rid of many of the comforts his soldiers had become used to and thereby lightening the load of its baggage. Once he was confident he commanded real soldiers, Scipio marched on Numantia.

Rather than fight head-on, Scipio's army established itself around Numantia, building fortified camps and encircling the city with defences. Attacks against the Roman positions were repulsed and the siege remained unbroken for eight months, during which the defenders slowly starved. Eventually the Celtiberians offered peace terms but were informed that only total submission was acceptable. Some of the Celtiberians killed themselves rather than surrender. Those who survived were sold into slavery.

Scipio Aemilianus made an example of Numantia, razing it to the ground and dividing the lands of the Arevaci among friendly tribes. Resistance to Rome collapsed, though parts of Iberia remained beyond Roman control for another century. Nor was Romanization pursued with any vigour. Some veterans settled in Iberia, but it was not until the time of Augustus Caesar (63–14 CE) that full control of the peninsula was attempted.

The Cantabrian War

The campaign against the Cantabri of northern Iberia was led by Augustus himself, and was characterized by guerrilla tactics on the part of the Cantabri. The tribe was defeated in what became known as the Cantabrian War of 26–25 BCE, and revolted in 22 BCE and 19 BCE. Even when defeated, many warriors committed suicide by blade or poison rather than submit.

The Cantabrian War brought about the end of resistance to Rome in Iberia, and thereafter the region was Romanized. Celtic influences were still present, but the Celtic homeland of Iberia was no more. Its history thereafter was as the Roman province of Hispania.

THE ECLIPSE OF THE CONTINENTAL GAULS

The inhabitants of Cisalpine Gaul were a problem for their Roman neighbours, though not exclusively. Even when some tribes were in conflict with Rome, others could be persuaded to assist or be hired as mercenaries. During Rome's wars with Macedon, it moved forces through Cisalpine Gaul, and Carthage did likewise during the Punic Wars. Cisalpine Gaul was eventually pacified, but the Gauls of the Rhône Valley continued to be a complicating factor in Roman affairs.

THE ALLOBROGES AND THE ARVERNI

The chief powers in the region were the Allobroges and the Arverni. The Allobroges occupied a territory from the Isara (modern Isère) River to the Alps and were bounded to the northeast by Lake Geneva. In Roman times this was referred to as Lacus Lemanus. The capital of the Allobroges lay at Solonion. The Arverni gave their name to the modern region of Auvergne, occupying a region around the Loire and Allier Rivers. They ruled over a number of other tribes in the region and had their capital at the hillfort of Bibracte.

It is possible the Allobroges were associated with the Celtic group identified as Roman writers as the Gaesatae, who served as mercenaries for their cousins in Cisalpine Gaul. However, the first direct mention of the Allobroges in history refers to them both assisting and opposing Hannibal's march towards Italia in 218 BCE. This came about as a result of two chieftains vying for supremacy. One sought and received Hannibal's support and in return assisted his army in crossing the lowland part of the Allobroges' territory.

The Highland leaders decided to ambush Hannibal as he entered their territory but were not subtle about their preparations. When the attack came, the Carthaginians were ready and the Gauls were repulsed with heavy casualties on both sides. While the Allobroges were in home territory and could absorb the losses, Hannibal was at the end of a long supply line which had already been cut in Iberia. This reduction in his force would be keenly felt in the campaign to come.

Over the next century, Rome was more concerned with events in Iberia and its wars with Carthage and Macedon than in Gaul. The Gauls themselves left little record of their doings during this time, but it is likely there were squabbles and skirmishes between the tribes and the occasional small war. Feuding and raiding were a regular part of tribal life, a way for young warriors to make a reputation for themselves and to test their skills in combat.

CONSTANT TRIBAL CONFLICTS

It may seem strange in modern times that constant minor conflict was considered important to the wellbeing of the tribe.

However, this was a different era. A tribe that did not present a fierce face to the world might be seen as a victim by more aggressive groups, and lack of experience among its warriors could be disastrous.

Limited conflict was used throughout the ancient world to maintain a martial character, and even in peacetime there were measures in place to ensure the population did not become squeamish. Rome had its gladiatorial contests, which not only presented a gory spectacle but also included set-pieces recreating famous battles to remind citizens of their glorious past. In Sparta, the helot (slave) population could be murdered at will and men were encouraged to beat and mistreat their slaves. Bloodshed, of one form or another, was believed to be necessary to the long-term wellbeing of a society.

As a result of this near-constant skirmishing, Celtic society had a ready supply of warriors willing to prove their bravery and skill in the hope of winning approval and social advancement. The price was constant loss of life among those who were raided, along with some of the raiders, but the situation was tolerable to the tribe as a whole. Those who made good decisions in the long term gained in power and status, receiving the submission of other tribes.

THE NATURE OF CELTIC LEADERSHIP

There was never any real prospect of a 'Celtic Empire' emerging, however. The decentralized nature of Celtic society made it impractical to govern a huge area, and the ambitions of those who wanted to do so were at odds with tribal customs. Governorship systems seem to have varied. In some tribes there were kings – at least according to outside observers. This is subject to the usual disclaimer that outsiders might not have understood what they were seeing. Other tribes had a council of nobles or a group of elected magistrates.

Tribal leadership might be a complicated matter when viewed from the inside, even if there was an apparent king or chieftain. Nobles held varying degrees of power and those who commanded the loyalty of a sufficient number of people – particularly warriors – would have a say in governance. This was a matter of courtesy and respect, but also a recognition that the tribe needed the support of its internal power structures and in a worst-case scenario might face civil war if powerful individuals felt disenfranchised.

FOSTERING AND HOSTAGE-TAKING

The practices of fostering and hostage-taking created bonds of loyalty between families and tribes. Fostering was a custom whereby children from the upper echelons of one tribe were sent to be raised in another. It was a matter of honour to provide a good education and to treat the child well, and bonds between foster families often became close. Hostage-taking was sometimes quite similar; a tribe sent some of its people to live in another as a guarantee of good relations.

In modern parlance the word 'hostage' has unpleasant connotations, and it is true that hostages might be mistreated or killed if their tribe became hostile. Much of the time, however, hostages were respected members of their host society in a similar manner to fosterlings. Hostages were not captives, as such, but might be considered more like ambassadors who were held responsible for the conduct of their people. Giving hostages to another tribe was a way for the subordinate group to impress their overlords, so it was not uncommon for hostages to strongly support their hosts in war and politics.

Fostering and hostage-taking were opposite sides of the same coin. When the system worked well it created bonds of friendship between the participants, turning tribes and even tribal confederations into hugely extended families who would unite against an outsider even if they had their own internal differences. There was a limit to how large a confederation could grow and still maintain the bonds that held society together, though a suitably serious external threat might prompt an alliance on an unusually large scale.

MILITARY POWER AND POLITICAL CAPITAL

The larger tribal confederations were significant military powers in their own right, but for military power to be useful it had to be translated into political capital by demonstrating a willingness to use it. Plunder and revenge for old grievances were valid reasons for raiding, along with the need to ensure potentially hostile neighbours continued to respect the tribe. As a result, the frontier between Gaulish and Roman territory was never entirely quiet, but so long as the troubles remained at a tolerable level a large-scale Roman response was not triggered.

For example, by 154 BCE the Salluvii tribe was becoming a real nuisance around Massilia. Roman forces made an essentially defensive response, repelling attacks and hoping to deter the

Salluvii by making further raiding too costly. There was no real attempt to conquer or drive off the Salluvii. The lands north of the coastal strip between Italia and Iberia had not been of much interest until this point, but a threat to Massilia impacted the Roman economy and disrupted troop movements in the area. With attention still on Iberia, it was enough to deal with the threat and move on to other problems.

When raiding resumed in 125 BCE or so, the Roman response was more aggressive. By this time, Rome was secure elsewhere and had become accustomed to regular conquests. The southern Transalpine Gauls were a convenient enemy for a state where political advancement came by way of military leadership. A Roman expedition soundly defeated the Salluvii, whose survivors were absorbed by the Allobroges.

Further raiding, including attacks on the sometime-allies of Rome, the Aedui, prompted a further expedition which began in 121 BCE. The pretext for this expedition was protection of allies and the refusal of the Allobroges to hand over Teutomalius (dates unknown), king of the Salluvii, who had taken refuge among them. The Allobroges were assisted by the Arverni under their king, Bituitus (dates unknown), but were defeated near Vindalium. No details are available, but some Roman sources give enormous casualty figures for the Allobroges.

The Allobroges remained independent after their defeat, but the Arverni did not. They were resoundingly defeated, along with their allies, at the Battle of the River Isara and their king captured. Bituitus was paraded before the Roman masses as part of the traditional Triumph, but was not publicly executed as later Celtic leaders would be. Instead, he was sentenced to exile and his people thereafter were ruled from Rome. The region was subsequently recognized as a Roman province. It was originally named Gallia Transalpina, but would become better known as Gallia Narbonensis.

THE CIMBRIAN WAR

Nothing happens in isolation. Just as the fate of the Celtiberians was decided by conflict between Rome and Carthage, the Celts of Gaul were heavily influenced by a migration of Germanic tribes into their territory. These were the Teutones and the Cimbri, who had left their homes in Jutland and were looking for somewhere to settle. Some sources describe the Cimbri as Celts.

In 113 BCE, the Teutones and the Cimbri pushed into Noricum, a region in modern Austria and Bavaria dominated by a Celtic culture overlaid on an earlier Illyrian society. The Celts of Noricum were friendly to Rome and requested assistance, which was granted. The migrating Germanics found resistance too strong and began to move off, explaining that they wanted no conflict with Rome and did not know the local population were its allies.

The local Roman commander, Gnaeus Papyrus Carbo (dates unknown), made the fateful decision to engage in a rather typical piece of Roman treachery. He outwardly accepted the tribes' apology and offered assistance in their migration, then set up an ambush. There are few accounts of the battle, but it appears the Roman force was enormously outnumbered and suffered a catastrophic defeat. Facing disgrace, Carbo committed suicide.

The Cimbri and the Teutones continued their wanderings. They were not at that time enemies of Rome as such, just people looking for a home. However, they gained a low opinion of Rome and its politicians from this incident, along with confidence that Roman forces could be defeated in the field.

Disaster for Rome

The arrival of these two large and powerful tribes in Gaul naturally caused consternation and disruption among the people already living there. Assistance again was requested from Rome, which responded by sending two consular armies. Encountering the migrating Germanics near Arausio, the Roman leaders opened negotiations... then attacked anyway.

The Battle of Arausio, in 105 BCE, was another disaster for Rome, and an event that had implications for the entire ancient world. Up until that point, the Roman military system required those serving to provide their own equipment, which in turn dictated their status within the army. Only the more affluent citizens could afford the full equipment of a heavy infantryman or a cavalryman.

While this had some advantages in terms of ensuring the lower orders remained in their place, the system was becoming unworkable. Long campaigns took the wealthier citizens away from their businesses for years at a time, and casualties were becoming hard to replace. The solution was a radical reform of the Roman army, which turned it from essentially a militia into a professional fighting force.

Roman Army Reforms

The Roman solution was to recruit poor people to fight for the Republic. The law was changed so soldiers would be provided with equipment and weapons at the state's expense, and service was made more attractive by the promise of a land grant at the end of their term. This provided the poorer elements of society a route towards personal advancement, albeit at the cost of years of harsh and dangerous service, and even possible death in some far-flung barbarian wasteland.

This change provided not only plenty of recruits to the Republic armies, but, more importantly, the prospect of long-service veterans in stable units who could use their experience to train new recruits. Personnel were paid a salary, unlike barbarian warriors who fought for plunder rights and their duty to their leaders. This gave us the word 'soldier', from the Latin *soldat* – a piece of money.

The reforms carried out on the Roman army in the wake of Arausio had immense repercussions for every enemy of the Republic – and the later Empire – faced. The troops became lighter and quicker on the field, with standardized weaponry and improved fighting tactics. Each man was equipped with a short sword – the Gladius Hispaniensis copied from the Celtiberians – along with a large shield and a set of pila, or javelins. Rather than the maniples of previous times, the legion would now be subdivided into cohorts which could serve as a self-contained fighting detachment at need.

The reforms created a Roman army that lost fewer battles than its predecessor, and when directed correctly could defeat almost any opponent that met it head-on. The practice of granting retiring soldiers land in conquered areas contributed to Romanization and the long-term stability of the Roman state. On one hand equipping a legion was expensive, but the hidden cost of having wealthy citizen-soldiers away for long periods at a time was removed. This was the army that would ultimately destroy the Celts of mainland Europe, but there were huge challenges to face in the meantime.

Romans Battle the Teutones

In 104 BCE, the Teutones were reported to be marching towards Italia, but in fact entered Iberia. Consul Gaius Marius took the opportunity to train his army and to conduct diplomacy with local tribes. He set his troops to building a canal to simplify logistics around his base, establishing the practice of using legions to build roads, forts and other strategic works when not engaged in military operations. By the time the expected threat materialized, Marius's army was a cohesive force with experience of operating in the field.

The Cimbri and the Teutones had parted ways in Iberia. The Cimbri and their allies launched a campaign of raiding which resulted in several defeats and a retreat into Gaul, while the Teutones and the Ambrones, who were allied to them, had already moved in that direction. Next, the Cimbri in alliance with the Tigurini attempted to move into Italia by way of the Alps. The Tigurini were a part of the Helvetii tribal confederation, a Celtic group dwelling in what is now Switzerland.

Marius was positioned across the route of the Teutones, protected by a fortified camp. He was in no hurry to confront his enemies but merely watched them as they set up their own camp. The Teutones tried to taunt the Romans out to fight them. They were big men, much taller than the average Roman, and given to displays of martial noisiness that could be unsettling to less experienced soldiers. The standoff enabled Marius's troops to get used to their rather frightening opponents, reducing the psychological impact of their appearance and demeanour.

The Teutones Bypass the Romans

The Teutones assaulted the Roman camp and were repulsed with heavy losses. After repeated attempts failed, their leaders decided to stop wasting warriors and march towards Italia. If the Romans lacked the stomach for a proper fight they could be safely bypassed. It is said that the army of the Teutones was so large it took six days to pass the Roman camp, during which its members constantly taunted the occupants to come out and fight.

Once the Teutones were past, Marius had his army form up and march after them. Following more lightly equipped enemies had in the past been disastrous for Roman armies, as their opponents' superior mobility allowed them to break contact or get into an ambush position if they chose to do so. This was a new Roman army, however, stripped of much of its previous encumbrance. The troops were still heavily burdened, but they were in excellent physical condition.

The Romans Attack

As the Teutones approached Aquae Sextiae, a settlement recently built north of Massilia to protect it from Gaulish raids, Marius offered battle. He constructed a fortified camp atop a hill, while the Ambrones and the Teutones were camped on low ground along a river. Romans sent to obtain water clashed with tribal warriors, drawing in more fighters from both sides. The Ambrones' response was piecemeal due to some of their men having to struggle across the river from their camp, and they were resoundingly defeated.

The battle had pulled men from the construction work, leaving Marius in a dangerously weak position by nightfall. Perhaps fearing a repeat of their earlier experiences, the Teutones did not attack and likely lost their chance at victory. After a few days, Marius marched his force out of the camp, detaching around 3,000 infantry to take up a concealed flank position. The Teutones saw this as an opportunity and readily accepted battle. Although they would have to attack up a slope, they outnumbered the Romans two or perhaps three to one, and they did not think highly of their enemies.

The Germanic assault was repulsed by a volley of javelins followed by a charge downhill against the disordered tribal warriors. The Roman force drove their enemies down the hill, inflicting heavy casualties, but once on level ground the Teutones managed to rally. As they formed a shield wall, they were hit from behind by the Roman flanking detachment and routed. Losses as high as 60,000 killed or captured were recorded, in return for around 1,000 Roman casualties.

The Cimbri Invade Italia

Although the Teutones and the Ambrones were shattered by this victory, the Cimbri and their allies fared better. The Roman army opposing their passage through the Alps was not so well led as that of Marius, nor was it properly prepared, and was driven from its positions without difficulty. The Cimbri then entered Italia but did not exploit the advantage they initially held. One reason for this was in outlook. The Romans were fighting to defeat an enemy, while the invaders were looking for somewhere to settle down, or at least to gain some plunder on the way. Had they marched on the Roman capital or other major strategic objectives, the Cimbri might have inflicted a serious defeat on Rome, but instead they remained in northern Italia.

In 101 BCE, Gaius Marius was once again elected as consul and led an army to confront the invaders. Denying their offer of peace in return for land to settle upon, Marius offered battle despite being outnumbered two to one or more. Under a flag of truce, the opposing leaders agreed to fight on the plain of Vercellae, whose exact location today is unclear.

The Battle of Vercellae

The Roman force was ready first, and took up a position that forced the Cimbri to advance with the sun in their eyes. The Cimbri and their allies approached with as many as 15,000 cavalry in the lead, becoming tired as they marched across the plain towards their waiting opponents. Once they were close enough, the cavalry launched a charge but veered suddenly away. Whether this was a feigned retreat or an attempt to sweep onto the flank is debatable; it may be that the cavalry recoiled from charging directly into a solid wall of Romans.

Whatever the reason for the turn, some of the legionaries saw an opportunity and advanced against the tribal cavalry. Infantry rarely succeed in charging cavalry, and this occasion was no exception. The now-disorganized Romans were attacked and roughly handled, but the Cimbri force also lost its cohesion. A counterattack by Roman cavalry drove the tribal horsemen into their infantry.

A general advance by the Roman infantry brought about a close-quarters battle in which the steadiness of the legionaries proved decisive. As the battle became a slaughter, the Cimbri began surrendering, though their leaders preferred a dramatic last stand to becoming captives. It is claimed the Cimbri lost as many as 100,000 people, some of them families of the warriors. The survivors were largely sold into slavery, and the power of the Cimbri was permanently broken.

At this time there was still a distinction between 'Roman' legions, which were manned by Roman citizens, and 'Latin' legions, which came from allied cities. Marius extended Roman citizenship after the battle to all who had fought alongside him, stating that he could not tell Romans from Latins in action. This angered the Senate, which had not granted permission, but Marius was too powerful to censure. Thereafter, there was no distinction between legions raised in Rome and those whose soldiers came from elsewhere in Italia.

Impact on the Celtic People

The Celtic people were, at first glance, on the periphery of these events. However, there were profound implications for the Gaulish tribes in particular. The Roman army forged by Marius was optimized for defeating tribal forces like those of the Celts, and would be wielded ruthlessly in later years by Julius Caesar to conquer them. It is notable that some of the auxiliary forces fielded by Marius were Ligurians, a people of uncertain origins who are known to have been heavily influenced by neighbouring Celts. For this reason, they are sometimes referred to as Celt-Ligurians, though some sources suggest a connection with the Ambrones.

Although generally described as Germanic, both the Teutones and the Cimbri have been described as Celtic or Celtic-influenced in some sources. Whether or not this is the case, they brought about events that would have enormous consequences for the Celtic people of Europe.

JULIUS CAESAR AND THE HELVETII

Gaius Julius Caesar (100–44 BCE) was born in 100 BCE, just after Marius won his great victory over the Cimbri. Indeed, it was Caesar's father who brought word to Rome of the battle. Caesar's early life was impacted by considerable internal conflict within the Roman Republic; a revolt by allied Italian cities and a civil war between Marius and his great rival Sulla. As a member of a powerful family he saw first-hand how the Republic worked; military and political power were inextricably linked. Caesar himself gained great power by the fairly standard method of spending huge amounts of money to win over supporters. This resulted in advancement but also potential bankruptcy.

In 59 BCE, Caesar was appointed governor of Cisalpine Gaul, a lucrative post. Caesar's ambitions went much further, however. He sought to win glory and enrich himself, and for that he needed a war. Cisalpine Gaul was peaceful by that time, but just over the mountains lay Transalpine Gaul, home to tribes who were not always friendly to Rome. Caesar was in a position to intervene in events there, and in 58 BCE a suitable opportunity arose.

The Helvetii Migrate into Transalpine Gaul

Two years earlier, Orgetorix (d. 60 or 61 BCE), a powerful nobleman among the Helvetii tribe, had proposed that his people migrate from their traditional homelands to Transalpine Gaul. It is probable this was due to pressure from Germanic tribes encroaching from the north, though Orgetorix apparently had larger plans. He had orchestrated a conspiracy within his own tribe and its neighbours to overthrow their existing magistrates and make Orgetorix king. It appears that he intended to forcibly unite the Gauls under his rule. Whether he or anyone else could have held a large Celtic kingdom together for long is an open question, but the Roman conquest of Gaul would have been at least set back by this move.

The conspiracy was discovered and Orgetorix brought to trial. However, when a large number of his followers threatened violence, he was released. Before the situation developed any further, Orgetorix died, probably by suicide. The idea of a migration to Transalpine Gaul lived on, however, and in 58 BCE the Helvetii began their move. The migration included the Boii, Latobrigi, Rarici and Tulingi tribes, with total numbers estimated at 250,000 to 300,000 people. About a quarter of this number were warriors, or at least capable of fighting, with the remainder transporting everything they owned. They moved in large groups that foraged for supplies and would quickly strip an area if unopposed.

The planned migration route would take the Helvetii through Roman territory, which could be seen as a threat to local stability or an outright attack if the foragers were too enthusiastic. The Helvetii asked for safe passage and gave assurances of their peaceful intentions, but Caesar wanted conflict. He had at the time only one legion available, which was not nearly enough, so he initially acted as if he might grant permission. He succeeded in stringing the Helvetii along with mixed messages while he gathered more troops.

Caesar also ordered the destruction of the Rhône bridge at Geneva and the construction of fortifications. Only then did he issue a clear answer – No. The Helvetii had burned their villages before they marched and had nowhere to return to. Denied permission to enter Roman territory, they took a more northerly route into the lands of the Aedui, who were generally, if not enthusiastically, friendly towards Rome.

Caesar Attacks the Helvetii

The Helvetii were granted permission to migrate through the lands of the Aedui by Dumnorix (d. 54 BCE), although he had no right to do so as it was his brother Divitiacus (dates unknown) who led the tribe. Dumnorix had been part of the conspiracy led by Orgetorix to overthrow tribal leaders, including Divitiacus, and was related by marriage to many other powerful Gauls. He was opposed to Rome, unlike his brother.

Divitiacus rescinded the permission and sent warriors to oppose the Helvetii as they began crossing the River Arar (modern Saône). He persuaded Caesar not to punish his brother, but also asked for Rome to provide military assistance against the Helvetii, as it had previously against the Allobroges and the Arverni.

Although most of the migration had already crossed the Arar when Ceasar arrived with six legions, the Tigurini tribe had not yet made the move. This tribe had accompanied the Cimbri during their march around Iberia and southern Gaul and had intended to follow them into Italia. The defeat of the Cimbri caused the Tigurini to return home instead.

Caesar was unlikely to have been motivated by a desire to crush a past and potential enemy of Rome or to take revenge for their attempted participation in an invasion of Italia, though a victory over the Tigurini could be spun that way if it suited his purposes. Caesar was on a more important mission, to him at least, and the Tigurini were no more or less than a handy target.

Three legions were ordered to advance during the hours of darkness, and caught the Tigurini by surprise. The resulting Battle of the Arar was a complete victory for Rome. Caesar claimed there were heavy casualties among the tribal warriors, but it is possible the tribe was dispersed rather than shattered. Afterwards, the legions built a bridge across the river, enabling a rapid pursuit of the Helvetii.

The Helvetii tried to negotiate, but Caesar wanted a victory and was not receptive. The march continued with Caesar's force in pursuit, until a lack of supplies forced him to redirect his troops towards the Aedui capital of Bibracte. There, he hoped to obtain provisions from the friendly tribe. Realizing the Romans were moving away, the Helvetii decided to attack them rather than break contact. They were delayed by the Roman cavalry rearguard, giving Caesar's legions time to take position on a nearby hill.

The Helvetii Counterattack

Having cleared the Roman cavalry aside, the Helvetii launched an uphill attack against the outnumbered legions. According to his own account of the battle, Caesar ordered his horse and those of other officers to be taken to the rear. By so doing he ensured there would be no retreat. As the Helvetii approached, the Romans unleashed their usual volley of pila and charged downhill into the dense masses of Gaulish warriors.

The Helvetii were thrown back and began to retreat in disorder, but as the Roman pursuit reached level ground the tribal rearguard, consisting of the Boii and Tulingi, hooked into the Roman rear. The main Helvetii force rallied and counterattacked, trapping the Romans. The resulting hand-to-hand fight pitted Roman staying power against Celtic numbers and prowess, and eventually the two tribal forces were driven apart. Fighting went on into the night, with the Helvetii camp stormed and their forces defeated.

The next day, the remnants of the Helvetii marched into the lands of the Lingones. The Roman force was in no condition to pursue for three days, but once it caught up, the Helvetii surrendered. Most were returned to their homelands, though the Boii were allowed to join the Aedui at the request of that tribe's leaders.

Whether or not there was any need for this conflict beyond Caesar's personal ambitions, it was over. Julius Caesar had eliminated the threat to the provinces he governed, as well as protected an allied tribe, and had won a great victory. It is unlikely he started out with plans beyond defeating the Helvetii, but an opportunity was soon presented to him for further glory. What should have been a clear-cut campaign became a series of conflicts known to history as the Gallic Wars, in what must be one of the most outrageous examples of 'mission creep' in all of history.

THE GERMANIC INVASION OF GAUL

Casear's next opportunity was furnished by the never-ending conflicts between Celtic tribes. The Sequani of the Upper Arar Basin had been at odds with the Aedui for a long time, aligning themselves with the Arverni. Sometime before 61 BCE, they requested assistance from the Suebi against the Aedui. The Suebi were a Germanic tribal group who gave their name to modern-day Swabia.

Under the leadership of Ariovistus (dates unknown), the Suebi crossed the Rhine and made war on the Aedui. The Sequani did not benefit from this, as the Suebi occupied a large swathe of their territory as part of their expanded homeland, and other Germanic groups were inspired to make a nuisance of themselves. This may have been a factor in the decision of the Helvetii to migrate: pressure from powerful Germanic tribes may have been too much to withstand.

The Aedui were heavily defeated at Magetobriga in 63 BCE by an alliance of the Arverni and Sequani, assisted by the Suebi. They requested aid from Rome but received only a promise, as a revolt among the Allobroges distracted Roman attention. The decree made by the Roman Senate, that the Aedui should receive military assistance, was interpreted rather loosely by Caesar when it suited his purposes.

Caesar Attacks the Suebi

The Germanic tribes had a certain martial mystique among the people of the Roman Republic. Clashes with the Cimbri and the Teutones left an impression of fearsome warriors who might threaten the Roman way of life. Defeating the Suebi would further enhance Caesar's reputation, so, since he already had an army in the field, he set about it. He had a pretext in the Senate's decree and a renewed plea for aid from Celtic leaders resulting from Ariovistus's demands for tribute and hostages from the nearby tribes. He could also claim that the Suebi were a destabilizing influence that might inspire the Allobroges to rebel once again.

Caesar's six legions marched on the Sequani capital at Vesontio (modern Besançon) and took control over it, though the Roman troops were nervous about confronting such large numbers of the fearsome Germanics. Nevertheless, order was restored and the army marched out in search of its enemies. Once the two armies were in proximity, a parley took place between Caesar and Ariovistus.

This was a meeting of two massive egos, both of whom considered they were in the right. Caesar had his many pretexts for action, plus his own desire for a military victory, and Ariovistus could argue that he was now the legitimate ruler of the area having fulfilled his agreement with the Sequani. Negotiations, perhaps unsurprisingly, came to nothing.

A period of skirmishing ensued, with both sides attempting to place fortified camps in advantageous positions. According to his own account, Caesar learned that Ariovistus wanted to delay battle until after the new moon, as a divination had told him he would be victorious in that case. Romans were great believers in divination and conducted their own before a battle. Some major defeats had been attributed to incorrectly performed or omitted divinations. Given that Caesar placed such faith in divinations, it was natural that he would want to deny Ariovistus the benefit of his.

Caesar forced a battle by attacking the Suebi camp, bringing about a hard-fought close-quarters struggle which eventually resulted in a collapse of the Suebi army. The survivors, including their leader, escaped across the Rhine. Ariovistus disappeared from history at this point, while Caesar moved on to his next conquest.

SUBDUAL OF THE BELGAE

According to Julius Caesar, there were three broad groups of people in Gaul and the surrounding areas. The Arverni and the Gauls (Caesar mentions they called themselves 'Celts') lived on opposite sides of the River Garonne, and the Belgae lived across the Marne and the Seine from the Gauls. The Belgae, Caesar stated, were the boldest of these peoples. He attributed this to them not being made soft by the luxuries traded by Roman merchants.

It was to the Belgae that Caesar turned his attention after chasing the Suebi out of Gaul. As before, it is unlikely he intended to pick a fight with this new opponent at the beginning of the campaign, but he was riding a wave of victory and saw a mix of opportunity and perhaps necessity. The Belgae were, quite reasonably, concerned about Roman military adventures close to their lands and began drawing together an army over the winter of 59–58 BCE.

Caesar saw this as a threat or a pretext, and called for the raising of additional forces to augment his existing army. This brought his strength up to eight legions plus auxiliary and allied forces. The Remi, a Belgic tribe who gave their name to the city of Reims, were induced to ally with Rome. They had several oppida – enclosed settlements that in other times and places might be called duns – including one at Bibrax on the River Axona (modern Aisne).

Bibrax and the territory of the Remi could be used as a staging point for a Roman incursion, and perhaps the leaders of the Belgae wanted to demonstrate that friendship with Rome meant enmity with the rest of the tribal confederation. They marched under the command of Galba (dates unknown), king of the Suessiones, to attack Bibrax.

The Belgae Harass the Countryside

The attack was unsuccessful, so the Belgae began to ravage the countryside. This was a normal part of tribal warfare, which served to keep warriors interested while yielding some plunder and supplies. Ravaging also weakened the victims economically, so that even if they avoided battle they would be diminished. A tribal leader who sat in his oppidum while enemies rampaged around the countryside would seem weak, so might be drawn out for a battle on unfavourable terms.

The Roman force moved into the area and deployed some light troops to harass the Belgae, who responded by advancing on Caesar's camp. His response was cautious, but after some skirmishing Caesar decided to offer battle. Naturally, he wanted this to be on his own terms, so had his troops set up field fortifications. A marsh to his front further protected Caesar's army.

This presented the Belgae with a problem. They hoped the Romans would advance through the marsh and become disordered, but they did not do so. Faced with the prospect of doing the same in the opposite direction and then attacking troops in prepared positions supported by field artillery, the Belgae wisely decided this was a losing prospect. Instead, they attempted to attack the Roman camp by crossing the River Axona in its rear.

Battle at Axona

The assault was a failure due to a stout defence by lighter Roman troops, and the Belgae fell back. After considering their options, they decided to retire to their homeland and pulled out in some disorder. At first Caesar did not pursue, perhaps fearing a trap like those sprung by other Celtic peoples. It was not, and once the legions did begin a pursuit, they caught the disorderly rear elements of the march by surprise. Caesar stated that his men inflicted heavy casualties for very little loss.

The Battle of the Axona was of little consequence for the Belgae in and of itself. Their strike against the Remi had been driven off, but their forces were intact. The Roman attack on the rear of the column was more embarrassing, and the fight seems to have gone out of some tribes. Caesar advanced into the lands of the Belgae in early 58 BCE, and despite a pledge to aid one another against Rome, most of the tribes surrendered.

The Atrebates, the Atuatuci, the Nervii and the Viromandui continued to resist. Caesar was informed that the Nervii were the most dangerous of these, so launched a campaign against them. As his army advanced into the lands of the Nervii, the Atrebates and Viromandui sent contingents of warriors to assist their allies. The Atuatuci did likewise, though they arrived too late to take part in the ensuing battle.

Caesar Battles the Nervii

According to Caesar's account, the Nervii attempted to concentrate against his army while it was still on the march, intending to overwhelm the leading legion before assistance could arrive. Aware of this, the Roman army began to advance on a frontage of six legions with two in the rear to guard the baggage train. This meant that it was not possible to march all units along the most advantageous route and would make the advance slower but made isolating the head of the column impossible.

As the Romans approached the River Sabis, where they intended to camp, the cavalry and light troops were sent forward to clear any opposition. The Nervii had concealed their forces in a wood, and launched their attack with great speed. Despite having few or perhaps no cavalry of their own, the tribesmen managed to cross the river and drive off the Roman advance guard before charging at the troops who were beginning the work of constructing a fortified camp.

What ensued was an extremely hard-fought action, ultimately won by Roman discipline and fighting power – and the heroic leadership of Caesar himself, if his own account of the battle is to be believed. The Belgae managed to enter the Roman camp, and pressed their opponents so hard that some allied cavalry fled the battle. They returned to their tribe with a lurid tale of Roman defeat and slaughter.

In reality, the six advanced legions managed to withstand the Belgic onslaught, and gradually manoeuvred into position to support one another. Light forces and cavalry were, according to Caesar, heartened and returned to the fray with gusto while the two rear legions hastened to assist their hard-pressed comrades. The battle became a slaughter of the Nervii fighting men.

Having come so close to defeat, Caesar naturally made much of the prowess and courage of his opponents. He also exaggerated the number of casualties sustained by the Nervii, but even so the tribe was devastated by its losses. The surviving leaders surrendered and, perhaps to their surprise, were treated leniently. The Nervii would keep their lands, and Caesar sent messengers to other tribes warning that he had offered protection to his defeated enemies.

Caesar Marches on Atuatuci

This was more likely to be a political gambit than mercy inspired by admiration. The message was clear – Rome was a kind friend and a deadly opponent. The point was underscored when Caesar's army marched on the Atuatuci, who gathered their population together in their strongest hillfort. The fortifications, combined with a naturally defensible position, were formidable, and the

Atuatuci conducted an active defence at first. Their warriors harassed the Romans as they attempted to build the usual circle of field fortifications.

The Atuatuci were not familiar with the Roman style of siege warfare and did not at first appreciate the significance of construction work going on behind their defences. Once it became apparent that the Romans had built engines to breach their wall, the Atuatuci attempted to negotiate. They offered to surrender on condition they would not be disarmed. This would leave them defenceless against their rivals.

Caesar was unwilling to grant this condition, but offered to do as he had with the Nervii. Neighbouring tribes would be warned not to harm those who had submitted to Rome. The Atuatuci agreed to these terms and began throwing their weapons out of the hillfort... but not all of them. Having convinced the besiegers they had submitted, the Atuatuci launched a night attack on the Roman positions. Caesar speaks highly of their courage and fighting skills, but they were defeated with heavy casualties. The entire tribe was then sold into slavery.

The Tribes Submit

It required little more to persuade the Belgae that further opposition to Rome was foolish and dangerous. The tribes submitted and were required to support Caesar's army when it went into winter quarters. This caused resentment that would become open defiance in 56 BCE, but towards the end of 57 BCE the situation was entirely satisfactory – from the Roman point of view anyway.

Caesar had made enough money to clear his debts and secure his political future, and was welcomed back to Rome as a conquering hero. He returned to his provinces over the winter to manage their affairs, but it is likely he expected to undertake further campaigning in Gaul whether or not there was a need. Leaving his legions in Gaul might have been no more than common sense, ensuring the tribes remained submissive and kept their promises not to molest those Caesar had disarmed, but it was also offensive to the proud tribes forced to supply them. Further conflict was more or less inevitable.

The Veneti

After the defeat of the Nervii and the destruction of the Atuatuci, other tribes surrendered to relatively small detachments of Caesar's army. Among these were the Veneti, whose name is given in various ways by different writers. It seems to be derived from an ancient word for white, in this case referring to the blond hair of most tribe members. The Veneti were related to the Belgae, though rather distantly. They were extremely important in the Celtic world due to their sea power.

The Veneti lived along the Atlantic coast and were great mariners, dominating the sea links between the mainland and the British Isles. Many of their settlements were inaccessible other than by sea, which may have been a factor in their decision to defy Caesar. Their ships were greatly superior to those available to the Romans since they had been developed to handle the Atlantic coastal waters rather than the relatively benign Mediterranean.

The ships of the Veneti were larger and more seaworthy than Roman vessels, with a strong prow and stern which made them resistant to ramming attacks. They also used sails, which Roman designs did not. These vessels were primarily used for trade up and down the coast and across the English Channel but could be an effective platform for combat.

Naval Warfare

Naval warfare in this era was fought at extremely close range. Ship-mounted artillery weapons were unavailable or ineffective, so, with the exception of ramming attacks, a sea battle was little different to one fought on land. Bows and javelins were used to weaken enemy crews, and boarding followed by hand-to-hand combat produced decisive results. Ramming attacks could be directed at the hull in the hope of sinking a vessel, or against the oars. This would not only break off several oars on one side but would cause the inboard end to move violently, injuring or killing crew members.

When Roman emissaries arrived demanding supplies of grain, the Veneti refused and began making defensive preparations. The Romans responded by constructing a fleet and attacking Veneti towns. This did not go as well as the Roman commanders hoped. Some settlements were captured but Veneti naval superiority enabled them to evacuate a threatened town or move reinforcements along the coast faster than the Romans could march.

The Roman fleet also underperformed. Its vessels were not well suited to conditions along the Atlantic coast and were unable to venture out much of the time due to weather. When Roman ships clashed with those of the Veneti, their ramming attacks generally failed, and the higher sides of the Veneti vessels made javelins ineffective.

What Rome had, however, was organization and resources. Additional ships were sent to reinforce the fleet operating off

Gaul, and one by one the Veneti settlements were captured. As the noose tightened, the Veneti decided to seek a decisive naval engagement, which seems to have taken place close to the Gulf of Morbihan in the Bay of Biscay. The outnumbered Veneti tried to break off after losing several ships but were unable to do so due to calm conditions. With a wind, their sails made Veneti ships much faster than Roman vessels, but without one the Romans could row faster.

The Veneti fleet was overwhelmed and most of its vessels captured. Afterwards, the tribe surrendered; but this time Caesar was not inclined to be generous. The Veneti leaders were executed, and the remaining population sold into slavery. Caesar then campaigned along the coast, subduing additional tribes.

In the meantime, detachments of the Roman army had conquered several tribes in what would become Normandy, and moved into Aquitania. They were harassed by tribal warriors using hit-and-run guerrilla tactics, but eventually managed to force a decisive battle by attacking the enemy's camp. Caesar himself was less successful, largely since the tribes he targeted would not come out to fight and be defeated in the manner he hoped for. The winter of 56–55 BCE saw the Roman army camped between the Saône and Loire Rivers, with the burden of supplying it falling on recently defiant tribes.

CAESAR SHOWBOATS

The beginning of 55 BCE saw Caesar's political position secured with five more years of governorship, giving him time and authority to continue his Gallic wars. He was in alliance with

Gnaeus Pompeius Magnus (Pompey the Great, 106–48 BCE) and
Marcus Licinius Crassus (115–53 BCE), forming what is known
to history as the First Triumvirate. Together, the three were
enormously powerful, but they were also rivals with their own
ambitions. Naturally, Caesar distrusted his allies and wanted to
be more powerful than them. His actions in 55–54 BCE were more
about winning fame and glory than any real necessity. The same
can be said about the entire campaign, but what followed the
conquest of the Veneti was particularly unnecessary.

Roman writers seemed to consider anyone living on the right
bank of the Rhine to be Germanic, and those on the left to be
Gauls. This is not a terrible generalization, but there were Celtic
people in what the Romans called Germania. The Tencteri and
Usipetes tribes were therefore referred to by Caesar as Germanic,
though they may have been Celts. Either way, they were driven
across the Rhine by pressure from the Suebi and requested
permission to find a home in Gaul.

Caesar refused this, and confidently sent a force of auxiliaries
to repel the tribes. This was roughly handled by their cavalry,
prompting Caesar to launch an attack on the tribes' camp and
slaughter everyone his troops encountered. Afterwards, the
legions built a bridge across the Rhine and crossed into the lands
of the Suebi. After a short campaign of raiding, the Roman army
re-crossed their bridge and destroyed it.

It is possible to argue that Caesar wanted to prevent the Suebi
becoming too powerful or to deter them from making forays into
conquered Gaul, but, in reality, it is more probable that Caesar
attacked the Suebi because he could. The campaign could be spun
back home as a daring exploit to chastise the nasty barbarians and
keep the Republic safe, and glory was always a good thing to have.

Caesar Invades the British Isles

Next, Caesar invaded the British Isles. His stated reason was that the Britons had assisted the Continental tribes against Rome, but, again, it is more likely he carried out the adventure as a public relations exercise. The tribes of south-eastern Britain were forewarned, and assembled an army to meet the Roman expedition. Caesar had to find an alternative landing point, and, even then, was soon faced with strong opposition.

Only two legions had made the crossing, with no cavalry support. Despite this, the Britons were reluctant to give battle at first. They were quite willing and able to ambush foraging parties, however, and having inflicted casualties on the invaders they were inspired to make a serious attempt to repel them. Their assault was unsuccessful, but Caesar could not attempt a pursuit for lack of cavalry. It was clear nothing decisive could be achieved and, as the 55 BCE campaign season drew to an end, the Romans retired to the Continent.

Despite not really achieving anything, these expeditions won Caesar even greater approval in Rome, which he decided to build on by making a proper invasion of the British Isles. This was carried out with great success in 54 BCE, though the Roman army was back in Gaul by the end of the year. Caesar's activities in Britain are covered in the next chapter.

THE REVOLT OF AMBIORIX

The destruction of whole tribes by Roman forces disrupted the balance of power in Gaul. In the case of the Atuatuci, their elimination freed the Eburones from subject status. The Eburones are described by Caesar as Germanic, but they are likely to have had Celtic influences given their location between the Meuse and the Rhine. They were not a large tribe; according to Caesar they managed to raise 40,000 warriors with help from three other tribes.

At the end of 54 BCE, Caesar wintered his legions in Gaul as he had done before, but lack of provisions required greater dispersal. This provided Ambiorix (d. 53 BCE), the leader of the Eburones, with an opportunity to strike at Rome. Archaeological evidence is scant, but the popularly accepted version of the story is that the Fourteenth Legion was quartered at Atautuca – whose actual location is uncertain – and the Eburones were expected to provide supplies. The year had been very dry, and food for the tribe was short, so having to give up a proportion of what little they had did not sit well with the Eburones.

A Roman foraging party was attacked by warriors from the Eburones tribe, which may or may not have been part of a plan. It is possible that Ambiorix feared savage Roman retaliation and decided he was now committed to fighting Rome. If this is so, then – as Caesar would later remark after crossing the Rubicon – the die was cast. It is claimed that Ambiorix was persuaded to rise up against Rome by other tribal leaders, but whether or not he intended to pick a fight with the Fourteenth Legion at that particular time remains unclear.

The Roman camp was too well fortified to attack, so Ambiorix took advantage of the good relations he enjoyed with the occupying Romans. As the story goes, he offered an apology to the Romans and told them his tribe was being coerced into attacking them. Worse, a huge army of Germanic warriors was on the way! The Roman garrison could not resist such a force, but Ambiorix would offer them safe passage to join up with their comrades elsewhere.

The Romans Ambushed

The Roman commanders disagreed on whether to accept the offer, but eventually came to a decision. The garrison marched out and, predictably perhaps, was ambushed in a ravine. Although the cohorts were able to form up into fighting order and repel hand-to-hand attacks, they were worn down by javelins thrown from above. Ambiorix agreed to discuss surrender, but this was another ruse. While he dragged out the preliminaries, his warriors moved into a better position and launched a charge that broke part of the Roman force. The remainder was gradually overpowered.

Some survivors managed to get back inside their camp, but killed themselves when they realized the hopelessness of the situation. Ambiorix told nearby tribes of the great victory, inspiring them to send warriors to assist him. He then marched on another Roman camp and caught its occupants unawares. A sudden assault eliminated those caught outside the fortifications, but Ambiorix was unable to enter the camp. He attempted the same deception as previously, but these Romans were more resolute. Far from accepting safe passage to retreat, they made a counteroffer that amounted to demanding immediate surrender.

Ambiorix now had sufficient strength to break a Roman camp, though his force took serious casualties in its first attempts. The defenders managed to hold out until a messenger reached Caesar, who marched immediately to their relief. His force was rather small for the task and behaved timidly. This was a ruse on Casear's part; he had managed to get a message to the fort and planned to draw in the Gaulish force so that the garrison could attack its rear.

As the Gauls advanced on Caesar's position, the garrison launched a rapid assault, disordering their opponents and bringing about a close-quarters battle that saw the Eburones scattered, with heavy casualties. Ambiorix escaped, along with his immediate followers. He is known to have crossed the Rhine to seek refuge, but beyond that his fate is unknown. The Eburones were subjected to typically vicious reprisals and effectively ceased to exist.

The Treveri Tribe Revolts

The Treveri tribe of the Moselle Valley were also in revolt. According to Caesar, the Eburones were a subject people of the Treveri. They were certainly a martial tribe who had attempted to resist Roman expansion under the leadership of Indutiomarus (d. 53 BCE). Once Caesar's army arrived in the lands of the Treveri, support for Indutiomarus dissipated and he was sidelined in favour of Cingetorix (dates unknown).

The Treveri supplied excellent cavalry to serve as Roman auxiliaries, led by Cingetorix, but while he was away, Indutiomarus reclaimed his position and made preparations for a revolt. It is possible that he was the instigator of the uprising among the Eburones, though how he persuaded Ambiorix to take up arms against Rome remains unclear. Indutiomarus stripped Cingetorix of his wealth and power, and renewed his preparations for war. Cingetorix brought a warning to nearby Roman forces, who defeated and killed Indutiomarus before reinstalling Cingetorix. Thereafter, the Treveri were generally friendly to Rome.

The uprising of the Eburones was unusually successful, due to a combination of circumstances and cunning leadership. Had it not been necessary to disperse the legions, there might have been no opportunity – and perhaps no need – for a revolt. A better harvest might have made the imposition of feeding the Roman army more tolerable. Be that as it may, Ambiorix and his tribe were all but expunged from history for many centuries.

It is interesting to ponder what might have been if Caesar had arrived just a little later or if the Roman garrison had hesitated to charge the Eburones' rear. Could Ambiorix have triggered a general uprising? Might his cunning and use of deception have defeated Caesar? Ambiorix did not have to defeat Rome to alter the course of history; all he had to do was break Caesar's winning streak – and he came close.

The Effect of Ambiorix's Revolt

Ambiorix's revolt was a pivotal moment in history, though at the time it may have seemed like just another Roman conquest or a shift in the power structure among the tribes of Gaul. Julius Caesar was a man who changed the world using the power he gained through his military escapades. A big enough dent in his reputation might have derailed the rise that led to Caesar gaining control of Rome and its subsequent transformation into an empire.

Ambiorix was rescued from obscurity when the modern nation of Belgium began seeking its cultural identity. His defiance of an overwhelmingly powerful invader – and the fact that he won a notable victory where others had been easily crushed – made him an obvious candidate for national hero status. It seems that he was a good choice; modern Belgium has twice faced a similarly overpowering invasion and each time given a good account of herself.

THE REVOLT OF VERCINGETORIX

In 52 BCE, several tribes rose in rebellion against the Roman occupation, under the overall leadership of Vercingetorix (82–46 BCE). Vercingetorix was a chieftain of the Arverni, one of the most powerful tribal confederations in Gaul, but to stand a chance against Rome he needed to forge an alliance or – better – unify the Gauls under his banner. This was a risky prospect; Vercingetorix's father Celtillus (dates unknown) had attempted to do so and was burned to death by his opponents.

The Arverni had no love for Rome, having suffered a crushing defeat in 121 BCE. They continued their rivalry with the Aedui, both seeking to be foremost in the Celtic world. Since the Aedui were at least sometimes friendly to Rome and the Arverni were not, whichever was in ascendance at any given time might have implications elsewhere.

Despite the risks – from his own people as well as Rome – inherent in trying to build a large Gaulish alliance, Vercingetorix began putting an army together by means of diplomacy and force. Caesar recorded that his supporters included the Aulerci, the Carduci, the Lemovice, the Parisii, the Pictones and the Turones. The Senones also joined the alliance, which may have been a significant factor in both Gaul and Rome. The Senones had plundered Rome itself in 390 BCE.

Not all the tribes were willing to join Vercingetorix. The Bituriges resisted and requested assistance from the Aedui, who were their overlords. This was promised but did not materialize. It has been suggested that the Aedui wanted to join the revolt or suspected some treachery. Either way, without the support of the Aedui, the Bituriges were forced to surrender to Vercingetorix.

Taking hostages from among the tribes to ensure their compliance, he demanded a proportion of their fighting strength be placed under his command.

The strengths and weaknesses of Roman forces were by now well known to tribal leaders such as Vercingetorix, who had commanded allied troops in Roman service. Defeating a Roman legion in direct battle was difficult, and an organized army was even tougher. Vercingetorix could not afford to be defeated if he hoped to retain the confidence of the tribes. Thus, he exploited the main Roman weaknesses – troops needed to be supplied and Roman infantry was relatively unwieldy.

The Early Campaign

The early campaign took the form of guerrilla attacks on exposed or small Roman detachments, particularly foraging parties. Supply lines were also raided, and when a response was mounted the attackers slipped away. This was a low-risk strategy for Vercingetorix; even if a raiding party was brought to action, a defeat was of no great consequence. The Roman units dispersed in Gaul were unable to achieve any sort of decisive result, and, in the meantime, they were worn down by endless pinpricks and a shortage of supplies.

At this point in the campaign Vercingetorix had the strategic initiative. He could choose when and where – and indeed whether – to engage Roman detachments. The Romans would inevitably concentrate their forces sooner or later, but it might be possible to keep some isolated or to prevent Caesar from taking command of a concentrated army. Vercingetorix was more than a match for lesser commanders, so isolating Caesar was a war-winning strategy if it could be achieved.

Another factor was denial of supplies to the invaders, which could cause an army to disperse or withdraw and at the least was a strategic consideration which could influence enemy actions. For example, a concentrated force marching to besiege a strategic town might be the best option at that time, but if there were insufficient supplies the operation could not be mounted. Likewise, a force might have to abandon a poorly supplied position or make a risky attack in order to obtain adequate supplies of food.

Scorched-Earth Strategy

Attacking the foraging parties was only one of the options available to Vercingetorix. He used what would become known as a 'scorched-earth' strategy, ordering towns, villages and farms to be burned in order to prevent the Romans from obtaining food. This was harsh and demanded great sacrifices from ordinary Gauls. Some might be willing to do so, perhaps in the expectation that their leaders would compensate them generously after the Romans were driven out. Others had to be compelled, which in turn required warriors to believe fervently in the necessity.

Diplomacy was also a factor in denying supplies to the enemy. Ideally, tribes would join the revolt and add their fighting strength to the Gaulish army. Some might not be willing to commit but could be persuaded to resist Roman demands for supplies. If they were attacked, they would have reason to join the rebellion.

Vercingetorix relied heavily upon Lucterius (dates unknown), a leader of the Cadurci tribe, which was subordinate to the Arverni. His mission was to persuade other tribes to join the rebellion, which was often best accomplished by marching an army into their territory to demonstrate Gaulish strength. After moving through the lands of the Nitiobroges, Ruteni and Gabali tribes, Lucterius was about to invade the Roman province of Narbonensis when Caesar made his appearance.

Caesar had naturally responded when word reached him, but he was at that time in Cisalpine Gaul while his army was dispersed in winter quarters. Taking with him what troops were available locally, he positioned his force to challenge Lucterius near Narbo. The Gauls retreated, freeing Caesar to gather his army and march into the lands of the Aedui. One of his main concerns was how to feed his troops during the campaign, and whether allied tribes could be relied upon to provide supplies when he required them. This concern directed the strategy of both sides for much of the conflict.

Nevertheless, the Romans had to act. If requests for aid were ignored, more tribes and their settlements might go over to the Gaulish cause. Militarily, the most effective response would be to wait for the campaign season to arrive, gather supplies, then launch an offensive on Roman terms. This was not an option at this time; by triggering his revolt in late winter, Vercingetorix forced Caesar to operate under difficult conditions in which a large army might be nullified by denying it provisions. The Gauls had a similar problem, but they were in friendly territory and less likely to have to fight for supplies.

The Siege of Gorgobina

Vercingetorix laid siege to the town of Gorgobina, which belonged to the Boii tribe. They had migrated over the Alps in 58 BCE along with the Helvetii, and unlike the other tribes involved in the movement they were permitted to remain as part of the Aedui tribal confederation. Caesar informed the Boii he was coming to

CELTIC   ANCIENT   ORIGINS

their assistance, but actually doing so was more complicated than simply marching up to break the siege.

Needing to secure his line of supply, Caesar went first to the town of Vellaunodunum in the lands of the Senones. His writings indicate he was uneasy at leaving a potential enemy at his rear. Roman forces surrounded the town and began siege preparations, and when the occupants asked for terms, Caesar demanded supplies, hostages and the surrender of weapons. With Vellaunodunum secured, the next target was Genabum, capital of the Carnutes. The Roman army pillaged the town to resupply themselves before advancing across the Loire.

The concept that it was possible to defend one place by attacking another was a stratagem well known to ancient generals, and Caesar decided this was his best option. He did not break the siege of Gorgobina by direct action, but instead surrounded Noviodunum. This caused Vercingetorix to abandon his own siege and march to the town's relief. Noviodunum had just surrendered when what they thought was the Gaulish army appeared, and quickly closed its gates to the Romans.

In reality, the Gaulish force was just some cavalry moving in advance of the army, and was driven off after a hard fight with Caesar's cavalry. The battle was turned by Germanic horsemen serving as auxiliaries with the Roman force. Faced with a Roman attack and the vengeance likely to be visited upon them, the leaders of Noviodunum opened the gates and surrendered a second time.

It appears that Caesar was too preoccupied with his immediate campaign movements to punish Noviodunum. After the usual hostages had been taken and the town disarmed, the Roman army marched towards Avaricum. This was the most prestigious town of the Bituriges, and was seen by Caesar as a strategic objective whose capture might undermine the Gaulish alliance.

Vercingetorix had instructed the Bituriges to burn their towns – including Avaricum – and to conduct a guerrilla campaign intended to deny the Romans any useful amount of supplies. The order was partially carried out, but the Bituriges preferred to keep Avaricum intact and to defend it. There was some merit in this suggestion; Avaricum was in a strong position with marshes and the confluence of two rivers providing a natural defence. However, it presented Caesar with the chance to follow another age-old military axiom – if you want to force an enemy to accept battle, attack something he has to defend.

The Siege of Avaricum

The Roman army made its usual fortified camp close to the town, and preparations for siege and assault began. The Gaulish army under Vercingetorix made its own camp nearby and began harassing Roman foraging parties. This placed Caesar in a difficult position as his force had limited provisions and could not be assured of more arriving from the Aedui tribe. As preparations for an assault on Avaricum neared completion, Vercingetorix moved his force closer with the intention of increasing the pressure on the Romans. Caesar responded by forming up for battle but what resulted was a standoff across a marsh neither side was willing to enter first.

The methodical siege warfare of the Roman army had initially been highly effective against the Gauls, but by now they were familiar with the methods they faced. An attempt to tunnel under the defences was countermined, and the Gauls had responses available for most Roman attacks on their walls. For twenty-five days Avaricum resisted, until the final Roman assault was ready.

The Romans had been constructing a mound, or ramp, up to the walls, which would be used by a large siege tower they had built. This was a proven method of breaching even the strongest walls, used by ancient civilizations at least as far back as the Assyrian Empire. The only hope for the defenders was to set the tower afire or cause the mound to collapse.

Constructing a siege ramp was slow and tiring, requiring a disciplined force willing to brave enemy missiles and keep working despite casualties. At first the construction was merely back-breaking, since the beginning of the mound was far from the defenders, but as it approached it had to be built higher – and therefore more slowly – and under fire. Less disciplined forces could not attempt such a feat, but to the Romans it was a routine part of soldiering.

The Gauls at Avaricum had among them a great many iron miners, who were put to work tunnelling under the mound. Once they were ready the wooden supports of the tunnels were set afire and the miners retreated. Gaulish warriors rushed out of their city and attacked the external supports of the siege ramp with burning pitch. Confused fighting took place in the darkness, but ultimately the sally was unsuccessful.

The Roman Assault

The following day, the defenders made preparations to break out of the town and join the army of Vercingetorix, but once it became apparent the Romans had become aware of the plan it was abandoned. The Roman assault came soon after, and reached the top of the defensive walls. The Gauls pulled back and prepared to resist in their town, but then made a disorderly attempt to escape through the gates.

The Romans used the height of their own walls to rain down pila upon the Gaulish warriors, many of whom nevertheless did get out of the town. They encountered Roman infantry outside the gates and suffered heavy casualties, after which the survivors were run down by cavalry. Once the fighting was over, the town's population were massacred. This may have been out of annoyance at the long siege, but is likely to have been a political gambit to demonstrate the price of defiance. Caesar must have had a reason to pass up the riches gained by selling a town or a whole tribe into slavery, suggesting the massacre was intended to dishearten others. Alternatively, it may be that killing everyone was easier than trying to get them past Vercingetorix's army.

For his part, Vercingetorix faced some hard questions over his failure to rescue the defenders of Avaricum, but was apparently able to retain or restore the confidence of his followers. He even had a chance to gain the Aedui as allies, which would have the double effect of adding yet more troops to the Gaulish army and robbing Caesar of his best source of supplies and auxiliary cavalry.

Caesar Splits His Army

As the weather improved into spring, Caesar detached four of his legions, sending them north to subdue the Parisi and the Senones. The remaining six were under his personal command as he marched on Gergovia, capital of the Arverni. Capturing this town might end the revolt at a stroke, due to the heroic style of leadership common among the Celtic peoples. If Vercingetorix could not defend the capital of his own people, his followers would surely desert him.

Caesar's logic seems sound, but he faced a number of problems. The first was the possible defection of the Aedui to Vercingetorix's cause. Leaders among the tribe were divided on whether to ally with Vercingetorix or to stay loyal to Rome. Caesar visited the tribe and passed judgment on who was senior to whom, naturally giving control to those favouring Rome. He demanded a large contingent of troops be sent to assist his army and returned to it.

Vercingetorix attempted to stall the Roman advance at the River Allier, which was high due to spring rains and would be a formidable obstacle. His army was drawn out of position by a deception operation in which four legions began very obviously marching southwards along the riverbank. Once the Gauls were out of the way, the two remaining legions emerged from concealment and bridged the river.

Vercingetorix withdrew to a position close to Gergovia, and the Romans established themselves nearby. The Celtic habit of building strong places on high ground paid off; Gergovia was not vulnerable to a simple assault. The Roman army began preparations for a formal siege but had not made any progress when the Aedui made an appearance.

The Aedui Revolt

This was not the reinforcement Caesar had hoped for. Having decided to join Vercingetorix after all, the Aedui leaders sent the requested detachment away for a few days, only to return with a lurid tale of how the Romans had massacred their comrades who were already with Caesar's army. The tribe naturally revolted against Rome.

While the Aedui assembled their main strength, the detachment approached Caesar's army. Forewarned, Caesar confronted the approaching Gauls and sent emissaries to their leaders. What followed appears to have been a form of large-scale armed democracy, in which the majority of warriors decided to throw in their lot with Caesar. Their former leaders escaped to join Vercingetorix.

With the Aedui in revolt, even if some of its warriors had joined him, Caesar needed a greater force than he currently commanded. The solution was to march north to join the four detached legions, but abandoning the siege of Gergovia would look like a defeat. Just as did Vercingetorix, Caesar needed to maintain his reputation. He resolved to launch an attack on one of the Gaulish camps, and, according to his account, this was to be the limit of the operation.

The attack went well at first, capturing the camp. However, whether through vague or mistransmitted orders, or, as Caesar stated, out of a desire for plunder, most of the attacking force continued and attempted to storm the town walls. Despite gaining a foothold on the walls, the Romans were driven back, with heavy casualties. Mistaking their Aedui allies for enemy reinforcements some units began to panic, resulting in a disorderly retreat back to the Roman camp.

Caesar found a way to retreat with his reputation intact. He drew up his army and offered battle, and when Vercingetorix did not oblige, he was able to claim he had faced down the Gauls. This piece of spin gave Caesar an excuse to withdraw from Gergovia and reunite his army. Vercingetorix was still in the field, however, and had the support even of former Roman allies such as the Aedui.

THE SIEGE OF ALESIA

With his army concentrated, Caesar had a significant advantage over any Gaulish force in terms of straight battle-winning power. However, the supply situation could become disastrous and the Gauls had more and better cavalry than the Romans. They could harass the Roman army until it collapsed from lack of food without ever engaging in a decisive battle. In an effort to counter this disadvantage, Caesar employed a force of Germanic cavalry to replace those that would have been supplied by his allies – if they were not currently fighting against him.

This brought about one of the most decisive events in the Celtic world: a defeat of the Gaulish cavalry by their Germanic counterparts, which in and of itself seemed to be no great thing. However, Vercingetorix hurriedly sought refuge in the fortified town of Alesia where he would become trapped and face total defeat. He sent his cousin Vercassivellaunus (d. 46 BCE) with a force of cavalry to fetch assistance.

Preparing the Siege

Unable to simply storm the town, the Romans set about preparing a siege. Vercingetorix was now trapped in Alesia, a situation he had avoided in the past by insisting on camping outside towns even if they were well defended. The food situation now favoured the Romans; Vercingetorix had only a month's supply at most and was completely surrounded. With foraging impossible, the Gauls forced all but their warriors out of the town. Vercingetorix had hoped that noncombatants might be allowed to depart, but the encircling Romans turned them back. Unable to re-enter the city the women and children of Alesia starved between its walls and the Roman siege works.

The siege preparations were elaborate. First Caesar had his men build a line of circumvallation: a ditch-and-mound defence completely enclosing the town. This was strengthened with towers and stone walls, and with emplaced artillery weapons such as ballistae. To protect against a relief force, a line of contravallation was then built, facing outward with the Roman camps in between the two.

Laborious as this construction was, its worth was proven when Vercassivellaunus returned with a large Gaulish army. It is estimated that as many as 240,000 warriors were assembled by the Aedui, the Arverni, the Atrebates and other tribes. They set up camp within striking distance of the Roman positions, where the defenders could see them. This permitted a co-ordinated attack from within and without the siege lines.

After two days of unsuccessful attacks, the Gauls became aware of a gap in the Roman defences. Vercassivellaunus is said to have personally led a force of some 60,000 Gauls in an assault upon it, while other attacks were made elsewhere. Vercingetorix led another attempt to breach the inner defences at the same time.

Caesar naturally claimed personal credit for defeating these powerful thrusts. According to his account, he donned an easily recognizable red cloak and entered the combat personally, inspiring his troops by his example. It is possible this actually happened; Caesar was a physically courageous man who knew what was at stake. Better to die fighting with his ambitions alive than flinch and hold back with serious consequences later. The same could be said for Vercingetorix and Vercassivellaunus, though their fate would be more immediate if they failed.

Caesar led a force out of the defences and got into the Gaulish rear, where his attack caused a panic. As Roman and allied cavalry exploited the situation, Vercassivellaunus was captured. The remainder of the outer force, while still huge, lost heart and began a retreat that was turned into a rout by a vigorous pursuit. This left Alesia besieged, short of provisions and with no hope of relief.

Vercingetorix Surrenders

Vercingetorix was as much a hero in defeat as in war. He presented himself to Caesar to offer the surrender of the city and its army, and was taken to Rome to be displayed in Caesar's Triumph. After the procession was over, Vercingetorix was imprisoned for five years then executed by public strangulation – not for him the comfortable exile of some of his predecessors.

The collapse of the Gaulish army at Alesia was the turning point of the Gallic Wars, and the moment where conquest and Romanization became inevitable. Had Vercingetorix not allowed himself to become trapped, he might have worn down the Roman army or even defeated it in the field. This would likely have derailed Caesar's ambitions and changed the course of world history.

But it was not to be. The great Gaulish revolt did not end immediately, but there was no one with the charisma of Vercingetorix to hold together a grand alliance of the tribes. Lucterius, Vercingetorix's trusted lieutenant, continued to harass Roman forces and managed to gather some remnants of the revolt to his banner. He even attempted another invasion of Narbonensis.

Facing superior Roman forces, Lucterius abandoned his plan and fell back on the fortified town of Uxellodnum. He used it as a base but did not take his army inside its walls, fearing he would

THE ECLIPSE OF THE CONTINENTAL GAULS

become trapped as Vercingetorix had. His continued defiance threatened to undermine Caesar's self-made legend, so the town came under heavy attack and was ultimately captured. Caesar showed a sort of mercy towards the defenders, merely ordering their hands cut off rather than executing them.

Lucterius was able to escape the defeat and returned to the Arverni in the hope of raising another force. Instead, he was handed over to Rome and the great revolt fizzled out. Romanization proceeded quickly thereafter, and the people of Gaul gradually became something that was Celtic-influenced but no longer Celts as such. Resistance to Rome continued to cast a long shadow over the former Gauls; as the modern nation of France found its identity, Vercingetorix became a national hero.

THE PACIFICATION AND ROMANIZATION OF GAUL

Caesar's exploits in Gaul – and his well-written account of them – catapulted him to superstar status in the Roman Republic. To some extent, he owed his success to the calibre of opponent he chose. Victory over a lesser enemy might not have impressed the Roman people so much, but Caesar had defeated the ferocious Gauls. He did not get to enjoy the spoils of victory for long, however. Civil war was followed by assassination in 44 BCE, and by the time the dust had settled, Rome was an empire ruled by Augustus, Caesar's adopted son.

Gaul was gradually Romanized by settling veterans, and what might be termed cultural imperialism. Latin was adopted by the upper classes, though intermixed with Celtic words. Likewise, there was some give and take in the absorption of Gaul. Some crafting techniques and artistic preferences found their way into mainstream Roman culture.

This process was interrupted by unrest and the occasional major revolt. In the early years of the Roman Empire, there was usually a tribe or two causing a nuisance, but this could be easily contained. More serious was a Roman defeat in 16 CE that led to an uprising five years later. This was less about Gauls fighting for their cultural identity and freedom than a Romano-Gaulish province objecting to high levels of taxation.

In the ensuing years, Gaul became more and more a Roman province, and served as a bastion against the Germanic tribes across the Rhine. Among these were the Franks, who were repelled when they first attempted to enter Gaul. The failing Roman Empire was unable to resist in the long term, and eventually the Franks became established in what is now Belgium.

In time, the Franks came to dominate the land that still bears their name. In so doing, they absorbed Gallo-Roman culture and the Celtic influences that remained within it. The Celtic identity was overlaid by successive groups migrating west under pressure from the Huns, and by the time the Huns were decisively defeated in 451 CE, at the Battle of the Catalaunian fields, it was thoroughly buried. Nevertheless, the Huns were finally turned back in what had been Gaul, and perhaps the spirit that inspired Vercingetorix and Ambiorix lived on in the Franks.

THE CELTS IN MAINLAND BRITAIN

The **Insular Celts**, those who lived in the British Isles, were aware of the Roman expansion in Europe through regular contact with their cousins on the Continent. It would have come as little surprise when a Roman vessel began scouting the southern coast of England in 55 BCE, and soon afterwards contacts on the Continent sent word that Julius Caesar was planning an expedition into their lands.

The expedition consisted of two legions carried aboard eighty transport vessels, with a cavalry force transported separately. As the fleet approached what is now Dover, it became apparent the Britons were expecting visitors and were not in a welcoming mood. Caesar tried to find an alternative landing point and is believed to have eventually come ashore at Thanet. Although today Thanet is attached to the mainland, it was at that time an island a short distance off the coast of Kent.

This was no rapid amphibious assault. Hundreds of Roman soldiers had to get down into the water from their ships and wade ashore, which was inevitably a slow process. As they arrived, tired and disordered, the Celtic cavalry and chariots harassed them. The chariots could make drive-by attacks with javelins or deliver warriors close to their opponents and pick them up again if resistance grew too strong.

Having eventually managed to establish themselves ashore, the Romans were harassed by additional attacks interspersed with diplomatic overtures from the Celts. With his cavalry unable to get across the Channel due to weather and an uncomfortable situation ashore, Caesar agreed to accept hostages from the tribes in return for peace. He was now able to say the expedition had been a success, so he returned to Gaul.

A Second Invasion

The following year, 54 BCE, saw a much larger force assembled for a new invasion. Five legions and supporting cavalry were transported by vessels modified to enable them to come closer inshore. Perhaps intimidated by the size of the Roman army, the Britons did not contest the landing this time. After constructing a fortified camp and making repairs to storm-damaged ships, the Roman army pushed inland.

Opposition emerged in the form of an army under the leadership of Cassivellaunus (dates unknown), leader of the Catuvellauni tribe. Like other tribes of south-eastern Britain, the Catuvellauni were Belgic in origin. Celtic guerrilla tactics slowed the Roman advance but could not halt it, and several tribes surrendered to Rome. As Caesar's army approached the Catuvellauni capital, Cassivellaunus requested his allies make an attack on Caesar's base camp. Had it succeeded, this might have placed the Roman force in a perilous situation. When it did not, Cassivellaunus was forced to sue for peace.

After agreeing to tributes and hostages from the tribes of the Britons, Caesar returned to Gaul. It is not clear whether the Britons ever intended to honour the agreement, nor if Caesar cared. He had more victories to celebrate – this time he had crossed the Channel and conquered the Britons. If the displaced Gauls did not meet their obligations, he could also go back and win more glory punishing them. Having served its purpose, Britain was largely ignored by Rome for the next century.

The Ensuing Century

There are few records of what happened in the British Isles during that time. Raids, skirmishes and the occasional serious war between tribes would be interspersed by periods of peace. The seasons turned and people went about their business in a typically Celtic manner – but not entirely in isolation.

The Celtic tribes of the mainland were now under Roman control, and, since contact was not broken, the Insular Celts were trading with people who were becoming increasingly Romanized. Cultural influences would have worked both ways, and the Britons would have been aware of events all over the known world. Accounts of far-off events may have been garbled, but the people of mainland Britain were aware – at least vaguely – of the wider world.

Thus, the Celtic people of Britain, particularly south-eastern Britain, would know about the conquest of Gaul and the reinvention of the Roman Republic as an empire. They would have plenty of time to form an opinion on whether or not they wanted to be part of that empire. In many cases, there seemed to be clear advantages.

Trade vessels regularly crossed the Channel from Continental ports, enabling the south-eastern British tribes to enrich themselves and use those riches to buy luxury Roman goods. One of the most profitable exports from Britain was slaves, which were obtained by making war on the more northern and western tribes.

The hostages sent to Rome returned with tales of splendour and opportunity, and they also made Roman culture seem a little less alien to their home tribes. The hostages would have come from noble families and would eventually take positions of power in their tribes. If their experiences in Rome had been positive, they might well be inclined to lead the tribe towards membership of the Empire.

CUNOBELIN, KING OF THE BRITONS

Cunobelin (d. *c.* 43 CE) became king of the Catuvellauni tribe around 9 CE, which also gave him overlordship of the Trinovantes, as they had recently been conquered. Under other circumstances that might have caused problems with Rome, but its attention was elsewhere. A disastrous expedition into Germania led to the loss of three entire legions and a need to pacify that frontier. The Roman Empire had been expanding vigorously up to that point, but after 9 CE there was a shift towards protecting Roman territory from Germanic attacks rather than conquering Germania, which may have been accompanied by a general change in policy.

Rome agreed to recognize Cunobelin as king of both tribes, and referred to him as 'King of the Britons'. This was not the same as 'King of Britain' as there was no concept of countries at the time, and Cunobelin only ruled a part of the territory that would eventually be recognized as the nation of Britain. Still, he was immensely powerful and capable of influencing other tribal leaders to follow his policies. Recognition might have been an expedient made necessary by problems on the Germania front, but it also furthered Roman interests. So long as Cunobelin was kept friendly, the rest of the Britons would most likely fall in line.

During the reign of Cunobelin, his seat of government at Camulodunum (modern Colchester) could be considered the capital of the Britons. However, around 40 CE Cunobelin's health declined, and he died within a year or two. It has been suggested he suffered a stroke. By this time, events had been set in motion which would lead to the Roman conquest of Britain.

Cunobelin's Successors

Cunobelin's three sons were divided in their stance towards Rome. Adminius (dates unknown), probably the eldest, was pro-Rome while Togodumnus (d. 43 CE) and Caractacus (d. 50 CE) were not. Adminius was given authority over Canticum – modern Kent plus some surrounding areas – around 35 CE but was later driven out by his brothers. This was around the time of Cunobelin's decline, and may or may not have been done with his blessing.

Adminius went to Rome, seeking assistance in regaining his position. The emperor at that time was Gaius Caesar Augustus Germanicus (12–41 CE), who is better known to history as the crazed tyrant Caligula. His madness was perhaps due to the amount of lead used to sweeten wine to his taste. Some accounts of his antics were written by those hostile to him, and since he died by assassination, it is possible that there has been some exaggeration in an attempt at justification.

That said, it does seem that Caligula was a dangerous person to be in charge of anything, let alone the most powerful empire of the ancient world. In 39 CE, he marched his army to the coast along the Channel, but then, for some reason, decided not to invade Britain after all. Instead, according to Roman accounts, he had his soldiers attack the sea with their weapons and bring him shells as trophies of victory. Then, having taught the English Channel a lesson about obedience to Rome, Caligula marched home.

Perhaps unsurprisingly, Rome did away with Caligula in 41 CE, replacing him with the rather more stable Tiberius Claudius Caesar Augustus Germanicus (10 BCE–54 CE), better known as Claudius. By this time, Caractacus had conquered more tribes. This might have been accepted by Rome, as his tribe's earlier conquests had, but for Caractacus's anti-Roman stance. A 'King of the Britons' who was friendly to Rome might be an asset, but a hostile one was a clear threat. Among the tribes diminished by Cunobelin and his successors were the Atrebates, whose king Verica (dates unknown) led a resurgence that came to an end at the hands of Caractacus and his army. Verica requested aid from Rome. This suited the purposes of the Roman Empire; replacing an anti-Roman King of the Britons with one who owed his position to the emperor would have long-term benefits. Verica may or may not have regained his throne after the Roman invasion; records are unclear.

Cunobelin is mentioned in the *Historia Brittonum* (*History of the Britons*), thought to have been compiled in the ninth century CE by the monk Nennius (dates unknown). This work was once thought to have been factual but is now regarded as largely pseudo-history. At some point, the *Historia Brittonum* crosses the line from myth to historical fact, and Cunobelin is on the fact side of that line. Much later, he was made the subject of the play *Cymbeline* by William Shakespeare (1564–1616 CE).

THE THIRD ROMAN INVASION

In 43 CE, a Roman army numbering around 40,000 was assembled on the shore along the Channel and, despite delays due to storms, was able make the crossing in three divisions. Roman sources mention the use of three separate forces but are not clear as to whether this means a staged crossing or three divisions each seeking to gain a foothold at the same time. This would make strategic sense, as it increased the chances of finding an undefended landing point or establishing a beachhead against light opposition. In this case, additional forces could be called in from the other groups without the possibility of more disruption due to storms.

The forces faced little or no resistance and were able to establish themselves ashore at what is now Richborough in eastern Kent. There was no large-scale attempt to drive the Romans back into the sea, though the local tribes engaged in skirmishing. When word reached Camulodunum that the Roman army was heading in that direction, Caractacus and Togodumnus set out to intercept it with the forces they had immediately available. They hoped to slow the Roman advance sufficiently that a sizable force could be assembled at the River Medway for a decisive battle.

Roman sources record that the Dobunni tribe surrendered to the advancing army. This raises questions, since the Dobunni had their centre of power in what is now Gloucestershire. It may be that this was a part of the Dobunni tribe that had fallen under control of the Atrebates. This was one of the problems facing Caractacus. He might be called 'King of the Britons', but he was no absolute monarch. Roman emissaries might be able to negotiate the surrender of individual tribes on favourable terms, robbing Caractacus of his supports one by one.

The Battle of Medway

The River Medway was a significant obstacle to the Roman advance, and a natural point to seek a battle. The Roman army needed to secure a crossing point, and Caractacus hoped to deny them that. In addition to auxiliaries, the Roman force comprised four legions, of which one was commanded by Caesar Vespasianus Augustus (9–79 CE), who would become the Emperor better known as Vespasian.

Caractacus did not believe the Medway could be crossed without a bridge, and may have been complacent about the security of his army. According to Roman accounts, the heavy infantry engaged in a great deal of activity opposite the Celtic host, fixing the attention of its commanders, while a detachment crossed the river out of sight. This was a large force of Batavians who were trained to swim or otherwise cross deep water in full gear.

The Batavians' attack was no general nuisance raid, but a targeted strike intended to weaken the Celts' most effective weapon: their chariots. The Batavians killed or wounded as many horses as possible then withdrew before a coherent response could be made. The attack would have been demoralizing whatever the target, but the nullification of an elite force such as the chariots was as serious from a morale point of view as it was in terms of raw fighting power.

While the Celts were distracted by this surprise attack, two legions found a suitable crossing point and reached the far bank undetected. Had their crossing been opposed it might have been a different story, but these legions were able to repel the counterattack launched once Caractacus realized they were present. Outnumbered and with a river to their backs, the legions were in a dangerous position from which they could not readily retire. Perhaps the future Emperor Vespasian might have been killed here, altering the course of the Roman Empire's history, but his force held on until support arrived.

Reinforced during the night by additional troops and the overall commander, Gnaeus Hosidius Geta (20–95 CE), the Roman force renewed the battle the following day. Although demoralized, the Celts were still in the fight, launching an assault to try to capture the Roman commander. Geta was the sort to lead his soldiers personally, which won him great rewards, but it was a risky gambit that almost undid the entire invasion plan. Had the Roman commander been taken, the battle might have had a different outcome.

The Celts Retreat

The attempt failed and the Celts were gradually outfought, making a retreat to wetlands on the Thames. They knew the ways through the area and the Romans did not, granting them some temporary security. However, the Batavian contingent was able to cross the marshes. Under heavy attack Caractacus again retreated, inflicting damage on the leading Roman units as he went.

Togodumnus was killed in the fighting at the Thames, possibly during skirmishing as Roman sources do not speak of a major battle. As the Romans forced a crossing of the Thames, Caractacus appears to have decided the war could not be won there, if at all. The south-east had submitted to Rome and his disheartened army was disintegrating. Caractacus fled westward to find a way to carry on the struggle, while his capital at Camulodunum became a Roman base.

Caractacus found new support from the Silures and the Ordovices. He was something of a national hero by this point – inasmuch as the Celts could be considered a 'nation' – and a symbol of resistance to Rome. The Silures made their home in what is now Glamorgan and Monmouthshire, in south-eastern Wales. According to the great Roman historian Publius Cornelius Tacitus (56–120 CE), the Silures were darker of complexion than other Celtic groups. He believed they may have migrated from Iberia.

The Ordovices lived to the north of the Silures, and joined with them to fight the encroaching Romans. What followed was a long period of gradual Roman advance and vigorous Celtic resistance, with Roman camps established to retain control of areas that might otherwise revolt as soon as the opportunity arose.

The Celts Defeated

Caractacus was finally defeated at Caer Caradoc around 50 CE. He was by then losing support as the Romans ground down the Celtic army and occupied more and more territory. Caractacus needed a decisive victory to encourage his supporters or to gain some new ones, and offered battle on terms advantageous to his followers. They fortified a hill with a river in front of it and awaited the Roman attack.

Despite the disadvantageous terrain, the Roman commander, Publius Ostorius Scapula (15–52 CE), decided to accept battle. The legionaries faced heavy opposition as they crossed the river but reached the far bank in good order. The Celts retreated uphill, showering the Romans with javelins as they went. The legionaries were able to advance under cover of their testudo formation, with shields held overhead to ward off missiles. It is not clear when this tactic was invented but there are records of its use almost a century earlier. Perhaps experience fighting the Gauls inspired this innovation.

No formation is entirely immune to missile fire, but the Roman testudos were able to reach the Celts' fortifications and begin demolishing them. Ferocious hand-to-hand fighting saw the Celts driven back and their formations pushed apart, after which the lighter Roman auxiliaries were able to pin some groups for the heavy legionaries to break. The remnants of the Celtic force were able to retire, but Caer Caradoc was a decisive victory for Rome.

It is likely that Caractacus realized his supporters were unable or unwilling to continue the fight. He fled to the Brigantes, whose territory centred on what would become Yorkshire. Caractacus sought the protection and support of Queen Cartimandua (d. 69 CE), only to find that she had other plans. The Brigantes had chosen to become a client of Rome, retaining their autonomy and receiving support if necessary. Cartimandua secured this status by surrendering Caractacus to Rome.

Caractacus Captured and Exiled

Not everyone was pleased with this arrangement, and there was resentment within the tribe. Cartimandua's husband Venutius (dates unknown) became estranged and the two divorced. It is not clear whether this was entirely over their differing stances towards Rome, but whatever the reason, Venutius's attempt to claim the kingship failed; at that point at least the Brigantes preferred to be led by their queen. Venutius then led an armed insurrection which was put down by Roman forces.

In 69 CE, Venutius tried again, and this time was successful. Cartimandua was evacuated by Roman forces, leaving the powerful Brigantes under the control of the anti-Roman Venutius. Caractacus was long since out of the picture by this time, though he was not dead. He was paraded as part of the Roman victory celebrations and no doubt expected to be gruesomely executed as had been Vercingetorix.

Caractacus made a speech in the presence of Emperor Claudius, which impressed the Emperor greatly. Part of his argument was that by being such a potent enemy, Caractacus enabled Claudius to demonstrate his greatness, and now when he was humbled he offered a chance for the Emperor to demonstrate his mercy. Whatever he had intended, Claudius chose to pardon Caractacus for his resistance and granted him and his family a comfortable life in exile.

SUPPRESSION OF THE DRUIDS

Resistance to Roman rule did not end with the defeat of Caractacus. The tribes which had benefited most from trade with the Empire were mostly in the south-east, and arguably this area was Romanized to some degree even before the invasion. Elsewhere the benefits – real or imagined – of being part of the Empire were less apparent and there was less inclination to accept the situation. This was particularly true in what is now Wales.

An aggressive campaign against the tribes that continued to resist made progress, but military conquest alone would not guarantee a future free from revolts and low-level resistance. For Britain to become anything more than a drain on resources it needed to be pacified and made to stay that way. One of the key tools in this endeavour was economics – people who are affluent tend to be content and unwilling to risk losing the nice things they have. The usual methods did not work so well in Wales, largely due to opposition from the Druids.

It is one thing to accept a change in the political landscape, but quite another to hear that the gods will be displeased with those who bow down before the invaders. The Druids therefore had tremendous influence over their people. In addition to their religious significance, the Druids were also the educated class among the Celtic peoples. They may have seen the situation more clearly than the average tribe member and made reasoned arguments for resistance against the invasion.

This made the Druids as a social class the enemies of Rome. Destroying them would undermine the will to resist. There may also have been a genuine spiritual element to the Roman campaign against the Druids; by eliminating their religious leaders the Romans could weaken the Celtic gods. In an age where divine favour was known for certain – rightly or wrongly to the modern mind – to bring fortune in battle, taking out the enemy's gods was an entirely valid military strategy.

The Anglesey Campaigns

In 58 CE, Gaius Suetonius Paulinus (dates unknown) was appointed Roman Governor of Britain. He campaigned against the tribes in Wales and, in 60 CE, launched an expedition to break the power of the Druids by capturing the island of Anglesey. Lying off the coast of Wales, Anglesey was an important centre for the Druids, which made it a military and political objective for Rome.

There may have been more to the matter than the long-term security of the Empire. It has been suggested that Paulinus wanted a military exploit to raise him above his rivals, or that he had come to believe there were rich resources on Anglesey. Whatever the reason behind it, Paulinus's expedition was initially successful but had no lasting effect. He was forced to abandon the endeavour and rush his army back to the supposedly pacified east due to a revolt among the Iceni tribe.

In 77 CE, a new expedition was launched under the command of Gnaeus Julius Agricola (40–93 CE), who had previously served with Paulinus. The Roman historian Tacitus produced an account of his life which mentions both Anglesey expeditions. Tacitus married Agricola's daughter, so it may be his writings are biased towards the glorification of his father-in-law, but no other accounts survive. Tacitus records that Paulinus's army used shallow-draught boats to cross the Menai Strait to the island but encountered fierce resistance as they came ashore.

The curses hurled by massed Druids were particularly terrifying to the superstitious Romans, whom Tacitus states were initially paralysed by fear. Mixed in with the Celtic warriors were women who seemed possessed by supernatural fervour. Nevertheless, the Romans gathered themselves and fought a brutal close-quarters action which saw the Britons finally defeated.

The intent was to destroy the Celtic holy places and garrison Anglesey, but Paulinus was forced to withdraw quickly due to events elsewhere. Anglesey was reoccupied and its remote location meant that Rome did not turn its attention that way for some years. In 74 CE, an expedition defeated the Silures tribe, and in 77 CE Agricola launched the second and final assault on Anglesey.

This was no easy matter. The Silures might have been put out of the fight for the time being, but the Ordovices were still capable of resistance. They eliminated a cavalry force based in their territory, inspiring hopes and fears of a general uprising. This might have occurred had Agricola not taken immediate measures. Despite only being able to gather a small force and the difficulties inherent in campaigning late in the year, Agricola confronted the Ordovices at an unknown location and soundly defeated them.

Agricola then set about subduing Anglesey. He had no boats, so sent some of his auxiliary troops to swim across the Menai Strait. This was a risky enterprise but had the advantage of surprise. Not seeing a Roman fleet, the defenders did not muster in time and were quickly overrun. The Druids and those associated with them were massacred. After this, the Romans withdrew from Anglesey, keeping it under observation from a fort at modern-day Caernarfon.

Defeat of the Druids

The massacre of the Druids at Anglesey seems to have broken their power as a social class, but their eclipse was probably not instant; they could not all have been killed at Anglesey. However, Romanization would have changed society to the point where the function of Druids could be fulfilled by bards or by scholars who operated in a Roman rather than Druidic style, and the Romans no doubt persecuted the remaining Druids with great vigour.

Even so, the Druids might have staged a comeback but for the great weakness of oral traditions. The death of so many Druids at once meant that there was no one to remember the old lore and to teach new candidates. Druidism was doomed to a slow demise as a result, and the loss of so much accumulated wisdom and history would have had a profound effect on future generations of British Celts.

The lurid tales of human sacrifice, wicker-men and perverse rituals told by Roman writers are more than likely untrue, or at least wildly distorted. The Druids are portrayed as savage nature-wizards, though exactly why is open to question. It has been suggested that this was an attempt to justify the massacre and suppression, but the Roman Empire never felt the need to justify itself. In any case, a society that practised sacrifice of a great many kinds, and which engaged in crucifixion of its enemies as well as bloody gladiatorial shows, could hardly object if someone else did similar things.

It is possible that the Roman accounts are intended to be genuine but based on hearsay and rumour, or that they are an attempt to play up the savagery of the enemy for the glorification of the Roman leaders. Victory over another bunch of barbarians was no big thing, but if they were particularly savage and backed up by a caste of supernatural magic-wielders, that was a bit more impressive – or a good excuse when a campaign did not go according to plan.

Whatever the reason, Roman accounts of the Druids are biased at best, and quite possibly invented. Nevertheless, this is the version that has passed into the popular modern mythology and is now reinforced by depictions in movies and adventure games. There was something of a 'Druidic revival' in Victorian times, but this was at best based upon conjecture and pseudo-historical quackery.

BOUDICCA AND THE REVOLT OF THE ICENI

The suppression of the Druids was interrupted by a revolt among the previously friendly Iceni tribe. The Iceni inhabited what is now Norfolk and Suffolk, and were not initially inclined to resist Roman encroachment. They were forced into rebellion in 47 CE when the Roman authorities attempted to disarm the tribe, but were defeated and became a client of the Roman Empire.

Under the rulership of King Prasutagus (d. 60 CE), the Iceni caused little trouble for Rome, but upon his death the king left his throne jointly to Emperor Nero (37–68 CE) and Prasutagus's daughters. It is likely this would be seen as an insult to the Emperor, as Roman society was extremely sexist. The idea of a woman being in charge of anything was uncomfortable to the Romans, so the Emperor sharing power with barbarian girls was entirely unacceptable.

Rome annexed the lands of the Iceni and treated the royal family harshly. Boudicca (d. 60 CE), widow of Prasutagus, was flogged and her daughters raped. The Romans may have thought they were teaching the Britons a lesson, but in reality all they achieved was triggering a revolt. Boudicca led the Iceni in an uprising and drew in other tribes as allies. It is said that she was able to muster some 120,000 warriors under her banner.

Boudicca Takes Command

If the Romans had any doubts that a woman could lead men in war, Boudicca dispelled them. Her army marched first on Camulodunum, which had been taken over as a Roman colonia. These were settlements for Roman veterans and their families, creating a Romanized enclave that would exert cultural influence and help defend the conquered territories.

Camulodunum was caught unprepared and quickly stormed, with great destruction ensuing. Once the capital of the Trinovantes, the town was now the symbol of a Roman occupation that had become unbearable. The town was burned and the population massacred despite an attempted intervention by the Legio IX Hispania and some auxiliary troops.

Having defeated the Ninth Legion in the field and all but destroyed it, Boudicca advanced on the trade hub of Londinium. By this time Gaius Suetonius Paulinus, Governor of Britain, had heard of the revolt and was marching his army back from Wales to counter it. He reached Londinium but decided he lacked the forces to challenge Boudicca's Celtic host. Instead, he escorted as much of the populace out as he could. It is notable that the richer citizens had already departed by this time.

Boudicca burned Londinium and moved on to Verulamium (modern-day St Albans) and also destroyed it. In the meantime, Paulinus made preparations for a decisive battle. Some accounts place the Celtic army at over 200,000 or perhaps even 300,000 by this time, though there are doubts about these figures. It does seem that the Romans were heavily outnumbered but had chosen terrain that would channel the Celts and restrict their ability to attack the flanks.

Boudicca Defeated

The surviving Roman accounts state that the Celtic assault was blunted by the usual hail of javelins, followed by a countercharge. As the Britons were pushed back, they became trapped against a line of wagons and chariots they had set up to protect themselves and were subjected to great slaughter. Once defeated, the Celtic host broke up and Boudicca herself died. Some accounts say she took poison, some that she had fallen ill.

Boudicca's rebellion was crushed, but it took the pressure off the tribes of Wales and the Druids holding out in Anglesey. Ultimately, this only bought a few more years, and Wales was eventually pacified. Despite not altering the course of the Roman conquest of Britain, the revolt would have been particularly shocking to the conquerors – and not merely for the extent of the damage. Barbarians were supposed to bow to Rome, not to burn its settlements and defeat its legions; and to have suffered such defeats at the hands of a woman was particularly galling to the sexist Romans.

As Roman literature became popular in the Renaissance era, there was renewed interest in Boudicca as an embodiment of national defiance. During the struggle to gain voting rights for women, she became a symbol of the suffragette movement, and to this day remains one of Britain's national heroic figures.

WEST AND NORTH

The suppression of Boudicca's revolt allowed Roman attention to return to conquest and pacification. Much of Wales remained rebellious or potentially rebellious, and no real attempt had yet been made to subjugate the northern tribes. It was perhaps inevitable that Rome would want to conquer the whole of mainland Britain sooner or later, for whatever reason. Rich resources, or rumours about them, might tempt an expedition, or one might be mounted out of concerns about security resulting from troublesome tribes.

Personal ambition was always a factor. A tribe might not possess anything worth taking but if a Roman official needed an enemy to win glory they were still not safe. The only possible long-term defence against Roman expansion was for a group to be more trouble than it was worth. Those who could combine force of arms with difficult terrain stood a chance of remaining independent or even curtailing Roman expansion in that area. For everyone else it was just a matter of time.

The Brigantes

Based in the north-east of what is now England, the Brigantes were a powerful tribal confederation who had accepted client status. This might have allowed them to keep their independence for a long time, depending upon events elsewhere, but their own internal politics resulted in a shift in their relations with Rome. When Caratacus sought shelter from Roman forces, Queen Cartimandua of the Brigantes thought it better to surrender him. This might have been the only viable option but it was an unpopular decision among many of the tribespeople.

After an initial attempt to seize sole power failed, Cartimandua's husband Venutius was successful in 69 CE. Cartimandua received protection from Roman forces but was unable to remain in control of the Brigantes. Over the next few years Rome made war on the Brigantes, bringing the tribe into the Empire as a conquered people. The frontier pushed north in both the east and west of England, supported by fleets moving supplies up the coast to camps established by the land forces.

Roman Conquest of Wales and Scotland

Few records were left of this period, other than expressions of satisfaction on the Roman side. Likewise, from 76 CE onwards, the conquest of Wales resumed. Even after tribes were defeated in battle and accepted Roman overlordship, they remained troublesome on a lower level. Tribal leaders would be held accountable for the actions of their people and would generally find it to be in their interests to keep the peace. However, the number of outposts and forts built in Wales suggests that peace was neither universal nor constant.

Agricola was appointed Governor of Britain in 78 CE, continuing the conquest with campaigns in Wales and Scotland. After suppressing the Ordovices in Wales and stationing garrisons throughout the territory, he campaigned in Scotland and conducted maritime operations around its coasts. His biographer, Tacitus, described these northern waters as heavy to the oar, with a general feeling of apprehension. This is hardly surprising, given that the Imperial heartlands were warm countries around the Mediterranean. The far north was cold and wet, had very different vegetation and wildlife, and it was populated by wild tribes who could launch an ambush from behind any blade of grass.

What is now Scotland was at that time populated by Celtic tribes and the people known as Picts, who may or may not have been Celts. Few records remain, though the Picts left behind a considerable number of carved stones. The name used for these people was assigned by the Romans, meaning 'painted people'. We do not know what they called themselves. Roman writings create an image of people so savage that the barbarians living to their south were scared of them, and the name refers to the supposed practice of extensive tattooing or body painting. There is little evidence for or against any of this.

The term 'Pict' was used very loosely by the Romans, usually to refer to uncivilized (by which they meant non-Romanized) people living in Caledonia. The reality was probably similar to other regions, with tribes interacting with their neighbours and being influenced by them. The Picts' reputation for savagery may be the product of Roman exaggeration. Alternatively, their vigorous and generally successful resistance to Roman intrusions may have been a factor. After all, it is a little embarrassing to have your expedition repelled by the local barbarians, but it might not be so humiliating if they are the most ferocious people ever encountered.

The term Caledones was also loosely used for anyone in the region, though it was also the name of a specific tribe according to Roman writers. Whether these people were Celts or Picts, or if those were more or less the same thing, is a matter of conjecture. The tribes may have been a composite of indigenous Picts and people from more southerly areas who had migrated north ahead of the Roman expansion. What is clear is that they made such an impression on the Romans that the whole region – Caledonia – was named after them.

The Caledones Resist Rome

According to Roman sources, the Caledones were led in their resistance to Roman expansion by a man named Calgacus (dates unknown). As with other such leaders, he may have been a composite character or might not have existed at all. The high-water mark, as it were, of Roman expansion into Caledonia was marked by victory over forces allegedly commanded by Calgacus at a place known as Mons Graupius.

The location of this battle has long been debated. It was conjectured to be somewhere in Perthshire or Fife, though recent rethinking suggests somewhere much further north in Aberdeenshire. What is known for sure is that while the Romans may have won a battle, they entirely failed to conquer the people they called the Caledones – and they knew it. Tacitus lamented that these people could not be pacified as long as there were two of them left to stand together. The Caledonian tribes, for their part, had been on the receiving end of an unpleasant demonstration of Roman fighting power.

The result was a gradual stabilization. Agricola withdrew his forces and stopped trying to conquer the Highlands. The frontier could be protected in other ways; notably by having good relations with tribes whose lands lay adjacent to the unconquered Picts and Caledones. These tribes could be gradually Romanized and made dependent on the Empire for luxury goods. If their wilder northern neighbours wanted someone to raid or to fight with, any harm would fall upon non-Romans.

For the tribes along the frontier, trade relations and a general mutual non-antagonism were preferable to further conflict, and as a result a frontier gradually emerged. This was not, presumably, the original Roman intention. There were no frontiers, just areas that had not yet been incorporated into the Empire. Yet as with the Germanic tribes at the beginning of the century, Rome came to realize that the cost of pacifying the Caledones was simply too high to justify the attempt.

The Roman Empire could have conquered Caledonia, but the cost might well have been so high as to cripple the Empire. The Caledones achieved what few others had: they made themselves more trouble than they were worth and ensured that ambitious Roman leaders preferred to look elsewhere for their share of glory. Tacitus wrote admiringly of their vibrancy and courage, stating that they were just like the Gauls of the Continent before Rome crushed them.

In what amounted to an admission that further expansion would be too costly, as well as a practical measure to protect the new frontier, the Roman army built a line of fortifications along the Gask Ridge in Perthshire, just north of the River Earn. To protect the construction work from attack, forward-positioned 'glen-blocker' forts were set up. This indicates the level of threat Rome felt despite the victory at Mons Graupius. Once Gask Ridge was fortified and garrisoned, the glen-blocker forts were abandoned. These were the first permanent fortifications at the frontier of the Empire, though they would be followed by more impressive works.

Hadrian's Wall

Emperor Hadrian (76–138 CE) ordered the construction of more elaborate fortifications at the frontiers, marking a shift in thinking in the top echelons of the Empire. From conquering everything in sight, the Empire had moved to a policy of protecting what it had. There is a discernible life cycle for empires; once growth ceases, they tend to enjoy a 'golden age', which is often the early stages of decline. If some great crisis rejuvenates the Empire, it may have a new lease of life, but if not, it will stagnate and gradually crumble.

The Caledones did not in any way precipitate the decline of the Roman Empire, but they ensured their culture would survive it. In 122 CE, work began on a solid line of fortifications right across the narrowest part of England. Known as Hadrian's Wall, this was – and still is – an impressive obstacle, but not one capable of withstanding a massive attack. Its function was in part political and in part to be a strategic tripwire.

The wall limited movement and contact between tribes north and south of it, facilitating the Romanization of the Britons and enabling Rome to restrict the benefits of trade with the tribes beyond the wall. Those who were friendly got Roman goods and the occasional 'goodwill' gift from the Empire. Those who were not would be impoverished by comparison.

The wall could repel small raiding parties, and good communications ensured that reinforcements were available in the case of a serious threat. It could be breached and crossed by larger forces, but this would draw a heavy response that ensured few warriors would get home again. Thus, while it was not an impenetrable barrier, Hadrian's Wall was a stabilizing influence and a useful political tool.

Hadrian's Wall was also a physical admission that Rome could not control the tribes of the north, and not everyone agreed with that. His successor, his adopted son Titus Aelius Caesar Antoninus (86–161 CE), launched a campaign of conquest and pacification that began with the Brigantes and pushed north of the wall. In 142 CE, work began on a new fortification, known as the Antonine Wall. This ran from the Firth of Forth to the Firth of Clyde and pushed the Roman frontier further out – but it was still an admission that the Caledones beyond were ungovernable.

The Antonine Wall was abandoned in 162 CE, with the Roman frontier moving back to Hadrian's line. Occasional attempts were made to reoccupy it, along with expeditions into the far north. In 209 CE, Emperor Septimus Severus (145–211 CE) made the last serious attempt to conquer the Caledones. Victories in battle were followed by massacres, but the Roman position was untenable. At the end of a long supply line and constantly harassed by bands of raiders, the Roman army had to abandon the enterprise and return to positions behind Hadrian's Wall. The subsequent strengthening of the wall indicates a defensive mindset thereafter.

ROMAN DECLINE

Plans for a renewed campaign into Caledonia were mooted from time to time, but there was usually something more urgent or less risky to occupy Imperial attention. As late as the early 300s, the Empire still hoped to conquer and pacify Caledonia, though by that time its troubles were intensifying. Having ascended to the imperial throne in 305 CE, Emperor Constantius I (c. 250–306 CE) presumably hoped to cement his authority with a successful military campaign.

He chose Caledonia as a suitable victim and claimed a notable victory in late 305 or the very beginning of 306 CE. He had planned to continue the campaign the following year but died at Eboracum during the winter. His son Constantine (c. 272–337 CE) was proclaimed Emperor but had to deal with opposition resulting in civil war. Eventually, Constantine was able to reunify the Roman Empire and became known to history as Constantine the Great. He was the first Roman Emperor to become a Christian, resulting in a huge surge of popularity for the religion across the whole Empire.

The Roman Empire was by that time too large to be effectively governed, and suffered greatly from internal divisions. These often centred on the actions of ambitious men, who might seek advantage in the internal politics of the Empire rather than dealing with the very real problems facing the Empire as a whole. Large numbers of troops were expended on internal conflict even though the borders were under pressure.

Emperor Constantine the Great attempted to rectify the situation by reforming the Roman army, eventually resulting in a two-tier system. Local garrisons were intended to keep the peace and provide security under normal conditions, with mobile forces available to support them or to undertake any offensive campaigns that might be necessary. This was a very different army from the one that had conquered in the name of Rome, and increasingly it was unable to defend the Empire.

One solution was to permit tribes to settle in Roman provinces on the condition they defend the frontiers. The Franks were one such group, as well as the Goths. The Empire was trying to adapt to changing conditions, but the decline was too far advanced by this point. With all available forces needed to defend the heartland of the Empire, Roman troops were withdrawn from the British Isles and its people advised to look to their own defence.

Arrival of the Huns

The face of Continental Europe was completely changed by the arrival of the Huns from the east. They were nomadic horsemen, whose origins are still debated. What is known is that they crossed the Volga into Europe in 370 CE and overran the territory of the tribes they encountered. This sparked a period of mass migration in which some tribes marched the length of Europe and even entered Africa seeking a safe place to settle.

Some of the Gothic tribes settled in Gaul alongside the Franks and the existing Romano-Gaulish population. By 450 CE, this region was sufficiently powerful that the diminished Roman Empire had to treat it as a political equal despite still nominally claiming to control it. The high point of the Hunnish invasion saw an army under the command of Attila (*c.* 406–43 CE) reach Gaul after plundering its way across Europe. A joint force of Romans, Franks and Goths inflicted a decisive defeat on the Huns in 451 CE. This did not end the Hunnish threat at a stroke, but it gradually diminished until they settled in the Danube Valley and became part of the European politico-cultural landscape.

AFTER THE FALL OF ROME

By the mid-400s, there were essentially two Roman Empires. The eastern component would endure for centuries more, becoming the Byzantine Empire. The western Empire, with its seat at Rome, had already declined to the point where it was no longer an influence on events. The last western Roman Emperor was deposed in 476 CE by Odoacer (d. 493 CE), a Germanic tribal king.

By this time, a new society was developing in Europe. The Franks, Goths and post-Roman Gauls would in time merge to form the Frankish Kingdom, which dominated Western Europe during the ensuing centuries. Migrating tribes found themselves a new home – or fought for one – and gave their names to regions they now occupied.

The Celtic peoples of these regions were subsumed into the new societies, forming part of these 'barbarian kingdoms'. Their unique culture was all but lost amid the emerging spirit of these new societies, to the point where there was nothing really 'Celtic' about them. Small enclaves of Celtic-speaking people did survive here and there, notably in Brittany, and these were joined by migrants from the British Isles.

In the meantime, Caledonia remained outside the Roman Empire, though not beyond its sphere of influence. Cross-border trade carried ideas, art and culture with it, though events in most of Caledonia were little more than vague rumours. As a result, there is little recorded history from the region. Meanwhile, the conquered parts of Britain became gradually more Romanized. The Romano-Britons retained a Celtic flavour to their society, especially among poorer people who could not afford the Empire's luxuries.

There was also a genetic influence. The people of a given region tend to develop a genetic identity, such as the Celtic trend towards being tall with red or reddish hair. Especially where there are natural barriers to movement, a population can develop prominent characteristics, but there is always some movement and exchange. Even in Neolithic times, people moved around far more than might be supposed, and in an age where narrow waters such as the English Channel and Irish Sea could be reliably crossed there was significant population drift. This brought in new genes which mixed with the existing pool.

Although this had always happened, to a greater or lesser degree the Roman era saw deliberate movement of people on a large scale. Troops were raised in one province and sent to another as garrisons, reducing the chance of a successful revolt in either location. Some of these personnel settled when their service was up, or fathered children in the meantime. Veterans of the legions were given a land grant to become gentleman-farmers and thereby slotted into the upper echelons of local society.

This influx of new genes has been repeated several times in the history of the British Isles, and it also worked the other way. Auxiliary troops raised in a Celtic area might serve in Africa or Asia Minor, and some would stay there. The effect was much less prominent in areas that were not conquered or were too remote to be important to the Empire. Thus, Ireland and Scotland did not see such an influx of non-Celtic genes, nor did parts of Wales and the south-west of England.

THE COMING OF THE SAXONS

The Germanic tribes of what is now Denmark and the North Sea coast of Europe had interacted with the people of the British Isles during the Roman occupation. They traded and sometimes served as mercenaries, and from around 410 CE onwards began to settle in south-eastern England. There is much debate as to whether there was a 'Saxon invasion' or a 'Saxon migration', or perhaps a bit of both.

New power structures emerged among the Romano-Britons once the Empire withdrew, and these kingdoms warred against one another. Continental mercenaries were highly useful, bringing Angles, Saxons and Jutes into Britain. Some of them settled along the coast, creating what would become known as the 'Saxon Shore'. It is possible that some local rulers encouraged this settlement, as it placed the newcomers in the path of any raids launched from their former home regions.

Resistance to raids was piecemeal now that the overarching Roman organizational structure had been withdrawn. It was a time of change, in which leaders had to adapt to a new situation and did not always make good decisions. These were also the early years of Christianity in the British Isles. Churchmen were the only significant literate class, and of course they had an agenda.

Earliest Reference to King Arthur

One of the few sources dealing with the Saxon incursions into Britain is attributed to Gildas (d. c. 570 CE), a Welsh monk whose opinion on the reason for the attacks and gradual migration is clear. Where modern scholars theorize that climate change forced the Saxons and their neighbours to seek new homes, Gildas was adamant that the Saxons were divinely sent as punishment for a lack of piety and a love of luxury among the leaders of what would become England.

Gildas's great work, *De excidio et conquestu Britanniae* (*The Overthrow and Conquest of Britain*), contains an account of the Saxon takeover of parts of England, and is also the earliest known reference to the King Arthur figure of British mythology. Additional information – though whether it is true or not is an open question – was added in the *Historia Brittonum*. This work is attributed to Nennius (dates unknown), and is thought to have been compiled in the 830s or so.

According to Nennius, large numbers of Saxons were invited to settle in Britain in return for mercenary service. This was at the command of Vortigern, a rather dissolute king who preferred to let others fight for him while he concentrated on having a good time. The Saxons were led by Hengist and Horsa (dates unknown), who plotted to gain additional land from Vortigern and to bring over more of their people to settle it.

Eventually, the Saxons betrayed their hosts in what is known as the Treason of the Long Knives. They proposed a feast to which everyone would come unarmed, and would sit Saxon beside Celt in friendship. The Saxons concealed knives about their person, and upon command set upon the defenceless Celtic leaders. Gildas made no mention of this incident, and it is likely to be fiction or at best loosely based upon a similar but smaller event.

By portraying Saxons as willing to betray hospitality laws and to engage in violence at an event ostensibly intended to bring about lasting peace, Nennius, and those who repeated the tale, were making it clear the invaders were the villains in this version of events. Whether or not the Treachery of the Long Knives happened, there was certainly conflict between the newcomers and the existing population. It is likely this was a series of small-scale incidents and large skirmishes rather than a deliberate attempt to take over the whole country.

Few records remain from this time, but there is a consensus that the Saxons suffered a major defeat at Mons Badonicus – Mount Badon – whose location has never been discovered. The Britons are said to have had a war leader named Arthur, who single-handedly slew a large number of Saxons. This is the earliest known reference to 'King Arthur', though in this early version of the tale his brother Uther was the king.

The Saxon Takeover

There are also references to a Romano-British leader named Ambrosius Aurelianus (dates unknown) leading the defence against the Saxons. Whatever happened – or did not happen – the Saxon takeover was relatively slow. It is commonly stated that the Celtic people of Britain were driven north and west, but it might be better to say that the Celtic culture was pushed in this direction. Some people would have relocated, but others accepted Saxon overlordship and became part of their new kingdoms.

Seven Saxon kingdoms emerged: East Anglia, Essex, Kent, Mercia, Northumbria, Sussex and Wessex. These gradually coalesced into three: Mercia, Northumbria and Wessex. In the meantime, Saxon dominance spread. The kingdom of Wessex defeated a Brythonic army in 577 CE and gained control over Gloucestershire, Oxfordshire and Somerset. Resistance continued, but a heavy defeat near Chester around 615 CE ended any chance of a Celtic resurgence.

THE 'VIKING ERA'

Celtic groups remained in control of the western parts of the British mainland – Cornwall and Wales – along with Scotland, but elsewhere the Romano-Britons were subsumed into the new Anglo-Saxon culture. This was challenged by the emergence of the Norsemen – the so-called Vikings – who began raiding the coasts of England from 793 CE. Correctly speaking, those first encountered by the Britons were indeed Vikings, in the sense that they were engaged in a 'vik', or expedition. Once they settled, the term did not apply. They were commonly referred to as Danes – no matter what part of Scandinavia they hailed from – or Norsemen.

The trading and raiding expeditions undertaken by the Norsemen were made possible by advances in maritime technology, which created vessels capable of crossing the North Sea and provided a means of navigation whilst out of sight of land. Prior to this, an open-sea crossing of any distance was simply not possible. This rules out any possibility of the ancient Celts crossing the Atlantic and exploring the Americas, though claims of this sort still surface from time to time. The Norsemen did eventually reach the Americas – barely – but to do so they had to leapfrog by way of Iceland and Greenland.

In the meantime, Norse raids became ever more serious. Around 800 CE, three ships constituted a major expedition. A century later, the Norsemen were capable of assembling hundreds of ships and thousands of warriors. Their expeditions were not always about conquest. If there was more money to be made from trade, the Norsemen would trade. They would also settle and conquer. The struggles between Saxons and Norsemen for control of England did not greatly affect the western Celtic people, though Norse incursions up the rivers of Scotland troubled those who lived nearby.

THE NORMAN CONQUEST

The 'Viking Era' is generally held to have ended in 1066 CE. By this time, the Frankish kingdom had emerged as a great European power, and had granted the right to settle in what became Normandy to a large number of Norsemen. As their cultures melded, what emerged was a Franco-Norse political entity with a long warrior tradition on both sides.

In 1066 CE, Duke William of Normandy, later known as William the Conqueror, attempted to seize the disputed crown of England. He faced opposition from the Anglo-Saxon candidate, Harold Godwinson, but defeated the English army at Hastings. A rapid campaign of pacification and fort-building secured control over the kingdoms of the English. Attempts to conquer the rest of Britain were less successful, however. Had the Normans succeeded in taking over Wales and Scotland there might never have been a United Kingdom in the modern sense; there would have been no separate thrones to unite in 1707. Celtic resistance to the Normans ensured there would be no single 'Kingdom of Britain' in the 1100s – or in any later century.

THE CELTIC STRONGLANDS

South-western **Britain**, Wales, Scotland and Ireland retain strong Celtic traditions to this day, as does Brittany on the Continent. Written records of their histories are scanty, and much of what does exist is intertwined with mythology and folktales. Many details – and perhaps some hugely significant events – have been lost through the centuries, while other stories have become distorted. Nevertheless, it is possible to piece together a narrative that starts as myth and becomes history somewhere along the way.

When the Celts arrived in the British Isles, beginning around 1000 BCE, they found humans already living there. Very little is known about these people. They were the descendants of hunter-gatherers who had migrated into the British Isles as the ice sheets retreated, and were probably quite diverse in culture and technological sophistication. Although not large compared to the Eurasian continent, Britain has a wide range of terrain and climate types. It is likely that natural barriers resulted in a number of different cultures developing, and that these influenced the nature of the Celtic societies that overlaid them.

The Celts did not come as conquerors, at least not in the sense of an organized invasion and takeover attempt, but neither had they any intention of turning around once they had arrived. Groups may have had to fight for the land they wanted, perhaps displacing the indigenous people, or absorbing them. Celtic culture spread across the British Isles due to migration rather than conquest, but spread it did. It is not clear, for example, whether the Picts were an entirely different group or were actually Celts. It is possible they were a mix of Celtic newcomers and the original population of Scotland.

Similarly, as the Celts drifted west into Ireland from around 500 CE onwards, they found a population already in place. Irish mythology mentions several invasions, which may be interpreted as the arrival of successive waves of settlers from the British mainland or perhaps Iberia. It is possible that some of the newcomers were displaced by Roman incursions into Britain or conflict between the tribes that emerged there. It is known that the Irish Celts interacted with their cousins in Wales and Scotland, and that some of the traditional Irish legends are inspired by characters and conflicts from history.

LEGENDARY KINGS OF WALES

The primary tribes emerging from the Celtic migration into what is now Wales were the Silures, who occupied the south-eastern region, and the Ordovices who lived to the north-west of them. The Demetae lived to the west of the Silures. It appears they had relatively little conflict with Rome. The Deceangli occupied the north, with the Cornovii holding lands in the east of Wales and parts of Shropshire. All were eventually brought under Roman rule, though this was loosely applied from regional centres. After the Roman withdrawal, new power structures began to emerge.

The early history of these new polities is preserved in legend, and some parts may be entirely mythical. Much of what is known comes from the *Mabinogion*, a collection of ancient Welsh tales and poems which is itself based on the fourteenth-century *Red Book of Hengest*. It is likely that these are ancient tales preserved orally by the bards, and therefore subject to embellishment and retelling in the Bardic tradition. Some of these tales are also told by Geoffrey of Monmouth (d. *c.* 1155) in his *Historia Regum Britanniae* (*History of the Kings of Britain*). Geoffrey of Monmouth's work was based on earlier writings and continues their tradition of wild pseudo-history, though it does eventually begin to resemble provable history.

Beli Mawr

Several royal dynasties trace their lineage back to Beli Mawr, who may have been a real individual but whose tale is shrouded in mythology. Early references claim descent from Aeneas, hero of the *Aeneid*. This is an epic poem by Virgil (70–19 BCE), in which Aeneas and his followers escape the fall of Troy and eventually settle in Italia. This not only leads to the founding of Rome but also to the exile of a man named Brutus. During his wanderings, according to the poem, Brutus not only founds cities in Europe but also discovers Britain and becomes its ruler.

As if this were not enough, Beli Mawr is also said to be married to a cousin of the Virgin Mary. His descendants can therefore trace their lineage back both to the family of Jesus Christ and, by way of the Trojan heroes, to the Greek gods. Among them were Cassivellaunus and his descendants Cunobelin and Caractacus, all leaders of the Catuvellauni tribe. Their dynasty was ultimately eliminated, but other branches of the family came to rule the kingdoms of Wales.

Eudaf Hen

Among the (at least semi-) mythical kings in Wales was Eudaf
Hen. According to Geoffrey of Monmouth, Eudaf Hen was
the half-brother of Constantine the Great, Emperor of Rome,
though in the *Historia Regum Britanniae* he is given the pseudo-
Latin name Octavius. When Constantine left Britain to take up
office as Emperor, Eudaf Hen rebelled against the governor he left
behind and became King of the Britons.

Constantine's response was to send three legions to Britain,
which were defeated near Winchester. The remnants of the
Roman army then fell back towards Scotland and began pillaging,
drawing a response from Eudaf Hen, which was in turn defeated.
With the assistance of British rebels and the King of Norway, Eudaf
Hen was able to inflict a decisive defeat on the Roman forces.

Coman Meriadoc

Caradocus, ruler of Cornwall, proposed a peace settlement
between Britain and Rome whereby Eudaf Hen's daughter
would marry Maximinianus, son of the Roman Emperor. Conan
Meriadoc (c. 305–395 according to legend), son or nephew of
Eudaf Hen depending on the version of the tale, was opposed
to the idea. He initially fought against Maximinianus with the
assistance of warriors from Caledonia and Pictland, but after
being defeated chose to ally with him. He was rewarded with lands
in Brittany, where he settled his followers.

Women from the Brythonic Kingdom of Dumnonia, located
in modern Cornwall and Devon, came to marry Conan's warriors
and he married Ursula, the daughter of the king. The marriage did
not last long; Ursula wanted to be a nun and agreed to the union
only on condition she be allowed to undertake a pilgrimage in

Europe. She died at Cologne. Afterwards, Conan married again, with some versions of the tale stating that his new bride was the sister of Saint Patrick. Conan's holdings in Armorica (Brittany) and Dunmonia passed to his sons upon his death around 395 CE.

An alternative version of the story appears in the *Mabinogion*. In this variant, the Emperor of Rome is named as Macsen Wledig, referring to Emperor Magnus Maximus (335–88 CE). Like other emperors of that troubled time, Magnus Maximus was proclaimed Emperor by the army – or at least, by the part of it he led. He inflicted a serious defeat on the Caledones in 383 CE, leading to his elevation, and appears to have withdrawn all the available forces from Wales in order to fight this campaign. The year 383 CE is therefore a highly significant one in Wales; the point where Roman rule ended and the local population could begin seeking their destiny. Magnus Maximus was killed in 388 CE.

Macsen Wledig

In the *Mabinogion*, Macsen Wledig dreamed of a beautiful maiden and initiated a search to find her. She was located in Caernarfon Castle along with her brothers Conan Meriadoc and Gadeon. Macsen proclaimed Eudaf Hen as King of the Britons, but soon found that his position had been usurped in his absence. With the assistance of Gadeon and Conan, he was able to overthrow the usurper. As with other versions of the tale, Macsen rewarded his allies with lands in Brittany. This relates to the migration of Brythonic people into the region in the post-Roman era.

The Kingdom of Gwynedd, occupying the north-west of Wales, is said to have its origins in these events by way of the Votadini tribe of south-eastern Scotland. Although living north of the Roman wall, they were friendly to Rome and were treated generously provided they defended the northern flank of the Empire against other tribes. After the Roman withdrawal, the Votadini became known as the Gododdin. They warred with the kingdoms of Bernicia and Deira, established by the Anglo-Saxons in the north-east of England.

Cunedda Wledig

A force of warriors from the Gododdin, under the leadership of Cunedda Wledig (386–460 CE), were deployed in what would become Gwynedd to defend against Irish pirates ravaging the coasts. Cunedda is stated to be a descendant of Conan Meriadoc, though this raises problems regarding exactly when these events are said to have taken place. After driving off the Irish, Cunedda settled down in Gwynedd, founding a royal dynasty. These events appear to have taken place around 350–450 CE, though there are contradictions which make a closer estimate difficult. Cunedda himself may have been a mythical figure or based upon one or more real rulers.

Cadwallon Lawhir ap Einion

Around this time, the Saxons were putting pressure on the British tribes to the east of Wales, though this slacked after they were heavily defeated at the Battle of Badon Hill. The main threat to Gwynedd came from Ireland. Pirate raids harassed coastal settlements while other Irish groups settled in Wales and Anglesey. Successive generations of kings of Gwynedd fought against them until Cadwallon Lawhir ap Einion (Cadwallon Long Hand, dates unknown) finally drove them out. The nickname Long Hand is probably a reference to the reach of his power. There are claims that Cadwallon Lawhir ap Einion had arms so long he could pick up objects from the ground without bending down, but this is almost certainly an invention of later writers.

It is difficult to put a date to any of these events, though the situation does become clearer as the years advance. One reason for this was the coming of Christianity to the British Isles. The conversion of Constantine the Great in 312 CE made Christianity an official (and later *the* official) religion of the Roman Empire, but most people in the British Isles were quite happy with their fire festivals and pagan gods. Maelgwyn Hir ap Cadwallon (Maelgwn the Tall, dates unknown), son of Cadwallon Lawhir ap Einion, was a patron of the early Church and benefited from having literate people at his court.

EARLY KINGDOMS OF WALES

Gwynedd

Maelgwyn Hir ap Cadwallon is also known as Maelgwyn Gwynedd, after whom the realm became known. His reign, probably around 520 CE or so, represents the beginning of clearly recorded history in the region. He was followed by a succession of kings who expanded the power of Gwynedd to the point where some are referred to as the High Kings of the Britons.

In the early 600s, Gwynedd came under pressure from Northumbria, an Anglo-Saxon kingdom formed from the merging of Bernicia and Deira in northern England. King Edwin of Northumbria (c. 568–633 CE) may have spent his early life in Gwynedd as an exile or a foster child in the tradition of the times. In 616 CE, he was at the court of King Raedwald of

East Anglia (d. c. 624 CE), and was clearly a favourite. After the conquest of Bernicia and Deira by Raedwald, Edwin was installed as a puppet king.

Raedwald was at this time the most powerful of the Anglo-Saxon kings. The *Anglo-Saxon Chronicle*, a chronological account of events in Anglo-Saxon and Norman England, created three centuries after his death, recognizes him as the High King over the Britons. After his death around 624 CE, Edwin of Northumbria expanded his newly independent kingdom. He was an aggressive ruler, routinely attacking his neighbours to gain territory or tribute. This placed him at odds with both Gwynedd and the Saxon kingdom of Mercia.

Edwin's invasion of Gwynedd forced its king, Cadwallon ap Cadfan (d. 634), to flee his stronghold on Anglesey. In alliance with King Penda of Mercia (c. 606–55 CE) and other Welsh leaders, Cadwallon ap Cadfan confronted Edwin at Hatfield Chase in 633 CE, defeating his army and killing the King of Northumbria. This caused the recently united kingdom to splinter back into Bernicia and Deira, which, according to some accounts, Cadwallon ap Cadfan pillaged mercilessly. He was killed in battle near Durham in 634, resulting in the reunification of Northumbria.

Northumbria and Mercia

The wars between Northumbria and Mercia – and her Welsh allies – continued after the death of Cadwallon ap Cadfan. The death of Penda in battle against King Oswiu of Northumbria (c. 612–70 CE) diminished the reputation of Gwynedd, whose forces had just departed for home. The kingdom spent the next two centuries in relative eclipse. In the meantime, King Oswiu made a pivotal decision which affected the entire Celtic world.

By this time, Christianity had strongly taken hold in the British Isles, and two rival identities had emerged. The Roman Church closely followed the orthodox approach prevalent elsewhere, while the Celtic Church incorporated themes and concepts derived from earlier Celtic religion.

In 664 CE, Oswiu sponsored the Synod of Whitby, at which it was decided how to determine when Easter should fall. He also responded to urgings from prominent churchmen by declaring that his kingdom would follow the Roman Church. This decision was likely political, as the unified Roman Church was a stronger ally than the fragmented Celtic one. Oswiu was at the time the most powerful king in Britain, so naturally his decision had a huge impact. The Celtic Church was gradually eclipsed, though vestiges remain to this day.

Mercia continued to be a threat to the Welsh kingdoms. During the reign of King Aethelbald (d. 757 CE), its power increased to the point where Aethelbald was recognized as controlling all the Saxon lands south of the Humber. He was assassinated in 757 CE and, after a period of internal strife, was succeeded by the extremely ambitious Offa (d. 796). Offa increased the power of Mercia at the expense of her neighbours. When not fighting other Saxons for dominance, he led campaigns into Wales on several occasions.

Offa is primarily known for the construction of Offa's Dyke, an earthwork formation facing Wales. Taking the form of a long ditch-and-mound, Offa's Dyke would make a reasonable obstacle if vigorously defended, but may have been more in the way of a political statement than a line of defence. As with ancient hillforts, the work required to construct such a fortification demonstrated power and wealth, and might serve as a reminder to those who saw it that they faced a potent enemy. Welsh warriors might well penetrate past the dyke, and other fortifications elsewhere, but they would know they were quite literally crossing a line from which there might be no coming back.

Powys

Gwynedd was by no means the only powerful Welsh polity. In the turbulent times after the Roman departure other powers had emerged, typically defined by the good farming land they controlled and confined by natural barriers. Among them was Powys. Where other Proto-kingdoms failed and were absorbed into more successful ones, Powys grew to dominate what is now the England/Wales border region.

Perhaps the most important figure in the history of Powys was Vortigern, who was recognized as King of the Britons around the mid-450s CE. This was not a great time to be a High King, since the Saxons were gaining in power on the eastern shore, and Vortigern was apparently not a very good king. It was he who, according to most surviving accounts, invited large numbers of Saxon mercenaries to fight his wars while he lived a life of luxury.

Powys was eventually absorbed by Gwynedd by way of a political alliance. Merfyn Frych (d. c. 844 CE) was the first king of Gwynedd not descended through the male line from Maelgwn Gwynedd. His claim to the throne was through his mother's family and was considered tenuous. However, after a power struggle left the kingdom with no more solid candidates, Merfyn Frych emerged as monarch. He is primarily known to history as the father of Rhodri Mawr ap Merfyn (Rhodri the Great, c. 820–78).

Rhodri Mawr ap Merfyn came to the throne in difficult times. Internal divisions, plague and pressure from neighbouring Mercia had weakened both Gwynedd and Powys, though fighting among the Saxon kingdoms reduced the significance of Mercia and granted Gwynedd time to recover. Rhodri Mawr ap Merfyn gained the throne of Powys through inheritance and that of Seisyllwg through marriage.

In addition to creating a powerful kingdom, Rhodri Mawr ap Merfyn had to deal with Norse raiders and settlers. As the power of the Norsemen increased, they followed the coasts ever farther afield, even raiding in the Mediterranean. They also settled or took over coastal communities, creating Norse enclaves that would serve as forward bases for future expeditions. Rhodri Mawr ap Merfyn led the Welsh resistance to these raids, inflicting a sharp defeat on a Norse army in 856 CE. He was defeated a decade later and fled to Ireland, but returned the following year. Although he regained his kingdom, Rhodri Mawr ap Merfyn was killed in battle against Mercian forces.

After the death of Rhodri Mawr ap Merfyn, his realm was divided again. His son, Anarawd ap Rhodri (855–916 CE) attempted to create stability by forming alliances. At that time, much of eastern England had been conquered by Norse armies, while British resistance was led by Alfred the Great of Wessex (848–99 CE). The British alliance held, but that with the Norsemen did not. Anarawd ap Rhodri repelled a Norse invasion of northern Wales in 894 CE and incursions against Anglesey in 980–982 CE.

Other Welsh Kingdoms

In the meantime, the fortunes of other Welsh kingdoms ebbed and flowed. Dyfed, in south-eastern Wales, was troubled by raids for all of its history. Some of these came from Ireland, others from the Anglo-Saxon kingdoms. Eventually Dyfed morphed into Deheubarth as the result of the actions of Hywel ap Cadell, also known as Hywel Dda (d. c. 950). He was a descendant of Rhodri Mawr ap Merfyn, and ruler of Seisyllwg. Some accounts state that he conquered Dyfed, others that he gained it through marriage. During his reign, he came to control most of Wales and is recorded as a King of the Britons. Hywel ap Cadell is known to history as a lawmaker, with a reputation for fairness and justice. That did not rule out wars of conquest, however; he invaded Gwynedd and for a short period ruled it before being driven out.

The Kingdom of Gwent, in the south-east of Wales, had mixed fortunes. Largely based on the Silures tribe, it retained some Roman power structures and important locations in the post-Roman years. The kingdom was heavily beset by Saxons around 630 CE. Athrwys ap Meurig (c. 605–55), is credited with leading the resistance and is considered by some to be a possible basis for the legendary King Arthur. Conflict with the Saxon kingdoms continued, along with pressure from other Welsh kingdoms.

In 896 CE, Gwent was subjected to large-scale raiding by Norse armies and declined thereafter, though eventually there was a resurgence. Gruffydd ap Rhydderch (d. 1055 CE) seized control of Deheubarth in the 1020s and 1030s, repelling Norse incursions until he was killed in battle against Gruffydd ap Llywelyn (c. 1010–63 CE), King of Gwynedd and Powys. This made Gruffydd ap Llywelyn king of a unified Wales.

NORMAN INVASIONS

The internal politics of Wales was rarely entirely peaceful. Power struggles and dynastic disputes sometimes resulted from external events such as a defeat by the Anglo-Saxons, Norse or Irish. On other occasions, foreigners were able to exploit the weakness of a polity weakened by internal squabbles. The reign of Gruffydd ap Llywelyn was a time of strength and stability for Wales, which may have worried the King of England, Edward the Confessor (c. 1002–66 CE). The death of Gruffydd ap Llewelyn in 1063 CE might have encouraged an English campaign into Wales, but no action was taken before Edward's death in 1066 CE. Afterwards, there were more pressing matters.

The English succession was disputed, with Harold Godwinson (c. 1022–66 CE), claiming the crown and defeating rival claimant Harald Hardrada in the north of England. Godwinson then marched south to confront the other claimant, Duke William of Normandy. William was victorious, bringing about the end of Anglo-Saxon rule in Britain and ushering in the Norman era. By this time, there was no longer a unified Wales. The successors to Gruffydd ap Llewelyn fought and schemed among themselves, eventually resulting in the kingdoms of Gwynedd and Deheubarth emerging as stable powers by the early 1080s.

In the meantime, the Normans had consolidated their control over England and now looked to secure the frontiers. King William installed his favoured followers in locations where they could best defend his new kingdom and perhaps engage in military adventures in the manner of their Roman predecessors. These 'Marcher Lords' gained further territories over time, securing them with fortifications. At first, these were motte-and-bailey constructions, built of wood atop a mound surrounded by an outer palisade. Over time they were replaced by stone castles.

Norman incursions were delayed by internal politics in the new realm, but gradually the lowlands at least were overrun. The Norman style of warfare favoured cavalry armoured in chain mail, who were potent on flat ground but of limited use in the hills. Difficult terrain made supplying Norman forces a problem in the same manner it had impeded the Romans. Nevertheless, the Welsh were gradually pushed back, and the lands of the Marcher Lords became at least somewhat 'Normanized'. One factor in this was the practice of bringing in foreign mercenaries to fight for the Norman crown, then settling them in the newly pacified territories.

William the Conqueror died in 1087 CE, but this did not halt the gradual encroachment. The year 1094 CE saw a resurgence in Gwynedd, which coincided with a period of civil war in England known as the Anarchy. This came about as a result of disputed succession. Henry I of England wished to be succeeded by his daughter Matilda, whilst many nobles favoured the easily manipulated Stephen of Blois. Some Welsh leaders became involved in the conflict, which did not end until 1153 CE.

Powys also regained some of its former glory, at least until the death of Madog ap Maredudd (d. 1160). After this, Powys was divided and greatly diminished. In the meantime, the Kingdom of Deheubarth had regained some of its strength and came to an agreement with Henry II of England (1133–89 CE) to become a tributary but autonomous state.

The reign of King John of England (1166–1216 CE) was disastrous for England, with the loss of almost all the realm's holdings in France. This period of weakness coincided with the rise of Llywelyn ab Iorwerth (Llewellyn the Great, 1173–1240 CE), a king of Gwynedd who ultimately came to rule almost all of Wales. Llywelyn ab Iorwerth married Joan, illegitimate daughter of King John, but was forced to surrender hostages as a guarantee of his kingdom's behaviour. Despite this, Welsh forces were involved in the revolt of the Barons in England, which pitted a group of powerful nobles against the ineffectual and unpopular King John. The conflict was ended in 1215 CE by the signing of the Magna Carta, which included a number of provisions dealing specifically with Wales and its interests.

Welsh power worried King Henry III of England (1207–72 CE), to the point where he refused to permit Dafydd ap Llywelyn (1215–46 CE) to inherit the lands of his father Llywelyn ab Iorwerth outside Gwynedd. This resulted in war between Wales and England, which ended due to internal conflict in Gwynedd after the death of Dafydd ap Llywelyn in 1246 CE. From this power struggle emerged Llywelyn ap Gruffudd (1223–82 CE), also known as Llywelyn the Last. Despite being recognized as Prince of Wales by the English throne – the only Welsh leader to receive this title – Llywelyn ap Gruffudd fought against the English aristocracy installed in Wales. He was killed at the Battle of Orewin Bridge near Builth in Powys.

Thereafter, Wales was ruled by the English. Welsh fighting men – notably archers – served admirably in the many wars of the medieval period, which at times pitted them against the Scots. English rule has not always sat comfortably in Wales, and the Welsh have refused to give up their Celtic traditions. The Brythonic Celtic language family has survived into modern times and continues to demonstrate its resilience. Of all the Celtic languages, Welsh is the only one not considered endangered.

A MYTHICAL HISTORY OF IRELAND

The ancient Celts are thought to have entered Ireland around 500 BCE, and found people already living there. These had been isolated to a greater or lesser degree since the flooding of the land bridge between Ireland and the mainland. A rather distorted version of the interactions between the Celts and the indigenous population survives in the form of myths and legends. These were preserved by endless retellings and naturally their content 'drifted' over time. They were eventually written down by outsiders, whose understanding may have been flawed or viewed through a biased lens.

The 'Book of Invasions'

The body of lore relating to these early times is known as the 'Mythological Cycle', within which the 'Book of Invasions' deals with five 'invasions' of Ireland. In this context, the arrival of unwelcome settlers might be considered an invasion; there was probably no mass assault. Instead, new people arrived, settled and competed for land and resources with those already in place.

It is difficult to correlate the mythological invasions with population movements as there are few written records. In any case, the 'invasions' were likely to be small-scale in any one area, with lulls in between. Only when something unusual occurred would it be possible to identify characteristics. For example, a period of quiet might result from events occurring in an invader's homeland, causing them to focus their attention there for a time before resuming an invasion, creating the impression of two waves or separate incursions. In reality, this was nothing more than interrupted population drift.

Even once the land bridges were submerged, the likely avenues for migration would not change. What was once land was now shallow and relatively sheltered sea that could be crossed in small boats. People could move relatively easily from Wales to Ireland, or from Ireland to south-western Scotland. The Isle of Man could act as a stopover for those crossing from what became western England. Movement from Iberia into Ireland required more seaworthy boats, but could be accomplished by way of Devon and Cornwall.

Cesair and the Great Flood

According to the 'Book of Invasions', the first people in Ireland were refugees from the Biblical Great Flood. Their leader was Cesair, granddaughter of Noah, whose foster father was an Egyptian priest. He warned her about the impending flood, and when Noah refused her and her followers a place on his Ark, she built one of her own.

Cesair's aim was to find a place where humans had never lived, in which case there could not have been any sin committed there. Such a land would be spared the effects of a Great Flood sent to cleanse the world of sin. She referred to her destination as Inis Fáil, or the Land of Destiny. Cesair's Ark (or Arks, as some seem to have been lost in transit) set off and some years later found a suitable place on the shores of Ireland.

There were fifty women and three men aboard the surviving Ark, so Cesair decided her people would divide into three groups with one man in each. Two of the men, Bith and Ladra, died of exhaustion as a result of their efforts to populate the new land. Cesair's partner Fintan Mac Bóchra, who was shared with many other women, decided to escape before he shared the same fate. He turned himself into a salmon and swam away.

Cesair died of grief at Fintan's loss, and soon afterwards it became apparent her people had not escaped the Great Flood after all. Ireland was inundated, and of the women, only one named Banba survived. Some legends state that after the waters receded Fintan and Banba produced offspring who became the race known as the Formorians. It is likely that early Christian scholars heard the tale of Cesair, a mythological figure, culture-hero or goddess, and retconned her into a biblical character. Her fate in this version of the tale fits the Christian agenda – she tried to dodge the will of God, but only Noah had divine permission to build an Ark, so the Flood got her in the end.

The Partholon Invasion

There are several links between Celtic mythology and ancient Greece and Egypt. It is likely this has something to do with scholarship in the Roman period. Observers might try to conflate what they saw with what they had been taught about the ancient Mediterranean civilizations. Bards would also use these places as handy references when spinning their tales. The average audience member would be familiar with Egypt or Greece as far-off, exotic places where incredible events might have taken place.

Alternatively, it is possible that the second wave of invaders really did come from Greece. According to legend, a band of wanderers led by Partholon arrived from Greece 312 years after Cesair. This raises questions, since Partholon is said to have been an exile who had murdered his parents. Exile suggests a stable society to be exiled from, which is quite an achievement given that the entire population other than a handful on the Ark were wiped out just three centuries before. It is likely that these plot holes are the result of Christian scholars wanting everything to fit with their agenda, regardless of the internal contradictions.

The 'Book of Invasions' states that the Partholonians landed in the spring, perhaps in Donegal Bay. They cleared land and began creating a civilization but soon came into conflict with the indigenous Formorians. These hideous people had only one leg and one arm, and were not mentioned in the tale of Cesair. One version of the myth states that they were descended from Fintan and Banba, survivors of the first invasion.

The tale is probably a heavily dramatized reference to the struggles between the early Celts, who possessed advanced metalworking and other technologies, and the relatively primitive indigenous population. Perhaps the locals really were unpleasant to gaze upon, but more likely they were turned into monsters for the sake of a good story or to exaggerate their primitive culture.

It is worth noting that at the time the Roman Empire was building advanced galleys and equipping its troops with complex armour, many remote regions were still populated by Neolithic hunter-gatherers. This technological gap gave huge advantages to the more advanced cultures. While the early Celts were not as organized as the Romans, their warriors had good iron weapons and chain mail body armour. It may be that the concept of 'cold iron' being effective against supernatural creatures had its origins in fights between outnumbered Celts and savage opponents, in which iron was the decisive factor.

Be that as it may, the Partholonians defeated the Formorians and drove them to take refuge on Toraigh (Tory) Island off the north-west coast of Ireland. They then built a culture which thrived (on the sites of modern cities, including Dublin) before all suddenly dying of a plague. In some versions of the tale, there was a survivor named Tuan. He was the sole Partholonian inhabitant of Ireland for thirty years, and was apparently not troubled by the Formorians.

The Nemedian Invasion

The next band of invaders were known as the Nemedians, after their leader, Nemed. Accounts of their origins vary, though Nemed appears to have inherited a penchant for maritime adventures from his ancestor, Noah. The Nemedians are variously described as having come from the west and from Iberia. Either way, Tuan tried to avoid contact with them by transforming himself into a variety of animals, including a stag, a boar and an eagle. While disguised as a salmon, he was eaten by the presumably unsuspecting wife of a man named Cairill.

Cairill's wife gave birth to a child named Tuan mac Cairill, suggesting the pregnancy was something to do with the magical man-fish she had ingested. This concept appears elsewhere in Celtic mythology, with other characters being reborn after being eaten. In this case, Tuan mac Cairill became the author of the 'Book of Invasions'. What he recorded, however, was rather grim for the Nemedians.

The Formorians re-entered Ireland at some point, and came into conflict with the Nemedians. Weakened by plague, they could not effectively resist and were enslaved by the Formorians for many years. The Nemedians eventually freed themselves and drove the Formorians back to their stronghold on Toraigh Island, but by the time the war was won there were only thirty Nemedians left.

Among these was Britán Máel, who led a handful in a migration to Alba – Scotland. It is claimed in the *Lebor Gabála Érenn* (*The Book of Invasions*) that Britán Máel gave his name to the British Isles. Another group found a refuge in 'the far north', though there is no indication of where that might have been.

The remainder of the Nemedians sailed away and eventually reached Greece, where they were enslaved and put to work carrying bags of soil as part of an agricultural development programme in Thrace. They became known as Fir Bolg, or 'bag men', for their sacks which gradually became so impregnated with dirt they were waterproof. This enabled the Fir Bolg to rebel and sail away on their dirtbags. They naturally made their way back to Ireland in this manner.

The returning Fir Bolg were able to defeat the Formorians this time, but soon encountered a new tribe. This was the Tuatha Dé Danann (Danu's Tribe), who were also descendants of the Nemedians. They had returned from whatever place of safety they had found and had as good a claim to the territory of the Nemedians as the Fir Bolg did.

Ascendency of the Tuatha Dé Danann

It seems that at first the two tribes sought to live in peace, but the Fir Bolg broke the truce. This was unwise, as the Tuatha Dé Danann had mystical knowledge the Fir Bolg lacked. In addition, they possessed magical weapons and artifacts. Among these was the spear of Lugh, which no warrior could withstand, and *Fragarach*, the sword of Núada, which could cut through anything and compel anyone to tell the truth.

In order to wield the sword Fragerach, a warrior had to be worthy to rule as High King. This was indicated by the *Lia*

Fáil, or Stone of Destiny, which made a roaring sound when the king touched it. Núada, King of the Tuatha Dé Danann, was thus confirmed as the rightful High King of Ireland. The Tuatha Dé Danann also possessed the *Coire ansic*, the Dagda's cauldron, which could feed any number of people.

With their logistical needs provided for and magical weapons available, the Tuatha Dé Danann possessed great advantages. Their leader was acclaimed by the Stone of Destiny, which would surely have raised morale. Just to be sure, the Tuatha Dé Danann made an alliance with the Formorians, which was sealed by marriage. This resulted in the birth of Lugh or Lug, who would become one of the most important Celtic gods.

The First Battle of Mag Tuired

Having stacked the deck to every possible extreme, the Tuatha Dé Danann landed in Ireland and burned their boats behind them. They met the army of the Fir Bolg in the First Battle of Mag Tuired. After some rather basic negotiations, the Fir Bolg decided to fight. The battle went on for four days, during which Sreng, champion of the Fir Bolg, cut off the hand of Nuada. Despite this setback, the Tuatha Dé Danann were winning and offered a truce for further negotiations.

The Fir Bolg were granted a province to settle, which they accepted rather than fight to the death against their clearly more powerful opponents. They had suffered 100,000 casualties, according to legend, and faced annihilation if they resisted further. Some of the Fir Bolg are said to have joined the Formorians, while others migrated to the western Scottish islands and the Isle of Man.

The maiming of Nuada created problems for the Tuatha Dé Danann. To be eligible to rule a king had to be whole, and Nuada was missing a hand. Although a new hand of silver was made for Nuada by Dian Cecht, god of physicians, he was replaced as king by Bres, who was not a popular ruler due to his favouritism towards the Formorians.

Bres was the son of Ériu, a noblewoman of the Tuatha Dé Danann, and the Formorian Prince Elatha. It seems that Formorians were no longer hideous, as Elatha was easily able to seduce Ériu and cause her to fall in love with him. From their union came Bres, a beautiful child who grew with supernatural speed. Everything of beauty in Ireland came to be compared to him, such was his appearance, but his loyalties lay with the Formorians.

Soon after Bres became king, the Formorians began to oppress the people of Ireland and demand great tribute from them. They enslaved noble members of the Tuatha Dé Danann such as Dagda, who was put to work digging ditches and creating fortifications to protect the Formorians. Bres even ignored the laws of hospitality, resulting in him being devastatingly satirized by the bards. This was his undoing. The Tuatha Dé Danann asked Bres to stand down as king, and he agreed to do so in seven years' time.

Bres had no intention of honouring the deal, he just needed time to gather support. He went to the Formorians for assistance and was granted the services of warriors, including Balor of the Evil Eye. Known throughout Celtic mythology by various names, Balor was mutated by exposure to a Druidic potion and grew a giant eye. When opened by his attendants the eye could kill everyone it gazed upon, turning them into statues.

It is said there were so many ships in the Formorian host they stretched all the way to the Hebrides. The Tuatha Dé Danann made their own preparations, including the use of prophecy to predict enemy movements. The Dagda was sent to delay the Formorians while the Tuatha Dé Danann concentrated a gigantic number of warriors. Fortunately for the Tuatha Dé Danann, the Formorians decided to ridicule the Dagda. They provided him with an outrageous amount of porridge, into which they cooked whole sheep and pigs, and told him he had to eat it all or be put to death.

The Dagda ate all the porridge, and was swollen up to a huge size by the time he finished. As a result, he was not at his best when he met Breg. This highly attractive woman was the daughter of Indech, one of the Formorian kings. She was unimpressed with the Dagda's appearance, and both struck him and verbally abused him. She then demanded the Dagda carry her home. Along the way, the effects of the porridge wore off and the two became lovers. Despite doing her level best to convince the Dagda not to join the battle, Breg eventually relented and agreed to use her magic to help him.

The Second Battle of Mag Tuired

The clash between the Formorians and the Tuatha Dé Danann is known as the Second Battle of Mag Tuired. It pitted huge numbers of fighting-men against one another, though it was the actions of heroes that decided the outcome. This is a common theme in Celtic mythology that remains popular today.

Balor of the Evil Eye was particularly destructive, killing many of the Tuatha Dé Danann warriors with his fearsome gaze. Among them was Nuada, who was leading the Tuatha Dé Danann as their reinstalled king. He was avenged by Lugh, whose well-aimed sling stone penetrated Balor's eye and slew him. The eye was knocked out and rolled around on the ground, killing many Formorian warriors.

Although defeated, the Formorians were able to cause further mischief. Some of them stole the Dagda's magical harp. This did not work out well for them; the harp would come to Dagda when he called it, and when he did it crushed the Formorians who were in its path. The Dagda was able to use the Three Noble Strains from the harp to first make the Formorians sad, then happy, then sleepy. He and his men then escaped with the harp.

After the defeat of the Formorians, the Dagda ruled Ireland and ushered in an age of prosperity. The Tuatha Dé Danann gained knowledge from their former foes, including secrets of agriculture given up by Bres in return for his life. After the Dagda died, his tribe continued to prosper until they were displaced by the final wave of invaders to arrive in Ireland. This was a tribe known as the Milesians after their leader Mil Espaine.

The Milesian Invasion

The Milesians had travelled far, all the way from Scythia through Egypt and Iberia. There may be some truth to this, though it is also possible these places were used by the bards to make the Milesians more impressive without any regard to whether they really did sail across the known world. Whatever the truth may be, the Milesians are said to have arrived in sixty-five ships despite attempts by the Tuatha Dé Danann to prevent them from getting ashore.

There are several variants of the story and no definitive account of exactly what happened. Some accounts state that the two tribes entered into negotiations which broke down into violence, others that there was a tragic misunderstanding with the same result. Either way the Milesians decided to take the land by force.

Initially, the Tuatha Dé Danann tried to cause the Milesians to get lost in a sea fog they created using magic, and when that failed they summoned a storm. The Milesians had bards of their own who could counter such magic and were able to land their forces. The wives of the three brothers who ruled the Tuatha Dé Danann at that time met with the Milesians, each asking the newcomers to name the land after her if they were victorious. It is not clear why this occurred; perhaps each hoped to elevate her position in the new order if one emerged. Eriu was chosen, giving Ireland its traditional name: Erin.

Eriu conspired with the Milesians, assisting them in defeating the Tuatha Dé Danann in battle. They were, however, not destroyed. The god Manannán mac Lir allocated the surviving members of the Tuatha Dé Danann places in the Sidhe, or fairy mounds, enabling them to retreat into the magical Otherworld and escape their enemies. The Milesians gained control of the natural world in Ireland, but they lived in fear of the Tuatha Dé Danann thereafter.

HEROES AND GODS

Lugh Lámhfada

The characters of the mythological history of Ireland often straddle the line between heroes and gods. Some are portrayed as talented mortals or semi-supernatural heroes who later are worshipped as gods. Among them was Lugh (or Lug) Lámhfada, also known as Lugh of the Long Hand. He was one of triplets born to Ethlinn, the daughter of Balor. This immediately raised problems for Balor, who knew of a prophecy that a child of Ethlinn would kill him. The other children were slain, but Lugh was rescued and raised among the Tuatha Dé Danann.

Lugh was trained in smithing but seems to have been some kind of polymath (or even omnimath). He earned the nickname Lugh Samildánach, which means 'skilled in all the arts'. While the tribe had others who had mastered any one of Lugh's skills, he was the only one who could rival all the masters in all of their skills. He was eventually murdered by the sons of a man named Cermait. Cermait had seduced Lugh's wife and was killed in retaliation.

The Morrigan

Some mythological figures seem to be considered gods at times and supernatural beings at others. The Morrigan is one such being. Variously referred to as Morrigan or the Morrigan, this sometimes-deity is a complex figure. As a goddess she is made up of three aspects, though references vary as to their identities. As a mythical being she is a shape-changer who prophesies the future and interferes in the fortunes of tribes and heroes.

Morrigan is associated with conflict and rulership and is a rather vengeful figure. She can change shape into various animals, including an eel, a heifer and a raven, and can appear as a beautiful maiden or a hag depending on her purposes at the time. She represents sovereignty over Ireland as well as fertility and war, and is sometimes called the 'queen of demons'. Like other Celtic gods, she appears to be the inspiration for characters in various tales, such as Morgan le Fay in the legends of King Arthur. Sometimes the names of these gods are used out of context, particularly in today's video games and popular entertainment. This, arguably, is in the Bardic tradition; a familiar name is used to give an impression of a character, enabling the story to move along without much need for exposition.

The 'Book of Invasions' is concerned with how Ireland came to be, in a spiritual sense. Successive waves of invaders (and re-invaders) were defeated by the Tuatha Dé Danann, who then became gods when the Milesians inherited the non-supernatural world. This world is not as mundane as our modern times, as the stories of the ancient Irish Ulaid Cycle and Fenian Cycle tell. Many of these feature heroes with supernatural powers and talents, opposed by equally overpowered villains.

The Ulaid (or Ulster) Cycle is primarily concerned with the adventures of a group of warriors known as the Red Branch, who formed an elite bodyguard for their king and dealt with serious problems as they arose. The warrior caste was well established in Celtic society as representatives of the leaders, engaging in what nowadays might be termed 'soft power projection' by their reputation and intimidating appearance (and if that failed, they would crush their king's enemies). The stories of the Ulaid Cycle were based on this normal part of Celtic culture, just with larger-than-life characters and events.

Cú Chulainn

Greatest of the Red Branch heroes was Cú Chulainn, whose father was none other than Lugh Lámhfada. Lugh was by that time a god, but interacted with the mortal world from time to time, as did others of the Tuatha Dé Danann. He fathered a child with the daughter of the Druid Cathbad, who originally named the baby Sétanta. Sétanta grew into an adventurous youth with a fondness for the game of hurley. This quintessentially Celtic sport is described in a modern movie as 'a cross between hockey and murder'. Sétanta was clearly of a combative disposition even at an early age.

Sétanta was also less than completely respectful of authority. He was supposed to meet Cathbad at the home of Culann, the master smith, but preferred to finish his game before setting off. He arrived late, and was confronted by the fearsome guard dog owned by Culann. Naturally, Sétanta clobbered the dog with his hurley stick, to the annoyance of Culann. Wild and violent he might be, Sétanta was also honourable. He agreed to guard the home of Culann for a year while a new guard dog was sought and trained, and became known as Cú Chulainn – the Hound of Culann.

At this point Cú Chulainn was an athletic and aggressive young man, but not yet a hero. That changed when Emer, daughter of a chieftain, declared that any husband of hers must be capable of performing heroic feats. Cú Chulainn set off for the isle of Skye where he believed he could obtain training that would enable him to fulfil his potential.

Cú Chulainn learned much, and when his mentor was challenged by the female warrior Aife, Cú Chulainn naturally stepped up to meet her. Aife was a superior warrior, so Cú Chulainn distracted her by pointing out an injury to her chariot horses. This turned out to be a trick, but it sufficed to enable Cú Chulainn to defeat Aife. Despite her being the better warrior and him winning by deceit – or perhaps because of it – Cú Chulainn and Aife became lovers.

The training received by Cú Chulainn was not merely in the use of sword and spear. He learned how to enter a berserk rage that gave him supernatural strength. When in this state, Cú Chulainn's organs moved around in his body and blood sprayed out of his forehead. He could apparently be brought out of his rage by rapid cooling, though anyone trying to plunge him into a container of cold water was taking their life in their hands.

THE 'CATTLE RAID OF COOLEY'

The tale of the 'Cattle Raid of Cooley', or Táin Bó Cuailnge, is considered the greatest of Cú Chulainn's legendary feats. It also gives an insight into some facets of Celtic life in Ireland. Among these is the concept that wealth should ideally be balanced between husband and wife. This was the case with Queen Medb of Connacht and her husband Ailill, and had it remained so everyone would have been much happier. However, a good story needs conflict as a driving force, and this had its roots in a decision made by Finnbennach, a magical white-horned bull.

Finnbennach was once a man named Rucht, a swineherd who quarrelled with his rival, Fruich. This was no trivial dispute; it took on a supernatural aspect that continued even when they were transformed into other creatures. While in the form of a water-worm, Rucht advised Medb to marry Ailill and shortly afterwards he was eaten by a cow. This resulted in Rucht being born as the magical bull Finnbennach.

Finnbennach was part of the herd owned by Medb and formed a significant part of her wealth. For whatever reason, Finnbennach disliked being owned by Medb and made it known he wanted to be part of her husband's herd. This created a disparity in wealth, which Medb tried to rectify by sending emissaries to Ulster in the hope of trading for Donn Cuailnge – the magical brown bull of Cooley.

Ulster was not willing to make the trade, so Medb resolved to steal the bull instead. Despite prophetic warnings that disaster would ensue, she sent her army into Ulster. The timing seemed to be in Connaught's favour as the warriors of Ulster were out of action at that point. This was due to a curse called the Pangs of Ulster. Depending on the version of the tale, a woman, goddess or supernatural person named Macha had suffered terribly as a result of her husband's boastfulness.

This man was Crunnchua who was at a horse race and overheard the King saying that nothing could run faster than his horses. Rather unwisely, Crunnchua bragged that his wife – then heavily pregnant – could. The King called him on this boast, and a race was organized. Macha was willing to race a horse (or chariot in some versions) but asked that the event be postponed until she had given birth.

This request was denied, and Macha raced the horses. She won, but gave birth on the finishing line and, in some versions of the tale, died. Her suffering resulted in a curse that every five years the men of Ulster would feel the pain of childbirth – for the next nine generations.

Cú Chulainn Fights the Connaughts

Being made of less stern stuff than Macha, the men of Ulster were unable to defend their homes or cattle against Medb's warriors. Cú Chulainn was not affected by the curse, and launched a single-handed guerrilla campaign that delayed and depleted the advancing Connaught army. He sniped at them with his sling and raided their camp, and made such a nuisance of himself that the men of Connaught negotiated a deal. They would send a champion to fight Cú Chulainn at a prearranged spot, and were permitted to continue their march while the warrior was still alive. Once Cú Chulainn killed his opponent, as he surely would, the army would halt until a new champion was found.

Although suicide for the champion, this reduced casualties among the men of Connaught while allowing them to make some progress. The Morrigan became involved at this point, offering assistance to Cú Chulainn if he accepted her sexual advances. He did not, so she used her magic to impede him. As a result, Cú Chulainn was wounded during a fight with a warrior named Loch. The army of Connaught continued to advance.

Cú Chulainn and Ferdiad Mac Damann

Eventually Connaught sent Ferdiad Mac Damann against Cú Chulainn. Ferdiad was his foster brother, under the system of fostering the children of powerful families among their allies and friends. Cú Chulainn did not want to fight but was threatened with being satirized by bards powerful enough to destroy his reputation. For the first two days of their battle, the heroes fought, but then dressed each other's wounds in the evening and slept under the same blanket.

This can be interpreted in many ways. It may be an illustration of the close bond between foster brothers, or something more. The ancient Celts did not seem to have any hang-ups about same-sex relationships, other than when they destroyed a marriage. Whatever was the case, the two did not sleep together after the third day, and on the fourth Ferdiad came close to killing Cú Chulainn. He was downed and badly wounded, and forced to take desperate measures. Cú Chulainn had a magic spear named Gae

Bolg, which was thrown with his foot. Depending on the account, it had thirty barbs or multiple heads. Either way, it rent Ferdiad's body and slew him.

In the end, it was all for nothing. The army of Connaught reached Ulster and took possession of the brown bull Donn Cuailnge. As a last-ditch measure, Ulster sent out a force made up of boys too young to be affected by the curse, who were easily swept aside by the warriors of Connaught. Cú Chulainn was furious and killed seventy of the enemy, but Ulster was plundered and the bull carried off.

Cú Chulainn led a pursuit once the men of Ulster were able to join him, and defeated the army of Connaught. He spared Queen Medb, which he would later regret. In the meantime, the two magical bulls had fought. Finnbennach, the bull of Connaught, was defeated and slain. Donn Cuailnge was mortally wounded, surviving only long enough to get home. The conflict left nobody with a magical bull and countless warriors dead on both sides.

Cú Chulainn and the Curse

The tale of Cú Chulainn also includes a curse or *geis* as a plot device, something still common in popular entertainment. One geis caused Cú Chulainn to kill his own son. This was Connla, who came from the union of Cú Chulainn and Aife. The boy was under a geis not to reveal his name, and also never to back down from a fight. When he was seven years old, he was sent to Cú Chulainn, who for whatever reason thought he was a threat. When the child refused to reveal his name Cú Chulainn hurled Gae Bolg at him and slew his own son.

Another geis – that Cú Chulainn could not eat dog meat but also could not decline any offer of hospitality – led to his death in one of the most epic last stands of all time. He was tricked into accepting food that contained dog meat, thereby breaking his geis and weakening him. Depending on the version of the tale, he was goaded into throwing Gae Bolg at satirists who were taunting him or he was attacked with magical spears created specifically to kill kings. His enemies were warriors serving Queen Medb or whose relatives he had previously killed. Whether it was his own spear flung back at him or specially made kingslayers, Cú Chulainn's charioteer and his horse – both 'kings' in the sense of being the greatest of their kind – were slain and he was pierced by the third cast. A spear, possibly the barbed Gae Bolg, tore open his belly. Cú Chulainn used his own entrails to tie himself to a boulder so that he could remain upright. Although they were now enemies, the Morrigan appears to have greatly respected Cú Chulainn. She took the form of a raven and sat on his shoulder while he was still alive, and it was not until she flew away from his corpse that any of his enemies dared approach.

THE FENIAN CYCLE

The Fenian Cycle revolves around Fionn mac Cumhaill in a later era of Irish mythological history. He was a descendant of King Nuada and had special hunting hounds named Bran and Sceólang. Their mother, Fionn's aunt Uirne, had been turned into a dog while pregnant. Although she returned to human form, her children did not. They proved intelligent and loyal companions to Fionn mac Cumhaill. This concept of animals who are family members is encountered outside Celtic mythology; the Norse god

Odin's horse Sleipnir is – by way of a truly bizarre set of events – also his nephew.

Fionn mac Cumhaill demonstrated his worth through heroic feats that gained him a magic banner and sword, and he thereby became clan chief. Fionn mac Cumhaill possessed the Oxter Bag, one of the treasures of Ireland. No matter what the owner needed, all he had to do was reach into the bag and it would be there.

As a youth, Fionn mac Cumhaill gained great knowledge as a result of an accident. He had been helping Finn Eces, a great poet or bard, cook the Salmon of Wisdom. Finn Eces had been trying to catch the supernatural fish for seven years, but when he finally succeeded he was robbed of his prize. Fionn burned his thumb and reflexively put it in his mouth, thereby gaining the knowledge of the salmon.

The vast knowledge now possessed by Fionn mac Cumhaill allowed him to defeat a supernatural enemy named Aillén Mac Midgna who had been terrorizing Tara, seat of the High Kings of Ireland. On each Samhain for 23 years, Aillén Mac Midgna would burn Tara's halls. He rendered the defenders helpless by playing one of the Noble Strains on the harp, sending everyone to sleep. He then breathed fire on the walls and retired to the Otherworld to plan further mischief.

One of the warriors at Tara, a man named Fiacha, had a poisoned spear that could kill Aillén Mac Midgna, but like everyone else he was rendered helpless by the strains of the harp. Fionn inhaled the fumes from the spear, which rendered him temporarily immune to the Noble Strains. He was then able to ambush Aillén Mac Midgna and stab him. For this deed, Fionn was given command over the Fianna Éireann, a band of elite warriors once led by his father.

Like other heroes, Fionn mac Cumhaill was something of a maverick. He caused a war by having an affair with the French king's wife, leading to a battle that lasted a year and a day. Eventually, the French were driven out by the intervention of the Tuatha Dé Danann. Fionn mac Cumhaill also became rather spiteful in his later years, leading to the murder-by-wilful-negligence of Diarmuid, one of his warriors who really deserved better. Diarmuid is credited with slaying hundreds of warriors in a single battle and saving Fionn's life. He was by all accounts a decent and loyal man whose foster father was the god Aengus Óg.

Gráinne and Diarmuid

Fionn invited Gráinne, daughter of the Irish High King, to his court hoping she would become his lover or wife, but Gráinne was more attracted to Diarmuid. The loyal warrior declined her advances but gave in when Gráinne used a geis on him. The lovers fled with the aid of a cloak of invisibility. When he found them, Fionn mac Cumhaill was persuaded by Aengus Óg not to take vengeance. However, Fionn still harboured resentment. During a boar hunt near Benbulben in County Sligo, Diarmuid was gored and mortally wounded. It was in Fionn mac Cumhaill's power to save him, as water drunk from his hands had healing properties. Twice he let the water run through his fingers, and by the time he relented and tried to let Diarmuid drink it was too late.

The tale of Diarmuid and Gráinne is remarkably similar to the story of Tristan and Iseult, which forms part of the King Arthur narrative. Both tales may have a common origin. There are other parallels with the Arthur legend. In some versions of his story, Fionn mac Cumhaill does not die but instead sleeps in a secret place awaiting his return. Other variants end in a violent demise. One version again involves a geis, this time not to drink from a horn. Fionn does so and smashes his head on rocks while attempting to jump the River Boyne.

A rather more heroic, if reprehensible, version has Fionn acting as kingmaker. As the leader of the Fianna Éireann, bodyguard of the High King of Ireland, he was one of the most powerful people in the land. A man named Caibre had ambitions of becoming the next High King, and Fionn was willing to help him in return either for a large amount of money or the right to sleep with Caibre's daughter. This escalated into open conflict as Caibre and other Irish leaders tried to break the power of the Fianna, and eventually Fionn mac Cumhaill was either ambushed or killed in battle.

THE BEGINNINGS OF RECORDED IRISH HISTORY

At some point the myths cross over into real history, or at least touch upon it. The mythological events are particularly difficult to pin down due to a lack of non-contradictory external references. The Celts began moving into Ireland around 500 BCE, so it can be assumed the myths of invasion and conquest equate to that period. However, some stories appear to allude to the aftermath of the Siege of Troy, though others apparently took place shortly after Noah and his followers escaped the Great Flood. This places them much earlier in the mythical timeline.

Time does not seem to work the same in the mythical world as in the natural world, often as a result of retellings, conflations, confusion or agenda on the part of observers. It may be best to consider history and the ancient myths as a panorama seen from a tall hill. What is close by can be discerned quite clearly and details confirmed. More distant parts of the scene are blurry and may be obscured by mist, clouds, smoke from the fires of war or intervening terrain. Looking at two points the same distance apart but close by, we can be reasonably sure they are within the same time frame. On the other hand, two parts of the far horizon, though each the same distance from our viewpoint, are not necessarily as far from us as from one another.

Just as distance blurs the far horizon, so does time – and to a varying degree. How much blurring occurs depends on what records remain and how reliable they are. There are ways to bring these distant places closer, at least apparently, but each lens has its flaws. Archaeology may present a different image of a given time to folktales from the same era, and the formal records of outside observers may present yet another distorted image. In short, the further back we look, the more difficult it becomes to determine anything for certain.

The pre-Celtic people of Ireland built megalithic structures but left no other records of their lives, and the early Celtic settlers likewise did not write anything down. Some of the structures left behind were intended to venerate the dead, others were designed to align with the sun or moon on certain days of the year. Whether this was to accurately determine solstices and equinoxes – which would be important to an agricultural society – or to exploit the extraordinary conditions believed to be in force on those days is uncertain.

It seems likely there was no 'Celtic invasion' as such, but a gradual 'Celticization' resulting from newcomers with their advanced weaponry settling in Ireland and rising to the top of local power structures. These would form the basis of the

Celtic tribes who controlled Ireland in Roman times. The Romans referred to Ireland as Hibernia and its people as Scoti and, although they never conquered Ireland – nor, apparently, made any serious attempt to – they interacted with the Scoti from time to time. There are records of an Irish prince-in-exile accompanying Agricola in his campaigns on the British mainland.

The Celtic people of Ireland, Wales and Scotland were sometimes collectively known as Gaels, though the term was at times used more specifically. There was considerable interaction with what are now Wales and Scotland, which sometimes had wider implications. Indeed, the modern country of Scotland got its name as a result of these interactions.

The Great Conspiracy

Late in the Roman era, as the power of the Empire was waning, Romano-Britain came under attack from multiple sources. This was described as the Great Conspiracy, or Barbarian Conspiracy. A Saxon force arrived from mainland Europe while Picts or Caledones crossed Hadrian's Wall and marched south. The Scoti also sent forces, and the combined weight of barbarian warriors overwhelmed Roman forces in the north and west.

Rome responded by sending a force to secure its province, which may have included future Emperor Magnus Maximus. After establishing a headquarters at Londinium, the Romans discovered that the Great Conspiracy, if ever it had been well organized, had become a general free-for-all of pillage and personal advancement. Local imperial forces had in some cases joined in due to a collapse in morale and faith in the Empire, or because they had not been paid for an extended period.

There was no large army to fight, so the Roman force was divided into detachments that chased down the bands of raiders. Those who had defected to join the barbarians were offered amnesty so long as they assisted in pacifying Britannia. There were also expeditions into the north of Britain, supported by naval operations, though these appear to have been punitive rather than an attempt at conquest.

It is largely through Roman records that Irish history of the period is known, though once Christianity took hold records began to be kept. It is likely that Christian missionaries were active in Ireland before the Roman withdrawal from the British Isles, though the earliest certain record is of a bishop sent by the Pope in 430 CE.

CHRISTIANITY IN THE CELTIC WORLD

Christianity spread throughout the Roman world despite opposition from the Empire, and after the Edict of Milan, issued by Constantine the Great in 313 CE, could be practised without penalty. The Romanized Britons were relatively receptive, but spreading the faith among the Celtic peoples of the British Isles was a difficult undertaking. Perhaps not coincidentally, a large number of saints are associated with Christianizing various regions. Among them is St Ninian (d. 432 CE) who is credited with bringing Christianity to Scotland.

Saint Patrick

Saint Patrick is credited with popularizing Christianity in Ireland, which was accomplished by making it palatable to the Celts.

Patrick integrated elements of the existing belief system with Christian tenets, laying the foundations for the Celtic Church, which was highly influential over the next decades. Exactly when he did this is open to debate, with 'sometime in the fifth century' being the general consensus. An official arrival date of 432 CE is recorded in the *Annals of the Kingdom of Ireland*, with his death placed anywhere between 460 and 493 CE.

Patrick was apparently captured by Irish pirates and enslaved as an animal-herd for several years. After escaping, he became a churchman and returned to Ireland as a missionary. He was hugely influential in the spread of Christianity and became known as the patron saint of Ireland – although he was never formally canonized. As a result of his work, Ireland gained a literate class, though as servants of the Christian Church they were biased in its favour. Some of the old Celtic legends were amended to better fit within the Christian timeline and agenda.

Much of the sea travel undertaken by early missionaries was rather more voluntary than Patrick's voyage to Ireland. Monasteries on the coasts of Ireland, Wales and Scotland were able to remain in contact with one another, and the Scottish islands – notably Iona – became a major centre for the emerging Church. There are records of Irish monks even setting up a community in Iceland. This was before the Norsemen discovered it, and the monks are said to have swiftly departed once they did.

The spread of Christianity suffered a major setback with the Great Conspiracy of 367–368 CE. The influence of Germanic paganism was increased for a time as a result of warriors from the Continent arriving in Britain. Similarly, Norse raids – which began in 793 CE – caused enormous damage to the Church. The Norsemen have been portrayed as 'enemies of God' for their attacks on monasteries, but the reality is far more mundane. Monasteries were rich, poorly defended and often in remote locations where the arrival of assistance was unlikely. The fact that many were built on the coast, in easy reach of a longship-borne raiding party, made them targets no self-respecting raider could pass up.

Celtic versus Roman Church

The 'Celtic Church' had a different flavour to that of Rome. One of the main differences was a lack of unity. Whereas the Roman Church was strict, formal and organized, the Celtic Church might better be described as 'local variations on the mainstream Church, with a Celtic undertone but no strong organization'. There were some factors in common, such as the timing of Easter, but otherwise there was no single Celtic Church.

The difference between Roman and local Celtic practices could be problematic. Some members of a household might be celebrating Easter while others were still fasting for Lent. The decision to create a definitive calculation was accompanied, at the Synod of Whitby in 633/634 CE, by a choice that the Anglo-Saxon kingdoms of England would follow Roman practices.

The lack of organization was ultimately what doomed the Celtic Church. The Roman Church was a powerful ally for the kings of the time while the local Celtic variation was just that – a local preference. However, Celtic influences did not disappear. Many of the great religious books created in the British Isles were decorated in Celtic fashion. The most notable of these was the *Book of Kells*, a manuscript containing the New Testament and associated material in Latin.

Exactly when the *Book of Kells* was created is open to debate. Traditionally, it is believed that the book was created on Iona but moved to the monastery at Kells to protect it from Norse raids. It is referred to in the *Annals of Ulster* as the great Gospel of Saint Columba. The *Book of Kells* was stolen in 1007 CE and later recovered minus its jewelled cover.

Christian Influence on Celtic Mythology

Much of what is known about the Celtic world was recorded by churchmen, such as the Venerable Bede (c. 673–735 CE) and Gildas, with later writers drawing upon the work of their predecessors. Misconceptions and biases were thereby continued and magnified. In many cases, the Celtic world is glimpsed only in passing as the writer was concerned with affairs more closely related to the Church. For example, Bede's *Historia ecclesiastica gentis Anglorum*, or *Ecclesiastical History of the English People*, has a clear purpose but touches upon mundane matters for context.

It may be that the Church had an influence on Celtic mythology, in the sense that mythical creatures and events were conflated with those familiar to Christians. Alternatively, churchmen may have played down the power and magnificence of some creatures, converting them into playful or spiteful minor spirits. Some medieval writers considered the 'wee folk' to be disgraced angels, while others stated they were spirits of the departed.

Modern Halloween has its origins in the Celtic festival of Samhain, by way of Christian superstition. The dead and various frightening spirits were thought to be abroad on All Hallows' Eve, and the practices of bribery with sweet things and dressing up were originally to do with protection from them. By disguising themselves as fellow monsters, people could hide from the more malicious creatures, while others might be placated with treats left outside the house.

The Christian Church both preserved and distorted the memories of the Celtic world, and left us with at least as many questions as answers. The meaning of the Celtic Cross is one. Some say it symbolizes the victory of Christianity over the old gods. In this interpretation, the ring is the sun, associated with the god Lugh. Others say the ring represents Christ's halo, though why Celtic crosses would depict this where others did not is an open question. The Celtic Cross is commonest in previously Celtic areas, but is today used elsewhere. It seems to have become a standard Christian symbol, as has the practice of using 'Celtic' style decoration in the form of swirls.

IRISH-SCOTTISH CONNECTIONS

The relative ease of crossing between north-eastern Ireland and south-western Scotland made cultural interactions and the creation of power structures inevitable. Greatest of these was the Kingdom of Dál Riata. It is said to have been founded in the fifth century CE, and reached its greatest extent in the sixth and seventh centuries. It is probable that the hillfort at Dunadd was its capital.

Dunadd was a good choice, providing a clear view in all directions and a significant obstacle for attackers. Even unencumbered by war gear, climbing the hill required considerable effort unless the obvious path was used. This ran across the least steep face of the hill, forcing intruders to run the gauntlet of objects thrown from above and arrive strung out while the defenders could muster in a group at the head of the path. While it was no stone castle, Dunadd was a secure location in which to find refuge. Visitors labouring up the hillside to meet the royalty of Dál Riata could hardly fail to be impressed.

The Kingdom of Dál Riata

The Kingdom of Dál Riata also contained the monastery on the island of Iona, where the *Book of Kells* may have been created. Iona was an important centre for early Christianity in Britain, with monks travelling to Ireland and Scotland aboard small but generally seaworthy vessels. The kingdom had a large fleet that was used to secure its territory and sometimes to conduct raids against rival polities.

Dál Riata suffered a heavy defeat at the Battle of Degsastan in 603 CE. At the head of a coalition including Irish and Briton forces, Dál Riata confronted Aethelfrith, King of Northumbria. Aethelfrith is recorded as being a savage tyrant who routinely attacked his neighbours. His army was smaller than the Dál Riatan force, but inflicted a tremendous defeat at a location that remains unclear. Most of the Dál Riatan force was slain, and the kingdom became subordinate to Northumbria thereafter. Its decline was hastened by a series of defeats, and, by 741 CE, Dál Riata was overrun by the Picts.

The Kingdom of Alba

There may or may not have been a Dál Riatan revival in the mid-700s, but the kingdom's maritime location became a liability once Norse raids began. With their superior vessels, the Norsemen could land wherever they pleased, then pillage and depart before an effective response could be mounted. Where there were clashes, the forces of Dál Riata were generally outfought by the Norsemen. Towards the end of the 800s, Dál Riata joined with Pictland to create the Kingdom of Alba.

Alba suffered further Norse raids, but was able for the most part to repel or withstand them. Its territory stretched from the north-east tip of mainland Scotland to Argyll in the south-west, though gradually the northern isles were taken over by Norse settlers. By the end of the 'Viking Era' – marked by the Norman conquest of England – Alba was a strong kingdom that expanded to take control of Cumbria, Lothian and Strathclyde. By this time, it was discovering a new identity. The kings of Alba became known as Kings of the Scots and in time Alba itself became Scotland.

The Five Kingdoms of Ireland

Ireland gradually coalesced into five kingdoms. Ulaid lay in the north-east and gave its name to modern Ulster. Like the other kingdoms, its fortunes waxed and waned. After Ireland was conquered by the Normans, Ulaid became the Earldom of Ulster. It was bordered to the west by Connaught, which today is one of the provinces of modern Ireland. Conflict between Connaught and Ulaid lies at the heart of the 'Cattle Raid of Cooley' story.

To the south of Connaught lay Mumhan, which is now the modern province of Munster, and to the east of Munster was Laighin, or Leinster. In the centre was Mide. The identities of these kingdoms changed over time, as did their relative power. Each was composed of smaller kingdoms ruled by an overking, and those kingdoms contained tribes and clans whose relations with one another might not always be cordial.

The High King at Tara

Above this hierarchy of chieftains and kings was the High King, whose seat was at Tara in what is now County Meath. The High King theoretically had sovereignty over all of Ireland, but in practice there were challenges and bargains, with the real power sometimes in the hands of someone who did not hold the title of High King. The Stone of Destiny, which, according to legend, cried out when touched by a true king, was held at Tara and used to determine the worthiness of a successor. Tara features prominently in Irish mythology as well as history. Legendary kings ruled from there and heroes visited. In history, Tara was a symbol of overlordship until at least the eleventh century. Thereafter, other political and economic centres such as Dublin and Limerick became more significant.

For a great many years the high kingship was held by the Uí Néill dynasties, whose pedigree went back to Niall of the Nine Hostages. Niall of the Nine Hostages appears to have been a historical figure, though accounts differ on when he reigned. Sometime in the late fourth century seems likely. It was not until late in the tenth century that his dynasty was replaced. This was the work of Brian Boru (c. 941–1014), who unified Ireland in a military campaign and led the Irish resistance to Norse incursions.

Norse Raids and the Norman Invasion

Norse raids in Ireland began around 795 CE, with settlers taking over coastal areas in later years. They did not come as a unified force, so settler groups became part of the local political landscape and got involved in the feuds and conflicts ongoing in their areas. At this time, there were well over a hundred leaders in Ireland sufficiently powerful to be called kings, and their overkings could command only loose allegiance much of the time.

In 1013 CE, an alliance of Norse warriors from the Dublin region and an army from Leinster attacked Boru's kingdom. The war went on into the next year, culminating in the Battle of Clontarf. This pitted the well-armoured Norsemen against the more numerous Irish, and ended in victory for Brian Boru after hard fighting. Additional casualties were inflicted on the Norsemen as they attempted to retreat, though Boru himself was killed. The Battle of Clontarf greatly diminished the power of the Norsemen in Ireland, but Boru's kingdom also declined. The High Kingship was seized by the Uí Néill dynasty.

In 1169 CE, the Norman invasion of Ireland began, leading to a period of harsh rule by the conquerors. Under the dominion of the Normans and the English, Irish culture was at times deliberately suppressed. Yet for all that, the myths and history of the Celtic people survived into modern times. Ireland, Scotland and south-western Britain remain Celtic stronglands to this day; places where the old languages are spoken and traditions are preserved.

LEGACY OF THE CELTS

The Celts of the Hallstatt and La Tène cultures are long gone, as are the Britons and the Gauls of the Roman era, but they continue to be hugely influential on the modern world. There is still much evidence of their lives to be uncovered by archaeologists working from Spain to Turkey, which may expand our understanding of ancient cultures and the history of Europe. There are also living traditions which have their origins in the Celtic way of life and, most particularly, in the tales told by the bards. These are the two main components of the Celtic legacy – the physical and the cultural. Whilst the physical remains of the Celts may not intrude into our modern lives very often – at least not obviously – their cultural legacy helped shape the modern world.

PHYSICAL LEGACY

The physical legacy includes a genetic component. A high percentage of people in Europe, though less elsewhere in the world, have a significant number of Celtic genes. This is particularly true in Ireland, Wales and Scotland as might be expected. The 'Celtic' traits described by ancient Roman writers – a tendency to be tall and have red or reddish hair – can come from other lineages of course, but there is a tendency to describe someone with these traits as a Celt even by those who have little idea what it means.

For the most part, the physical legacy consists of objects that have survived through the centuries. Many of these are mundane: tools and weapons or the remains of structures. It is possible to infer a great deal about Celtic society from these items. They made clothing in bright colours with a complex weave. There is no absolute need to do that; plain and simple clothing will keep the wearer just as warm. The ancient Celts must have cared about their appearance and delighted in beautiful things just for the sake of them.

We know that personal jewellery was common in Celtic society, and not just among the top echelons of society. As with clothing, functional items were decorated. There had to be a reason for this; a cloak pin is a cloak pin. Items that take longer to make represent additional work for the creator and therefore cost more. This is not the same as having greater intrinsic value – no matter how well decorated it may be, that cloak pin is still just a cloak pin. A plain one will do the same job, but what it will not do is attract admiring comments from other members of society or make the wearer feel good for owning it.

It is therefore clear that the ancient Celts were at least a little bit materialistic. This is no bad thing unless it gets out of hand and becomes runaway consumerism. They liked beautiful things and – it can be safely assumed – considered them to be status symbols. That has not changed into the modern era, and while a liking for fine clothes and objects admired by others is not a uniquely Celtic legacy, their society was one of those that eventually led to ours. Had the Celts preferred to dress in plain homespun and use only the most functional of items, our own society might have been different.

The physical legacy also includes items cast away for religious purposes, such as weapons, shields and the occasional human sacrifice found in bogs or bodies of water. There are also the remains of structures and everyday objects such as coins. We can learn a lot from these items (and bodies), but they have little direct impact on our modern world.

Perhaps the most impactful component of the physical legacy can go unnoticed. The ancient Celts flourished at a time when populations were expanding, and they moved into areas which had previously been sparsely inhabited – or not at all. They built their homes in logical places: on good farmland, near river crossings or close to easily obtained resources such as salt or iron. These places were rarely abandoned, though they may have been taken over by other societies.

This hidden legacy takes the form of communities all over Europe. The pattern of settlement, and in some cases even modern street layouts, can be traced back to the Celtic era when these towns and cities were first founded. We live on the same land they did, and often in the very same places. The world has changed in many ways, but the mountains, seas and rivers are the same for us as they were for our Celtic ancestors. Celtic origins can also be discerned in place names – a name ending in 'dun' indicates it was once a fort or strong place of the Celts, and many modern cities take their names from the tribes who once dwelled there.

The physical legacy also includes monuments such as carved stones, which serve as a reminder that others were here before us. The artistic patterns created by ancient craftsmen still survive in many cases, and can inspire modern creativity. Celtic-style art and jewellery may go in and out of fashion, but it never seems to fade away. It might be possible to come up with all manner of wild theories about ancient secrets locked in Celtic symbols, but it is more likely that the Celts simply made what they found pleasing and that modern people have similar tastes.

HISTORICAL LEGACY

The ancient Celts left an enormous historical legacy. They were on the losing side of many historical events, but their actions still helped shape those events. In many cases, the incident and its consequences have been completely forgotten. We may never know about the band of Celtic mercenaries who took part in a particular battle or expedition, or the trader who introduced an influential concept to people who later made great use of it. These people were 'there', and their actions, ideas and culture influenced the course of history in a multitude of small ways.

Greater events are known. The ancient Celts are credited with inventing chain mail armour, and may have created other important inventions. Whether or not they did come up with the idea of the animal-drawn heavy plough, they made good use of it, which would inspire others to do the same. The Hallstatt-era Celts may have learned about ironworking from others, but they helped popularize it.

The Iron Age dawned at different times in different places as the skills and techniques for ironworking spread across Europe. Switching from bronze to iron was no small matter, so a demonstration of the benefits was required. Again, this was not a uniquely Celtic endeavour, but their adoption of the new material helped make it prevalent. Had they made different decisions, the Iron Age might have occurred earlier or later, with huge repercussions for other societies.

The Celtic invasions of Greece and Italia were pivotal moments in world history. Had a successor to Alexander the Great's empire – or a significant part of it – emerged they might have created a stable state in the eastern Mediterranean. It is interesting to wonder if Rome could have risen so high in that world, or what might have been, if the sack of Rome by Brennus and his followers had been more thorough.

It is inevitable that accounts of the period focus on the societies that left a comprehensive written record, such as the Greeks and the Romans, but decisions made in Celtic hillforts were just as critical as the proceedings of the Roman Senate. What if a particular tribe had opposed Rome instead of allying? Would Julius Caesar have been able to build his legend? Might the Roman invasion of the British Isles have ended in ignominious retreat?

It is possible that, given enough time and outside influences, the loose alliances of tribes might have grown into medieval-style kingdoms or even empires. Alternatively, Europe might have remained a tribal land for much longer. Europeans would no doubt have arrived on other continents at some point, but conditions there might have been quite different if it had happened a few centuries later. The might-have-beens are intriguing, though beyond a certain point it is impossible to say what would have occurred. It is, however, possible to determine some might-not-have-beens. Had the Celtic tribes made different choices, our history would have been set upon an entirely different path.

CULTURAL LEGACY

The **greatest legacy** of the Celtic peoples is cultural. Many of the elements that have survived into the modern era are not uniquely Celtic but their transmission into our time owes much to the Celts and those who interacted with them. In many cases, this legacy is not recognized at all. There are plenty of people who celebrate modern Halloween without ever knowing – or caring about – the origins of the festival.

Many elements of Celtic mythology have found their way into what might be termed modern popular mythology. This is a composite of bits and pieces from all over the world, lumped together without much regard to context and used by creators of entertainment as they see fit. Game designers, moviemakers and authors routinely borrow from this mythological grab-bag, incorporating Druids, dragons and vampires into a story – or whatever other mix suits their purposes.

Modern popular mythology is also used outside entertainment. Advertisers may decide to incorporate a cute fairy or a grumpy troll in their efforts to sell us anything from high-performance vehicles to cough syrup. These elements are so embedded in our cultural psyche that we take them for granted. Likewise, mythical places, people and objects can be a handy shorthand for someone telling a story or selling us something. Odin's spear, the Dagda's cauldron of plenty or a manuscript from ancient Troy are easily recognizable without explanation.

Modern Popular Mythology

All of these elements got into the modern popular mythology somehow. The usual route seems to have been folktales written down by outsiders or by literate people late in the Celtic era. Historical accounts also sometimes mention beliefs and cultural practices in passing. It is also possible to make inferences from writings about better-documented societies, using fragmentary references to discern similarities. However, this approach does require many assumptions to be made.

Other elements of the Celtic way of life and worldview came down to us through historical records. Most of what we know about the Continental Celts was written by Romans, while the histories of the Insular Celts are at least alluded to by the writings of Christian scholars. These include the *Anglo-Saxon Chronicle*, which was created in the ninth century. It naturally focuses on the Anglo-Saxon kingdoms of eastern England but, since they interacted with both Celtic and Norse peoples, their chronicles give at least a glimpse of those societies.

The *Annals of Ulster* and the *Book of Leinster* provide a more direct insight. The former covers a period from around 430 CE to 1460, with earlier sections drawing on previous works. The *Book of Leinster* was created around 1160 CE and contains the tale of the 'Cattle Raid of Cooley'. These, along with other historical works, concentrate on the lives and deeds of kings. They give an impression of the 'big picture' of what was going on in Ireland at the time. Sources of this kind rarely tell us much about the daily lives of ordinary people.

Some insight can be gained from folktales, endlessly repeated through the generations and spread wherever people liked a good story. These would contain elements of mythology and religion, but should be treated with caution regarding what people actually believed. These tales were the books, games and movies of the era, and may present as distorted a picture of contemporary society as the typical Hollywood blockbuster.

Nevertheless, elements of Celtic mythology are still with us. The 'Celtic Revival' of the nineteenth century drew upon sources that might well be considered rather flawed, and modern representations still tend to be influenced by this image. The writer Sir Arthur Conan Doyle (1859–1930 CE) was part of a spiritualist revival and was instrumental in making popular the 'Cottingley Fairies'. These were photographs which apparently showed dainty winged creatures of a sort most people would associate with the word 'fairy'. The photographs remain controversial despite an admission that they were faked.

This impression of the 'fairy folk' as beautiful and benign or harmless creatures is very different from the nervous superstition of the ancient Celts. Today's leprechauns are jolly little men who like to play pranks on mortals and have a pot of gold hidden at the end of the rainbow. Early stories referencing them have leprechauns carrying off children or abducting adults. Like the rest of what can loosely be described as the fairy folk, they are dangerous.

The idea of a hidden realm, perhaps underground, pervades modern popular mythology and may be derived from other sources than the Celtic Sidhe. Endless stories revolve around humans getting caught up in the affairs of the otherworldly folk, sometimes explicitly the Celtic ones and sometimes a more general 'fae folk' based upon the concept.

Later writers have drawn heavily upon works influenced by these myths and folktales. Particularly influential was *The Faerie Queene*, an epic poem by Edmund Spenser (1552–99 CE). This is one of the longest poems in English, though the original intent was for it to be even longer. It was written as a rather blatant attempt to win favour – and money – from Queen Elizabeth I, but was described by its author as being an allegorical guide to fine and gentlemanly conduct. Relatively modern works, including science fiction movies, reference the chivalry and other virtues of Spenser's characters.

The Mabinogion and the Arthur Stories

The two most influential bodies of work, in terms of transmitting Celtic ideas and mythology into the modern era, are the *Mabinogion* and the *Matter of Britain*. The former takes its name from four of the 11 tales contained within it. These are known as the *Four Branches of the Mabinogi*, with 'branch' in this case meaning 'part'. These four stories are interrelated, forming a mythical history of Wales and the surrounding lands. The tales are traditional, with the earliest dating from the eleventh century, though the *Mabinogion* was first published in English in 1840. Most of the other stories concern the legendary King Arthur.

The *Matter of Britain* revolves around the mythical Arthur figure. It owes a great deal to Welsh mythology and traditional tales originating there, but the Arthur stories concern the whole of the British Isles and touch on elements of history corroborated by other writings and archaeological evidence. It is unlikely there ever was a single person identifiable as the 'real King Arthur', but there are parallels with real events in the stories as well as incidents echoed in other mythology.

Many versions of the Arthur story have emerged; in some Arthur dies, and in others he journeys to the magical land of Avalon to await the time when he will be needed again. These conflicting variants are further confused by later reinterpretations and the incorporation of tales from other cultures. The legends of King Arthur lie somewhat outside the ancient Celtic myths yet are heavily influenced by them, much as later society adopted various Celtic concepts.

Arthur, Mythical King of the Britons

The Arthur story begins – in the sense that a recognizable Arthur character appears – in the *Historia Brittonum*. This is attributed to Nennius, who lived around 800 CE and was strongly connected with the Church in Wales. Literacy at that time was only common among churchmen, but, despite his Christian background, Nennius would be familiar with the mythology and the folktales of the Welsh people. It is not clear whether *Historia Brittonum* was Nennius's own work or if he compiled earlier writings.

In this work, Arthur is not a king but a war leader defending Britain against Saxon invaders. The story is therefore set around 500 CE. This Arthur is not the chivalrous knight depicted in most modern versions of the tale; the code of chivalry would not be developed for several centuries. Nor is he a 'knight in shining armour' – articulated plate did not exist. The Arthur of the *Historia Brittonum* is a Celtic or Romano-British warrior equipped with a coat of chain mail, a large shield, a spear and a sword.

The *Historia Brittonum* was written by a churchman, and naturally has a Christian agenda. Arthur was fighting against the invading Saxons, whose depredations are described by Nennius as resulting from over-indulgence and lack of piety on the part of the leaders of the Britons. Arthur is a war leader in the service of his brother, Uther Pendragon. In later versions of the tale, Uther is the name of Arthur's father.

Arthur is most definitely a hero in this tale, though his great victories over the Saxons are ascribed to divine favour rather than personal fighting ability. Whatever the origin of his prowess, this Arthur performs great feats of arms that echo the actions of other legendary Celtic heroes such as Cù Chulainn and Fionn mac Cumhaill. Indeed, there are parallels to many other legends, which suggests a certain amount of cross-pollination.

It is possible the hero-tales of this era were based – if rather loosely – on the exploits of real warriors. A nobleman trained for war and equipped with the best armour and weapons had a huge advantage over poorly armed commoners. Although described as warriors, most of these people would be farmers or minor craftsmen who were following their leaders out of obligation. Equipped with a spear, shield and perhaps a knife or hand axe as a backup weapon, these men would be a match for a similarly out-of-their-depth opponent but hopelessly outclassed against a professional or – worse – a group of professionals practised in working together.

The primary weapon of the professional warrior was the same spear everyone else was using, but how they used it made all the difference. A professional made fewer 'rookie mistakes' and even if something went wrong they might avoid serious injury due to their armour or the intervention of a skilled friend. It is entirely possible that tales told at the after-battle feast, speaking of dozens of enemies slain with spear or sword, might not be exaggerated. For people who had seen someone they knew defeat 10 men, a hero who could slay 100 or even 1,000 would seem at least borderline plausible.

There are various candidates for a 'real Arthur' of this era. Among them is a Romano-British noble named Ambrosius Aurelianus. According to the accounts of the era, Ambrosius led

the Romano-Britons to a great victory over the Saxons at a place
called Badon Hill. This battle has become part of the Arthur
legend, though its location is unknown.

As previously stated, the first reference to Arthur as a king
rather than a war leader is found in the *Historia Regum Britanniae*
(*History of the Kings of Britain*), by Geoffrey of Monmouth. Like
Nennius, he was a churchman connected with Wales. Geoffrey
of Monmouth was writing after the Norman conquest of most of
Britain, and was influenced by the technology of the time.

The battlefield of 1136 was dominated by armoured cavalry,
who might be described as 'knights' though they did not have
the chivalric or heraldic trappings of later eras. There was still no
shiny plate armour; Norman cavalry wore a long coat of mail and
an open helm. Their primary weapon on horseback was a long
spear or lance, though it was rarely used in the manner depicted by
most movies. The lance could be couched under the arm but was
more commonly used to stab to the side as the horseman passed
close to the target – ideally just out of reach of their own weapon.

Similarly, the tourneys described in early versions of the
Arthur story were not the grandiose gatherings of later tales.
A tourney was originally an informal meet-up of a few warriors
for the purpose of testing their skills against one another. Live
weapons were used, and sometimes warriors were injured or
killed. This constant low-level bloodshed was deemed necessary
to maintain the skills of the fighting elite, even if it had to take
place semi-covertly.

The tale of Arthur as presented by Geoffrey of Monmouth
draws upon the *Historia Brittonum*, including its supernatural
elements. Arthur's equally mythical predecessor King Bladud is
noted as being some kind of wizard, though he met his death

trying to fly using magical wings. He was succeeded by his son Leir, whose tragic story was the basis for Shakespeare's play *King Lear*. After a period of 'do-nothing kings' – rulers whose reign was not marked by any great events or disasters – a series of civil wars wracked Britain, resulting in a north-south split along the line of the River Humber.

Geoffrey of Monmouth describes how the northern faction was aided by a fleet sent by the King of Norway. Of course, there was no Kingdom of Norway in that time, and ships capable of crossing the North Sea were yet to be invented. The king of the defeated southern faction – Brennius – went to Gaul and became the king of the Allobroges tribe. These events take place around 400 BCE, when Rome is known to have been attacked by Celtic people whose leader is sometimes named as Brennus. Geoffrey of Monmouth weaves these events into his narrative, along with references to a migration from Spain to Ireland. There is genetic evidence this happened at some point, and Irish legends mention such a movement. It appears that at some point Geoffrey of Monmouth goes from outright fiction to an account that could possibly be based on real events.

This is not to say that the narrative becomes real history at this point. Having paid a brief visit to reality, Geoffrey of Monmouth's account tells how King Morvidus had to deal with giants and dragons around 340 BCE, after which nothing much happened for several generations. The meeting point for Geoffrey of Monmouth's work and something resembling history seems to be the life of the Celtic leader Cassivellaunus, who fought the Roman invasion of 54 BCE.

Geoffrey of Monmouth's version of these events seems to have been almost entirely made up; afterwards his work has a closer relationship with reality. He tells the tale of Cunobelin, who resisted the Romanization of the Britons, and of Vortigern, who invited the Saxons into Britain.

Le Morte d'Arthur

The definitive version of the Arthur story was published in 1485 CE. It was apparently written by Sir Thomas Malory, though there are questions over exactly who he was and when he lived. *Le Morte d'Arthur* tells the tale of an Arthur who battled Saxons, discovered Iceland and conquered Rome before being undone by treachery among his followers. After the decisive Battle of Camlann, Arthur is taken to the magical land of Avalon where he waits until he is next needed. Celtic legend has a number of such places, including Tír na nÓg, the land of eternal youth where the Tuatha Dé Danann dwell.

The Arthur tale has a great many elements in common with the Celtic hero stories. His magical sword Caliburn (Excalibur in later versions) can cut through anything, which is just as well as Arthur has to battle giants and monsters in addition to hordes of enemies. He is cryptically advised by Merlin, who is sometimes referred to as a Druid. As in all the best tales, Merlin's advice tends to be more suited to moving the plot along than actually solving Arthur's problems.

The creation of the Round Table as an institution may be a Celtic influence. At the time *Le Morte d'Arthur* was written, the kings of Europe stood at the head of a rigid hierarchy. The pomp and ceremony associated with royalty, and the general difficulty in even approaching a monarch, was in part intended to remind everyone of their importance. A king who sat at a round table with his knights was being humble, and humility was a character flaw in a ruler of the time. If too many people thought they were the equal of the king, he would not be able to command them any longer.

The Round Table may be a reference to the Christian virtue of humility, but it might instead harken back to an era of warrior brotherhood. Rather than being a stuffy medieval king, Arthur was presented as treating the best and finest of his knights as the equal of a king. Perhaps there are echoes of ancient Celtic war bands like the Fianna Éireann in this; they were a group of brothers-in-arms who held themselves above the nobility of the land by way of their membership and voluntarily accepted the leadership of the greatest among them.

It is also possible to draw a parallel between the Holy Grail sought by Arthur's knights and the various magical cauldrons of Celtic legend. Whereas the Dagda's cauldron could only make porridge – though an infinite amount of it – the Holy Grail could create fabulous delicacies and cause an entire feast to materialize out of thin air. In addition to the cauldron parallel, the Arthur story features a number of magic weapons. Caliburn, or Excalibur, is the best known of course, but the Arthur tale also features the Bleeding Lance – the weapon used to wound Christ on the Cross.

The Grail Quest section of the Arthur story is rather tedious despite featuring an England beset by magical creatures. The Holy Grail was guarded by the Fisher King. He was gravely wounded and unable to do much but fish, hence his name, and the wound he bore also caused the land around to become barren. The Fisher King, and all England, could be healed by the Grail, but first a perfect knight must find it.

This looks like the setup for a truly epic tale, but the style of writing had changed by the time the Grail Quest was penned.

Early Arthur stories were graphically violent, but the Grail Quest skips over the fights. Instead, it dwells for pages and pages on lectures delivered by hermits to knights who need to be more pious and humble. This would appear to reflect the views of the authors, and represents a move from the rough-and-ready world of the early tales – and their Celtic predecessors – to a rather more formal and Church-dominated world.

SORCERESSES, BARDS AND DRUIDS

The *Mabinogion* and the legends of King Arthur contain several people with magical powers. The best known of these is the wizard Merlin, who is referred to as a Druid in some tales. There is considerable variation in Merlin's backstory, but in all cases he is mysterious and powerful. His role is, however, advisory for the most part. Modern fiction does include stories focusing on Merlin rather than Arthur, but the Arthurian legends are just that – stories of Arthur and his knights rather than his friendly wizard.

Merlin

Merlin appears in the Arthurian cycle as a facilitator and a source of unreliable advice. This role can be referred to as an 'oracle', which most heroic stories have in some form or other. The oracle provides information that is sufficient and reliable enough to set the heroes on their path, but is somehow misleading or misinterpreted. This is just as well for the tale, as it would be far less interesting if the hero was given detailed instructions and everything they needed to carry them out. Instead, they plunge into a dragon-infested swamp the oracular figure forgot to mention and have many wonderful adventures trying to get back out. Tiresome as this may be for heroes, it makes a better story and is, unsurprisingly, a common element in heroic fiction of many kinds.

Merlin also advised Ambrosius Aurelianus on how to construct a great monument to those murdered by Saxon treachery – namely, Stonehenge. In modern times we know that Stonehenge is thousands of years older than anything built during the Saxon invasions, but there are many who insist the stones could not have been moved without magical assistance.

After Ambrosius was killed by a treacherous Saxon, his brother Uther Pendragon took command. He was a flawed character who became infatuated with the wife of his ally Gorlois. The resulting conflict culminated in the capture of Tintagel, Gorlois's stronghold. During the final battle, Merlin used magic to allow Uther to pass as Gorlois in order to sleep with his wife. She became pregnant with a child who would become King Arthur. In this variant, Uther is Arthur's father, and the magic facilitating his conception seems to imbue him with superhuman abilities but also makes him the focus for tragedy.

Merlin is a plot device. He turns up from time to time to make Arthur aware of something he needs to do but rarely assists in a meaningful way. He does set up the incident of the sword in the stone, which can only be removed by someone worthy to rule the Britons. This weapon is commonly assumed to be Excalibur, but in fact was an entirely different weapon. It has been suggested that getting a sword out of a stone might be a metaphor for iron-smithing skills and that the story has its origins in ancient legends from the beginning of the Iron Age.

Be that as it may, the sword in the stone is one of the most iconic mythological images in Western culture. Even today, there are wild tales of how it has been found in some obscure corner of Europe and claims this proves the Arthur story – or whatever narrative the writer is peddling. This 'discovered' sword is inevitably still embedded in the stone despite the fact that Arthur removing it was the crux of the original tale.

Merlin is less influential in the Arthur tale than many people might imagine. He was trapped in a cave and robbed of his magical powers by Nimue, and thereafter played no part. Nimue may or may not be the same person as the Lady of the Lake, who gave Arthur the magical sword Excalibur. At the end of his story, as Arthur was dying, he instructed that Excalibur should be flung back into the lake. There is an obvious symmetry to returning the weapon, but the gesture may be inspired by the ancient Celtic tradition of making religious offerings of swords thrown into bodies of water.

After the departure of Merlin, the stories still need a source of semi-reliable information, so the role of oracle is taken on by Nimue or the bard Taliesin. This 'oracle' tradition is as common in modern fiction as in ancient legends. Often the more active of the protagonists will be sent down the wrong road by partial information emerging early in the crime lab's analysis or passed on by a convenient bystander.

Taliesin

The bard Taliesin features in both the *Mabinogion* and the Arthur legends. He may have been a real figure who has been turned into a legend, or a combination of real and legendary people. He is, or is implied to be, the observer who tells the tale in some of the *Mabinogion* stories. His origin story may seem familiar to those conversant with the earlier Celtic legends.

In the *Mabinogion*, the sorceress Ceridwen was the wife of Tegid Foel, a giant who extorted tribute from the people of Powys. They had two children, of whom Creirwy was beautiful and clever while Morfran was misshapen and cursed. In an effort to help her son, Ceridwen attempted to create a potion which would grant him wisdom and allow him to shift into any shape he pleased. She hired a servant boy named Gwion Bach to tend the cauldron in which she was making her potion.

Three drops of the almost complete potion burned Gwion's thumb, which he naturally put in his mouth. This was sufficient to grant him great knowledge and wisdom; any more of the potion would have killed him. As it was, he attracted the anger of Ceridwen and tried to escape. Using his new knowledge Gwion changed shape repeatedly, but she did likewise. While in the form of a hen Ceridwen ate Gwion Bach while he was hiding among a pile of grain. Even in the form of grain, Gwion Bach's power was considerable, and caused Ceridwen to become pregnant.

There are clear parallels in this tale to the way Fionn mac Cumhaill gained his power, and also to the way Tuan mac Cairill gained wisdom that eventually enabled him to write the Irish 'Book of Invasions'. The idea that eating a magical person or creature can cause a supernatural pregnancy appears in several Celtic mythological stories, though whether it is derived from a single original tale is an open question. In this case Gwion was reborn as a human. He was so beautiful that Ceridwen decided not to kill him as she had intended, but instead mercifully tied him into a bag and threw him in the sea.

The infant floated for nine days before being caught by Elffin, nephew of the King of Wales, who was out fishing. His disappointment at catching a nine-day-old infant presumably turned to great surprise when the baby sang him a poem of consolation and recounted his adventures. Elffin was ridiculed for bringing home a baby instead of a fish, but that attitude disappeared when the baby spoke clear words of wisdom and produced a great light shining from his forehead. He announced that he was the reincarnation of Gwion Bach, but Elffin named him Taliesin and adopted him as foster son. Taliesin provided good advice to his foster family, helping them with many difficulties, and eventually found himself at the court of King Arthur.

The tale of Taliesin mentions King Maelgwn Gwynedd, making him a contemporary. According to legend, Elffin annoyed Maelgwn Gwynedd with his constant boasting. Taliesin was able to 'prove' all the boasts were true, albeit by means of some quite spurious logic at times, and thereby save his foster father. This must have happened, if it happened at all, around 520–40 CE. On the other hand, the *Book of Taliesin*, attributed to Taliesin, contains material originating as late as the fourteenth century CE. It is possible that some of these writings were created by the original bard, with the rest added by later writers in the same tradition.

Modern fiction has characters who are explicitly Druids or bards, and a range of parallels, including wizards, sorcerers and alchemists. Typically, such characters have some explanation as to why they can do things ordinary mortals cannot. Accidents with magic potions are one possible reason for supernatural powers.

The Scheming Sorceress

The character of Morgan (or Morgana) le Fay appears in Le Morte d'Arthur and some other versions of the Arthur story. She is rather complex, sometimes depicted as a sorceress or witch and sometimes as a mortal woman. In some versions she is the aunt of Mordred, Arthur's nemesis, though she is also one of the magical women who accompany Arthur to Avalon after Mordred is defeated. There are parallels to the Morrigan of ancient Celtic legend.

The scheming sorceress, usually beautiful but evil, appears in a great deal of modern mythology. A more enigmatic variant – dangerous but not necessarily inimical – may take the part of a story's oracle or an unreliable ally. As with Druids and wizards, these characters sometimes have a supernatural backstory which allows the storyteller to get on with the plot without having to explain too much.

RUNES AND ANCIENT SYMBOLS

Ironically perhaps, the Celts' own writing system did not convey much of their culture or mythology to the present day, but it did survive as a concept. From the fourth century CE, Ogham writing began to appear in Ireland and Pictish regions. Ogham characters are designed to be easy to carve into wood or stone using short, straight strokes, though their origins are debatable. Ogham may have been developed as a means to write the Latin alphabet, or it could have been developed as a whole as a purely runic script.

It is said that Ogham writing was carved into pieces of wood, and while there is little or no evidence for this, we know that the Norsemen did something very similar. They, like the Celts, preferred to retain knowledge in the minds of experts rather than entrusting it to paper or wood. Ogham-inscribed slivers might have been used to transmit messages, and there are many surviving inscriptions on stone. However, this would be a hugely laborious way of preserving an entire genealogy or a long story.

Ogham inscriptions were carved into stones and monuments which have survived to this day, as have the runic inscriptions of other European cultures. The idea of ancient symbols empowering an object is extremely common in modern fiction, though the term 'rune' is more commonly used than a reference to Ogham. This can be seen as a sort of cultural victory for the societies that used runes over the Irish Celts; a reference to Ogham writing needs explanation but a 'rune-inscribed blade' on a magic sword is familiar to almost anyone.

Runes and their equivalent symbols are common plot devices in stories and games. Characters may need to collect certain symbols or learn to read them in order to progress and gain advantages. Alternatively, the runes can serve as a plot device. Misread symbols can mislead the characters or let loose some new menace. Rune-casters can also provide (potentially dubious) information. This is extremely useful when the story needs to move forward without a long search for clues. The runes are cast and the story moves in a new direction, or a symbol is applied to remove an obstacle.

THE OTHERWORLD

The 'Otherworld' is a common concept in modern fiction. It comes to us from various mythologies, not all of them European, but our popular conception of it is heavily influenced by Celtic traditions. In the first tale of the *Mabinogion*, Pwyll, a chieftain from Dyfed, spends a year in the supernatural realm of Annwyn. This has parallels to the Irish Sidhe, though the Sidhe are earth mounds found all over Ireland which give access to the Otherworld.

Pwyll was out hunting, and committed the social gaffe of allowing his hounds to finish off a stag that had been run down by someone else's dogs. He may well have thought this was his right; as King of Dyfed, he had no social equals and could do as he pleased. Or so he thought. In fact, the other hounds belonged to Arawn, King of Annwyn.

Arawn was angered, and demanded Pwyll do him a service in recompense. He was to slay Havgan, Arawn's rival and also a King of Annwyn. Arawn and Pwyll swapped places – and appearances – for a year, during which time Pwyll did indeed defeat Havgan. He did not have sex with Arawn's wife, however, even though they slept in the same bed. At the end of the year, Arawn was pleased with Pwyll's deeds and rewarded him richly. Pwyll returned to his own lands to find they had prospered under Arawn's rule.

Not all interactions were so positive. Elsewhere in the *Mabinogion*, Arawn leads his army against the Kingdom of Gwynedd in retaliation for a theft. In this case, the magical land of youth and plenty seems rather less pleasant, spawning terrifying supernatural creatures. In some tales, Arawn is given the identity of Gwyn ap Nudd, who leads the Hounds of Annwyn.

This ties into the common European myth of the Wild Hunt, whose appearance usually presages death and disaster for anyone witnessing it.

The *Book of Taliesin* contains a story where King Arthur leads a party of knights into Annwyn where most of them meet their demise. This tale features the cauldron of Annwyn, which has a parallel in the Dagda's magical cauldron of plenty. In some tales the cauldron can bring back the dead, enabling its user to replace battle casualties as fast as the bodies can be recovered. It can be destroyed by a living person voluntarily being placed in it.

GIANTS, STARLINGS AND A CAULDRON

Also in the *Mabinogion* is a tale of conflict between Ireland and Wales. Historically, there was plenty of that, though this story features supernatural elements. In this tale, Mallolwch, King of Ireland, came to the court of the giant king, Bran the Blessed of Wales. They agreed that Mallolwch should marry Branwen, Bran's sister. This should have been a good thing, cementing ties between the two realms.

Bran's half-brother Evnissyen derailed the proceedings by mutilating Mallolwch's horses. This was something of an overreaction to not being consulted about the marriage. Bran smoothed over the incident with rich gifts, including a magical cauldron that could bring back the dead. Mollified, Mallolwch returned home with his new bride. Although she bore him a son, their happiness did not last long. An anti-Welsh faction at the court of Mallolwch persuaded him that he had been insulted by the paltry gifts given by King Bran. He began to mistreat Branwen, forcing her to work in the kitchens. She was able to recruit a starling to carry a message to her brother.

Supernatural elements of this sort are a wonderful boon for the storyteller. How could King Bran find out about his sister's mistreatment, triggering the war at the centre of the tale? A message might be smuggled by a sympathetic co-worker perhaps, or a wandering bard might have heard rumours. However, a talking bird allows the plot to move forward in just a sentence or two.

King Bran decided to punish Mallolwch and set off marching towards Ireland. He was tall enough to simply stride across the Irish Sea, though his warriors required boats. Bran also used his height to bypass other obstacles, such as the River Liffey after its bridge was destroyed by Irish warriors. Mallolwch then resorted to treachery. He invited Bran to a peace conference in a house where he had concealed 200 warriors in what he claimed were flour sacks.

Bran, or in some versions Evnissyen, undid the trap by squeezing the bags, pretending not to have noticed what was inside. With his warriors squashed, Mallolwch decided to go ahead with the peace conference as if he had meant to all along. Things might have turned out well but for the dangerously unstable Evnissyen. He burned alive Gwern, child of Branwen and Mallolwch, and thereby triggered a violent clash in which Mallolwch had a decisive advantage. Slain warriors were brought to the cauldron Bran had gifted him and returned to life. Evnissyen made recompense for his misdeeds by sacrificing himself, entering the cauldron alive and thereby destroying it.

The battle was a quasi-victory for the Welsh, though only seven of them survived, including the bard Taliesin. Bran was mortally wounded by a poisoned spear or sword, while Branwen died of a broken heart. King Bran's body was far too heavy for seven people to carry, so it was decided they would take his head home for burial. This they did, by way of an eighty-year stopover in a magical hall in Gwales. The concept of places where time works differently is found elsewhere in Celtic mythology, notably in the story of how Oisín visited Tír na nÓg.

A LASTING CULTURAL LEGACY

Where the physical elements may have disappeared or faded from notice, the cultural legacy of the Celts remains a powerful force shaping modern society. Our ideas of what a hero should be and how they behave can be traced to traditional Celtic stories. This may be the most enduring legacy of the Celtic people – they not only gave us ideas for elements of a good story but they helped shape our very concept of what a good story should be.

FINAL NOTES

Just as the ancient Celts were not a monolithic culture, their history was one of gradual but constant change. Technology advanced, new ideas were exchanged with trading partners, interactions with other groups caused a drift in beliefs and culture. In truth there can be no account of 'Celts as they always were'; only snapshots of a given place and time.

The Celts did not mysteriously disappear. They had their time and were eventually subsumed into later cultures. Theirs was a long era which saw the introduction of widespread ironworking in Europe, the rise and fall of the Roman Empire, the coming of Christianity and the beginnings of our modern countries. Celtic culture and mythology are part of the modern world – a world that continues to change just as that of the Celts did.

With so much history and mythology to study, there really is no need to invent Celtic history – and yet it happens. There are websites that confidently state the Celts arrived from outer space 50,000 years ago, just after their planet became our asteroid belt by means of a large but unexplained detonation. There are equally silly tales of what happened to them.

One such story claims that the Celts decided to escape imminent Roman domination by borrowing ships from the Carthaginians and crossing the Atlantic. There, they became overlords of the South American and Central American people. This is 'proven', we are told, by the discovery of a Celtic-type bronze axe in the Amazon jungle. Leaving aside the fact that all this is rather insulting to the magnificent cultures of the Americas, it is also patently ridiculous.

An Atlantic crossing was simply impossible for the ships of the time and even if Carthage had still been around to lend them, why would they? The bronze axe apparently dates from a period when the Celts had been using iron for generations. Equally, claims that Celtic explorers somehow reached the North American continent and set up communities there are distinctly implausible. The ancient Celts were not spacemen or transatlantic conquerors. What they were is... us.

The Celts Were Like Us

That is to say, the ancient Celts were people very much like us. Most just wanted a quiet life, filled with food, warmth and companionship. Some sought adventure or got involved in politics; they had their beliefs and their stories, their fears and their worries. They liked having nice possessions, like decorative pottery and the latest fashionable clothes. They fell out with their relatives but banded together with them against outsiders. These behaviours may seem oddly familiar.

We live in the same world as the ancient Celts, just with more advanced technology. Our own world is in transition, just as theirs was, and as they are a part of our heritage so we will carry on parts of theirs into whatever our society becomes in the next few centuries. In short, the Celts are not gone. They are no longer centre stage, but they are still part of the story. And if we look closely enough we find their influence in all aspects of our society.

We still create stories and retell them in the Bardic tradition. We are excited by the exploits of sword-armed heroes and their modern equivalents. We find the same attractively decorated goods desirable, and tend to admire those who possess them. We hold gatherings where those to be honoured sit in the most prominent places and are served their food first. And sometimes, when it is dark and cold, we huddle around the light and wonder what the strange noises outside may be.

The Celtic people are a part of the story of how the modern world came to be; which societies became prominent and shaped the future and which faded away; which settlements became prosperous and influential; which leaders were successful enough to impose their will upon the future. That story has not ended. Rather, it has flowed into the vast ocean of history and mythology, where its ripples can still be seen from time to time.

ANCIENT
KINGS & LEADERS

Ancient cultures often traded with and influenced
each other, while others grew independently.
This section provides the key leaders from a
number of regions, to offer comparative insights
into developments across the ancient world.

CELTIC & BRITISH LEADERS

This list is not exhaustive and dates are approximate. Where dates of rule overlap, emperors either ruled jointly or ruled in opposition to one another. There may also be differences in name spellings between different sources.

BEGINNINGS

The Celts were thought to have originated in central Europe at around 1400 BCE. Migrations across Europe began around 900 BCE and saw the Celts migrate west to parts of France, Spain, Italia, Greece, and into Scotland, England, Ireland and Wales. Broadly speaking, a Celt can be defined as someone speaking a Celtic language and being from a Celtic culture. The Celts that settled in Britain in around 300 BCE became the island's dominant ethnic group.

GAUL, IBERIA AND THE EUROPEAN CONTINENT

Ambicatus, Bituriges	*c.* 600 BCE
Bellovesus, Bituriges	*c.* 600 BCE
Segovesus, Bituriges	*c.* 600 BCE
Brennus, Senones	*c.* 390 BCE
Onomaris	*c.* 400–300 BCE

Britomaris, Senones	c. 283 BCE
Acichorius/Brennus	c. 279 BCE
Bolgios	c. 279 BCE
Cambuales	c. 279 BCE
Cerethrius	c. 277 BCE
Autaritus	d. 238 BCE
Aneroëstes, Gaesatae	d. 225 BCE
Concolitanus, Gaesatae	d. 225 BCE
Viridomarus	d. 222 BCE
Ducarius, Insubres	c. 217 BCE
Olyndicus, Celtiberians	d. c. 170 BCE
Punicus, Lusitani	c. 155 BCE
Caesarius, Lusitani	c. 155 BCE
Caucenus, Lusitani	c. 153 BCE
Tanginus, Celtiberians	c. 140 BCE
Tautalus, Celtiberians	c. 139 BCE
Virathius, Celtiberians	d. 139 BCE
Divico, Helvetii	c. 109 BCE
Orgetorix, Helvetii	c. 60 BCE
Casticus, Sequani	c. 60 BCE
Dumnoix, Haedui	c. 60 BCE
Viridovix, Unelli	c. 56 BCE
Acco, Senones	c. 54 BCE
Ambiorix, Eburones	c. 54 BCE
Cativolcus, Eburones	c. 54 BCE
Cingetorix, Treveri	c. 54 BCE
Tasgetius, Carnutes	d. 54 BCE
Indutiomeris, Treveri	d. 53 BCE
Camulogene, Aulerci	d. 52 BCE
Convictolitavis, Haedui	c. 52 BCE

Aegus, Allobroges	c. 50 BCE
Regus, Allobroges	c. 50 BCE
Vercingetorix, Averni	c. 80–46 BCE
Commius, Atrebates	c. 57-c. 20 BCE
Tincomarus, Atrebates	c. 30 BCE–c. 8 BCE
Eppillius, Atrebates	c. 20-7 BCE
Biatex, Boii	1st century BCE
Diviciacus, Suessiones	c. 70 BCE?
Verica, Atrebates	c. 15–c. 42 CE
Julius Indus, Treveri	d. c. 65 CE
Julius Sabinus, Lingones	c. 69 CE

KINGS OF BRITONS/BRYTHONS

Legendary Kings

This includes a selection of mythological rulers. There is much diversity of opinion over who the kings actually consisted of and the dates they ruled.

Brutus   c. 1115 BCE (23 years)
Founder and first King of the Britons, Brutus is thought to be a descendant of Troy. He divided the land between his three sons: Albanactus who gained Albany (Scotland); Kamber who gained Cambria (Wales); and Locrinus who gained Lloegr (roughly England), and was also high king of Britain

Pwyll Pen Annwn	King of Dyfed
Pryderi fab Pywll	Son of Pwyll, succeeded his father as king of Dyfed

Leir/Llyr	c. 950 BCE, possible inspiration for Shakespeare's King Lear
Beli ap Rhun	c. 500s, king of Gwenydd
King Arthur	5th–6th century, king of Britain, led the Knights of the Round Table

Historical Kings of Briton (c. 54 BCE–50 CE)

This section mainly covers people of England, Wales and southern Scotland.

Cassivellaunus	54 BCE; led the defence against Julius Caesar's second invasion
Carvilius (one of the four kings of Kent)	c. 54 BCE
Cingetorix (one of the four kings of Kent)	c. 54 BCE
Segovax (one of the four kings of Kent)	c. 54 BCE
Taximagulus (one of the four kings of Kent)	c. 54 BCE
Imanuentius, Trinovantes	c. 54 BCE
Lugotorix	c. 54 BCE
Mandubracius, Trinovantes	c. 54 BCE
Tasciovanus	20 BCE–9 CE
Cunobeline	9–40 CE
Tiberius Claudius	40–43 CE
Caractacus, Catuvellauni	43–50 CE
Togodumnus, Catuvellauni	d. 43 CE

Roman Era Onwards

This section mainly covers people of England, Wales and southern Scotland. These rulers may have only governed part of Briton, with many being based in and ruler of Wales, which itself was split into several kingdoms. Some are disputed.

Prasutagus, Iceni	d. 60 CE
Boudicca, Iceni	d. 60 CE
Cartimandua, Brigantes	c. 69 CE
Vellocatus, Brigantes	c. 69 CE
Venutius, Brigantes	c. 70 CE
Vortigern	mid-5th century
Riothamus	c. 469 CE
Ambrosius Aurelianus	late 5th century
Maelgwn Gwynedd	mid- to late-5th century
Selyf ap Cynan	c. 613 CE
Ceretic of Elmet	c. 614–617 CE
Cadwallon ap Cadfan	c. 634 CE
Idris ap Gwyddno	c. 635 CE
Eugein I of Alt Clut	c. 642 CE
Cadwaladr	c. 654–664 CE
Ifor	683–698 CE
Rhodri Molwynog	c. 712–754 CE
Cynan Dindaethwy	798–816 CE
Merfyn Frych	825–844 CE
Rhodri ap Merfyn 'the Great'	844–878 CE
Anarawd ap Rhodri	878–916 CE
Idwal Foel ap Anarawd	916–942 CE
Hwyel Dda 'the Good'	942–950 CE
Dyfnwal ab Owain	930s–970s CE
Maredudd ab Owain	986–999 CE
Llywelyn ap Seisyll	1018–1023 CE
Iago ab Idwal	1023–1039 CE
Gruffyd ap Llywelyn	1039/1055–1063 CE

MONARCHS OF ENGLAND (886-1066 CE)

House of Wessex (c. 886-924 CE)

The House of Wessex was founded when Alfred became King of the Anglo-Saxons.

Alfred 'the Great'	c. 886–899 CE
Edward 'the Elder'	899–924 CE
Aethelstan 'the Glorious'	924–939 CE
Edmund I 'the Magnificent'	939–946 CE
Eadred	946–955 CE
Eadwig	955–959 CE
Edgar 'the Peaceful'	959–975 CE
Edward 'the Martyr'	975–978 CE
Aethelred II 'the Unready'	978–1013 CE

House of Denmark (c. 1013-1014 CE)

England was invaded by the Danes in 1013. Aethelred abandoned the throne to Sweyn Forkbeard.

Sweyn Forkbeard	1013–1014 CE

House of Wessex (restored, 1014-1016 CE)

Aethelred II was restored to the English throne after the death of Sweyn Forkbeard.

Aethelred II 'the Unready'	1014–1016 CE
Edmund Ironside	1016–1016 CE

House of Denmark (restored, 1016–1042 CE)

Cnut became king of all England apart from Wessex after signing a treaty with Edmund Ironside. He became king of all England following Edmund's death just over a month later.

Cnut 'the Great' (Canute)	1016–1035 CE
Harold Harefoot	1035–1040 CE
Harthacnut	1040–1042 CE

House of Wessex (restored, second time, 1042–1066 CE)

Edward 'the Confessor'	1042–1066 CE

House of Goodwin (1066 CE)

Harold II Godwinson	1066–1066 CE

Following Harold II's death in the Battle of Hastings, several claimants emerged to fight over the English throne. William the Conqueror of the House of Normandy was crowned king on 25 December 1066.

HIGH KINGS OF IRELAND

Mythological High Kings of Ireland

Dates and rulers are different depending on the source.

Nuada	?–1897 BCE; first reign
Bres	1897–1890 BCE
Nuada	1890–1870 BCE; second reign

Lug	1870–1830 BCE
Eochaid Ollathair (the Dadga)	1830–1750 BCE
Delbaeth	1750–1740 BCE
Fiacha	1740–1730 BCE
Mac Cuill	1730–1700 BCE

Ireland was split into several kingdoms until the national title of High King began, despite mythological stories of unbroken lines of High Kings.

Semi-historical High Kings (c. 459–831 CE)

Most of these kings are thought to be historical figures, but it is disputed whether they were all High Kings.

Ailill Molt	459–478 CE
Lugaid mac Loegairi	479–503 CE
Muirchertach mac Ercae	504–527 CE
Tuathal Maelgarb	528–538 CE
Diarmait mac Cerbaill	539–558 CE
Domhnall mac Muirchertaig	559–561 CE; joint ruler
Fearghus mac Muirchertaig	559–561 CE; joint ruler
Baedan mac Muirchertaig	562–563 CE; joint ruler
Eochaidh mac Domnaill	562–563 CE; joint ruler
Ainmuire mac Setnai	564–566 CE
Baetan mac Ninnedo	567 CE
Aed mac Ainmuirech	568–594 CE
Aed Slaine	595–600 CE; joint ruler
Colman Rimid	595–600 CE; joint ruler
Aed Uaridnach	601–607 CE
Mael Coba mac Aedo	608–610 CE

Suibne Menn	611–623 CE
Domnall mac Aedo	624–639 CE
Cellach mac Maele Coba	640–656 CE; joint ruler
Conall mac Maele Coba	640–656 CE; joint ruler
Diarmait	657–664 CE; joint ruler
Blathmac	657–664 CE; joint ruler
Sechnassach	665–669 CE
Cenn Faelad	670–673 CE
Finsnechta Fledach	674–693 CE
Loingsech mac Oengusso	694–701 CE
Congal Cennmagair	702–708 CE
Fergal mac Maele Duin	709–718 CE
Fogartach mac Neill	719 CE
Cinaed mac Irgalaig	720–722 CE
Flaithbertach mac Loingsig	723–729 CE
Aed Allan	730–738 CE
Domnall Midi	739–758 CE
Niall Frossach	759–765 CE
Donnchad Midi	766–792 CE
Aed Oirdnide	793–819 CE
Conchobar mac Donnchada	819–833 CE
Feidlimid mac Crimthainn	832–846 CE

Historical High Kings of Ireland (c. 846–1198 CE)

It is disputed whether these were all High Kings.

Mael Sechnaill mac Maele-Ruanaid	846–860 CE
Aed Findliath	861–876 CE
Fiann Sinna	877–914 CE
Niall Glundub	915–917 CE

Donnchad Donn	918–942 CE
Congalach Cnogba	943–954 CE
Domnall ua Neill	955–978 CE
Mael Sechnaill mac Domnaill	979–1002 CE; first reign
Brian Boruma	1002–1014 CE
Mael Sechnaill mac Domnaill	1014–1022 CE; second reign
Donnchad mac Brian	d. 1064
Diarmait mac Mail na mBo	d. 1072 CE
Toiredelbach Ua Briain	d. 1086 CE
Domnall Ua Lochlainn	d. 1121 CE
Muirchertach Ua Briain	d. 1119 CE
Toirdelbach Ua Conchobair	1119–1156 CE
Muirchertach Mac Lochlainn	1156–1166 CE
Ruaidri Ua Conchobair	1166–1198 CE

RULERS OF SCOTLAND

Legendary kings

Fergus I	c. 330 BCE
Feritharis	305 BCE
Mainus	290 BCE
Dornadilla	262 BCE
Nothatus	232 BCE

Some of the significant rulers between 200 BCE and 800 CE are listed here.

Caractacus (King of the Britons, he was also considered king of Scotland in legend)   1st century CE, to c. 50 CE

Donaldus I (Some consider him to be the
    first Christian king of Scotland)

Calgacus, Caledones	c. 85 CE
Argentocoxos, Caledones	c. 210 CE
Fergus Mor	c. 500 CE; possible king of Dál Riata

The list ends around the time of Kenneth MacAlpin, who founded
the House of Alpin. Following the Roman departure from Britain,
Scotland split into four main groups: the Picts, the people of Dál
Riata, the Kingdom of Strathclyde and the Kingdom of Bernicia.
The Picts would eventually merge with Dál Riata to form the
Kingdom of Scotland.

Monarchs of Scotland (c. 848–1286 CE)

House of Alpin (848–1034 CE)

Kenneth I was the son of Alpin, king of Dál Riata, a Gaelic
kingdom located in Scotland and Ireland.

Kenneth I MacAlpin	843/848–13 February 858 CE; first King of Alba thought to be of Gaelic origin
Donald I	858–13 April 862 CE
Causantin mac Cinaeda (Constantine I)	862–877 CE
Aed mac Cinaeda	877–878 CE
Giric 'mac Rath'	878–889 CE
Donald II	889–900 CE
Causantin mac Aeda (Constantine II)	900–943 CE
Malcolm I	943–954 CE
Indulf	954–962 CE
Dub mac Mail Coluim	962–967 CE

Cuilen	967–971 CE
Amlaib	973–977 CE
Constantine III	995–997 CE
Kenneth III	997–25 March 1005 CE
Malcolm II	1005–1034 CE

House of Dunkeld (1034–1286)

Duncan was the grandson of Malcolm II. He founded the House of Dunkeld.

Duncan I	1034–1040 CE
Macbeth	1040–1057 CE
Lulach	1057–1058 CE
Malcolm III	1058–1093 CE
Donald III	1093–1097 CE
Duncan II	1094 CE
Edgar	1097–1107 CE
Alexander I	1107–1124 CE
David I	1124–1153 CE
Malcolm IV	1153–1165 CE
William I	1165–1214 CE
Alexander II	1219–1249 CE
Alexander III	1249–1286 CE

NORSE MONARCHS

This list is not exhaustive and dates are approximate. The legitimacy of some kings is also open to interpretation. Where dates of rule overlap, kings either ruled jointly or ruled in opposition to one another. There may also be differences in name spellings between different sources.

BEGINNINGS

The Norse people or Vikings migrated from Norway, Denmark and Sweden during the Middle Ages to many places including Britain, Ireland, Scotland, Normandy, Iceland, Greenland and even as far as North America. They brought their religious beliefs and mythology with them. The first two humans were created by three Norse gods, including Odin. Ask, a man created from an ash tree, and Embla, a woman created from an elm tree, went on to create the whole human race who dwelled at Midgard.

HOUSE OF YNGLING

Descendants of the family, whose name means children of the god Frey, became the first semi-mythological rulers of Sweden, then Norway. There are several versions of this dynasty showing different names or orders descending from Fiolner, son of Frey, son of Njord, who was part of the Vanir tribe. The family is also known as the Sclyfings.

Fiolner (son of the god Frey)
Sveigoir (son of Fiolner, mythological king of Sweden)
Vanlandi (son of Sveigoir)
Visbur (son of Vanlandi)
Domaldi (son of Visbur)
Domar (son of Domaldi)
Dyggvi (son of Domar)
Dag 'the Wise' spaki (son of Dyggvi)
Agni (son of Dag)
Alrekr and Eirikr (sons of Agni)
Yngvi and Alfr (sons of Alrekr)
Jorundr (son of Yngvi)
Aunn (son of Jorundr)
Egill/Ongentheow (father of Ohthere and Onela)
Ottarr/Ohthere and Onela (son of Egill)
Aoils/Eadgils and Eanmund (son of Ohthere)
Eysteinn (son of Eadgils)
Yngvarr (son of Eysteinn)
Onundr (son of Yngvarr)
Ingjaldr (?)

From the Yngling family came these semi-mythological kings.

Olaf the Tree-feller	approx. 700s CE
Halfdan Whiteleg	approx. 800s CE

Gudrod the Hunter	approx. 850s CE
Halfdan the Swarthy (Halfdan the Black)	821–860 CE

The following list runs from 872 which is when King Harald Fairhair was victorious in the Battle of Hafrsfjord, after which he merged the petty kingdoms of Norway into a unified kingdom.

FAIRHAIR DYNASTY (872-970 CE)

Dates for the Fairhair dynasty are estimated.

Harald I Halfdansson (Harald Fairhair)	872–928/932 CE
Eirik I Haraldsson (Eric Bloodaxe)	928/932–934 CE
Haakon I Haraldsson (Haakon the Good)	934–960 CE
Harald II Ericsson (Harald Greycloak)	961–970 CE

HOUSE OF GORM/EARL OF LADE (961-995 CE)

Harald Gormsson (Harald Bluetooth; ruled with Harald Greycloak)	961–980 CE
Earl Hakkon Sigurdsson (Hakkon Jarl, Eric the Victorious)	965/970–995 CE

FAIRHAIR DYNASTY (RESTORED) (995-1000 CE)

Olav I Tryggvason	995–1000 CE

HOUSE OF GORM/EARL OF LADE (RESTORED) (1000-1015 CE)

Sweyn Forkbeard; joint ruler	1000–1013 CE
Earl Eirik Haakonsson; joint ruler	1000–1015 CE
Earl Sweyn Haakonsson; joint ruler	1000–1015 CE

ST OLAV DYNASTY (1015-1028 CE)

Olav II Haraldsson (Saint Olav)	1015–1028 CE

HOUSE OF GORM/EARL OF LADE (SECOND RESTORATION) (1028-1035 CE)

Cnut the Great (Canute)	1028–1035 CE
Earl Haakon Ericsson; joint ruler	1028–1029 CE
Sweyn Knutsson; joint ruler	1030–1035 CE

ST OLAV DYNASTY (RESTORED) (1035-1047 CE)

Magnus I Olafsson (Magnus the Good)	1015–1028 CE

HARDRADA DYNASTY (1046-1135 CE)

Harald III Sigurdsson (Harald Hardrada)	1046–1066 CE
Magnus II Haralldsson	1066–1069 CE
Olaf III Haralldsson (Olaf the Peaceful)	1067–1093 CE

Hakkon (II) Magnusson (Haakon Toresfostre)	1093–1095 CE
Magnus III Olafsson (Magnus Barefoot)	1093–1103 CE
Olaf (IV) Magnusson; joint ruler	1103–1115 CE
Eystein I Magnusson; joint ruler	1103–1123 CE
Sigurd I Magnusson (Sigurd the Crusader)	1103–1130 CE
Magnus IV Sigurdsson (Magnus the Blind)	1130–1135 CE

GILLE DYNASTY (1130–1162 CE)

Harald IV Magnusson (Harald Gille)	1130–1136 CE
Sigurd II Haraldsson; joint ruler (Sigurd Munn)	1136–1155 CE
Inge I Haraldsson; joint ruler (Inge the Hunchback)	1136–1161 CE
Eystein II Haraldsson; joint ruler	1142–1157 CE
Magnus (V) Haraldsson; joint ruler	1142–1145 CE
Haakon II Sigurdsson (Hakkon the Broadshouldered)	1157–1162 CE

HARDRADA DYNASTY (RESTORED, COGNATIC BRANCH) (1161–1184 CE)

| Magnus V Erlingsson | 1161–1184 CE |

SVERRE DYNASTY (1184–1204 CE)

Sverre Sigurdsson	1184–1202 CE
Haakon III Sverresson	1202–1204 CE
Guttorm Sigurdsson	January to August 1204 CE

GILLE DYNASTY (COGNATIC BRANCH) (1204–1217 CE)

Inge II Bardsson   1204–1217 CE

SVERRE DYNASTY (RESTORED) (1217–1319 CE)

Haakon IV Hakkonsson (Hakkon the Old)   1217–1263 CE
Haakon (V) Haakonsson (Hakkon the Young) 1240–1257 CE
Magnus VI Haakonsson (Magnus the
  Law-mender)   1257–1280 CE
Eric II Magnusson   1273–1299 CE
Hakkon V Magnusson   1299–1319 CE

HOUSE OF BJELBO (1319–1387)

Magnus VII Eriksson   1319–1343 CE
Hakkon VI Magnusson   1343–1380 CE
Olaf IV Hakkonsson   1380–1387 CE

HOUSE OF ESTRIDEN (1380–1412)

Margaret I   1380–1412 CE

HOUSE OF GRIFFIN (1389–1387)

Eric III   1389–1442 CE

HOUSE OF PALANTINATE-NEUMARKT (1442-1448)

Christopher   1442–1448 CE

HOUSE OF BONDE (1449-1450)

Charles I   1449–1450 CE

HOUSE OF OLDENBURG (1450-1814)

Christian I   1450–1481 CE

Interregnum (1481–1483) in which Jon Svaleson Smor served as regent

John   1483–1513 CE
Christian II   1513–1523 CE
Fredrick I   1524–1533 CE

Interregnum (1533–1537) in which Olaf Engelbrektsson served as regent

Christian III   1537–1559 CE
Fredrick II   1559–1588 CE
Christian IV   1588–1648 CE
Fredrick III   1648–1670 CE
Christian V   1670–1699 CE
Fredrick IV   1699–1730 CE

Christian VI	1730–1746 CE
Fredrick V	1746–1766 CE
Christian VII	1766–1808 CE
Fredrick VI	1808–1814 CE

Interregnum (1814–1814) in which Christian Frederick served as regent

Christian Frederick	1814–1814 CE

Interregnum (1814–1814) in which Marcus Gjoe Rosenkrantz served as prime minister

HOUSE OF HOLSTEIN-GOTTORP (1814–1818)

Charles II	1814–1818 CE

HOUSE OF BERNADOTTE (1818–1905)

Charles III John	1818–1944 CE
Oscar I	1844–1859 CE
Charles IV	1859–1872 CE
Oscar II	1872–1905 CE

SLAVIC NATIONS TIMELINE & KEY LEADERS

This list is not exhaustive and dates are approximate. The legitimacy of some kings is also open to interpretation. Where dates of rule overlap, kings either ruled jointly or ruled in opposition to one another. There may also be differences in name spellings between different sources.

ORIGINS AND MIGRATIONS

Thought by many to have originated in Polesia, a region encompassing parts of Central and Eastern Europe and south-western Russia, the Slavic people were made up of tribal societies. Many of these societies migrated across Europe integrating with Czech, Russia, Bulgaria, Croatia, Bosnia, Poland, Hungary and other countries and cultures.

While their beliefs and myths diverge, some believe the legend of three brothers who founded three of the main Slavic peoples. The three brothers, Lech, Czech and Rus', were on a hunting trip when they took different directions to hunt their own prey. Lech travelled to the north, where he would eventually found Poland; Czech travelled west to found Czech;

and Rus' travelled east to found Russia, Ukraine and Belarus.

The timelines that follow chart the main migrations, key events and major rulers of several branches of the Slavic people.

WESTERN STEM

Czech

?	Czech founds what is now the Czech Republic (mythological)
623 CE	Samo, the first King of the Slavs, founds Samo's Empire which includes the kingdom of Moravia
626 CE	Samo leads the Slavs against the Avars
631	Samo leads his realm in the Battle of Wogastisburg, defeating the Franks
658	Samo dies. His sons do not inherit and the Slavic kingdom dissolves
?	Little is known about this period but it might have fallen under Avar rule
820s	Mojmir I founds the House of Mojmir and converts to Christianity
833	Mojmir unifies Moravia and Nitra (Slovakia) as the state of Great Moravia
846	Mojmir I is deposed. Ratislav becomes the second prince of Moravia
862	Prince Ratislav of Moravia converts to Christianity
872	Ratislav is dethroned by his nephew, Svatopluk I, who succeeds him as prince of Moravia
870/874	Borivoj I becomes prince of Bohemia, founding the House of Premysl

880	Svatopluk I 'the Great' is crowned king of Great Moravia
882	The Moravians invade Bohemia and Pannonia
895	The dukes of Bohemia under Spytihnev I separate from the Moravian kingdom
902/907	The Moravian kingdom collapses
912	Vratislav I becomes duke of Bohemia
921	Wenceslas I (posthumously declared patron saint of Czech) becomes duke of Bohemia
929	Boleslav I 'the Cruel' becomes duke of Bohemia after murdering Wenceslas I Bohemia conquers Moravia (Slovakia)
972	Boleslav II 'the Pious' becomes duke of Bohemia
999	Boleslav III 'the Red' becomes duke of Bohemia (first reign)
1003	After a brief revolt, Boleslav III is restored to the dukedom (second reign)
1003	Poland conquers Moravia and Boleslaw I (also duke of Poland) becomes duke of Bohemia
1013	Bohemia reconquers Moravia from Poland under Ulrich, duke of Bohemia
1038	Bohemia under Bretislav I invades Poland conquers Silesia and Wroclaw
1061	Vratislav II becomes duke of Bohemia
1085	Henry IV (Holy Roman Emperor) makes Vratislav II the first king of Bohemia (non-hereditary title) The House of Premysl continues to rule Bohemia
1158	German Emperor Friedrich I Barbarossa makes Duke Vladislav II of Bohemia the second king of Bohemia (non-hereditary title)

1198	The duchy of Bohemia officially becomes a kingdom
1253	Ottakar II becomes king of Bohemia and the kingdom grows
1278	Wenceslas II becomes king of Bohemia
1300	Wenceslas II of Bohemia becomes king of Poland
1305	Wenceslas III becomes king of Bohemia and Poland
1306	Wenceslas III of Bohemia is murdered, ending the House of Premysl

Poland

?	Lech founds what is now Poland (mythological)
c. 8thC CE	Krak I or Krok founds Kracow (mythological)
c. 8thC	Krak II founds Kracow (mythological)
c. 9thC	Piast 'the Wheelwright' founds the Piast dynasty and names his state Polska (semi-mythological)
960?	Mieszko I founds the duchy of Poland
966	Mieszko I converts to Christianity
992	Boleslaw I 'the Brave' succeeds his father Mieszko I on his death
999	Poland becomes a Christian kingdom
1000	Poland becomes part of the German Empire under Emperor Otto III
1025	Boleslaw I is crowned first Polish king by the Pope
1025	Mieszko II becomes king of Poland
1034/1040	Casimir 'the Restorer' becomes king of Poland
1058	Boleslaw II 'the Generous' becomes duke, then king of Poland
1079	Wladyslaw I becomes duke of Poland
1102	Boleslaw III 'the Wry-mouthed' becomes duke, then king of Poland

1138	Boleslaw III dies. The kingdom is divided among his sons, which begins the fragmentation of Poland
1226	Konrad I of Masovia asks the Teutonic Order (crusading knights based in Germany) to help subdue the pagan tribes of Prussia
1240/1241	The Mongols invade Poland, defeating a joint army of Henry I of Silesia and the Teutonic Order at the Battle of Legnica
1290	The Teutonic Order conquer all of Prussia
1295	Premysl II returns Poland to a kingdom with a hereditary title. Vytenis become grand duke of Lithuania and unites the country
1300	Wenceslas II of the house of Premysl, Bohemia, becomes king of Poland
1315/1316	Vytenis' brother Gediminas expands Lithuania to span from the Baltic Sea to the Black Sea
1320	Wladyslaw I Lokietek (known as Wladyslaw the Short) reunites the kingdom of Poland

EASTERN STEM

Russia and Former Soviet Republics

?	Rus' founded the Rus' people (mythological)
c. 800 CE	The Varingian Rus' found the state of Kiev
c. 862/870	The Varingian Rus prince Rurik begins the Rurik dynasty by founding Novgorod
879	Rurik's son, Oleg 'the Wise', becomes ruler of Novgorod

882	Oleg of Novgorod conquers Kiev and later unifies it with Novgorod to form what would become Kievan-Rus'
912	Oleg dies and Igor 'the Old', Rurik's younger son, becomes the ruler of Kiev-Novgorod
921	Igor moves the capital of the duchy to Kiev
941 & 944	Igor besieges Constantinople
945	Igor is assassinated and his widow, Olga, succeeds him
962	Olga of Kiev is succeeded by Sviatoslav I, her son
964–968	Sviatoslav launches a military campaign to the east and south, conquering first the Volga Bulgars and then the Khazar Empire
972	Sviatoslav dies. His son Yaropolk I is given Kiev, but civil war soon breaks out
980	Vladimir I 'the Great' of Novgorod conquers Kiev and creates a unified Rus. He soon begins a campaign to conquer the Baltic people
988	Vladimir, previously a pagan, converts to Greek-Orthodox Christianity. His kingdom now extends from Ukraine to the Baltic Sea
1015	Vladimir dies and civil war erupts again under the dubious claim of Sviatopolk I
1019	Yaroslav I 'the Wise' becomes the new ruler of Kiev
1054	Yaroslav dies, splitting the kingdom among his sons and leaving it weakened. He leaves Kiev and Novgorod to Iziaslav I
11–12thC	The kingdom remains divided. The Crusades further weaken the Baltic states and Constantinople
1237	The Mongols invade Kievan Rus'

1237–1239 Mongol leader Batu Khan raids Kiev
before sacking Vladimir, Moscow, and
many other Kievan Rus' cities
1253 Danylo Halitski of Galicia is crowned king by the Pope
1283 Daniil Alexsandrovich becomes the first prince of
Moscow and establishes the grand duchy of Moscow

Illyrico-Servian branch

South Slavs migrate and begin to settle in countries including
what are known today as Bosnia, Montenegro, Serbia and Croatia.

up to the late 500s   South Slavic tribes remain fragmented.
Invasions on territories take place, including
the Balkans, Dalmatia and Greece
558 CE Several South Slavic tribes are defeated
by the Avars. Many of the Slavs move
east from the Russian Steppes
600s–700s South Slavs begin to settle along the Danube, in
the Balkans, Bulgaria, Montenegro and Serbia.
There is some assimilation of the cultures; South
Slavs invade Greece, reaching Macedonia and
Thessalonica; States or kingdoms are formed
but many are threatened by invasion
870 The Serbs begin to convert to Christianity
925 The kingdom of Croatia is formed
under Tomislav, its first king
1042 Duklja in Montenegro gains independence
from the Roman Empire
1168 Stefan Nemanja founds the Nemanjic dynasty
in Serbia

1217	Stefan Nemanjic 'the First-Crowned', son of Stefan Nemanja, is crowned by the Pope as first king of Serbia. The kingdom of Serbia is formed
Mid-12thC	The Banate of Bosnia is formed
Mid-14thC	Principality of Zeta is formed, covering parts of what is today Montenegro

Magyars/Hungary

14 BCE	Pannonia which includes parts of Hungary is classed as part of the Roman Empire
5 CE	The Romans found Aquincum (now Budapest)
370–469	The Hunnic Empire invades much of Central and Eastern Europe, including Hung
c. 5thC	The Magyars migrate from the Ural Mountains in Russia. Some settle along the Don River in the Khazar Khanate
862	The Magyars raid the Frankish Empire and parts of Bulgaria and the Balaton principality
895/896	Arpad, head of the seven Magyar tribes and thought to be a descendant of Attila, founds the kingdom of Hungary with three Khazar tribes
906	The Hungarians defeat the Moravian kingdom and annex Slovakia
907	The Hungarians defeat the Bavarian army in the Battle of Pressburg
917–934	The Hungarians raid parts of France, Switzerland, Saxony, Italia and Constantinople
948	Bulcsu, a descendant of Arpad, signs a peace treaty with the Roman Empire and converts to Christianity

955	Bulcsu and his troops meet the German army led by Otto I 'the Great' and are defeated in the Battle of Lechfeld, resulting in an end to further Hungarian invasions
1001	Stephen I (Saint Stephen) is crowned king of Hungary and sets out to consolidate and extend his rule
1030	Stephen I repels an invasion led by the Holy Roman Emperor, Conrad II
1038	Stephen I of Hungary dies. There follows a series of civil wars
1077	King Ladislaus I becomes king of Hungary (he also becomes king of Croatia in 1091)
1095	Coloman 'the Learned' becomes king of Hungary. Over the next few years, he annexes Croatia (becoming its king in 1097), Slavonia and Dalmatia
1116	Stephen II becomes king of Hungary and Croatia,
1141	Geza II becomes king of Hungary and Croatia and seeks to expand his borders. For the next century, the country faces both expansion and revolt
1241	Bela IV (who became king in 1235) refuses to surrender to the Mongols under Batu Khan, but the Hungarian army is defeated. However, the Mongols retreat in 1242
1242	With the country weakened, Bela IV concentrates on rebuilding, including the castle of Buda
1272	Ladislaus IV becomes king of Hungary and Croatia
1290	Ladislaus IV is murdered and his throne is taken by Andrew III, a descendant of the Arpads

| 1301 | Andrew II dies, causing the Arpad dynasty to become extinct in the male line. Charles Robert I of Anjou, a 13-year-old Catholic, inherits the throne of Hungary |

Bulgaria

6th century–479 BCE	The Achaemenid Empire controls parts of what is now Bulgaria
341 CE	Philip II of Macedon makes Bulgaria part of his empire
3rd century	Bulgaria is attacked by the Celts
45 CE	Bulgaria becomes part of the Roman Empire
c. 381	The Gothic (Wulfila) Bible is created in what is now northern Bulgaria
482	Following migration, the Turkic-speaking tribes of the Bulgars mainly reside north-east of the Danube River. The tribes are fragmented and remain so for the next century. Some are under the control of the Avars
584	Kubrat of the Dulo dynasty unifies the main Bulgarian tribes
619	Kubrat converts to Christianity
632	Kubrat unites all Bulgarian tribes and founds the state known as Old Great Bulgaria
650/665	Kubrat dies. Old Great Bulgaria largely disintegrates
680	Under Kubrat's sons, the Bulgars migrate across parts of Europe. Asparukh, one of Kubrat's sons and thought to be a descendant of Attila, travel west towards the Danube
680/681	Asparukh establishes the First Bulgarian Empire

700	Tervel becomes king of Bulgaria following Asparukh's death in battle. Terval is also given the title of Caesar in 705
753	Sevar, king of Bulgaria, dies, ending the reign of the Dulo dynasty
753/756	Vinekh begins the Ukil dynasty. The period is marked by the short reigns and murders of many of its kings, and by a series of attacks on Bulgaria by the Byzantine Empire
777	Kardam becomes king of Bulgaria and restores order and power
c. 803	Krum 'the Fearsome' becomes king of the Bulgars, beginning the rule of the Krum dynasty
810	The Bulgars under Krum expand their empire and destroy the Avars
807–811	Krum's Bulgars are attacked by the Byzantine army, but defeat them in the Battle of Pliska, killing the Byzantine Emperor, Nikephoros I
814/815	Krum dies while preparing to attack Constantinople. He is succeeded by his son Omurtag, who signs a 30-year peace treaty with the Byzantine Empire. This marks a period of peace and expansion in Bulgaria
852	Boris I becomes king of Bulgaria, marking a ten-year period of instability
864	Boris converts Bulgaria to Christianity and is regarded as a saint by the Eastern Orthodox Church
893	Boris' son, Simeon I 'the Great', becomes Bulgaria's first tsar. Under him, the state becomes among the most powerful in Eastern and Southeastern Europe

927	Simeon dies and is succeeded by his son, Peter I. This ushers in a golden age of peace and prosperity
934–965	A series of raids by Hungarians, coupled by political insecurity, causes the start of decline in Bulgaria
969	Boris II, Peter's son, becomes tsar when Peter abdicates. He spends most of his reign in captivity of the Byzantine Emperor, Nikephoras II
997	Samuel becomes tsar. His reign is hindered by constant war with the Byzantines
1015	Ivan Vladislav becomes tsar
1018	Ivan dies, and the Byzantine Empire under Basil II annexes the kingdom of Bulgaria
1185	The Second Bulgarian Empire is established by Peter II. It remains a dominant power until the mid-1200s when the Mongols invade

SUMERIAN KING LIST

This list is based on the *Sumerian King List* or *Chronicle of the One Monarchy*. The lists were often originally carved into clay tablets and several versions have been found, mainly in southern Mesopotamia. Some of these are incomplete and others contradict one another. Dates are based on archaeological evidence as far as possible but are thus approximate. There may also be differences in name spellings between different sources. Nevertheless, the lists remain an invaluable source of information.

As with many civilizations, the lists of leaders here begin with mythological and legendary figures before they merge into the more solidly historical, hence why you will see some reigns of seemingly impossible length.

After the kingship descended from heaven, the kingship was in Eridug.

Alulim	28,8000 years (8 *sars**)
Alalngar	36,000 years (10 *sars*)

Then Eridug fell and the kingship was taken to Bad-tibira.

En-men-lu-ana	43,200 years (12 *sars*)
En-mel-gal-ana	28,800 years (8 *sars*)

Dumuzid the Shepherd (or Tammuz)   36,000 years (10 *sars*)

Then Bad-tibira fell and the kingship was taken to Larag.

En-sipad-zid-ana   28,800 years (8 *sars*)

Then Larag fell and the kingship was taken to Zimbir.

En-men-dur-ana   21,000 years (5 *sars* and 5 *ners*)

Then Zimbir fell and the kingship was taken to Shuruppag.

Ubara-Tutu   18,600 years (5 *sars* and 1 *ner**)

Then the flood swept over.

*A *sar* is a numerical unit of 3,600; a *ner* is a numerical unit of 600.

FIRST DYNASTY OF KISH

After the flood had swept over, and the kingship had descended from heaven, the kingship was in Kish.

Jushur	1,200 years
Kullassina-bel	960 years
Nangishlisma	1,200 years
En-tarah-ana	420 years
Babum	300 years

Puannum	840 years
Kalibum	960 years
Kalumum	840 years
Zuqaqip	900 years
Atab (or A-ba)	600 years
Mashda (son of Atab)	840 years
Arwium (son of Mashda)	720 years
Etana the Shepherd	1,500 years
Balih (son of Etana)	400 years
En-me-nuna	660 years
Melem-Kish (son of Enme-nuna)	900 years
Barsal-nuna (son of Enme-nuna)	1,200 years
Zamug (son of Barsal-nuna)	140 years
Tizqar (son of Zamug)	305 years
Ilku	900 years
Iltasadum	1,200 years
Enmebaragesi	900 years (earliest proven ruler based on archaeological sources; Early Dynastic Period, 2900–2350 BCE)
Aga of Kish (son of Enmebaragesi)	625 years (Early Dynastic Period, 2900–2350 BCE)

Then Kish was defeated and the kingship was taken to E-anna.

FIRST RULERS OF URUK

Mesh-ki-ang-gasher (son of Utu)	324 years (Late Uruk Period, 4000–3100 BCE)

Enmerkar (son of Mesh-ki-ang-gasher)	420 years (Late Uruk Period, 4000–3100 BCE)
Lugal-banda the shepherd	1200 years (Late Uruk Period, 4000–3100 BCE)
Dumuzid the fisherman	100 years (Jemdet Nasr Period, 3100–2900 BCE)
Gilgamesh	126 years (Early Dynastic Period, 2900–2350 BCE)
Ur-Nungal (son of Gilgamesh)	30 years
Udul-kalama (son of Ur-Nungal)	15 year
La-ba'shum	9 years
En-nun-tarah-ana	8 years
Mesh-he	36 years
Melem-ana	6 years
Lugal-kitun	36 years

Then Unug was defeated and the kingship was taken to Urim (Ur).

FIRST DYNASTY OF UR

Mesh-Ane-pada	80 years
Mesh-ki-ang-Nuna (son of Mesh-Ane-pada)	36 years
Elulu	25 years
Balulu	36 years

Then Urim was defeated and the kingship was taken to Awan.

DYNASTY OF AWAN

Three kings of Awan   356 years

Then Awan was defeated and the kingship was taken to Kish.

SECOND DYNASTY OF KISH

Susuda the fuller	201 years
Dadasig	81 years
Mamagal the boatman	360 years
Kalbum (son of Mamagal)	195 years
Tuge	360 years
Men-nuna (son of Tuge)	180 years
Enbi-Ishtar	290 years
Lugalngu	360 years

Then Kish was defeated and the kingship was taken to Hamazi.

DYNASTY OF HAMAZI

Hadanish   360 years

Then Hamazi was defeated and the kingship was taken to Unug (Uruk).

SECOND DYNASTY OF URUK

En-shag-kush-ana	60 years (c. 25th century BCE)
Lugal-kinishe-dudu	120 years
Argandea	7 years

Then Unug was defeated and the kingship was taken to Urim (Ur).

SECOND DYNASTY OF UR

| Nanni | 120 years |
| Mesh-ki-ang-Nanna II (son of Nanni) | 48 years |

Then Urim was defeated and the kingship was taken to Adab.

DYNASTY OF ADAB

| Lugal-Ane-mundu | 90 years (c. 25th century BCE) |

Then Adab was defeated and the kingship was taken to Mari.

DYNASTY OF MARI

Anbu	30 years	Zizi of Mari, the fuller	20 years
Anba (son of Anbu)	17 years	Limer the 'gudug'	
Bazi the		priest	30 years
leatherworker	30 years	Sharrum-iter	9 years

Then Mari was defeated and the kingship was taken to Kish.

THIRD DYNASTY OF KISH

Kug-Bau (Kubaba)   100 years (c. 25th century BCE)

Then Kish was defeated and the kingship was taken to Akshak.

DYNASTY OF AKSHAK

Unzi	30 years	Ishu-Il	24 years
Undalulu	6 years	Shu-Suen (son of	
Urur	6 years	Ishu-Il)	7 years
Puzur-Nirah	20 years		

Then Akshak was defeated and the kingship was taken to Kish.

FOURTH DYNASTY OF KISH

Puzur-Suen (son of Kug-bau)	25 years (c. 2350 BCE)
Ur-Zababa (son of Puzur-Suen)	400 years (c.2350 BCE)
Zimudar	30 years
Usi-watar (son of Zimudar)	7 years
Eshtar-muti	11 years
Ishme-Shamash	11 years
Shu-ilishu	15 years
Nanniya the jeweller	7 years

Then Kish was defeated and the kingship was taken to Unug (Uruk).

THIRD DYNASTY OF URUK

Lugal-zage-si   25 years (*c.* 2296–2271 BCE)

Then Unug was defeated and the kingship was taken to Agade (Akkad).

DYNASTY OF AKKAD

Sargon of Akkad	56 years (*c.* 2270–2215 BCE)
Rimush of Akkad (son of Sargon)	9 years (*c.* 2214–2206 BCE)
Manishtushu (son of Sargon)	15 years (*c.* 2205–2191 BCE)
Naram-Sin of Akkad (son of Manishtushu)	56 years (*c.* 2190–2154 BCE)
Shar-kali-sharri (son of Naram-Sin)	24 years(*c.* 2153–2129 BCE)

Then who was king? Who was not the king?

Irgigi, Nanum, Imi and Ilulu	3 years (four rivals who fought to be king during a three-year period; *c.* 2128–2125 BCE
Dudu of Akkad	21 years (*c.* 2125–2104 BCE)
Shu-Durul (son of Duu)	15 years (*c.* 2104–2083 BCE)

Then Agade was defeated and the kingship was taken to Unug (Uruk).

FOURTH DYNASTY OF URUK

Ur-ningin	7 years (*c.* 2091?–2061? BCE)
Ur-gigir (son of Ur-ningin)	6 years
Kuda	6 years
Puzur-ili	5 years
Ur-Utu (or Lugal-melem; son of Ur-gigir)	6 years

Unug was defeated and the kingship was taken to the army of Gutium.

GUTIAN RULE

Inkišuš	6 years (*c.* 2147–2050 BCE)
Sarlagab (or Zarlagab)	6 years
Shulme (or Yarlagash)	6 years
Elulmeš (or Silulumeš or Silulu)	6 years
Inimabakeš (or Duga)	5 years
Igešauš (or Ilu-An)	6 years
Yarlagab	3 years
Ibate of Gutium	3 years
Yarla (or Yarlangab)	3 years
Kurum	1 year
Apilkin	3 years
La-erabum	2 years
Irarum	2 years
Ibranum	1 year
Hablum	2 years
Puzur-Suen (son of Hablum)	7 years
Yarlaganda	7 years

| Si'um (or Si-u) | 7 years |
| Tirigan | 40 days |

Then the army of Gutium was defeated and the kingship taken to Unug (Uruk).

FIFTH DYNASTY OF URUK

| Utu-hengal | 427 years / 26 years / 7 years |
| | (conflicting dates; *c.* 2055–2048 BCE) |

THIRD DYNASTY OF UR

Ur-Namma (or Ur-Nammu)	18 years (*c.* 2047–2030 BCE)
Shulgi (son of Ur-Namma)	48 years (*c.* 2029–1982 BCE)
Amar-Suena (son of Shulgi)	9 years (*c.* 1981–1973 BCE)
Shu-Suen (son of Amar-Suena)	9 years (*c.* 1972–1964 BCE)
Ibbi-Suen (son of Shu-Suen)	24 years (*c.* 1963–1940 BCE)

Then Urim was defeated. The very foundation of Sumer was torn out. The kingship was taken to Isin.

DYNASTY OF ISIN

Ishbi-Erra	33 years (*c.* 1953–1920 BCE)
Shu-Ilishu (son of Ishbi-Erra)	20 years
Iddin-Dagan (son of Shu-Ilishu)	20 years

Ishme-Dagan (son of Iddin-Dagan)	20 years
Lipit-Eshtar (son of Ishme-Dagan or Iddin Dagan)	11 years
Ur-Ninurta (son of Ishkur)	28 years
Bur-Suen (son of Ur-Ninurta)	21 years
Lipit-Enlil (son of Bur-Suen)	5 years
Erra-imitti	8 years
Enlil-bani	24 years
Zambiya	3 years
Iter-pisha	4 years
Ur-du-kuga	4 years
Suen-magir	11 years
Damiq-ilishu	23 years (son of Suen-magir)

ANCIENT GREEK MONARCHS

This list is not exhaustive and dates are approximate. Where dates of rule overlap, emperors either ruled jointly or ruled in opposition to one another. There may also be differences in name spellings between different sources.

Because of the fragmented nature of Greece prior to its unification by Philip II of Macedon, this list includes mythological and existing rulers of Thebes, Athens and Sparta as some of the leading ancient Greek city-states. These different city-states had some common belief in the mythological gods and goddesses of ancient Greece, although their accounts may differ.

KINGS OF THEBES (*c.* 753–509 BCE)

These rulers are mythological. There is much diversity over who the kings actually were, and the dates they ruled.

Calydnus (son of Uranus)
Ogyges (son of Poseidon, thought to be king of Boeotia or Attica)
Cadmus (Greek mythological hero known as the founder of Thebes, known as Cadmeia until the reign of Amphion and Zethus)
Pentheus (son of Echion, one of the mythological Spartoi, and Agave, daughter of Cadmus)

Polydorus (son of Cadmus and Harmonia, goddess of harmony)

Nycteus (like his brother Lycus, thought to be the son of a Spartoi and a nymph, or a son of Poseidon)

Lycus (brother of Nyceteus)

Labdacus (grandson of Cadmus)

Lycus (second reign as regent for Laius)

Amphion and Zethus (joint rulers and twin sons of Zeus, constructed the city walls of Thebes)

Laius (son of Labdacus, married to Jocasta)

Oedipus (son of Laius, killed his father and married his mother, Jocasta)

Creon (regent after the death of Laius)

Eteocles and Polynices (brothers/sons of Oedipus; killed each other in battle)

Creon (regent for Laodamas)

Laodamas (son of Eteocles)

Thersander (son of Polynices)

Peneleos (regent for Tisamenus)

Tisamenus (son of Thersander)

Autesion (son of Tisamenes)

Damasichthon (son of Peneleos)

Ptolemy (son of Damasichton, 12 century BCE)

Xanthos (son of Ptolemy)

KINGS OF ATHENS

Early legendary kings who ruled before the mythological flood caused by Zeus, which only Deucalion (son of Prometheus) and a few others survived (date unknown).

Periphas (king of Attica, turned into an eagle by Zeus)

Ogyges (son of Poseidon, thought to be king of either Boeotia or Attica)

Actaeus (king of Attica, father-in-law to Cecrops I)

Erechtheid Dynasty (1556–1127 BCE)

Cecrops I (founder and first king of Athens; half-man, half-serpent who married Actaeus' daughter)	1556–1506 BCE
Cranaus	1506–1497 BCE
Amphictyon (son of Deucalion)	1497–1487 BCE
Erichthonius (adopted by Athena)	1487–1437 BCE
Pandion I (son of Erichthonius)	1437–1397 BCE
Erechtheus (son of Pandion I)	1397–1347 BCE
Cecrops II (son of Erechtheus)	1347–1307 BCE
Pandion II (son of Cecrops II)	1307–1282 BCE
Aegeus (adopted by Pandion II, gave his name to the Aegean Sea)	1282–1234 BCE
Theseus (son of Aegeus, killed the minotaur)	1234–1205 BCE
Menestheus (made king by Castor and Pollux when Theseus was in the underworld)	1205–1183 BCE
Demophon (son of Theseus)	1183–1150 BCE
Oxyntes (son of Demophon)	1150–1136 BCE
Apheidas (son of Oxyntes)	1136–1135 BCE
Thymoetes (son of Oxyntes)	1135–1127 BCE

Melanthid Dynasty (1126–1068 BCE)

Melanthus (king of Messenia, fled to Athens when expelled)	1126–1089 BCE
Codrus (last of the semi-mythological Athenian kings)	1089–1068 BCE

ANCIENT KINGS & LEADERS

LIFE ARCHONS OF ATHENS (1068–753 BCE)

These rulers held public office up until their deaths.

Medon	1068–1048 BCE	Pherecles	864–845 BCE
Acastus	1048–1012 BCE	Ariphon	845–825 BCE
Archippus	1012–993 BCE	Thespieus	824–797 BCE
Thersippus	993–952 BCE	Agamestor	796–778 BCE
Phorbas	952–922 BCE	Aeschylus	778–755 BCE
Megacles	922–892 BCE	Alcmaeon	755–753 BCE
Diognetus	892–864 BCE		

From this point, archons led for a period of ten years up to 683 BCE, then a period of one year up to 485 CE. Selected important leaders – including archons and tyrants – in this later period are as follows:

SELECTED LATER LEADERS OF ATHENS

Peisistratos 'the Tyrant of Athens'	561, 559–556, 546–527 BCE
Cleisthenes (archon)	525–524 BCE
Themistocles (archon)	493–492 BCE
Pericles	c. 461–429 BCE

KINGS OF SPARTA

These rulers are mythological and are thought to be descendants of the ancient tribe of Leleges. There is much diversity over who the kings actually were, and the dates they ruled.

Lelex (son of Poseidon or Helios, ruled Laconia)   *c.* 1600 BCE
Myles (son of Lelex, ruled Laconia)   *c.* 1575 BCE
Eurotas (son of Myles, father of Sparta)   *c.* 1550 BCE

From the Lelegids, rule passed to the Lacedaemonids when Lacedaemon married Sparta.
Lacedaemon (son of Zeus, husband of Sparta)
Amyklas (son of Lacedaemon)
Argalus (son of Amyklas)
Kynortas (son of Amyklas)
Perieres (son of Kynortas)
Oibalos (son of Kynortas)
Tyndareos (first reign; son of Oibalos, father of Helen of Troy)
Hippocoon (son of Oibalos)
Tyndareos (second reign; son of Oibaos, father of Helen of Troy)

From the Lacedaemons, rule passed to the Atreids when Menelaus married Helen of Troy.

Menelaus (son of Atreus, king of Mycenae,
    and husband of Helen)   *c.* 1250 BCE
Orestes (son of Agamemnon, Menelaus' brother)   *c.* 1150 BCE
Tisamenos (son of Orestes)
Dion   *c.* 1100 BCE

From the Atreids, rule passed to the Heraclids following war.

Aristodemos (son of Aristomachus, great-great-grandson of Heracles)

Theras (served as regent for Aristodemes' sons, Eurysthenes
    and Procles)
Eurysthenes   c. 930 BCE

From the Heraclids, rule passed to the Agiads, founded by Agis I.
Only major kings during this period are listed here.

Agis I (conceivably the first historical Spartan king)   c. 930–900 BCE
Alcamenes   c. 740–700 BCE,
                                          during First Messenian War
Cleomenes I (important leader in the
    Greek resistance against the Persians)   524 – 490 BCE
Leonidas I (died while leading the
    Greeks – the 300 Spartans – against
    the Persians in the Battle of
    Thermopylae, 480 BCE)   490–480 BCE
Cleomenes III (exiled following the
    Battle of Sellasia)   c. 235–222 BCE

KINGS OF MACEDON

Argead Dynasty (808–309 BCE)

Karanos	c. 808–778 BCE	Alcetas I	c. 576–547 BCE
Koinos	c. 778–750 BCE	Amyntas I	c. 547–498 BCE
Tyrimmas	c. 750–700 BCE	Alexander I	c. 498–454 BCE
Perdiccas I	c. 700–678 BCE	Alcetas II	c. 454–448 BCE
Argaeus I	c. 678–640 BCE	Perdiccas II	c. 448–413 BCE
Philip I	c. 640–602 BCE	Archelaus I	c. 413–339 BCE
Aeropus I	c. 602–576 BCE	Craterus	c. 399 BCE

Orestes	c. 399–396 BCE	Perdiccas III	c. 368–359 BCE
Aeropus II	c. 399–394/93 BCE	Amyntas IV	c. 359 BCE
Archelaus II	c. 394–393 BCE	Philip II	c. 359–336 BCE
Amyntas II	c. 393 BCE	Alexander III 'the Great'	
Pausanias	c. 393 BCE	(also King of Persia and	
Amyntas III	c. 393	Pharaoh of Egypt by end	
	BCE; first reign	of reign)	c. 336–323 BCE
Argeus II	c. 393–392 BCE	Philip III	c. 323–317 BCE
Amyntas III	c. 392–370 BCE	Alexander IV	c. 323/
Alexander II	c. 370–368 BCE		317–309 BCE

Note: the Corinthian League or Hellenic League was created by Philip II and was the first time that the divided Greek city-states were unified under a single government.

Post-Argead Dynasty (309–168 BCE, 149–148 BCE)

Cassander	c. 305–297 BCE
Philip IV	c. 297 BCE
Antipater II	c. 297–294 BCE
Alexpander V	c. 297–294 BCE

Antigonid, Alkimachid and Aeacid Dynasties (294–281 BCE)

Demetrius	c. 294–288 BCE
Lysimachus	c. 288–281 BCE
Pyrrhus	c. 288–285 BCE; first reign

Ptolemaic Dynasty (281–279 BCE)

Ptolemy Ceraunus (son of Ptolemy I of Egypt)	c. 281–279 BCE
Meleager	279 BCE

Antipatrid, Antigonid, Aeacid Dynasties, Restored
(279–167 BCE)

Antipater	c. 279 BCE
Sosthenes	c. 279–277 BCE
Antigonus II	c. 277–274 BCE; first reign
Pyrrhus	c. 274–272 BCE; second reign
Antigonus II	c. 272–239 BCE; second reign
Demetrius II	c. 239–229 BCE
Antigonus III	c. 229–221 BCE
Philip V	c. 221–179 BCE
Perseus (deposed by Romans)	c. 179–168 BCE
Revolt by Philip VI (Andriskos)	c. 149–148 BCE

SELEUCID DYNASTY (c. 320 BCE–63 CE)

Seleucus I Nicator	c. 320–315, 312–305, 305–281 BCE
Antiochus I Soter	c. 291, 281–261 BCE
Antiochus II Theos	c. 261–246 BCE
Seleucus II Callinicus	c. 246–225 BCE
Seleucus III Ceraunus	c. 225–223 BCE
Antiochus III 'the Great'	c. 223–187 BCE
Seleucus IV Philopator	c. 187–175 BCE
Antiochus (son of Seleucus IV)	c. 175–170 BCE
Antiochus IV Epiphanes	c. 175–163 BCE
Antiochus V Eupater	c. 163–161 BCE
Demetrius I Soter	c. 161–150 BCE
Alexander I Balas	c. 150–145 BCE
Demetrius II Nicator	c. 145–138 BCE; first reign
Antiochus VI Dionysus	c. 145–140 BCE

Diodotus Tryphon	c. 140–138 BCE
Antiochus VII Sidetes	c. 138–129 BCE
Demetrius II Nicator	c. 129–126 BCE; second reign
Alexander II Zabinas	c. 129–123 BCE
Cleopatra Thea	c. 126–121 BCE
Seleucus V Philometor	c. 126/125 BCE
Antiochus VIII Grypus	c. 125–96 BCE
Antiochus IX Cyzicenus	c. 114–96 BCE
Seleucus VI Epiphanes	c. 96–95 BCE
Antiochus X Eusebes	c. 95–92/83 BCE
Demetrius III Eucaerus	c. 95–87 BCE
Antiochus XI Epiphanes	c. 95–92 BCE
Philip I Philadelphus	c. 95–84/83 BCE
Antiochus XII Dionysus	c. 87–84 BCE
Seleucus VII	c. 83–69 BCE
Antiochus XIII Asiaticus	c. 69–64 BCE
Philip II Philoromaeus	c. 65–63 BCE

Ptolemaic Dynasty (305–30 BCE)

The Ptolemaic dynasty in Greece was the last dynasty of Ancient Egypt before it became a province of Rome.

Ptolemy I Soter	305–282 BCE
Ptolemy II Philadelphos	284–246 BCE
Arsinoe II	c. 277–270 BCE
Ptolemy III Euergetes	246–222 BCE
Berenice II	244/243–222 BCE
Ptolemy IV Philopater	222–204 BCE
Arsinoe III	220–204 BCE
Ptolemy V Epiphanes	204–180 BCE

Cleopatra I	193–176 BCE
Ptolemy VI Philometor	180–164, 163–145 BCE
Cleopatra II	175–164 BCE, 163–127 BCE and 124–116 BCE
Ptolemy VIII Physcon	171–163 BCE, 144–131 BCE and 127–116 BCE
Ptolemy VII Neos Philopator	145–144 BCE
Cleopatra III	142–131 BCE, 127–107 BCE
Ptolemy Memphites	113 BCE
Ptolemy IX Soter	116–110 BCE
Cleopatra IV	116–115 BCE
Ptolemy X Alexander	110–109 BCE
Berenice III	81–80 BCE
Ptolemy XI Alexander	80 BCE
Ptolemy XII Auletes	80–58 BCE, 55–51 BCE
Cleopatra V Tryphaena	79–68 BCE
Cleopatra VI	58–57 BCE
Berenice IV	58–55 BCE

In 27 BCE, Caesar Augustus annexed Greece and it became integrated into the Roman Empire.

ANCIENT ROMAN LEADERS

This list is not exhaustive and some dates are approximate. The legitimacy of some rulers is also open to interpretation. Where dates of rule overlap, emperors either ruled jointly or ruled in opposition to one another. There may also be differences in name spellings between different sources.

KINGS OF ROME (753–509 BCE)

Romulus (mythological founder and first ruler of Rome)	753–716 BCE
Numa Pompilius (mythological)	715–672 BCE
Tullus Hostilius (mythological)	672–640 BCE
Ancus Marcius (mythological)	640–616 BCE
Lucius Tarquinius Priscus (mythological)	616–578 BCE
Servius Tullius (mythological)	578–534 BCE
Lucius Tarquinius Superbus (Tarquin the Proud; mythological)	534–509 BCE

ROMAN REPUBLIC (509–27 BCE)

During this period, two consuls were elected to serve a joint one-year term. Therefore, only a selection of significant consuls are included here.

Lucius Junius Brutus (semi-mythological)	509 BCE
Marcus Porcius Cato (Cato the Elder)	195 BCE
Scipio Africanus	194 BCE
Cnaeus Pompeius Magnus (Pompey the Great)	70, 55 and 52 BCE
Marcus Linius Crassus	70 and 55 BCE
Marcus Tullius Cicero	63 BCE
Caius Julius Caesar	59 BCE
Marcus Aemilius Lepidus	46 and 42 BCE
Marcus Antonius (Mark Anthony)	44 and 34 BCE
Marcus Agrippa	37 and 28 BCE

PRINCIPATE (27 BCE–284 CE)

Julio-Claudian Dynasty (27 BCE–68 CE)

Augustus (Caius Octavius Thurinus, Caius Julius Caesar, Imperator Caesar Divi filius)	27 BCE–14 CE
Tiberius (Tiberius Julius Caesar Augustus)	14–37 CE
Caligula (Caius Caesar Augustus Germanicus)	37–41 CE
Claudius (Tiberius Claudius Caesar Augustus Germanicus)	41–54 CE
Nero (Nero Claudius Caesar Augustus Germanicus)	54–68 CE

Year of the Four Emperors (68–69 CE)

Galba (Servius Sulpicius Galba Caesar Augustus)	68–69 CE
Otho (Marcus Salvio Otho Caesar Augustus)	Jan–Apr 69 CE
Vitellius (Aulus Vitellius Germanicus Augustus)	Apr–Dec 69 CE

Note: the fourth Emperor, Vespasian, is listed below.

Flavian Dynasty (66–96 CE)

Vespasian (Caesar Vespasianus Augustus)	69–79 CE
Titus (Titus Caesar Vespasianus Augustus)	79–81 CE
Domitian (Caesar Domitianus Augustus)	81–96 CE

Nerva-Antonine Dynasty (69–192 CE)

Nerva (Nerva Caesar Augustus)	96–98 CE
Trajan (Caesar Nerva Traianus Augustus)	98–117 CE
Hadrian (Caesar Traianus Hadrianus Augustus)	138–161 CE
Antonius Pius (Caesar Titus Aelius Hadrianus Antoninus Augustus Pius)	138–161 CE
Marcus Aurelius (Caesar Marcus Aurelius Antoninus Augustus)	161–180 CE
Lucius Verus (Lucius Aurelius Verus Augustus)	161–169 CE
Commodus (Caesar Marcus Aurelius Commodus Antoninus Augustus)	180–192 CE

Year of the Five Emperors (193 CE)

Pertinax (Publius Helvius Pertinax)	Jan–Mar 193 CE
Didius Julianus (Marcus Didius Severus Julianus)	Mar–Jun 193 CE

Note: Pescennius Niger and Clodius Albinus are generally regarded as usurpers, while the fifth, Septimius Severus, is listed below

Severan Dynasty (193–235 CE)

Septimius Severus (Lucius Septimius Severus Pertinax)	193–211 CE
Caracalla (Marcus Aurelius Antonius)	211–217 CE
Geta (Publius Septimius Geta)	Feb–Dec 211 CE
Macrinus (Caesar Marcus Opellius Severus Macrinus Augustus)	217–218 CE
Diadumenian (Marcus Opellius Antonius Diadumenianus)	May–Jun 218 CE
Elagabalus (Caesar Marcus Aurelius Antoninus Augustus)	218–222 CE
Severus Alexander (Marcus Aurelius Severus Alexander)	222–235 CE

Crisis of the Third Century (235–285 CE)

Maximinus 'Thrax' (Caius Julius Verus Maximus)	235–238 CE
Gordian I (Marcus Antonius Gordianus Sempronianus Romanus)	Apr–May 238 CE
Gordian II (Marcus Antonius Gordianus Sempronianus Romanus)	Apr–May 238 CE
Pupienus Maximus (Marcus Clodius Pupienus Maximus)	May–Aug 238 CE
Balbinus (Decimus Caelius Calvinus Balbinus)	May–Aug 238 CE
Gordian III (Marcus Antonius Gordianus)	Aug 238–Feb 244 CE
Philip I 'the Arab' (Marcus Julius Philippus)	244–249 CE
Philip II 'the Younger' (Marcus Julius Severus Philippus)	247–249 CE
Decius (Caius Messius Quintus Traianus Decius)	249–251 CE
Herennius Etruscus (Quintus Herennius Etruscus Messius Decius)	May/Jun 251 CE

Trebonianus Gallus (Caius Vibius Trebonianus Gallus) 251–253 CE
Hostilian (Caius Valens Hostilianus Messius
    Quintus)   Jun–Jul 251 CE
Volusianus (Caius Vibius Afinius Gallus
    Veldumnianus Volusianus)   251–253 CE
Aemilian (Marcus Aemilius Aemilianus)   Jul–Sep 253 CE
Silbannacus (Marcus Silbannacus)   Sep/Oct 253 CE
Valerian (Publius Licinius Valerianus)   253–260 CE
Gallienus (Publius Licinius Egnatius Gallienus)   253–268 CE
Saloninus (Publius Licinius Cornelius
    Saloninus Valerianus)   Autumn 260 CE
Claudius II Gothicus (Marcus Aurelius Claudius)   268–270 CE
Quintilus (Marcus Aurelius Claudias
    Quintillus)   Apr–May/Jun 270 CE
Aurelian (Luciua Domitius Aurelianus)   270–275 CE
Tacitus (Marcus Claudius Tacitus)   275–276 CE
Florianus (Marcus Annius Florianus)   276–282 CE
Probus (Marcus Aurelius Probus Romanus;
    in opposition to Florianus)   276–282 CE
Carus (Marcus Aurelias Carus)   282–283 CE
Carinus (Marcus Aurelius Carinus)   283–285 CE
Numerian (Marcus Aurelius Numerianus)   283–284 CE

DOMINATE (284–610)

Tetrarchy (284–324)

Diocletian 'Lovius' (Caius Aurelius Valerius Diocletianus) 284–305
Maximian 'Herculius' (Marcus Aurelius Valerius
    Maximianus; ruled the western provinces) 286–305/late 306–308

Galerius (Caius Galerius Valerius Maximianus; ruled the eastern provinces)	305–311
Constantius I 'Chlorus' (Marcus Flavius Valerius Constantius; ruled the western provinces)	305–306
Severus II (Flavius Valerius Severus; ruled the western provinces)	306–307
Maxentius (Marcus Aurelius Valerius Maxentius)	306–312
Licinius (Valerius Licinanus Licinius; ruled the western, then the eastern provinces)	308–324
Maximinus II 'Daza' (Aurelius Valerius Valens; ruled the western provinces)	316–317
Martinian (Marcus Martinianus; ruled the western provinces)	Jul–Sep 324

Constantinian Dynasty (306–363)

Constantine I 'the Great' (Flavius Valerius Constantinus; ruled the western provinces then whole)	306–337
Constantine II (Flavius Claudius Constantinus)	337–340
Constans I (Flavius Julius Constans)	337–350
Constantius II (Flavius Julius Constantius)	337–361
Magnentius (Magnus Magnentius)	360–353
Nepotianus (Julius Nepotianus)	Jun 350
Vetranio	Mar–Dec 350
Julian 'the Apostate' (Flavius Claudius Julianus)	361–363
Jovian (Jovianus)	363–364

Valentinianic Dynasty (364–392)

Valentinian I 'the Great' (Valentinianus)	364–375
Valens (ruled the eastern provinces)	364–378

Procopius (revolted against Valens)	365–366
Gratian (Flavius Gratianus Augustus; ruled the western provinces then whole)	375–383
Magnus Maximus	383–388
Valentinian II (Flavius Valentinianus)	388–392
Eugenius	392–394

Theodosian Dynasty (379–457)

Theodosius I 'the Great' (Flavius Theodosius)	Jan 395
Arcadius	383–408
Honorius (Flavius Honorius)	395–432
Constantine III	407–411
Theodosius II	408–450
Priscus Attalus; usurper	409–410
Constantius III	Feb–Sep 421
Johannes	423–425
Valentinian III	425–455
Marcian	450–457

Last Emperors in the West (455–476)

Petronius Maximus	Mar–May 455
Avitus	455–456
Majorian	457–461
Libius Severus (Severus III)	461–465
Anthemius	467–472
Olybrius	Apr–Nov 472
Glycerius	473–474
Julius Nepos	474–475
Romulus Augustulus (Flavius Momyllus Romulus Augustulus)	475–476

Leonid Dynasty (East, 457–518)

Leo I (Leo Thrax Magnus)	457–474
Leo II	Jan–Nov 474
Zeno	474–475
Basiliscus	475–476
Zeno (second reign)	476–491
Anastasius I 'Dicorus'	491–518

Justinian Dynasty (East, 518–602)

Justin I	518–527
Justinian I 'the Great' (Flavius Justinianus, Petrus Sabbatius)	527–565
Justin II	565–578
Tiberius II Constantine	578–582
Maurice (Mauricius Flavius Tiberius)	582–602
Phocas	602–610

LATER EASTERN EMPERORS (610–1059)

Heraclian Dynasty (610–695)

Heraclius	610–641
Heraclius Constantine (Constantine III)	Feb–May 641
Heraclonas	Feb–Nov 641
Constans II Pogonatus ('the Bearded')	641–668
Constantine IV	668–685
Justinian II	685–695

Twenty Years' Anarchy (695–717)

Leontius	695–698
Tiberius III	698–705

Justinian II 'Rhinometus' (second reign)	705–711
Philippicus	711–713
Anastasius II	713–715
Theodosius III	715–717

Isaurian Dynasty (717–803)

Leo III 'the Isaurian'	717–741
Constantine V	741–775
Artabasdos	741/2–743
Leo V 'the Khazar'	775–780
Constantine VI	780–797
Irene	797–802

Nikephorian Dynasty (802–813)

Nikephoros I 'the Logothete'	802–811
Staurakios	July–Oct 811
Michael I Rangabé	813–820

Amorian Dynasty (820–867)

Michael II 'the Amorian'	820–829
Theophilos	829–842
Theodora	842–856
Michael III 'the Drunkard'	842–867

Macedonian Dynasty (867–1056)

Basil I 'the Macedonian'	867–886
Leo VI 'the Wise'	886–912
Alexander	912–913
Constantine VII Porphyrogenitus	913–959
Romanos I Lecapenus	920–944

Romanos II	959–963
Nikephoros II Phocas	963–969
John I Tzimiskes	969–976
Basil II 'the Bulgar-Slayer'	976–1025
Constantine VIII	1025–1028
Romanus III Argyros	1028–1034
Michael IV 'the Paphlagonian'	1034–1041
Michael V Kalaphates	1041–1042
Zoë Porphyrogenita	Apr–Jun 1042
Theodora Porphyrogenita	Apr–Jun 1042
Constantine IX Monomachos	1042–1055
Theodora Porphyrogenita (second reign)	1055–1056
Michael VI Bringas 'Stratioticus'	1056–1057
Isaab I Komnenos	1057–1059